DREAMWALKERS

S. PARNAM-HARRIS

For Gill (Gillibean) Baderman – Fellow dreamwalker.

'Eternity is an awfully long time, especially towards the end.'

— WOODY ALLEN

DREAMWALKERS

I dreamed I was teaching a man to fly. In that place you go to between sleeping and waking. Stretching out and pushing off with my toes, I was swooping up high over the trees, remembering how the air felt in-between my fingers as if the feathers of the past were still attached. The man was suddenly next to me and he smiled, because he already knew how to fly.

As a child it hadn't occurred to me that dreaming was something most people never had a choice about. When I closed my eyes, I played in the dusty noisy streets of what seemed to be a one- horse town in the early days of the settlers, a dirty child, who moved silently between the horses, touching their soft noses and breathing in their warm smooth coats that were muddy and sweaty from the rides into the hills which surrounded the town, and the long journeys of places I couldn't quite reach.

I became part of the puzzled expression on the faces of busy people trying to make the tough decisions of life in difficult times. The doors of houses were unlocked and I looked around without question, as if I was ET surrounded by children, and therefore just not that noticed. It wasn't invisibility, more as though I was someone you always expect to be there. These other children accepted me as part of the group; we played together in unbothered sunshine and sometimes hid in the warm untidy stables during cold, wet weather. That there were changing seasons was something I never questioned.

The farmers came in from out of town and brought their families with them. On the days when the market was in full flow, it was as if the usual underlying sleepiness buzzed with an unquantifiable energy. Sometimes strangers came in, rich with stories from the far-away places and the smell of money unearned, and the tired horses stood waiting in the streets with gentle patience, as the two bars became wild with noise and light.

People were afraid of these outsiders because they were rootless and destructive. I could feel the tension that they brought with them. It never occurred to me that I was a stranger also. Nothing about it seemed unknown. It was my other place.

I always assumed that the dream travelling was something everyone did until a curious teacher asked me about the 'story' I had written. We had a vicious row about me being a 'little liar,' she preferred the man-eating goats on a desert island that the boys in my class had lifted almost word for word from some illegal comic. I learned to be more circumspect with whom I talked to about the dream town.

I was the quiet one at the back of the class and embraced my inner geek with chess club membership and an unhealthy interest in physics text books. I wasn't gifted, just bothered by the things that I didn't understand, which when you're eleven, as I remember, is nearly everything.

My parents were the only two doctors in a south-west country practice, not really disinterested, just permanently exhausted from the desert that is the National Health Service in an English village. How they had me was a miracle, considering that they were so rarely both at home at the same time. I must have been conceived by a medical memo, as that was how they communicated most days. 'Buy inhalers for surgery. Pick up medical student from station. Check

Mrs Aldwich's prescription. Get pregnant.' Always on call, even at Christmas, they provided the absent-minded cuddles of the truly dedicated workaholic. I was their first and last 'mistake.' Mealtimes were accompanied by the postman's leg ulcers and the latest much-argued about treatment for diverticulitis. We had mugs of tea with the names of drug companies emblazoned on them and even now I found it easier to digest food whilst reading the latest copy of a medical journal, preferably with graphic pictures.

I told my mother, in a rare quiet moment, about the 'other place' and asked her where *she* went when she was asleep. After a protracted question and answer session, where a behavioural psychologist became a serious possibility, she finally banned me from watching western films for a month. It was the last time I told anyone about my night-time travels. I think I was twelve. Even *I* knew cowboys were nothing to do with anything. The place where I went was different. The people were mixed. They worked together. There was no taking the land from someone else, there was no someone else to take it from and the horses were not the only way to get around. It's just that with no roads it was easier. The post, which was not actually letters, came from a small craft that glided over the hills and hovered above the ground, making the dust swirl in a whirl-wind around it, before dropping down at the end of the town surrounded by excited people. The pilot was always welcomed like an old friend and given a meal, while people gathered to hear the latest gossip and to pick up the deliveries. Food, farming materials, technology and parcels from faraway families, all were unloaded and exclaimed over.

I gathered with them and listened to the chatter, stupidly hoping in my childish mind that someone had sent me something. No one ever did.

We never brought anything with us, but then children seldom journey with much baggage. The little group of faces changed occasionally as our numbers swelled and reduced. Our games grew as we did and we ventured further from the town centre, walking up to the gold-coloured cliffs that edged the settlement on two sides. I some-times took a horse from the stable and trotted out, hoping to catch a glimpse of the things beyond that I couldn't reach. Sometimes I would see the squat post craft swooping down low for an impressive landing. I always found myself resting nervously as the group of children got to the trees where the wind rustled through thick leaves. We all moved back to the safety of the town after silent agreement.

It didn't matter to me that I slipped easily into the places on the edge of reality. I was a child and it had always been. I questioned nothing.

As I reached puberty the possibility of sleep was no longer a foregone conclusion. Exams, family pressure, just growing up with that ache of longing for something not always understood. The geeky girl, slightly apart from the crowd. My parents seemed stunned that I wasn't the bright creature they should have created. I know I must have disappointed them, but they both died before their disbelief became my reality.

I wandered through two years of psychology at the big sprawling university city of Exeter, with the money carefully invested for me by my hopeful parents. The empty house was looked after by the woman who had worked for them and I came home at the weekends and in the holidays to memories and shadows. Somehow the last year got away from me and I just never went back.

That's the thing about some people; they drift through their own lives as if they are ghosts, never really making footsteps in the dust.

I had the luxury of a small annuity and spent far too much time reading old books and working in a charity shop with thoughtful octogenarians. They were almost without exception ladies who had done amazing things long ago in far-away places, like delivering babies in Mongolia, existing on yak tea and goat's milk. They had beautiful skin, the octogenarians not the goats and knowing eyes, and they treated me with the same love and care as the delivered babies. I envied them their memories and their beautiful skin.

I was at a dinner party one evening with people who wore the Exmoor uniform of baggy faded cavalry twill trousers and tweed. There were lots of Marks and Spencer green crimplene skirts with elasticised waists and white nylon cardigans and a liberal smattering of dog hair over everything. I was at least thirty years younger than the next oldest, but they had known my parents and were kind in a sort of puzzled, condescending way.

The 'young man' who had been invited to make up the numbers, was maybe only twenty years older than me. He was tall and muscular with thick blonde hair and blue eyes and a serious cravat problem. He tried to chat about the things he thought I would be interested in, but we had stumbled over ocean sized silences interspersed with questions like, "Do you ever go to the opera?" (Him).

"I'm more of a Hammersmith Odeon girl" (me). Until he noticed a book, I had stuffed into my leather backpack. It was an idiot's guide to quantum mechanics. He pulled the book out. I explained that I was the scientific equivalent of the awful people who go into art galleries and museums and tell anyone foolish enough to enquire, that they 'don't know anything about art but they know what they like.'

He began talking about his business and I tried again to say that I didn't understand most of it but I thought it was important to try. My host helpfully interjected that he'd never seen anyone with such a large collection of books that had titles he couldn't comprehend, never mind the contents. I replied that as there was nothing on *his* shelves except 'pheasant plucking for the slightly pissed' or 'fifty ways to skin a rabbit whilst talking to your broker,' I could understand his puzzlement. His loud laughter brought the room into the curve of the fire and the warmth filtered through my thoughts along with the huge quantities of alcohol.

I slept on the sofa with the dogs that night, a smelly blanket tucked around us. Their gentle rhythmic snoring and the hypnotising depth of the fire opened a door for a moment into my other place again. Only I saw it with different eyes. Older eyes. It closed again in the puppy breath and whiskers tickling me awake.

That was how I first met my boss Simon Knowles and how I got a job buying science and technical books for his shop. Several years later I was still working for him. The one small shop in Tiverton had seeded the chain of shops in the south-west and the Internet had given us the future in specialist books. He had hit on the, not exactly original, idea of putting books and cups of expensive coffee together. It just worked. Even online shopping didn't stop people wanting to pick up a book and read the first page before buying it. Simon said I was the only person he had ever met who knew what a quark was.

I worked in all the shops over the years, travelling from the house on the moor if I could, or renting locally and coming home on my days off when it was just too far to drive. If you need to hide you can do that in the pages of a book.

The changing seasons were filled with thoughts and dreams and I began to use my holiday time for prolonged trips abroad. I even took a sabbatical and spent three months in a Winnebago driving around the all the places my mother had thought I used to dream about.

The difference between a positive thought and a negative one is the difference between solitude and isolation. I had loved America. I liked the huge sky and the eggs over easy and people who thought you only had to work hard to achieve something. It was, at the time, a place where I felt at home and if I blurred my eyes a little, I could see the small town with the dusty streets and narrow men of my childhood dreams.

The years when I didn't dream travel hadn't bothered me. I had thought it was just time passing, and somewhere only children were able to go and my nights had been filled instead with subatomic particles and star systems. Every now and then an echo would follow me down the years and I would think that I saw something at the edge of my mind, which felt as though it was a book I had forgotten I once read, but somehow I knew what happened next.

In the spaces in-between I had tried some of the things that I didn't understand, along with skydiving and casual relationships. But eventually you arrive at a place where the four known forces in the universe collide, though of course there are probably more, these are the ones we are connected to, gravity, electromagnetic, strong and weak.

Courage comes in all shapes and sizes and so does cowardice, and if it feels as if you're alone, it's probably because you are. I think that was why I went back.

———

I was standing by the reception desk arguing with Richard, who was our IT geek. He worked in the computer section with two others, locating specialist books. I was hopeful about brane theory and he was one of those people who won't look at anything after Einstein. I know Einstein is of course 'the man,' it's just that I've always been keen on anything to do with the possibility of multiple universes and Richard was not.

Our receptionist Saffron slid past us, pink hair, nose ring, and skirt that should have come with a government health warning. "What is this?" She said, "Dirty talk for nerds?"

Richard turned the same pink as her hair. "Look," I said, "Einstein was not exactly against the possibility!"

Saffron began making snoring noises. Richard mumbled something about a local band and concert dates and Saffron did a double take. I realised that I had just become the conversational equivalent of wallpaper and made a slightly undignified exit.

As I turned the corner to my office, I glanced back. Richard, of the floppy hair and lanky frame was leaning over the reception desk, in the pretence of checking dates on a calendar. I caught his eye and he smiled. It was a wicked smile. He seemed suddenly younger, more like the students I used to know at the university, with that just starting out feeling.

"Millie!" I jumped guiltily and turned around. Simon was leaning into the corridor. "Are we going to have a meeting any time soon?" He saw the little tableau at the reception desk and a small frown crumpled the usually suspiciously smooth forehead. "Is that young man hitting on my secretary?"

I hid behind the non-lie and did my best mid-Atlantic accent. "I am not at liberty to say, sir."

"Maybe he'll be able to get her to wear a nice frock to work."

"*Frock*! Where are you from, the Dark Ages? Who even *uses* that word anymore?" I walked into his office, which was full of junk, mountains of paperwork and doing the literary geological equivalent of laying down substrata, some of it had been there so long. My fingers itched for a roll of rubbish bin liners and some bleach.

"Millie!"

"What?"

"You were thinking about tidying again, weren't you?" His tone was accusatory. In a moment of madness a few years previously after a really bad row, I had threatened to clean up. After paling in a way that would have got him a thermometer in the ear in my parent's house, he had taken to locking his office door. This was a man attached to his rubbish.

We talked about the financial forecast, which if the truth be told and it seldom is, I really didn't understand, and more awful, I didn't care. I gave him my lists, which I knew he wouldn't approve, and then we did some gossiping. This was a single guy who wore a cravat and had a serious addiction to ABBA. I don't think we had ever mentioned closets, but I felt more comfortable with him than just about anyone I had ever met. The gossip was the best part of the daily meeting anyway. Two lattes later I sailed out on a wave of caffeine fumes. Richard was still working on the artful Saffron. I contemplated a nose ring for nearly a quarter of a nanosecond, and then the thought of all that pain, and the possibility of wayward nasal discharge, put me off.

I went down into the shop and worked on the tills for a few hours. The sales staff were a cheerful bunch, who were mostly students working their way through university. They laughed and joked and had the serious discussions of the incredibly hopeful. It was the real reason I went down there, rather than the 'staying in touch with the customers' that I suggested when Simon asked. He sometimes did it himself, though the staff would sigh with exasperation, not because it put them off to have the boss around, but because he messed up the tills. The damn things went into a terminal state of pitiful beeping which required a lengthy visit from the IT department, which was Richard, to put right.

My feet ached and I juggled shopping as I pushed my front door open with my elbow. The cat wound itself around my ankles, which was strange because I don't have a cat. Two amber eyes blinked cupboard love up at me. "Cecil, you do understand that you live down the road, don't you?" More cat blinking. I dumped the food on the kitchen counters and went to run a bath.

Cecil was happy to share a really smelly camembert, crackers and brandy. I rang my neighbours and got their answer machine. A steady rain was flicking against the windows as Cecil and I looked at each other. I have never understood why people have animals but can't be bothered to look after them. He washed a tabby paw.

"Okay, I give in." We wandered upstairs and I turned off the lights as we went, the twitching tail making huge shadows on the walls.

Cecil settled to one side of my legs and I pulled a book towards me, a photographic tour through the galaxy. The lamp cast strange shapes into the corners of the room and my eyes blurred. The rain on the windows and the steady flickering of the light acted as though it was a hypnotist's watch. I slipped into my dream travel and into the other place.

I became aware of gunfire and at first, I thought it was the strangers in the town who were causing drunken trouble. Someone shouted at me, "Get down!" I tuned into the reality of the dream, the noise increased, there was a smell of smoke, and frightened horses shuffled their anxiety behind me. The voice shouted again and then a shape loomed out of the dark stables and rugby tackled me to the ground, knocking the breath out of me. In the half-light I could see furious, glittering eyes and feel the breath close to my skin. I shoved him away and he grunted. I'm not a small woman and I was angry and frightened, so it was a good shove. "Stay down!" He pushed me over to one side of the doorway as I tried to get to my feet.

"What's going on?" I shouted from the safety of the other side of the stable door.

"Borderers!"

I had no idea what that meant, but the sound of the word made my stomach turn over, so somewhere in my subconscious I must have heard it before. A hand touched my shoulder, I levitated for the first time in my life and turned to defend myself, which might have included quite a lot of screaming. The two men standing behind me were carrying something that looked as though they were guns. They made that universal placating gesture of hands outspread. "What's happening 'Oak?"

"The borderers hit a couple of hours ago, the town's full of them." He fired off a few rounds into the darkness, the gun seemed to be shooting a stream of light as well as a projectile.

"Great, just what I needed," one of the men behind me muttered. He looked at me and then pointed at himself. "Rari, and that's Joao." The other guy with him waved one hand while crouching down using the wooden door as cover, and began firing.

"Since when did this place become a war zone?" I muttered into the lull of sound that was several people checking to see if anyone was still out there.

"This is contested territory so, since forever," answered the grumpy one. He pointed at his chest. "Okan."

"Millie," I said. We waited in the spinning silence; all the little noises of the night seemed to be coming back.

I couldn't remember being so frightened in my childhood travels, things had always felt real, I could touch and smell and taste; when I cut myself in the dream place, I bled, but the wound had gone when I returned to the house on the moor, this was something else. I remembered that I always seemed to fall asleep here and wake up at home and I knew which the dream was and which was home.

A burst of violent noise broke the thoughts and I flattened myself back against the barn wall.

"Give me a gun!" I shouted at the grumpy one they had called Okan.

"Why?" He asked, as he fired back into the darkness.

"Because it's important to accessorise you idiot. Why do you *think*?"

The two other men had moved to the back doorway and were taking turns at firing out into the night. "Do you even *know* how to use a gun?" Grumpy Okan was reloading and I could see some shadows creeping towards us using the edge of the buildings as cover.

"The bad stuff comes out of the pointy end," I whispered, holding out a hand.

"Good enough," he whispered back, sliding a weapon across the dusty floor towards me.

I aimed carefully at the creeping shadows. Closing one eye and using the sight, I squeezed gently. A bark of soft sound and one shape slid down the wall. I gasped. Aiming a gun was not on the list of things I prided myself on and killing someone was awful on several levels. Okan nodded and the firefight began again.

I saw a movement out of the corner of my eye, some looming giant of a shape, the shine of eyes in the moonlight. The shadow was a caricature of wild hair and spiky fingers, a cartoon you would laugh at, only this seemed to freeze my heart and I found the idea of breathing in and out something I had to remember how to do. I pointed this out quietly to Okan and he turned very slowly to see what I was gesticulating about.

It was as if the cartoon and the reality because it would have been difficult to call it a man, coalesced into one creature. Still large, if Okan was anything to go by, it looked in our direction. You expect to be relieved when you see the shape behind the shadow, that the rabbit is really your dad's hand. This, however, was worse.

I backed in towards the darkness of the stable and the eyes flickered at the movement. Fixing on me it didn't seem to see Okan and came quietly forward. I swallowed my scream and raised the gun, not even bothering to aim, or to think, I just emptied the chamber. Bullets and light pulses hit, but the claw-like hands reached and I backed even further towards the terrified horses, clicking the empty weapon as the light pulse got weaker and weaker.

A stream of gunfire blasted at the head of this 'thing,' bits of brain and blood spattered over my face and clothes and I sank to my knees with the outstretched fingers inches away from me. Everything was quiet for a moment. "What is that?" I managed to get out.

Okan hauled me to my feet and brushed the muck off my face with the edge of his sweaty shirt, which endeared him to me forever.

"*That* was a borderer."

It could have been a man once, but the expression on the face was pure lupine. I couldn't see the eyes, but the way it/he had seen me in the darkened doorway made me think that they were more cat-like. I knelt down, curiosity hand in hand with too much adrenaline. Tattoos made dark patterns on the skin and the hair was like wire, something was wound into the twists that made me shudder. All the features were exaggerated, as if someone had decided more was better. He /it, must have been nearly seven feet tall.

"Oak! I think we should take some horses and make a run for it. Anyone with sense will have left hours ago." Rari came from the back of the stables, making me jump with the sudden sound of his voice so close to me. He looked at me standing in the shadows at the edge of the moonlight and then looked at the ground where the borderer was bleeding into the straw; a large dark puddle curled its way toward my feet. "Did you get that one, Millie?"

"No." I shook my head. "I can't say that I did."

He nodded but his expression was grim. I gave him my gun and he began filling it with bullets from his jacket pocket while he talked to Okan.

"I don't think there's anyone left here and you know they've probably already got whatever women and children they could find, back on the shuttle." I looked up. Okan was doing the cut off movement across the neck that meant shut up. Rari checked the gun and handed it back to me. "Safety is on. Can you ride, Millie?" I tucked the gun in the back of my pyjamas and nodded in answer to the question. Then thought about the fact that I was wearing the clothes I usually wore to bed. Somehow this didn't feel as if I was anywhere near Oz, never mind Kansas. Fortunately, I am one of those people who wear more to go to sleep than to go to work. The house on the moor had very little heating and I was wearing a sleeveless vest, pyjama bottoms and thick climbing socks.

As a child when I dream travelled, I had always arrived wearing the dungarees my mother thought would be ideal for me. There were lots of places to put a sandwich and the odd grasshopper and padded knees for the flying lessons off the garage roof that I gave myself.

I had, in the past, always gone to bed in my pyjamas and taken the clothes for granted. It was just as well I wasn't Simon; he told me once he usually found himself, in the dreaming hours, shopping for frozen peas in his skin and cravat and nothing else; a dream, he said, he always enjoyed very much.

Joao handed me a pair of muddy boots and a jacket that must have belonged to the man who mucked out. They were both big and smelly and very welcome. I tucked my pyjama bottoms into the boots and wrapped the jacket around me.

Pushing my messy hair back from my face and trying not to notice the little bits of gloopy stuff that stuck to my fingers, I helped Joao saddle four horses while Okan and Rari watched the two exits. Okan untied the other two horses and they snorted their gratitude. He helped me to get up by hooking his fingers together. The gun slipped from the back of my pyjamas and Okan caught it as it fell. He handed it back, smiling. It was warm from the contact with my skin and I realised why he was smiling and I blushed for the first time in several years, the combination of skydiving and working for an aging gay guy made embarrassment an unlikely sensation for me, but it had been an unusual night.

"Ready?" He leaned towards me and asked quietly.

"As I ever will be."

Rari was close to the stable door and was looking out into the dark; he turned on his horse and gave a half shrug.

I can't say I was ever any good at riding; my parents had made me have lessons in the hope that it would integrate me with the local children. In the way of the very young I did everything I could to avoid doing something they wanted me to do. Later, much later, I found some comfort from riding out on the moor on cold, clear winter mornings with a borrowed horse, an old cob that belonged to the same couple who invited me for dinner every chance that they had. I took their five dogs for extra company, and they would race up and down chasing old ghosts, totally ignored by the ancient, gentle horse, for whom plodding had become something of an art.

So, the raced standing start from the stable nearly unseated me. I clung on, because the alternative would have included me being crushed beneath the speeding hooves and lots of screaming. The horses with no riders were out in front. I think Joao was hoping they would distract anyone still watching. But no one fired at us and we made it to the trees without being shot at. Not that I would have been able to fire a gun if I'd wanted to, as hanging on was taking up most of my time.

I thought the borderers had lost interest for some reason or they had got what they came for. I hoped with all the brain cells I could spare, which was not very many, that the reason wasn't waiting for us in the dark trees. *Why* I should fear the forest I couldn't remember, but something had been planted deep in my memory telling me that I should *not* be heading for the trees.

The horses slowed and we stopped. Okan and Joao wheeled the nervous creatures around and watched the town for movement. Rari leaned over towards me. "Okay?"

I nodded, resting my head in my hands for a moment. "I'm going to be so glad to wake up," I whispered to myself.

Rari must have had ears like a cat because he snorted and answered, "It's not like when we were children Millie, I've been here for four weeks this dreamwalk."

Okan came over to us. "Nothing. I think they've gone."

"You think the one Millie got was the 'suicide' left behind?" Rari patted the neck of his horse and it shuffled, still not happy.

Okan shrugged. Completely ignoring that my part in the death of the borderer had been bait. He looked at me and then back at the town. "We can camp on the ridge for the rest of the night and go back in the daylight." It was a question of sorts and it included me, but the statement Rari had just made was beginning to filter through my numbed thoughts.

"How long?" I squeaked, much too loudly. The sound reverberated against the solid darkness and then it wasn't only the horses who looked nervous.

"Millie, not so loud! There are vildenbeasts in here. Don't you remember?"

Oh great, I thought, what's a *vildenbeast*? With expert timing something rustled in the undergrowth. I could feel my eyebrows sweating with suppressed nerves and the feeling that you get when you think you're just about to wake up with the covers on the floor gasping for breath.

"Millie?" Rari tried again.

"Sorry. I'm *trying* to do my best to catch up and no, I don't remember what's in these forests."

"It's a hybrid, of a breed of wild cat with a bit of pig," Okan whispered. "It's enormous and extremely bad tempered and I'd *really* rather not wake one up." He looked at the two other men and they shrugged in silent agreement. Joao turned his horse towards the cliffs and we made our way, as quietly as possible, staying close to the trees for cover. The horse's hooves were making a comforting sound on the fallen leaves, then I caught Rari looking nervously over his shoulder a few times and the back of my neck became ridged with tension again.

The air was getting colder as the night filled with stars. In the distance the town looked peaceful and quiet. The odd light showed in the house windows as if people had just settled in for the evening. I could see the horse's breath, and I shivered in my pyjamas and borrowed jacket. I tried to make sense of the last few hours, checking my watch's luminous dial to see how long I had been dream travelling. It had stopped. I shook my wrist, but it remained stubbornly still.

We reached the rocky outcrop that came before the cliffs and hills that edged the town. The moonlight was making dark shadows and there were shapes that loomed towards you. The ground became crisp as the leaves were left behind in the forest. Joao held up a hand and we all stopped. I slid gratefully from the horse's back and leaned into the creature, resting against its warm flank as it dropped its head, weary like me.

The three men moved in familiar silence, checking the small clearing in the rocks and pulling the horses in close. Rari removed a water bottle from the backpack he seemed to be welded to and began giving the eager animals a drink. I made a mental note to make sure I dream travelled with an emergency kit next time. I wondered wryly if that was actually possible, if you ever brought anything with you apart from your memories.

"You said you'd been here four weeks?" I asked Rari, taking the water bottle from him and helping myself to a swig before pouring some water into my cupped hand and giving my own horse a drink. Grateful whiskers tickled my fingers and the creature snorted, spraying me with fine droplets.

"Joao and I had gone with the post to the next town. We were on our way back when the postie noticed an incoming blip on his holo-screen. He chatted with Twin Rivers and they confirmed that they had put up the net." This made no sense to me but I nodded anyway.

"We persuaded him to put us down at the cliff edge and he gave us the guns."

Joao shrugged, "Just thought we'd see if we could help. Been coming here a lot of years. It's home I guess."

"Do you remember *me* Joao?" I asked softly. In the half light from the bright moon, he looked embarrassed.

"Yeah. Your hair used to be wild all over the place, and it hasn't changed."

I was stunned. He must have been one of the children from the gang who roamed the town like a pack of wild puppies. I couldn't remember his face, but something about the half-starved voice sounded familiar. I remembered a dark quiet boy older than me, who was always hungry.

"I think we'll risk lighting a fire." Okan interrupted my next question, which was the one Rari had avoided answering. "There's a cave back there," he pointed behind him. "It will shield some of the firelight from anyone who might be interested."

We moved the tired horses and Okan did something with one of the guns that meant it didn't shoot a bullet, but the flash of light ignited the little mound of leaves and moss. He added larger and larger twigs and eventually some wood.

Joao took first watch, he disappeared into the dark at the edge of the moonlight and I noticed his shadow follow him until he became the shapes of rocks and quiet.

There is something about a fire; it reawakens those atavistic feelings of security that have a mesmerising effect on the soul. We sat looking deep into the flames, as if the answers were all there if only you could decipher the code.

"Tell me about the borderers?" I broke the spell with my whispered thought.

Rari shrugged. He looked at Okan who also shrugged, in fact if I had, we could have started a club. What *is* wrong with some men, don't they realise it's a complete giveaway for 'should we tell the woman something scary?' I wanted to say try being one alone for a few minutes, it'll shock the hell out of you. Instead, I waited, as women have been doing forever, for men to get around to it.

"They live in space. I mean they don't colonise," he added, in answer to my puzzled face. "When the settlers began moving further out, it encroached on the borderer's territory."

"Is that why they attack? There's always death without motive, but all murders come with a reason. Even your common or garden psychopath has a motive to kill." I waved a hand in what I thought was the direction of the town. "It usually doesn't make any sense to anyone else, but it's there."

"At first, they just took foodstuff and cattle, things they could use. Then a few years ago they began taking women and children."

We sat in silence for a while as I thought about that. "What does that *actually* mean?" I looked from Okan to Rari.

"I think they don't," Okan cleared his throat, "Have access to women any other way."

I work in a bookshop and I have a whole relationship with science books that lowers my understanding of the real world and could be described as not quite healthy, but I can be quite quick if the need arises. "Great," I said. I must have looked a little queasy because Okan patted me on the back, much as you would a difficult child.

Joao suddenly appeared at the edge of the firelight. He didn't look at us, not wanting to destroy his night vision, but Rari got up to go as if an actual conversation had taken place. Joao sat down close to the fire and pulled a small foil wrapped snack from his jacket. "The postie gave us some rations."

He offered me the open pack and I took a small piece of the dark block, smelling it before I put it into my mouth, as if the smell would be any indication of taste, it wasn't. It was similar to eating salty cardboard, not that I've ever tried. Joao was not so fussy and he ate as if it were a long time since his last meal.

My back ached from the unaccustomed gallop and I was tired from one scare too many. "Where are you from Joao, I mean, when you're awake?" He hesitated and smiled, glancing for a moment at Okan. I saw the look but it didn't mean anything to me, he was just trying to gauge whether the information is going to get them into trouble. I could understand; I wasn't sure what I would say if they asked me. It's all very well meeting people in the dream travel, but I had often wondered if knowing someone in the waking world would be difficult. It *felt* as if it would be.

"Rari and me, we come from Canada. Okan's a New Yorker."

I nodded; he and Rari had that west coast soft 'not American' inflection and a New York accent is difficult to miss. I pointed at myself. "England." The formalities were finally over, as if we were at some stuffy dinner party, which was rather stupid because I was in my pyjamas and we'd already killed someone; something, I have always thought of as an ice breaker.

"It will be light soon, why don't you get some rest?" Okan took off his jacket and offered it to me as a blanket. I shook my head. The fire had warmed me through and in fact the cave was becoming stuffy. I stood up and stretched: my back and knees sounded like castanets in the quiet of the night.

"Won't I wake up at home if I go to sleep here?" I looked at both of them and the shadows seemed to stretch around us in the shape of lies not spoken.

"No, not necessarily." Okan shifted so that his back was against a convenient rock. "How much of this have you done?" He asked.

"Dream travelling? All the time when I was a child."

He smiled. "We call it dreamwalking. What about as an adult?"

"None." I sat down again and shared his rock, tucking my knees up and resting my chin. The flames from the fire were red gold, as if the wood burned with a special heat.

"You have more control and it will take some 'active' thinking to go back."

I was not sure how I felt about that and my silence must have been loud with unspoken thoughts. "Sometimes a situation will precipitate a return, or extreme pain." He tailed off looking uncomfortable.

Joao was watching us; he had stretched out and his long lean body took up the whole of the other side of the fire. He shook his head and the smallest smile caught the corners of his eyes. "Don't panic Millie. Okan always likes to give the bottom line on everything."

"Well, there *is* some panicking going on, but I will try and keep it to a dignified minimum."

"We both appreciate that," Joao said seriously. The dryness of his humour was not lost in the light of the distant stars. I held out a hand for some more salted cardboard and he handed me the folded packet. A man who was careful with food.

I sighed, "This place loses its charm when someone's shooting at you."

"Oh, I don't know," Joao smiled.

I wondered if they knew each other at home. I used to look at people who came into the shop and guess at the choice of book. Middle aged busy women loved murder, the higher the body count the better, I think that shopping for a family of four, whilst holding down a demanding job, would send anyone directly from the frozen peas to a Cathy Reichs. Each face would hide a wealth of quiet thoughts. It's impossible to see where people go when they sleep, maybe we all go somewhere.

The sharp stones stuck into my legs and I swept the ground beneath me, running the soft soil through my fingers. Being able to see, feel and taste in my dreams was not a novelty. A breeze made the fire crackle and I closed my eyes for a moment, leaning back against the rock. I felt Okan put his coat over me and surprisingly a cool hand touched the side of my face.

I must have dozed, because I could hear whispered voices and smelt something that couldn't possibly have been coffee, but my eyes opened. Rari smiled, he held out a large mug, the steam curled in delicate curves and I gratefully sipped. "Rari, you made coffee! If there's anything I can ever do for you, my first-born son."

"Ah, let me think about it." He began stamping out the embers of the fire and scattering them. There was no sign of Okan or Joao.

I stood up, trying to stretch my aching bones and keep the drink from spilling. In the early morning light, the 'camp' looked less a place of safety and more as though it was the home of some untidy carnivores, the grey dawn showed unpleasant things that had been chewed. I wondered where it had slept.

We rode down to the town, bringing the unsaddled horses with us. From a distance everything looked normal. Swirls of dust clouded the horses' hoofs. The stable doors swung back on their hinges banging in the wind, the saddest loneliest noise I had ever heard.

Okan and Joao appeared, standing in dishevelled silence on the walkway in front of the buildings. The sun was just up above the horizon in a pale blue-green sky. They seemed as if they were the strangers that I remembered who came into the town and caused trouble. It made me think that maybe some of them might have been dream travelling and I looked back in my memories with different eyes.

We took the horses into the stables and fed them, securing the doors open and letting in the light. I noticed the body of the borderer had gone and I realised why the two men looked so dirty and tired. They must have been back before dawn, burying the dead and hoping to find anyone left alive.

A voice made us all jump, "Saw your fire." Okan nearly dropped the man, but as he turned it was obvious from the tracks of blood on the man's clothes that he was incapable of any kind of fight. His face looked vaguely familiar. I touched him on the shoulder, the only place that didn't look damaged and Joao handed him a water bottle. He drank gratefully. He pointed at himself. "Til Duster."

I remembered him. He ran the larger of the two bars in town. His grey face was craggy and he seemed to be smaller than I recalled, but then everyone is tall when you're a child.

"They came without warning, we usually have time," his voice drifted off, "More and more lately, lost my Ginnie in the last raid." He suddenly sat down in the dust and I knelt by him, Rari was looking out to the rest of the town, he gestured with his chin and Okan nodded. He went off, leaving us in a little knot by the stable. I moved the man's hand away from the wet patch of blood on the side of his chest and pressed a cloth Joao gave me over the seeping wound. Til smiled the vacant, damaged smile of someone who isn't sure he has actually survived. Looking up to Okan he asked, "Did you find anyone else?" Okan shook his head. They were both referring to people from the town, everyone there knew that they'd found plenty of dead borderers.

"Come on," I said, "Let's get you home. Somewhere you can lie down." He staggered to his feet with my help and we walked as though we were the losers in a three-legged race, to the bar on one side of the street.

The place looked as if a small tornado had hit, but mostly it was mess rather than damage. We both carefully ignored the large patches of blood that dotted the ground floor. I helped him up the stairs to a small apartment that must have been decorated by his partner. Cushions and books, plants and pots. All the things that usually a woman would think important in a home. I sat him in a chair and he pointed to a cupboard in the open plan living room. It could have been a flat in a Manhattan loft. I pulled out boxes with first aid equipment, most of it identifiable, all of it would have been welcome in a city emergency department. It was one more reminder that I wasn't in a frontier town at the turn of the last century. I thought about this place, somewhere out there, in someone else's time.

He had pulled off his shirt with great difficulty and was examining the deep gash with bemused shock. I said, "Why didn't you come to us when you saw the fire?"

I cleaned the wound with something that smelt as if it was an antiseptic. It seeped, but was not bleeding badly. I hunted for a stitch kit.

He pushed my hand away and pulled out a small device similar to a stapler, and set the dial for length and depth of stitch. "I was scared."

He leaned back in the chair and I placed the gadget hopefully over the open wound. "I imagine this is going to hurt?" I asked.

"It's got the usual combi-anaesthetic, but yeah."

He took a deep breath and I pressed the catch. A neat loop covered the wound with something that seemed to be a very fine wire. I worked my way down the gash and each loop pulled the wound together in a smooth tight line. My parents would have been impressed. He pointed to a tube and I covered the area in a layer of clear gel. It solidified in a moment.

He looked pale with shock and I took his pulse, it was fast and thready.

"No other injuries?" I asked. I took in the quick shake of his head and helped him to the bedroom where he stretched out. "I'll come back and check on you."

"Can you see who else made it? Most people got out to the forest farms before they landed and I guess will drift back, and I think we managed to get a group of children and injured to the caves. Got caught trying to buy them some time." His face was twisted with desperation. I nodded. Speaking would have formed a lie and I didn't want to give him false hope. Though my mother always used to say 'in times of great grief anything that gets you through.'

I went downstairs, Okan and Joao were sitting at one of the tables, they had righted the chairs and were drinking something that smelled of good coffee. Both their faces were streaked with dirt and they were hunched over with exhaustion. I wondered how many graves they had dug and felt guilty that they had let me sleep. "Til said they sent some people to the caves. Do you know where that is?"

Joao looked up; his face suddenly took on an expression of surprise. "I think I know where he means. I'll go take a look."

"Be careful Joao," I said, "It could be mostly children, they'll be scared."

He looked at me with that complicated male expression. The one that says, 'I don't know how to put this.' "Okay," I said. We went towards the door. "Can you check in on Til?" I asked Okan, "He's probably suffering from shock. I know *I* am," I added quietly. Okan nodded and finished his drink.

He reached for the gun that rested on the table and we went out into the sunshine together, Joao and I to saddle up two tired, stressed horses and Okan to what was probably more digging. I didn't ask. It's not a question you really wanted to hear an answer to.

"Where's Rari?" I coaxed the tired horse out into the sunshine.

"The professor? I think he's on the lookout for a return visit. We may not have got all the borderers and they tend to leave their wounded behind."

I stopped and my mouth was open. The horse stood with horsey patience. "Maybe it's time I woke up."

Joao looked worried. "Do you really mean that?"

"No. I want to find out what happens next." I moved around to the side of the horse and Joao hooked his fingers, hoisting me into the saddle.

We trotted through the silent town, the sun was higher in the sky and the warmth gave a false feeling of security. We took the opposite way out of the town than the escape route of the previous night. Curving off through the spiky brush from the dusty road, it was a short easy ride to the cliffs. I turned to look back at the hunched buildings and was surprised to see a small wisp of smoke.

"What's Okan burning?" Joao didn't say anything, but left me to work it out. I realised eventually that the borderers were not going to be getting the dignity of a burial.

This part of the range of hills that surrounded the town was softer. More of the farmers had cultivated the surrounding area, and cattle grazed in the distance. It was vast and silent except for the sound of the wind in the trees and the cry of birds high in the sky. We could have been in British Colombia on a late spring day. But we weren't.

"I came here once with one of the local girls." Joao interrupted my thoughts. He smiled at the memory, pulling his horse onto a barely visible path. I stopped suddenly, causing an equine traffic jam. I pointed down to the edge of the trail, half hidden in the grass was a small shoe. Joao hopped off and picked it up, passing it to me. It was covered in dried blood.

"This can't be good," I muttered. I looked around for any other sign of life or death. There was nothing, but then I was not a trained tracker, something could have been staring me in the face and I wouldn't have known, as a bookshop in the south-west of England was not the place to learn these skills. I felt suddenly vulnerable again.

"Are you okay?" Joao asked, hopping skilfully back onto his horse.

I shook my head. "I can't say I am. You have to understand Joao, up until the borderer in the stables, this place was no more alien to me than Oregon."

"Yeah, I understand," he said dryly, "I've never stopped coming here so the borderer in the stables felt pretty normal."

"Don't you have a life somewhere else?" I asked curiously.

His back was to me as we followed the narrow trail, so I couldn't see the expression on his face, but his shoulders tensed. "Not much of one."

I left it at that and went back to another question that had been hanging around. "Why do you call Rari 'the professor?'

This time he laughed, "Because he is, he teaches history. Somewhere in New York." Joao stopped his horse and looked around. "We're here," he whispered. I could see quite a few trees, lots of grass and the blank gold cliffs. Joao slid down and came over to me. "I think we'll be less threatening if we walk."

I stood next to him while he tied the horses up on a loose rein and they began grazing undisturbed. "Joao did you *see* someone?" I asked quietly, getting a feeling from the man I couldn't understand.

"There's a lookout, over there," he pointed with his chin. "Don't want to get shot by some nervous, sleep deprived kid."

We walked carefully through an almost invisible cutting in the rocks, it brought us into a small clearing close to the cliffs and the muzzle of a gun in the middle of my back.

I stood very still, trying to think of something to say that didn't include the words, 'I'm going to die.'

Joao was slightly in front of me with his hands raised and well away from the gun he carried at his waist. I looked up to see a young teenager standing on the rocks above us with a rifle pointed very close to the man's head. Somehow the weapon looked more dangerous in the hands of someone who looked as if he still had puppy fat. Joao spoke very quietly, "Til sent us up from the town to see if you were okay." Nothing happened for what seemed like an hour but was probably only seconds. The gun was removed from my back. Very slowly I turned round.

A small child looked back, a dirty, frightened child with a large weapon in his hand. I reached out and he handed it over to me without a word. A tear slid gracefully down his cheek leaving a clear line from eye to chin. I knelt down and held out my arms, because sometimes there is nothing to say. He hesitated for a moment and then stumbled down the two steps and leaned on my shoulder and cried in complete silence. I had never felt more helpless.

Without letting go of the little boy I handed the gun up to Joao. He looked down at me with an expression I wouldn't have been able to decipher on my most perceptive female days and I don't have those very often. I think it was pity, but there was something there that looked like sadness and loss.

The older boy jumped down from the rocks, a cheerful smile on his face, the rifle slung behind him. He patted the smaller boy on the back. He looked about thirteen to me. In some cultures that would make him already a man. But there was something about the way he looked at us that made me think he would never be a child again in this world. "It's okay Lu, they've gone now." He checked with us for confirmation and Joao nodded. The boy pointed over to the cliffs.

"The rest of them are over there." He smiled. "I'm Solly." Joao held out his hand and Solly paused for a moment then shook it. I think it must have been the first time anyone had treated him like an adult. It made me wonder even more about Joao and the place he came from: we don't all grow up with enough to eat.

Lu took a step back and in that heart-breaking way of little hurt things said, "I'm okay now." I took his small, warm and very grubby hand and we followed the other two towards the caves.

It was difficult to see in the gloom, there were whispers and quick movement in the shadows. As my eyes adjusted, I could see children, lots of them. Lu still had hold of my hand. He pulled me over to a bundled shape. "Mum, they've come." Her face was pale with suppressed pain. I reached down and without a word she moved the blanket. Her huge eyes never left my face as I examined the wound. It looked as if it had been done with a serrated edge, and the blood was caked on the blanket.

"Joao!" He came over and knelt down beside me. "I think we're going to need help." I pressed the wound with a clean edge of the blanket.

"There are seven adults and three children badly injured," he said, shaking his head. "I don't know anything but the basics, what about you?"

"Both of my parents were doctors." Suddenly that made me the expert, so I tried not to sound desperate, "You'll have to go back to the town and get some transport. Is it safe for those who can, to start walking?"

He shrugged and then nodded. "I guess. Never heard of them hitting one place twice in a row." He stood up and began organising the children into groups while I took a look at the rest of the injured. If you know *anything* about medicine; it's how much you don't know that bothers you. All of it looked out of my league. I stood outside in the sun trying not to gag on the smell of blood and the thought of the small white face of the little girl who only wore one shoe.

Joao leaned down from his horse. "You going to be okay here?" I noticed that he had one blue eye and one green. He had dark floppy hair and a small scar on the side of his chin. I realised that he was tired and for the first time knew that I was, fear tired, something you usually wake up from. It was as if everything came into sharp focus.

"This is real, isn't it?" I whispered. He nodded. I turned to look around me, at the children getting ready to walk back to the town, at the green fields and the rich trees, my back was warm with the sun on it. I took a deep breath in and breathed things I didn't understand. Joao watched me and said nothing. "Can you bring a first aid kit?" I asked. "There's a good one in the bar in Til's place." He turned the horse around and sped off.

I helped Solly get three of the smallest children onto the back of my horse and he smiled his thanks. "Is my dad alright? He was shouting for me to get to the caves and I didn't see him after that. Til's my dad," he added.

"He had a bad slash wound, but he was fine when I left him, Solly." His expression hardly changed, but every part of him exuded relief.

The group of children set off in unnatural quiet, small faces looked back at me as if I were sending them off to school. One little girl waved and I found myself waving back. I turned and went back into the caves and the well of dark desperation.

"Why is it that people always ask 'can you move' then when you try, they say 'don't move!'" My pathetic attempts at humour brought a corner of a smile to the mouth of Lu's mother. He squatted on the cold stone floor next to her, a small hand pressed on the wound site as I had told him to do. Before they left, I commandeered all the clothing that could be spared from the other children to use as pillows, blankets and bandages. They had brought surprisingly little with them when they had fled the borderers.

I checked the little girl, curled up against a woman as if asleep. She had slipped into unconsciousness sometime in the night according to the injured woman.

"Are you her mother?" I asked. The woman shook her head. Running her fingers through the child's golden curls she tried for a more comfortable position on the hard ground. I checked the bullet hole in the woman's thigh that was beginning to go purple around the edges. Her leg was hot and her skin dry. The medical magazines and table talk of my past paraded a list of possibilities, blood poisoning, gangrene, internal bleeding.

"I'm her aunt. She's my little sister's child." The eyes of the woman filled with tears and I leaned down to put my arms around her. Which was not something you can find in a medical magazine, more a skill the octogenarians who delivered babies in Mongolia had taught me, because not all of the babies had survived. "Do you think they will be back soon?"

I looked at my watch and tutted, it was still not working. "I think so. Joao wanted to find some transport that wasn't horses."

She grabbed my wrist and examined the watch with some interest.

"My grandmother had something like this. I haven't seen one in ages." I pulled my hand away, suddenly conscious of wondering who these people thought we were. I rearranged my sleeve over the watch and smiled, trying to diffuse the moment. She patted my hand and with a perception that took my breath away said, "We call you people 'the travellers.' You've been around for as long as I can remember, though I don't think there is as many of you now as when my grandmother was a child." Her face took on wistful shadows of the past, as if the memories were the best part of her childhood. "My best friend when I was little was a traveller. I miss her." She looked at my worried face. "Most of the settlers don't notice; let's face it you're just people making your way in the system."

I tried not to say anything that would get me into trouble later and then couldn't think of anything that *wouldn't*. It felt as if my life had just got a whole lot more complicated. The sound of an engine, quiet though it was, brought the woman to her elbow and me to the edge of the cave, flattened against the wall, the small gun Joao had left with me held tightly down by my side. She opened her mouth to whisper to me and I put my finger to my lips. A huge shadow moved into the cave; I raised the gun as the figure came quietly in. The hand that grabbed the weapon was fast and I struggled for a moment until Okan spoke, "Joao told me you might try and shoot me."

I thumped him. Hard. "Couldn't you have said something!"

"I brought a medic; he's from Twin Rivers, the closest town to

Gold Cliffs." A small group of people came in carrying stretchers and the clutter that goes with saving lives.

I spent a few moments telling the three men and one woman what I knew, which wasn't much. I think they listened out of politeness.

I walked out into the sunshine with Okan. A small hover-vehicle, very like the one the postie of my childhood had used, was parked close to the caves. Which was good flying. I leaned against a warm rock, drawing in some strength from the solidness of it. Okan put his arm around me. "Are you okay?" he asked.

"You mean am I about to have a king-sized meltdown?" He looked puzzled. I realised I was pleased to see him. "I'm just having a moment about the 'why me' feelings." He nodded as if this was something he understood. The arm turned into a hug, which was odd, but nice and I rested my head against his chest and breathed in the maleness and felt not so bad, which was as odd a sensation as the 'pleased to see him' one.

"Okan! Do you think you can fly the hovvy straight into the trauma centre in Twin Rivers?" The medic stuck his head out of the cave.

He looked at the two of us. Okan was resting his chin on my head.

"Oh, sorry." He mumbled in our direction.

"I can try," Okan answered, without moving. The medic disappeared back into the cave.

I talked into his shirt, which was a bit scratchy and my nose was slightly squashed so my voice must have sounded a little strange, "The injured woman with the child? She seemed to know who I was. She said the ones who *do* notice call us 'the travellers.'"

Okan sighed. "I think they mostly just assume we're from one of the other towns. There seems to be a lot of movement between settlements and they don't have the same fear of people they don't know as we're used to."

The first of the stretchers began to appear and we broke apart. I looked up at him. It felt as if I had known him for some time, he just seemed familiar to me. Brown shadowed eyes, short dark curly hair, the configuration of features of an old friend. He smiled and I remembered something else about him; that he was trouble, a part of the group of my childhood; one of the older boys and *definitely* badly behaved.

"You used to dare me to jump off the stable roof!" I poked him in the chest.

"*You* used to think you could fly!" He laughed as he went to prep the hover-vehicle.

I helped them put the wounded into the craft. The stretchers had small jets at each corner to provide lift and support, there was still some weight, but mainly you just had to manoeuvre them into place. Inside the hover-vehicle the stretchers stacked neatly, if a little claustrophobically, down each side; leaving a small corridor from the door to the pilot seats.

Lu was standing by his mother who was on a bottom bunk. Her eyes were closed, but she looked a better colour to me and seemed to be out of pain. He patted her hand, then sat himself down on the floor with the obvious intention of staying there. Okan shrugged. The rest of the medical team stood in the narrow space watching over a patient each. I went to the doorway thinking about the walk back to town and my tired feet.

"Hey!" Okan called me and waved me towards him. He pointed to the spare pilot seat. "You might as well have a look at the country-side from the air."

I sat down gratefully and strapped in. Flexible bands crossed my waist and upper body. The window stretched around the front of the craft and as it lifted off in a smooth vertical upsweep, I could see that the cliffs became hills and then in the distance a snow-capped mountain range. Okan turned the craft carefully using the computer panel of lighted keys.

"Where did you learn to fly this?" I whispered.

"The postie liked to sleep on the long runs." He smiled. I remembered the smile from the ever increasingly dangerous dares of my childhood.

"I imagine you didn't have a break for adolescence." It wasn't really a question, more of a note to self, but his face changed and he looked bleak. It made me feel nervous. "I remember when this used to be a place where I felt safe and didn't need to wash too much," I sighed.

We passed over farms and patch fields and cattle. On one occasion people came out from the farmhouse and looked up at us. Gold Cliffs disappeared behind and we travelled for a while in silence. The hovvy was never more than a thousand feet up and seemed to be struggling with that. "Doesn't she go any higher?" I asked. Any good skydiver will tell you that it's the ground that hurts, not the air and the more height you have means the more time to put things right.

"Not with this load," Okan said. The medic in the back snorted his agreement. The sensation of being 'out there at the edge' was making itself felt; but I tried not to let it interfere with my innate nosiness, for which I have honorary Olympic status.

The fields gave way to a huge lake and then two rivers winding their way like lovers, intertwining and parting through the grasslands and the heavy trees. The town of Twin Rivers was much larger than Gold Cliffs and had established itself in the bifurcation as the two rivers curved into one.

We came in to land in the smallest space possible. I was tapping my foot on an imaginary brake as we dropped the last three feet in a cloud of dust. The medics held on with silent resignation. I however, whinged, " Okan, that was an arrival, not a landing." My teeth were aching where I had clamped them together in anticipation of the heavy bone crunching descent that didn't happen.

People with equipment ran to the hovvy as if it was a television series. In a whirl of organisation, the injured were lifted carefully off the makeshift transport and a willing Lu was escorted to the hospital by one of the medics. He waved to me over his shoulder as Okan and I stretched our legs on the walkways around the buildings.

"Have you been here before?" I asked. He nodded; his hands over his head. I resisted the childish urge to tickle him in the gap between his shirt and trousers as he looked dusty and tired. There was a patch of blood on his clothing which didn't invite a frivolous gesture.

"Can I fly on the way back?" I clambered into the left-hand seat.

"Sure." He pointed to the computer settings and gave me a brief account of what would happen if we didn't do a perfect vertical take off. I stuck my tongue out and put my hands on the lighted keys.

"Is this for balance?" He tapped his grubby finger on my tongue. I spat theatrically. "It works for me!" I went back to concentrating and did what I hoped was a reasonable job. In reality I think the craft really flew itself. The buildings gave me a bit of a scare as a sudden updraft buffeted the small vehicle.

Okan put his hands over mine and we settled into a smooth glide over the edge of the hospital.

"Why didn't the borderers didn't hit Twin Rivers?" I asked as we headed for what felt like home.

"They're not stupid. Twin Rivers has a very efficient defence net. Gold Cliffs can't afford one. Lots of the smaller settlements are easy pickings. Though it does seem to me that the Cliffs has had a beating lately." His face furrowed with concern.

I wondered if he was expecting me to ask what planet we were on, and then couldn't think why I hadn't asked. It was a long way from the dreams of my childhood and in the spaces in-between waking and sleeping, I thought that I could wait for answers, then I realised, actually no I couldn't. "Okan, what planet is this?"

The silence was the moment before a clap of thunder or wild applause. Disturbing, as in the sensation you get in the long dark corridors of really bad places with the click of footsteps behind you.

"It's a moon," he said, in the matter-of-fact tone that people use when they tell you something that means trouble.

We flew into the setting sun. It was green and gold, but I'm not fussy, I never turn down the opportunity of a sunset, you never know when you might see another one.

Gold Cliffs looked peaceful. It was nearly dark and I let Okan do the landing because I thought that both of us keeping our teeth would be a good thing. The shadows moved and swayed and Rari came out of the nearby trees and opened the door from outside. He helped me down from the little craft and I almost fell with the tired-ness that filtered through my bones and into my mind. The breeze played with my head and I could see my bedroom at home and the cat washing himself. Only I wasn't sure which was the place I really belonged any more.

Okan looked into my face with concern and asked quietly, "Is it time you went home?" He touched the side of my forehead as if checking for a fever.

"I feel very tired and a bit disorientated, I just saw my room and my neighbour's cat." He and Rari exchanged a glance. It was the sort of look that people who know something you don't give each other which was *very* irritating. "Why is it you two don't need to take a break from all this?" I waved my hand around and nearly fell over again.

Okan smiled and held me up until I found my balance. I felt drunk but without the pleasant glow. "We've been doing it a lot longer." He helped me over to the nearest patch of grass and I sank gratefully down and put my head on my knees to stop the spin.

"Are you ready?" Okan stroked my hair and knelt down in front of me.

"Will I be able to come back?"

"Do you want to?" His eyes were unreadable in the dark, but the question was a loaded one and I could sense that Rari was listening carefully.

"Of course." I said it without thinking, but as soon as I did, I realised that I meant it.

The tension eased and I was puzzled as to why it was so important to them. My head began to spin again and the thought whirled away in a sea of nausea.

"Millie, you'd better give me the jacket and the boots," Rari said, helping me out of the former as Okan undid the straps on the boots. "I need to give them back to the stable man," he added by way of an explanation. Which seemed to make perfect sense.

"Okay, ready?" Okan held my shoulders. I nodded. "Close your eyes. Allow yourself to fix onto the room, it's right there."

"Just don't tell me to click my heels and say 'there's no place like home,'" I laughed at their stunned silence. I'm always amazed that not everyone watches Judy Garland sing 'Somewhere over the Rainbow' every Christmas.

The sound of my own breathing and the wind in the trees became one thought and I caught a glimpse of a shadow at the edge of my mind. Something tipped sideways.

I opened my eyes. The room was full of old memories. Cecil blinked steadily at me and the rain battered the windows. "Okay," I said to Cecil. "That was interesting." Cecil was washing his nether regions with enthusiasm, so maybe he considered that was more interesting for him.

I moved my head on the pillows and a sharp pain at the base of my neck made me feel as if I'd been in a car accident. The rest of my body followed suit and stupidly I checked for bruises. I couldn't see any but they felt as if they were there and it smelt as though I had been sleeping with horses. I wondered if the memory of a smell was actually a smell.

Cecil was looking curiously at my head as a small curl of straw dislodged itself from my hair and spiralled down to the covers. I picked it up with dirty, shaking fingers.

Watched by Cecil's amber eyes I ran a bath. As I took my watch off, I realised it was working again and I checked the clock by the bed to see what the time was. No time had passed.

I swallowed a couple of pills with a gallon of water and sank into the bath. Cecil moved to the top of the loo seat, not wanting to miss any of the show. I had once read a manual belonging to the Royal Army Ordnance Corps. It said something along the lines of, 'if you see a bomb disposal technician running, try to keep up.' I had always thought it was meant to be a joke, but it made perfect sense to me at that moment.

In my childhood I had gone to sleep at night and woken up in the morning. If I felt a little grubby, all to the good, because I was getting one over on my mum, who was a washaholic. I had *never*

34

thought about time. The hot water helped with the muscle ache and I went back to bed with the now complaining Cecil, who was clearly asking me to make up my mind.

He did the cat equivalent of '*what now*' when I got up again to go downstairs and make a hot drink, but forgave me when he realised that the biscuit tin was coming out of the cupboard. The wind and the rain were unceasing in their assault on the side of the house and I hauled a load of books upstairs, making a nest of the pillows and downie. Cecil sighed his contentment with a biscuit all his own and he proceeded to make a mess on the bed covers. I dunked large chunks of chocolate chip in my drink until the bottom of the cup was full of soggy bits and then fell asleep over an introduction to gravity waves.

The sound of purring woke me and a soft paw tapped my still closed lids in the hope of attracting my attention, which worked. I opened my eyes. My parent's room had never been anything but theirs, even after all the time that had passed, I was always surprised to see the view from their window in the early morning light. I had come back from one term at university to find all my things had been moved from my small room into the big one. The meagre amount of life clutter that had belonged to them was packed care-fully away in the attic. Margery, the lady who looked after them never mentioned it and neither did I.

The rain had stopped and a clear watery sky was spectacular with the rising sun in stunning colours of peach and gold. The house, small and Edwardian, was built on the side of a hill above the town. It dealt with the south facing aspect and high winds in equal measure. The cat and I wandered down to the kitchen and made coffee and orange juice, though the cat just supervised. He sat on the table and looked hopefully at the fridge. I fetched a small plastic bowl of organic rice pudding that I was saving for an appropriate moment and pulled off the foil. "*This* is bad for you," I warned him. He decided that he would go for it anyway and I made a note on the wall memo pad that Margery and I used to communicate, for cat food to be bought.

It was shaping up to be autumn and Exmoor is really good at a stunning autumn. I wandered around the garden in my dressing gown and slippers, checking the pots and the view as if things could have changed in the nanosecond that I was away in the night. I sifted slightly damp soil through my fingers and clipped some late roses for my kitchen. The gritty soil *felt* as if it was real, and so did the warm sweet smell of the roses, but at the base of my skull I could feel a hum of thought that reminded me that the other place had felt just the same.

I don't think most normal people realise the existence of the magnifying mirror. Mine is a horrifying x10 which can give you a nasty fright on a *good* day. I wouldn't have noticed it if I didn't check my face in the mirror most mornings. The usual crop of stray eyebrows had grown in the night, which was my Groucho Marx look and I took full advantage of the sunlight shining directly onto my face to do some appropriate plucking.

It looked like a tiny mole, close to the hairline by my right eye. I touched it with my finger, and I could feel a slight bump. I fetched another smaller handbag size x10 mirror and held it to my cheek so that it reflected the image back onto the first mirror.

It wasn't a mole. It seemed to be fixed into the skin and the surface was not brown. I could see minute lines criss-crossing the top. I tried to get my nail under it to see if I could pull it away from the surface, but a sharp needle of pain stopped me.

I thought about a whole range of things on the way to work. Leaf covered roads and the river swollen with rainwater propelled me towards the city and I had one of those journeys where you don't remember actually travelling it and you hope that you didn't deposit any cyclist into the hedgerow in your absent-mindedness.

The shop was busy, full of early morning coffee drinkers taking advantage of the quiet and the daily papers scattered around. That people bought books before nine o'clock always surprised Simon, who couldn't do *anything* that required thought before his first two toasted bagels and a gallon of mind-altering espresso, but it made perfect sense to me.

I had worried at the 'mole' with anxious fingernails and the area was quite red, so I covered it with makeup and did the worrying inside my head instead.

Saffron smiled a morning greeting at me, the sun glinting off the multiple piercings and what looked as if it was a diamond in her front tooth. Ha! I thought, I bet I've got something you haven't, and then shuddered at the possibility. "How did your date with Richard go?" I tried to look interested.

"Cool. He's really great. Plus," she added, "His father owns everything."

"Okay, good." I wandered off, preoccupied with my own piercing.

Simon stuck his head out of his office door. "Millie!" He was about to add something and then looked carefully at my face. "You look different. Are you?" His expression took on the feral whiskers of the true gossip lover. He literally shoved me into his room and closed the door. "You've met someone!" The tone was accusatory. I sat down in the chair and found that somehow a small tear was trailing down my face. I wiped it away. "Oh honey," he said, "If you haven't felt like arming yourself at least once in a relationship then it isn't going to last."

I looked at him in astonishment. He had the kind of prescience that bordered on spooky. I had just been thinking that a gun might indeed come in handy the next time I spoke to Okan. Simon gave me a hug and made some coffee. "When will you be seeing him again?"

"The next time I close my eyes," I whispered.

"Huh?" He handed me the coffee. "What about some details? Nice arse? Huge income?" Simon's idea of a good relationship being based mainly on those two things.

"What are you," I sighed grumpily, "The paramilitary wing of computer dating?"

He hid his disappointment at the lack of forthcoming information not at all.

"By the way, did you know that Richard's father owns *everything*?" I did a passable impression of Saffron which was not that easy without the tongue stud.

Simon's eyebrows shot up. "No!" He took his coffee and slid down the corridor in search of a more hopeful line of gossip.

I did some work at my desk which took all morning, though most of me was on automatic pilot. Lots of publisher's emails, letters, sample books, and lists, it all got swept away in the worry of something not understood.

The shop was busy as I wandered out into the unusually warm autumn sunshine on the lunchtime forage. I walked through the park to the railway station where there was a good organic café, and ordered a fried egg sandwich, which is comfort food for the guilty, because it's somehow not quite such a sin if the egg is organic. I sat outside and watched the university students performing mating rituals with mascara and music. They passed by on their way to being other people. Little groups of hormones with uncomplicated thoughts.

I tipped my head back and drank in the sunlight with the last dregs of the coffee cup. Some creeping sensation in the base of my neck made me shudder. I looked around me. It felt as if a cloud had passed over my soul. I was suddenly frightened. I stood up abruptly, making a couple at the next table start. I apologised, "I'm late!" I tapped my watch. They looked away with pretend smiles.

The local park was full of students and the type of people who take short travel breaks when all the kids have gone back to school. Simon called them 'the sandals and socks invasion.' He shuddered when he said it, which was cruel but there did seem to be a high proportion of humanity wearing shorts with socks and sandals around, so maybe there was something in it.

I kept looking over my shoulder. I could feel that someone was watching me. Following me. Not having done the course on covert surveillance I didn't *actually* know what to look for. But I was doing my best to see in all directions at once, so much so that I smacked straight into somebody and we both jumped back. "Sorry!" I said, at exactly the same time as he did. A small bespectacled man was wiping coffee from his jacket. He looked as though he taught media studies to first year students. I handed over wet wipes and profuse apologies, feeling foolish as if the spell had been broken with the first wave of coffee.

He eventually glanced up at me, I was at least half a foot taller, and I found myself doing that fish out of water impression that I feel goes so well for me at parties. On this occasion, it wasn't because I was doing my best to 'make friends,' which was Simon's term for rubbing up to the clients, it was due to an overwhelming sense of evil.

People usually don't understand malevolence. It doesn't always exist in its entirety in the pages of a psychopath's mind, sometimes it can be seen in the actions of normal every day monsters, those people who really believed they were 'just doing their job.' The man fell into that category. He touched my hand in a friendly gesture of thanks and I almost lost the egg sandwich. This was not some psychic experience but the deep-seated genetic memory of self-preservation. Which is what keeps you alive when all your other senses are frozen in a modern-day cocoon of 'it couldn't possibly happen in daylight to me.'

I took a step back and moved around him as if he were a cobra having a difficult day. The expression on his face changed, from benign professor to something that looked to my puzzled brain as if it could have been greed. Incongruously I said, "Sorry again. Good-bye." He nodded. Much as, I would imagine, the Nazi guards did to potential camp inmates.

I stumbled off, blinded to the world around me, the one I was supposed to live in. No one in their right mind would miss the connection between the dreamwalking and the appearance of the monster. I can accept the possibility of coincidence, but this screamed, 'look at me!' I tried deep breathing and fast walking and then risked a quick glance over my shoulder. Nobody. In fact, if I'd been capable of denial at that point, I would have put it down to just my imagination, but unfortunately my fear was making it impossible.

The shop looked reassuringly normal and I found myself wandering along the shelves touching books and lifting them out of their place to flip the pages. There is a certain smell that goes with a new book;

nothing is more comforting than a waft of fresh pages, along with cut grass, the first smoke fires of the winter evenings and warm horses in the early dawn. I could feel my vertebrae uncrunching and my heart rate returning to pre-infarction levels. Someone touched my shoulder and I leapt at least a foot in the air, shrieking like the demented. A shocked shop assistant, one I vaguely recognised, stepped back, her hand over her own heart. We both remained speechless for a moment. "Sorry!" She finally managed, "I was just wondering?"

I looked behind her to the rest of the team as they stood together by the till, shaking with laughter at the performance. I looked back at her. The penalty of being the new girl was to find out what the senior staff were up to. Usually, we were disappointingly up to nothing, but it seemed important for them to check. Simon called it low level snooping.

The office was still in its pre-lunch state of disorder and I tidied up, which involved shoving several things in my bottom drawer and watering a pot plant languishing on the window sill.

I couldn't say anything much was achieved; my brain was scrambled with thoughts and I tried not to make more of it than it was. By the time the evening lights were turned on and I had collected my belongings for the journey home, I had *almost* convinced myself that the two things may not be connected after all.

Simon stuck his head around the door, making me jump. "Are you off?" As I was standing there with a scarf wrapped around my neck, a mountain of books in one hand and my backpack in the other, I just looked back at him. There was a sarcastic remark somewhere about, but I just couldn't seem to get hold of it.

He came in and sat down, fiddling with the paraphernalia I usually left out on my desk.

"What's up?" One of the things about Simon that I had noticed when I first met him was that he listened. Which was unusual for a man, I had assumed it was a gay trait. "You know Millie, other people have pictures of their families on the desk; you have copies of the periodic table."

"I find it comforting," I said defensively, sitting down again.

"Seven copies!"

"*Very* comforting." I shuffled the books which slid spectacularly onto the floor and we both began to pick them up, Simon tutting every time he read a title. He patted my hand as he put the last book on the stack.

"I will *always* be here for you," he said quietly, "Whatever it is."

For a moment, I thought about telling him and I think he realised it because his face changed from a talking one to a listening one. But I just *couldn't*. 'I dreamwalk at night and now I think someone is following me.' No one could understand that, not even my oldest and best friend. He seemed disappointed as we walked out of the office together and down the stairs, not speaking, but he put his hand on my shoulder and gave me a hug.

They were doing a good trade in the coffee shop, the young evening crowd noisy with plans. I waved to the supervisor, who was standing at the till. He waved back at me, a big smile on his face. "We need to start planning late opening for the Christmas trade soon," he shouted.

Simon shuddered. "Please don't let's think about it yet. I can't bear all those awful people!" He did the perfect imitation of a customer, gender unknown, "Can you tell me if this bestseller is any good?" He answered himself, "Of course it is you stupid thick *uneducated twit*, that's why it says *bestseller!*"

The drive home was full of rain clouds and the radio played the music you know the words to, but don't know how you do. I stopped on the edge of the moor near a bridge and got out of the car. It was still the grey of twilight and the trees were so close together their branches made a cavern that the road disappeared into, but it didn't feel dark or claustrophobic. I looked at the river and the sound of the swollen water hitting the stones filled my head like unanswered questions.

Most of us are bound to our lives by the people around us, parents, siblings, our friends, and by what we do. I didn't have enough to tie me to the place on the moor for it to matter, but in my dreams, I was never lonely.

Cecil was standing on the window ledge. He looked annoyed. I let him in and he went immediately over to the bag of cat food that was sitting on the work surface in the kitchen. There was one message on the answer phone, my neighbours telling me that they were away for two weeks in Spain and would I feed the cat. I could hear the tinny voice at the airport announcing the next flight to somewhere warm. I tipped cat crunchies into a bowl and made a large brandy for myself.

The view from the garden stretched for miles down the valley. Small lights on the hill opposite were farms and houses. I could smell wood smoke and the fresh clean edge to the wind that meant cold weather. Shivering in my pyjamas with Cecil winding himself around my legs, I looked above me to see a sky full of stars and took a breath. Each spark of light in the Pleiades looked back at me. I picked Cecil up and he settled on my shoulder purring into my ear. I stood there for a long time until I was shivering, watching the lights in the valley turn out one by one, until all that was left were the stars.

The cat and I shared a bowl of rice pudding in bed. The heating had gone off and I pulled the downie up around my shoulders. He grumbled his exasperation as I got out of bed again and put on underwear, jeans and a sweatshirt. I didn't know why I did, but it was something to do with the mole on my face and a head full of questions and not wanting to be the only one wearing Marks and Spencer striped pyjamas. I hopped back into bed. Cecil, grumbling, made himself a nest in the top cover and we went about our respective pre-sleep thinking. I had never been afraid of my dream place and as I drifted off, I realised I wasn't actually worried about going there. The worry seemed to be about something else apart from the clothes but I couldn't remember, in the quiet shadows of the room, what exactly that was.

The sun on my back was a puzzle and as I turned around, Rari was looking at me. He raised a hand in silent greeting and I found myself smiling hello. Joao was right, he did look like a professor of something, slim and blonde with that 'thinks about everything' expression. Somewhere, I thought, there was a pair of horn-rimmed glasses he couldn't find. He handed me a gun, so therefore, maybe he was not your *average* university professor; I tucked it into the back of my jeans, and he gave me a pair of stout looking boots. I could see the side of the stables and realised I had come back in closer to the town than when I had left. The sun had an early morning feel to it. I looked down at my feet, thick Exmoor socks looked back.

"Well done on the clothes," he said, looking slightly disappointed, hanging up the unneeded jacket. I sat down in the dirt and strapped up the boots, which fitted me better than the ones belonging to the man who mucked out. "I rather liked the striped pyjamas," he added wistfully.

"How did you know where I would be, Rari?"

He looked at me carefully, gauging a reply. "Well, I guess that might need an explanation," he paused, "The others are this way." We walked towards the bar belonging to Til.

"Does this have something to do with it?" I pointed to the small 'mole' by my eye.

He looked surprised. "How did you *ever* notice that?"

I thought I'd keep the secret of the female population's relationship with magnifying mirrors to myself for the time being. I stopped in the middle of the street. "What is it Rari?" I think my whole body was radiating that I was 'not going a step further until you tell me.'

"It's called a 'fixer.' It makes it easier to dreamwalk." He carried on up the steps to the bar and I found myself following. I knew the answer was much too fast for that to be the whole explanation, but it was something.

I suddenly realised the street had people in it. The kind that wasn't covered with blood and running from the borderers. Rari held the door to the bar open for me and I followed him in. It was quiet inside. A few people were sat at tables eating and talking quietly. Which made it feel as if it was more Exeter than Dodge.

We walked over to the sofas in the far corner where Joao and Okan slouched with Til, drinking what smelt as though it was a really good coffee. Til was looking at a handheld computer and was tapping the surface with a small pointer. He got up when he saw me and in an old -fashioned gesture reached for my hand and kissed it. "It's good to see you again Millie." His hand was warm and his grey eyes clear and genuine. Okan and Joao were also standing. I sat down and Okan passed me a cup of coffee.

"How is Solly?" I asked Til. It was an obscure dance of polite conversation. As if you were at a garden party in your underwear.

"Back at school and hating it. I think that boy would be happy if the borderers hit every day just so he could get out of going." I nodded as if I understood. "Well," he said, sensing something, "I'd better go and finish my stock ordering." He tapped the computer and went off towards the stairs, stopping to talk to one of his customers.

"Right," I said quietly, "What is this?" I pointed to the fixer. No one said anything, they looked as though they were the children I knew at school, who sat at the back of the class with their chairs leaning against the wall. It's odd but I had always *thought* that those kids were smarter than the teachers and now I knew they were.

They grow into the kind of people who pick up tiny bits of dust at a crime scene and make a perfect case, or take photographs of killer whales off the shores of Patagonia. If you are their passion, they can peel you like an onion and if they make that promise, the one that says 'no one hurts you, not while I'm here,' then they will do whatever they can to keep it. Which was why I was so angry.

"I'm still sitting here!" I said, helpfully.

"It makes it easier to dreamwalk," Okan answered.

"Yes, I got that from Rari."

Okan drank coffee and looked carefully at Rari with expressionless dark eyes.

"Hey, *she* asked *me*!" Rari shrugged.

I put my coffee cup down with a clatter and one or two people glanced our way. It was difficult not to overdo the exasperation.

"What are you not saying?"

"It interacts with your body at the subatomic level and allows you to dreamwalk with more than just your mind." Joao spoke quietly and without any reference to Okan, which I thought was interesting.

"We all have one." He pointed to a small dot on the side of his face over the pulse point by his eye. "It's not dangerous Millie, in fact it makes things safer. You don't want to know what happens to you if you can't get back to your body."

I am not *ever* speechless, but the thought that I might not be able to get back to my body had *never* actually occurred to me. "What do you mean exactly, that it's possible to be *lost* between the two places?"

"Oh yeah," Joao answered, "Not good." He finished his coffee. "Are we off, or what?"

"There are so many things I don't know," I sighed, as Rari and Joao got up to go. I felt as if I was the little kid running to keep up with the big boys.

"You coming?" Rari looked at Okan.

He shook his head and pointed at me. "I think I'd better stay and keep Millie company, just in case her head explodes." I thumped him on the arm. I watched as the odd couple made their way towards the door and out into the sunshine. Their shadows caught in the dust on the floor as they went.

"Where are they going?" I picked up my coffee.

"Trying to get a look at one of the space vehicles that the borderers have left behind. It crashed up in the canyon." I finished my coffee. We looked at each other for a moment and he leaned forward and touched my knee. "Are you okay?"

I pointed to the fixer. "What else does this do?" He seemed to be hiding behind his eyes for a second. I added, "I know it must have some identifying properties because Rari knew exactly where I was going to be when I came back."

He nodded, hunting for the words. "Sometimes, it's not that easy to do the right thing."

"You mean when you have to follow the rules," I said, with a flash of insight that I didn't really feel.

"Yes," he said, relieved, then sat back rubbing his face like a man with a problem.

"So, what rules are *you* breaking Okan?" There ensued one of those silences that happens when two people are deciding whether to trust each other.

"It makes the dreamwalker traceable in both places and helps the

45

process happen without doing any damage. Long term dreamwalking has had several irreversible side effects on some people."

I realised that there was enough that he wasn't telling me to sink a sizeable ship, but it felt as if that was okay and not too weird. I had known these people since I was a small child and though that didn't mean the same thing as trust, it meant something. The question that hung around in the air between us and the one I knew I wouldn't get an answer for was 'who's doing the tracing,' that part *was* creepy.

"Millie, Okan said, leaning forward, "You need to learn how to use the directional function."

"What exactly does that mean?"

"It's not always a good idea to arrive in the same place." I must have looked puzzled. He lowered his voice. From a distance we would have seemed like lovers whispering the things that they would find interesting. One or two of the customers on the other tables watched as he moved closer to me and you could see the shape of old memories flicker across their faces, because people always remember what love felt like even after it's long gone.

"Haven't you noticed that you always arrive near the stables?" Okan had the kind of grainy New York accent that made you think of rainy days in Central Park, strong black coffee and a lazy, laconic strength. "Millie?"

"Sorry." I did my best to remember what we had been talking about before I had gone off on the mental walkabout. "Yes, you were saying, arriving at the stables?"

He smiled and shook his head, then leaned forward again. "The 'fixer' will help you move location. You need to practice arriving at a different place. Just think about another area, try and be specific about the memory. It might save your life."

I thought about this for a while. Watching the door as people moved off to the rest of their day. "Okan, how long have I been away? From here I mean."

"Three days." He examined my reaction. But I couldn't say I had one. The time frame didn't seem to have any relevance. At home I was one day older.

"How is Lu's mother?" I asked.

46

He was surprised by the question. "She's not great. Still in the hospital at Twin Rivers."

"Where's Lu?"

"He's staying with Til Duster."

I poured myself some more coffee, which was still hot in the container. The smooth ergonomic silver shape seemed to have the ability to retain the temperature without any heat source. It reflected the movement in the room, as if I was seeing a world through the fisheye lens of strange forms. Okan held out his cup and I filled it. He drank it black and I drowned mine in lots of sugar and milk.

"When I dreamwalk I come back to the same place every time." It wasn't really a question. I was just settling some things in my mind. Okan nodded, looking wary. I thought back to my childish wanderings and realised that I had always arrived in or close to the stables. "The stable is a fixed point of entry." He said nothing that time, just watched as I tried to figure things out, he was much better at observing than I was at working things out.

"It doesn't have to be, it's the way the mind processes information. The more you know of the area the more places you can arrive." He leaned back with his coffee cradled in two hands and the tired look of someone who is treading carefully around a really big crater. The question of who had thought through the details, wasn't asked and therefore not answered, but my money would have been on the same people who had made the fixer and had done the tracking.

"Okay," I said, "I'll practice." I understood that 'something was going on.' I was not stupid. But it felt as if there was plenty of time and this was my other place.

I reached out and touched Okan's hand and he turned his over so they were palm to palm. "Do you think we could go and look at that borderer's ship?"

He seemed surprised and then not. "Sure." He pulled me up and put his coffee down in one move and we followed the trail of sunlight that fell through the windows in untainted brilliance to the doorway and outside. "Til!" He shouted back into the dark bar, "Can we borrow the runabout?"

"Yeah. Not a problem. Be back before sunset. The vildens are breeding."

The runabout was a small vehicle that looked similar the four wheeled quad bikes they used on Exmoor to round up sheep, except that there were no wheels. It had the usual hover-jets that seemed to be the main type of ground vehicle power.

I sat behind Okan and put my arms around his waist as he started the engine. I felt as if I was a biker but with only the one tattoo. Til Duster came running around the end of the building with a small, brightly coloured bag in his hand. "Can you drop this off at the school? Solly forgot his lunch today." He pulled a square of jelly-like substance out of his pocket. "Weldon left this behind last night. You have to go past their place to get to the 'dropdown.'" He laughed, "His partner Tara has just called me on it to see where it was."

I put the two things in the square lidded container tucked behind me that Okan pointed out. My sweatshirt must have ridden up, uncovering the small gun that Rari had given me. Til tapped the exposed weapon. "You need to get a holster for that. Don't want to be losing it over some bumpy ride, not in these times." He looked bleak and I realised that it was not long since he had lost his partner. I leaned over and gave him a hug. He smiled and hugged me back, patting me like a restless horse. "Be safe now," he said.

The small town was a blur as we set off, Okan twisting the power up, like a race track rider. I grabbed him to stop from being unseated and he laughed.

The school was in easy walking distance of the town and had a serious set of white interconnecting buildings, with large windows. We arrived to see children playing in the grounds. There were a lot of battles going on, borderers and settlers. Kids everywhere, forever, goodies and baddies linked in the endless noisy war of growing up.

Solly yelled, "Okan!" He came over to us and took the package I handed him with a big smile. Lu appeared from a knot of curious children and I pulled him up by his outstretched arms to sit on my lap. He leaned into me and I hugged him, squeezing until he giggled. His sharp little face was shadowed with the worry you only see on people who are desperately afraid. I kissed his forehead and he smiled again, slipping down to join his friends who asked loud questions.

Okan took off again and we settled into a routine of me saying, "Oh look," and him explaining just what I was pointing at. Water towers, solar power units. A weather station, which also doubled as the early warning security centre, as the town didn't have a 'net.'

The track leading to the hills was coated with a glittering dust and I asked Okan if he knew what it was. He told me the moon had a very high level of mineable minerals and the trail led from the cliff mines to the town.

We headed out towards the place where Joao and I had found the survivors and then carried on past, staying on the track. A turning appeared after miles of fields and cattle interspersed with dense trees. The slopes of the snow-capped mountains seemed to be closer here, though I knew they were miles away. It reminded me of travelling through Montana in late spring.

A small sign on one side of the trail said 'Weldon.' Okan turned the runabout and it dipped over on one side like a boat in a gale. We arrived up at the house to see a woman on the porch with a large gun. She smiled and leaned the weapon against the doorway when she saw us.

I hopped off the runabout with the grace of a pregnant goat. It gave you the kind of sea legs that made you feel woozy when you got off a ship onto dry land after a rough crossing. She held out a hand.

"You must be Millie. I'm Tara Weldon." She had a firm warm hand, toffee coloured skin, clear green eyes and was tall and slim in dusty trousers, jacket and boots.

"Are you stopping for coffee and a visit, Okan?" It looked as if we were as he followed her into the house. It was large and comfortable with a view of the mountains from the back windows. "Weldon's out checking the cattle," she said over her shoulder.

"Did you lose much?" Okan asked her, settling himself down into the kitchen chair as she mixed hot water and coffee. A large cake with icing an inch thick came out of a cupboard.

"Quite a few." Her face was lined with tiredness and worry. "They hit us hard."

I gave her the small square of jelly. "Til sent this."

"Weldon's com. He loses this thing at least once a week!" She smiled.

While she cut the cake, I had a quick look at the com. It had interconnecting fibres woven through it and a series of square indentations around the outer edge with raised symbols.

"Do you know how Jarry Wang is?"

I had no idea who that was but Okan answered, "Not so good, still at the hospital in Twin Rivers." I realised that they were talking about Lu's mother.

She tutted, handing over enough cake to feed a London Welsh prop forward. "Those borderers sure love their knives! What they can't steal they spoil." She sat down with us and we drank coffee for a moment. "We all really appreciated your help Okan, you and your friends."

"That view is breathtaking," I said, breaking a small silence that threatened to be a big one.

"Yeah," she said, "It never gets old."

The cake was so good I pinched the icing from Okan's plate. He looked astonished. "What?" I said, "You should eat faster." I had learned the hard way *not* to leave cake lying around working with a gay guy and a bunch of teenagers.

"You on your way to the dropdown?" Tara asked. Okan nodded, draining the last of the coffee, which could have easily cleaned the barnacles from a nuclear submarine. Tara shuddered. "I wouldn't go near the thing if you paid me. There's one that's never going to be picked clean by the salvagers."

She stood in the doorway waving until we turned the corner.

Nothing changed, even in my dream place. Strong women were still holding things together in the middle of nowhere.

The sky was blue-green and clear with small clouds on the mountains. It felt cold on the runabout and I curved myself against Okan, using him as a shield from the wind. It was possible to talk but we were both silent. As if Tara's 'normal' had fed us more than cake.

A small copse of broken trees and a trail of scorched earth pinpointed the dropdown. We pulled up next to the ship. I could hear Rari and Joao talking. They appeared from the inside.

"I thought you might turn up." Rari smiled.

I jumped down, my curiosity overcoming the unpleasant burnt smell. The ship was an 'egg on its side' shape, with small windows in the front and an entrance halfway down. It looked as if it had had a really bad landing; the ground was pushed up around the craft and curled, in a wave of earth and stones.

"Can I look inside?" I asked.

"It's not too wholesome in there Millie, are you sure?" Joao said. I shrugged. My parents on the really busy days had sometimes 'bandaged' in the kitchen. They were the kind of doctors that answered the door to 'can you just fix this for me.' Leg ulcers were not an unusual sight at mealtimes. I remembered the smell of a neglected gangrenous limb and my parents horrified faces. Some sweet old lady who hadn't wanted to bother them at work. It's not the ghastly sights that affect you the most, it's the smell.

I touched the smooth side of the craft with my fingers. It gave off a slight fizz as if the forces of electromagnetism had crossed the dreamwalking barriers as easily as the taste of coffee. The doorway was gloomy and the work surfaces had the lighted consoles of flying vehicles everywhere. The outside was not much bigger than the inside. There was possibly room for six normal sized people. I stood for a moment, my eyes getting used to the light level. The two seats at the pointy end were facing forward and I could see lumpy shapes which my brain tried to identify. I realised that there were bits of the occupants still remaining.

Joao and Rari were discussing the ship with Okan. I pointed.

"Yeah. We were hoping to have removed the bodies before you got here," Joao said.

"Where's the rest of them?" I breathed carefully through my mouth.

They all shrugged. Rari said, "We think there may have been a

fight on board that caused the crash. I guess they were the losers."
I took a shallow breath and had a look. The human body is a
rather frail thing when it comes up against metal at speed. I
couldn't see anything that might have been a seat belt and no sign
of airbags.

"How fast does this ship go?"

"Light speed."

I thought I would be astonished when the surroundings were
more conducive. The bodies were mashed. "I don't think there was a
fight. I think they were going too fast when they hit the ground; they
may have bounced through some kind of barrier to slow them down.
But my guess is these are impact injuries. I suppose the ship is made
of sterner stuff because it doesn't seem badly damaged." I glanced
up. Three pairs of eyes regarded me with sceptical expressions.
"Imagine a tin can with sharp pointy things in it and put two soft
squashy things inside. Then shake vigorously." They all nodded,
looking slightly grim.

I moved away from the bodies and decided to get some fresh air.
A few deep breaths made a difference to the possibility of Tara's cake
being seen again. I leaned against the ship, feeling again the slight
fizz of something, which was the crackle before a thunderstorm.

"Joao!" I called, "Is there some kind of power source still on
inside?" He stuck his head out of the open doorway. "Look," I said,
putting my hand an inch away from the ship's surface. You could see
a small electric shock pass across. Joao came out, his face a mask of
puzzlement. He called the others. I demonstrated the trick again,
sucking my fingers afterwards, because it hurt. Something was
communicated silently between them that made me feel as if I was
the last person to get the joke. "What?" I asked.

"Well," Okan searched for words. He held his hand close to the
surface of the ship and we all watched as nothing happened.

"What does that mean?"

"These ships are biomechanical," he explained. I think I was
doing an impression of a large plank of wood because he tried again.

"They program them with the ability to connect to a certain
biochemical response. The locals usually strip anything that drops

down from the sky for useful parts because no one can fly them without the connection."

"Why do I have a connection?" I touched the surface again, suffering the shock for the sake of curiosity.

"Good question." Joao's smile had the depth of things not said and then he said it. "Millie, do you have biogenetic manipulation where you come from?"

"Joao!" Okan shouted and Rari shook his head, raising his eyes up in exasperation.

"Okan. She didn't flinch when she looked at those two bodies, which frankly turned *my* stomach. I don't think she's the type of person who's going to have a problem with the truth!"

I realised of course, immediately. But somehow it just wouldn't filter through and I had to ask the question anyway. I said carefully as if the words would bite me, "Don't we come from the same place?" Each face expressed what was behind the eyes as a reply. "I *thought* it was something to do with *time*." I sat down on a well-placed smooth rock and was stunned into silence for several minutes.

"It's more complicated than that." Okan sat on the ground next to me. We looked as though we were a gathering of garden gnomes, as Joao stretched out on the grass. Rari went back into the craft and began making comforting geek twiddling noises.

"I don't actually think there *is* anything more complicated than time travel."

"Have you heard of multiverse?" Okan spoke gently, but I began to feel very dizzy and I put my head down. I know I groaned which was slightly theatrical.

"Multiple universe theory," I said to my knees.

"You're not taking this as well as I thought you would Millie," Joao said curiously.

"*Really!*" I was still talking to my knees. I was never a scientist. I had always classed myself as a science nerd, someone who gets a buzz out of quantum mechanics and star systems. Reading about gravity waves is better than chocolate, but it doesn't mean I will ever understand it. "So basically, what you're saying is," I sat up and looked at them, "I *am* in Kansas, just not my Kansas?"

Okan shook his head. He had an 'let's hope this gets better' expression on his face. "Not exactly."

A shout from the end of the track had all of us jumping as if we were kids caught behind the bike sheds. A man came skidding up on a runabout similar to the one we had borrowed from Til Duster. He hopped off and came over. "Hey!" He smiled. They all tapped fists in something that looked similar to a gang handshake. "You must be Millie?"

"Yes," I said, smiling, "I'm thinking of changing my name by deed poll to include 'you must be.'" I stood up and came over to join the male bonding session.

"Weldon." He pointed to himself and we shook hands.

"I brought some clearance bags; thought you might need them. Anything useful on the ship?"

Okan and Joao took on the roles of second-hand car salesmen steering the buyer towards a questionably better deal. It was difficult for them to carry it off with the sounds of Rari in the background going 'ooh' and 'ahh' in an enthusiastic geek voice.

"Oh, and Tara sent cake and hot coffee." Weldon, who didn't seem to have a first name, reached over for the bags, which were light grey and looked too fragile to put body parts in.

Rari's head appeared out of the doorway. "Did someone mention cake?"

The little group of men stood about talking and eating, it could have been anywhere, anytime, which considering the circumstances, pretty much covered it. I went inside the craft and had another look around. The two bodies were stinking and slightly bloated. From what was left I could see that they were similar to the borderer I had met in the town. Larger than average size and those odd feline looking eyes. Even the pupil, milky in death, had the slashed shape of a cat's eye, which was probably designed so they would be able to see movement in the dark.

I reached carefully over the seats and, trying not to touch anything slimy, I tapped the console keys. Small lights appeared and a steady hum began somewhere in the heart of the ship. I could feel the fizz inside my head, as well as my fingers.

"Hey!" Okan shouted, making me jump. "What are you *doing*?"

I pulled my hands away and tried not to look as if my mother had caught me on the garage roof again.

"Unless you know how to fly this, I don't think starting it up is such a good idea."

He spoke with the kind of reasonableness that teachers have for their most difficult pupils, checking the console which had gone back to 'pre fizz' dormancy and then looking at me. His eyes glittered dark in the shadows. "Would you mind if I took a DNA sample?"

"We haven't even had a date yet!" I laughed. The 'dead bodies in spaceship' effect was making me feel slightly off balance. He took a small kit from a pack he had brought in with him. "Do you use the epithelial tissue from the mouth?" I asked.

He shrugged. "That will do." He leaned toward me and I opened my mouth. The implement he used wasn't a swab, but similar to a suction tube. "Are you sure you've never had any genetic manipulation?"

"Aah," I said, as the tube was in my mouth. He removed it.

"No. I don't think so. It's not something we do at home yet." We were standing so close together I could feel his breath on my skin and his fingers were still holding my chin. He took a short, sharp inhalation and then a step back, putting the tube in a small container.

"You having a party in there?" Rari came in with the bags the rancher had brought. I could hear a runabout disappearing into the distance.

"Weldon gone?" Okan asked.

"Yeah. It wasn't easy to persuade him after Millie did her thing." Rari looked exasperated.

"Sorry." I shrugged. "I didn't realise I was actually *doing* something."

"What?" Okan asked me, puzzled.

"It just felt natural." I couldn't explain it. "The ship seemed to be alive and we could have a conversation, if only I knew the right words."

Both of them looked as if they were struggling with the layers of meaningful words, which made them seem similar to most men in existence from the beginning of time.

Rari spoke first. "Do you think those bodies are carrying anything I should be worried about?"

"Rari, you should know that most viruses need a live biological environment to survive and," I added, "*We're* dreamwalking."

"There's something to do with bacteriology that I don't understand that makes it possible," Rari answered grumpily, avoiding my eyes,

He began to manoeuvre body parts and Okan opened up the bags, they had a system which suggested that it was not a first time for either of them. For half a second, I thought about offering to help and then made a feeble exit.

Joao was inspecting the outside of the ship, checking dents and running his hand over the barely discernible joints in the hull. I followed him around like an extra leg, getting in the way. "Put your hand here Millie." He pointed to a small unit that had appeared when he touched a set of lighted keys by the door. I held my hand over the squashy square. It began to fizz alarmingly and he moved my too-close fingers. "Good, there's plenty of power."

I looked up at the sky and stretched my back which felt as if I had been sitting for too long, though I hadn't. "Joao, why is the sky so green here?"

He turned to me, his odd eyes thinking of something else. "What? Oh, well, you know the way sunlight scatters when it hits the air?"

"Yes, Rayleigh scattering. As it hits the atmosphere the longer yellow, orange and red wavelengths pass through unobstructed, but blue and violet light is scattered by air molecules in all directions."

He looked impressed for a second, which made me feel insulted for slightly longer than that. "Well, there's something in the upper atmosphere that affects the wavelengths closer to the 500 to 550 nanometre range."

"What thing?" I asked to his back, as he pushed at a small scrape and tutted as it bubbled out.

"That would be the weather net."

I nodded. The dream place of my childhood had a weather net and suddenly the journey had gone from the distance of a moment when your eyes closed, to an epic.

"Ah!" I shouted. Joao dropped into a crouch and held his gun in front of him. Okan and Rari leapt from the doorway of the craft, Okan doing an impressive roll to hide behind a rock. It went very quiet. I sat down abruptly. When the expected attack didn't manifest into anything, the three men stood around looking helplessly at each other.

Rari and Joao silently voted Okan as spokesman and slid with relief back into the ship. Both of them were trying not to look as if they had got the better deal with the dead bodies, rather than the existential crisis.

"Millie," Okan said calmly, "I take it you're having a bit of trouble dealing with this."

"Well, we *are* talking straight to an alternative live streaming site?"

He nodded his head slowly which turned into a shake. "I really have no idea what you just said, but I think that would be yes." He sat down next to me and sighed, then gave me a cuddle, which was the nose squashing kind, but somehow comforting.

"I'm not sure about my reality anymore." My voice was muffled against the scratchy shirt.

"Millie, reality comes from the human mind, not the body or brain."

"Ah!" I said again, but quietly.

"I don't have all the answers," Okan said, ruffling my hair which was not as irritating as it ought to have been.

"Who knew, you're human after all."

"You're really very sarcastic," he said.

"Is it safe to come out yet?" Joao shouted, "Has Millie finished having a crisis?"

I sighed and got to my feet, pulling Okan up. I went over to the ship and took one end of the bag that Joao was carrying. We manoeuvred it out of the doorway, its contents were alarmingly squashy against my legs.

"Whoever made these people so violent?" I asked, huffing with the weight of what must have been a small part of a borderer. Joao was concentrating on an answer. "They were *made* in a test tube?" I added.

"Well, they were genetically modified. We all have prehistoric genes in us Millie. We carry the code of our violent past in our DNA. You just have to find it."

"You only have to see a game of ice hockey to know *that's* true." I balanced the weight on my knee for a moment, rubbing my sticky hands for a better grip. We pushed and pulled the soggy bag into a hole that the two men must have dug while Okan and I were drinking coffee with Tara.

"Do the 'they' that Okan keeps referring to know *how* we are here?" I pointed at myself and then him.

Joao stopped in full walking mode, which made it look as if he was doing a small dance and I smiled. Okan and Rari were bringing another bag which they threw into the hole. Joao looked at Okan and then said, "Some people have a strong connection to this place. It's similar to wiring."

"Do you mean mine's different?"

"Something like that."

We went back into the ship and pulled another bag out through the doorway. A strip of bloody fluid streaked across the floor. Small scraps of flesh were caught on the pilot's seats. I thought that a whole bucket of bleach wouldn't clean the smell away. Then I remembered something my mother had told me. "We need lemon juice." Joao looked puzzled. "The smell of adipocere gets into everything, including your hair and clothes."

He looked even more puzzled. "Decomposing body fat," I explained, pointing to the unattractive bits that seemed to have become attached everywhere. "Lemon juice works." I picked up my end of the bag.

"It's usually caused by moisture and microbes and I think, low oxygen and," I said helpfully, "There's something to do with bowel flora that I can't quite remember."

"Well thank goodness for that," Joao muttered.

"Sorry, I get carried away." The bag slipped and slithered, and holding on was painful so we concentrated for a moment on the task.

I asked, "Have they tried putting a fixer on someone who doesn't *actually* dreamwalk?"

"Yes." Joao hefted his end of the bag.

"What happened?"

He looked serious. "Not so good."

I stretched my back again and watched while Okan and Rari added their burden to the hole in the ground. The air felt warm and fresh and the smell from the rotting flesh was like a swarm of hornets stinging the breeze. You couldn't see any houses or any sign of people and except for the animals grazing in the distance there was nothing. I wondered about the early days of the native Americans and settlers in in the west, if the country had been this empty. My eyes went from the mountains to the ship. Maybe it was not quite the Oregon trail.

Joao cleared his throat, "You're not going to have another crisis, are you?"

I thumped him on the arm. "I was just *thinking*!" I waved my arms around, nearly catching him on the chin, he ducked back in a theatrical fashion and I laughed. He joined in and then stopped abruptly, as if it was something he hadn't done for a long time. His odd eyes looked puzzled again.

"We're going to have to do some cleaning before we try and start it up." Okan reached down and lit the corner of one of the bags with a small square stone that could have been a thermo block, but it was self-igniting. It flamed bright blue, smoke spiralled into the sky and I remembered the last time I had seen that, at the back of the town.

We stepped away as the funeral pyre crackled with the human fluids of death. There's was nothing kind or loving about this end. Just three dream warriors and a lonely woman.

We worked on the ship all day. Okan went off to see if he could get some lemon juice from Tara Weldon and came back with something that appeared to be a hybrid of several fruits. It had a sharp citrus smell when I squeezed it, so I mixed it with some water that Joao had produced from the river and heated over an instant fire he had made. Tara had thoughtfully provided a few old cloths that looked as if they had been clothing in a past life. I cleaned the seats and the floor of the craft and left a bucket of strong solution inside for a while with the doorway closed.

I took some of the fruit down to the river and stripped off. The water was freezing, but I stood close to the bank and rubbed the fruit skin over me, rinsing off in one brave breathless dip.

"Millie! Are you decent?" Okan shouted.

"No! Don't come any closer." I used my vest to dry off and put my clothes back on. I pulled the sweatshirt over my head and came around the bushes to see Okan with his back turned. It made me laugh.

He looked around. "We were wondering if you were up to a test drive?"

"How long have you been there?"

"Long enough." He grinned.

I thumped him on the arm. "I'm not going anywhere with you lot until you wash."

"You're joking?" Joao looked suspiciously at the squeezed fruit and then back at me. I shook my head. "Let me get this, okay? You want me to cover myself in fruit juice and then jump into a freezing cold river!" I nodded. "But why?"

"You *stink* and I'm *not* getting into something the size of a tin can with you." The three of them looked back at me with the expressive schoolboy horror of soap and water.

"We can't negotiate?" Rari tried hopefully.

I shook my head again. "It's my best offer."

"You know," Joao said over his shoulder as he walked down the path to the river, "When my mother retires, *you* can have the job."

I stood by the fire and waited for them. Okan had declined my kind proposition of holding their clothes, with a snort. The grey was deepening around the edges and the evening seemed cool and quiet. I looked up at the new stars and saw a moon, which was small but very bright. I wondered, fleetingly, what the albedo reading for light reflection was. A large shape that loomed as a shadow in the night sky was puzzling. As if I was seeing something through a curtain. It was a huge striped saucer, but not very well defined in the early evening and the stars, which were bright everywhere else, but had been blocked out by whatever it was.

The fire provided the comfort that you would expect, I reached out my hands feeling the warmth and it felt as if the flames reached back.

I could hear the soft voices of the men coming back from the river, laughing quietly, easy in their friendship. "So, how's this?" Rari turned himself around for inspection.

I sniffed with exaggeration. "You'll do."

The ship was a shadow in the corner of my eye. Joao did a last-minute inspection of the outside, using a torch. Okan and I went and sat in the pilot seats and Rari doused the fire. "Okan," I asked, "Is there a moon around this moon?"

" It was necessary, something to do with the tides and a whole lot of astrological science"

He was examining the pilot's console which was small sections of squashy coloured lights with several sets of hieroglyphs written above them.

I thought about this for a while. I could hear Rari talking to Joao as they finished the visual check of the ship. "What you're saying is, these people moved another moon into an orbit around this one?"

He looked up. "Yes," he said.. He looked down again. "There's a rational explanation that involves crop rotation, insects and breeding cycles that makes your eyes glaze over."

"I was *actually* thinking of the 'moving a moon,' how does *that* happen?" I leaned over to see what he was doing with a black marker pen that wrote in luminous ink. There were one or two suggestions as in, 'start up here' and several exclamation marks.

"Nothing that high tech. You just need a really big bang in the right place," he explained.

I didn't know what was the most difficult to get hold of. The shifting of a large moving mass in space and the creation of an orbit, or the fact that Okan didn't know what most of the keys on the pilot's console were for.

Rari closed the ship's door and I tried not to think about claustrophobia. He and Joao pulled two seats out of a blank wall and sat down close to us. Okan looked at me.

"What now?" I asked him. He shrugged and pointed to the console. "Abracadabra!" I said as I wiggled my fingers and put my hands on the console keys, trying to avoid the exclamation marks. "Do you know abracadabra is a mix of three ancient Hebrew words, meaning father, son and holy spirit?" All three pairs of eyes were incredulous. "Do you think I only graze in the science section?" Joao shook his head slowly.

There was something odd happening to the ends of my fingers, apart from the electrical shock that was visible in the gloom of the ship. It started as a slight fizz and ended up somewhere in the bones of my back. The men were all straining to see what was going on and then the console lights began flashing as the ship recognised my DNA signature. "Hey!" I pointed at the lights. "It likes me!"

"Try this one, Millie." Okan indicated the keys he had marked with the hopeful word's 'power' and 'take off.' I tried the power first. We shot back in our seats as the ship responded, like a scandalised chicken on a collision course with the trees. Joao and Rari shouted completely pointless advice and Okan indicated the 'possible take off' key. I hit it with about two feet to spare.

We were out of control but this time in a different direction. Up. Okan tried using the console, but the ship wouldn't speak to him. "Let's try a bit of steering," he said, pointing to a double row of keys that were flashing up and down, one red one green. I put the fingers of my right hand on the green and my left on the red. It was like stirring a pudding with your tongue. Eventually the ship seemed to slow down and settle, and the collective sigh of relief was audible. It was really just a single engine aeroplane. The red was the power and the green was directional. If you got it down to a fine art you could do left and right with the same fingers, though it made your eyes cross. I played around with the keys, swimming around in the air, skimming the trees and doing near-vertical pull ups. The console had produced a dizzying set of unreadable information on the hiero-glyphic head-up display in the same language that was written all over the ship. It would have looked at home on the side of an Egyptian tomb.

The sky was evening dark and we flew in a tight circle over the quiet fields and up to the edge of the mountain range. "What about fuel?"

"It's a regenerating biomechanical unit." Okan was watching my hands and trying to keep from taking over. I wondered if it was the first time he'd had to sit back and let someone else do the difficult things. I had some uncharitable thoughts about how good it would be for his personal growth.

"Let's go and see if this is space-worthy." Okan was pointing at the power key. I held my finger on the top red squashy square and eased the rest of my fingers down the other red squares. At the same time, I pushed hard on the green keys. We shot upwards and the ground blurred into the grey shadows of early evening. We passed through the layers of cloud and the sky became a strange colour with small floating black shapes that looked as if it was the game you play with noughts and crosses. I thought my eyes were objecting to the sudden upward trajectory and the cells that wander around the vitreous at the back of your eye were collecting together.

Okan pointed. "That's the weather net. The satellites link up to provide the layer of weather control."

We were climbing at a terrific rate, but the craft seemed to slide through the atmosphere with little inertia. Suddenly the sky was full of stars and we were away from the moon and out into space. Both Rari and Joao hopped out of their seats and came over to the front window.

I gasped and then, moving my hands away from the console, I pointed. The ship, not appreciating the lack of directive, began to swirl, which had Okan jittering and trying to do something. He even-tually pushed my hands back onto the keys. I didn't look at him. The window occupied my whole conscious thought. "Jupiter!" I said, the striped saucer shape was now making sense. I turned the ship back to look at the moon and pointed with my chin.

"It's Europa." Okan answered.

"The only one with water," I whispered. A small moon was spinning around the larger one. I pointed again without using my hands.

"Leda," Joao said. He was smiling as he leaned over the chair that I was sitting in. I noticed that his front teeth were slightly crooked.

We were all quiet for a long time. I kept the ship in a high orbit above Europa, which was a posh way of saying my fingers were on the controls, rather than wafting about in the air where they usually were when I was looking and thinking at the same time.

"Is there a satellite tracking system around here?" I asked, "We are in a borderer ship."

"There is a basic system linked into the main port," Okan said. "They will know that someone is up here, but not who or what. This settler group doesn't have the money to pay for anything more sophisticated. If we stay here much longer without making contact, someone will start to get very nervous."

"Then who moved the moons?" I was still having some difficulty with the thought that anyone actually could.

"Not these people," Rari answered.

Joao had gone to check on a blinking light at the doorway. It seemed to match the one I had on the upper edge of the pilot's console.

Suddenly a string of information was running at speed across the holo-screen in front of me. I couldn't read it. It looked like a combination of hieroglyphs and shorthand. I pointed at it helpfully.

Joao flicked one of the small blue squares that they all carried around to make a fire. He blew it out quickly and watched as the spiral of smoke twisted its way towards the door. "Right. I think we'd better get back to dry land." He and Rari sat down again and I slithered my fingers down the keys, pushing the craft towards the high cloud layer around the moon. The flashing lights were joined by a buzzing noise.

"Do you suppose that means the air supply is getting low?" I asked Okan.

"I think that's pretty much a given." He sat with his arms folded, suppressing huge amounts of impotence and frustration. His fingers twitched to take over and land the craft and I was twitching with the thought of actually having to do so.

"Where should we put down?" I asked, my voice shaking slightly with nerves.

"Anywhere would be good," Rari shouted from the seats behind me, trying to be heard over the incessant awful buzzing, as he and Joao fumbled with the now available safety straps that were unused by the borderers.

We spun through the cloud layers and the noughts and crosses of the weather net. The green tinge filled the cabin and each face took on the shadow glow of the unhealthy. Okan was straining against the straps that held him into his seat, trying not to jerk my fingers away and fix the noise and crazy descent. My hands became sweaty and cramped, and I resisted the temptation to flex them.

The cloud layer was full of storm and we came out under thousands of feet of wild grey into a world where the horizon merged into mountains, the huge towers and anvils of cumuli nimbus swirled and growled with threatened rain and thunder.

The little craft was spinning from the rotation caused by the surface and upper air patterns. In the back of my head was a stray thought about jet streams and thunder clouds and organised storms. "Okan, does this moon have tornados?"

It was as if we were being grabbed by the ground and thrown back into the air. I did as much as I could, but the craft couldn't cope with the dynamics. "Okan!" I struggled. He looked helpless and furious. We were descending far too fast and much too steeply. My fingers were slippery with sweat and I could feel my contact and communication with the ship beginning to fray at the edges. It was sluggish to respond, as if we had stopped speaking the same language and it needed to think carefully before replying.

The mountains were dark, full of snow and mean sharp winds, and we were an out-of-control rollercoaster of power and noise. Nothing seemed to slow us down. I leaned over and quickly rubbed my forehead with the sleeve of my sweatshirt without taking my hands off the controls. My arms were shaking with the strain and I took a mind freezing moment to wipe one set of sweaty fingers. The ship took a slight list to port which I tried to correct. "Maybe if we get out of this, some flying lessons and a short course in the local meteorology would be useful?"

"Is there *any way* you can slow us down?" Rari shouted. Okan looked back at him.

We were getting closer to the ground, no more than a few thousand feet.

"Try and stay away from the mountains," Okan said.

"I think I need to make it clearer to you just how out of control this is." I pushed the power keys at their squashy base and the craft began to oscillate, too little power too close to the ground would make us drop out of the sky. The winds were fierce and whirls of debris funnelled around us making the chance of hitting something a real possibility. "Can the ship cope with a mid-air collision?" I shouted. Large branches were flying around us. A huge clang made the inside ring like a bell. We all held our breath.

"I think that's yes," Okan said. Then he pointed. "Look, over there!"

"I see it!" Close to the mountains and *much* too close to a large body of water. We seemed to have come out on the other side of the range. I thought I would add a navigation lesson to my to do list. Nothing on the computer screen made any sense. It was trying to tell me where we were, how high we were, how fast we were going. I just couldn't read it. Little red lights began to blink all over the console.

The take offs and landings that I had practised in the fields behind Weldon's farm had been mainly done by the ship, easy, no off the scale winds, no funnels of debris. No leaking air and not so dark.

As we got closer, I realised the 'landing strip' was little more than a beach between the tree line and the water. It seemed to be getting smaller the closer we got, but I hoped that was my brain playing silly little games with my eyes. The winds were, if anything getting stronger, pulling the craft in different directions, one moment rushing us at the ground, the next on a bubble of updraught.

I tried to focus my mind on the patch of beach in front of me. I realised we would not actually suffocate anymore; because death would probably be in the way of the two borderers we had found, squashy.

The landing was a short glide and a long slide, with lots of crashing and bumping. Everything was quiet, even the warning buzz had given up. No one spoke. My hands were numb and shaking. I put them in my lap and dropped my head. Eventually Rari got up and I tapped the doorway to open. A rush of wild salt-filled rain swept into the cabin. The storm pushed its way into the small space, rattling the craft. I closed the door again. "How long do you think we're going to be here?" I asked, still shaking.

"I think the worst of it will be gone by morning," Okan said, stretching himself up. "Well," he said suddenly, making me jump, "That wasn't too bad, was it?"

Rari was already pulling the covers off the ship's workings, trying to check for damage. "Come over here and put your hand on this, Millie." A small fizzy light appeared to be pulsing happily at the core of lots of gel-covered wiring.

Joao produced some of the food Weldon had brought us out of a bag, and a flask of a hot fruit flavoured drink. It was camping, but without being outside. Okan was trying to seal the pinhole damage with something that looked as if it could be cake frosting, but behaved the way that mercury does. "What do you think caused that?" I pointed.

"Micro meteor maybe." He shrugged. "When the weather gets better, I'll have a go at the outside. Should be okay." He was corralling the substance towards the damage. It funnelled down the hole as if it was alive, which was creepy but in a chemically satisfying way.

The banging and crashing continued. I curled up in the pilot's seat, which had been designed with much bigger occupants in mind, so it felt as though you were a child in your granddad's chair. Not that I had ever known either set belonging to my parents. I watched Rari and Joao fixing things, helping out when they needed a 'fizz' check from me. Okan was trying to get to grips with the language on the computer. The view through the front windows was distorted by the dark and rain, a battering of sound and water. I could see huge waves, walls of moving green and grey. Trees bent and tore at themselves like demented creatures with terrible secrets. The ship rocked a few times in an alarming way and we all stopped for a moment of collective anxiety.

None of us had been able to go outside. I said, "Does this have a loo?" Rari pointed to the back of the craft and a sliding doorway. I went through. It was little more than a large cupboard, but squashed in were folding bunks and units that looked as if they contained medical equipment and stores. It was well organised, which made me think about the borderers. Tidy and efficient didn't really go with the blood and mesentery as a choice of hair care.

Something that was hopefully a bathroom was across one corner. It was a tight squeeze for me, the average borderer would have had to be a proficient limbo dancer. It was clean in an anti-static way. There was an inappropriate comfort to thinking that everyone peed in much the same way, even if they were trying to kill you. I chucked my clothes on the nearest bunk and turned on the shower, letting hot water cascade down over my head and shoulders. There was nothing much to the hieroglyphs, which were off and on, with a slide for temperature. As I turned the water off a wash of warm air filled the tiny room. I was dry apart from my hair in a few minutes.

"We were just about to send out a search party." Okan didn't look up, but his voice had that trace of dry laughter which made me want to pinch him hard.

"I've been thinking." I pulled my fingers through my hair. He looked up, face in shadow, eyes unreadable. "Can two people exist together in the same universe? As in another me."

"That's parallel universe theory, not multiverse." I sighed in my exasperation. "You're still thinking about this as a separate place," he said, "They're interconnected." He put down a small handheld computer that I had seen him use before and leaned back in the pilot's seat with his arms folded. "You know about multiverse theory?"

"Open multiverse, bubble theory, big bounce and many worlds interpretation. Most of which I don't understand, plus there's M theory which has to do with string theory and two-dimensional space, *all* of which I don't understand."

He watched me for a moment and I noticed that Rari and Joao had paused in their twiddling. Whatever relationship existed between these men, it was obvious that they were reliant on each other. As if their safety was not a forgone conclusion and they all walked a high wire, tied together and if one of them fell, they all did.

"It's really a combination of most of those. Something that looks like a network of atoms in a crystal, all the universes are connected in a lattice by the same big bang. The energy fluctuations that occur in the quantum foam create tiny wormholes between them. Most of the universes are structurally identical with the same physical laws and values. The difference in the theories and this," he waved a finger in the air, "Is the fact that 'information' can pass between them." I pointed at myself. He nodded.

"You're saying no to another me?"

"I think it's safe to say that you're unique." He picked up his com again and sighed.

Joao stuck his hand in the craft's innards and swore when it bit him. Rari laughed they poked each other with deadly fingers for a moment. Okan pointed at the main computer. "Put your hand on this for me Millie." It lit up and a steady march of information appeared. He muttered with exasperation. I looked over his shoulder at the small computer in his hand. I could see the hieroglyphs from the main screen and the translations Okan had made.

"It's a pity that you couldn't download something, as in a program, or a virus. You know, when you buy a gismo and it asks you what language you want it to speak before you set it up." He stared at me for so long that I pinched him on the arm to see if he was still in there.

"Mothership calling Okan?"

Joao looked up. "That's actually *not* that funny Millie, as it could be around any time soon."

"The borderers have a *mothership*?" I spun in my seat.

"*That* is a good idea." Okan went over to the cover on one wall and pulled at it. A section of jelly and intricate wiring was exposed.

"I suppose we're not talking about the borderers," Joao said, helping with the main computer cover. He leaned the metal by a seat and Rari moved over to stand next to Okan.

"Millie's idea," Okan said, "We download the language directly from this into that." He pointed at the handheld and then the ship's innards. They then had one of those computer conversations that I think is more effective than ten milligrams of diazepam for knocking you out. I dozed. It was dark, the rain was lashing against the windows, I was tired and where computers are concerned, I had nothing to contribute, not even an opinion. I kept one hand on the main power so that they had some fizz, and then curled up in my seat. In my head I could see the bedroom at home and I fought not to go back. If I went, I couldn't be sure of getting the return place right and they wouldn't be able to fly without me. I seemed to swim over a cone of light that swirled with a darker accretion disk of rippling colour around it. There was no sound, it felt as if it should have been a waterfall of noise, but there was nothing. I could still hear the quiet words of Okan and Joao arguing about the computer, and the sound of rain and wind. I willed myself to stay with the voices.

I awoke with my head leaning on the console and a really bad crick in my neck. I think there may have been some dribbling. The door to the craft was open and bright sunlight made a triangular pattern on the floor. The wind had died down, except for that wonderful 'trees on the beach sound' that had waves mixed into it.

I stretched and my vertebrae cracked as if someone had dropped castanets. Leaning in the doorway I watched as Okan and Joao swam up and down, splashing each other and shouting. Rari sat on a rock, his face up to the sun, one foot in the water. He turned as if sensing me there. "Hey Millie!"

I pulled off my borrowed boots and bed socks and walked through the sand and the waves at the edge of the sea to join him.

We sat in silence for a while. Okan and Joao swam out to where the sea became dark blue and then turned and raced each other. They reached the shallow water at almost the same time, with several episodes of severe cheating going on. Joao stood half out of the sea and then flopped into a curved dive. I looked at Rari. "What are those marks on Joao's back?" He was wearing next to nothing in the way of underwear and you could see deep angry grooves in the skin, brown from age.

"Joao comes from a place where vagrancy is seen as a crime. He lives off the grid."

"I thought you were all from the same place?" I said, puzzled.

"Okan and I come from one place, Joao from another." He looked sad. "Things are more complicated than they look, Millie."

"I don't *actually* think that's possible Rari." The silence spun out between us, a thin wisp of smoke in the air.

"Joao's verse is post war, and they live, what's left of them, in a pretty frightening time."

"What about your verse Rari, yours and Okan's?"

He sighed. "I really should let Okan explain the details."

"What, so he can stretch it out, a bit at a time and tell me what he thinks I should know?" I may have sounded grumpy.

Rari shrugged. "It's not easy to take in all at once." He looked away, swishing his feet in the waves. I could tell by his expression that even to him, it sounded thin for a reason. "Developmentally this one is the most advanced. Have you heard of the classification of civilizations according to their energy consumption?"

"Yes," I said, "Nikolai Kardashev, a Russian astrophysicist in the sixties defined three types. Type one is planetary." I squinted up at the sky, in the hope of finding details. "Able to exploit the energy falling from the sun and hydrogen from the oceans and volcanos and control the weather. Type two could control the energy output of the sun, solar flares, antimatter. Which in theory would make them immune to an ice age, meteors and possibly, supernovas. Type three would be capable of controlling the output of the galaxy, derive energy from black holes and stars, Planck energy, which means we're back to wormholes and space/time foam."

He smiled. A big brother grin of epic proportions. "You *really* are a science geek, aren't you?" He flicked water at me with a foot. "Your verse is a type zero, isn't it?"

"Sadly yes, oil and coal are still a big issue for us." I looked up to watch Okan and Joao trying to drown each other. "What about you?"

"Close to a type one and we have other technology that means we're out there," he pointed up with a stick he had found on the rock next to him, "But we also have some serious problems." Rari stabbed at the sand. "This verse is type two."

I gaped, because that was really impressive. He grinned again and then flicked me with more water. I flicked him back and somehow, he got pushed off the rock. I laughed out loud and shuffled out of the way so I couldn't be pulled in by my feet.

I thought for a moment with my head tipped upwards, dizzy with the sky. Rari swam lazily on his back. "Did the same person define the three types in your verse?"

"Now you're getting it!" Rari grinned. The teacher in him was a halo of learning. "No, it was a Frenchman and at the turn of our twentieth century."

It was one of those things that drifted into the subconscious and didn't just appear like a light bulb on a dark evening. "So, Rari. There's a type three out there, isn't there?" I didn't look at him and he didn't answer.

I was gazing at the horizon which seemed to be less defined than it had been. Rari dried off with a shirt that was probably Okan's.

"Is that another storm coming in?"

Rari whistled at the two men still messing around in the shallows.

"Okan!" Rari pointed out to sea and we all squinted.

"Okay, maybe it's time to leave." Okan snatched the shirt from Rari. "Feel like another go at this Millie?"

"Is there still a hole in the ship?" We were walking up the beach, Joao had reluctantly come out of the water and was looking wistfully over his shoulder.

"No, I fixed it!" Okan sounded slightly insulted.

"In that case," I said, "Sure." All three of the men were getting dressed as they walked, a skill I very much admired. I've always needed to be stationary to put my jeans on. We ducked into the shadowed doorway of the craft.

"We also have a little surprise for you." Joao looked very pleased with himself. He tapped the console with a sandy finger. "Fizz her up, Millie."

I put my hand on the power keys and the ship responded with lazy acquiescence. The computer screen wobbled as Joao hooked up the handheld Okan was usually welded to, with what looked as if it could be a twig and a sticking plaster. I watched as the computer made a monumental effort to communicate in two languages and then it settled down in defeat. A steady march of information that appeared vaguely recognisable flashed onto the screen. "When did you do that?" I asked, impressed.

"While you were snoring." Joao smiled, as I tapped the doorway key and checked it as it slid shut.

We pulled up over the bay and swept out low across the deep water. Small fishing boats seemed to be clustered around a large pontoon that had thatched houses on it. "What's that?" I asked, pushing the power so we could get closer.

"Sea gypsies," Okan answered, "They live completely on the ocean. Fish. Trade with the settlements, mostly in minerals. Don't bother anyone. Nice people."

"Nice life," Joao said quietly, from the back seat.

A few of the people in the sea village below came out and pointed up at the craft. I wondered if they thought it was the start of a borderers' raid. "Okan, we have to do something about this ship, to try and make it look less of an attack craft. Someone's going to get nervous and start shooting at us."

"Good idea," he said, "What do you suggest, we paint the outside with 'we're not the borderers!'" Okan was watching the screen. It was still unintelligible, but now in a recognisable way.

"Don't be so grumpy! Oh, and by the way, you said you would bring Til's runabout back before dark and it's the next day."

"Damn!" Okan thumped the console and the computer shimmered.

"Don't do that!" I pointed. We all held our breath as the computer decided to think in hieroglyphs for a moment. Eventually it stopped wobbling.

"Maybe we could mark the outside with the international symbol of peace," Rari said, shrugging, "We could try, it might help." Neither Joao nor Okan seemed to think so, by their expressions.

"What about their police force, don't they have some sort of law enforcement on the moon?"

A stunned silence followed my question.

"Well," Okan said, "Europa is more an outpost of the settler movement. They have an internal local system of law that punishes people if they steal or kill, but the borderers are usually dealt with by the Navy and it's not something that they consider a priority as they don't hit the central planets."

We swept back over the land and climbed several thousand feet to avoid bumping into the mountains. The jagged snow-covered peaks were beautiful in the morning light, in the way of special things that can really hurt you if you're foolish enough to underestimate them. The blue-green sky was cloudless as we came over the range into the river valley of farms and small settlements. I stayed high, not wanting to cause any distress to the locals who might see the craft.

Okan pointed to the Twin Rivers settlement. "Don't get too close to that, we'll ping their security net."

"Is it possible to change the configuration of the ship so that it doesn't come up on the computers as the enemy?"

Okan shrugged. "I really don't know."

It surprised me. I suppose I had been thinking up to that moment that they had the edge, when in fact they were mostly just feeling their way in the dark like me.

I turned at the bend in the river to head back to Gold Cliffs and what felt as if it was home. The little craft was low over Weldon's farmhouse. Tara came out, her hand over her eyes and I waggled the controls, making the ship do a wicked shimmy to give her what I hoped would be a signal that it wasn't the borderers. "What was the dance for Millie?" Joao laughed.

"Just trying to let Tara know instead of getting the guns out she can put the kettle on." I lowered the ship down gently in the clearing where we'd taken off, there was no sign of Til Duster's runabout, something that I didn't point out to Okan.

He stuck a dirty finger on my tongue as I concentrated. "Doing that balancing thing again?" He smiled.

Before we had time to open the door, Tara was there, driving the missing runabout. She was laughing as she grabbed a huge bag of food from the back of the vehicle. "How did you ever get that to work? I had Weldon pick up the runabout, and told Til you were off on some quest." As she talked, she handed out the food, slabs of bread and cheese and hot coffee, with small sweet cakes the men didn't even bother to chew. It was wonderful and I put my arms around her. She hugged me back and over the edge of her shoulder I saw Joao, his face was a mask of loss and pain and the longing that comes with thinking you're never going to touch anyone again. It took my breath away with its intensity.

The morning consisted of more twiddling with the computer system. Okan went off on the runabout to see Til Duster and apologise for not returning the vehicle. He came back an hour or so later with more food as I was having one of 'those' conversations.

"What you're saying is this verse has tethered an asteroid for collecting water, minerals and to use as a low gravity launch site to other planetary settlements."

"Well technically other moons, but yes." Joao seemed to be taking far too much pleasure in turning my brain inside-out.

"They really are a type two!" I had my hand pressed over the power so they could get some fizz, while they worked on trying to get the computer to stop looking as though it was a borderer ship, which was something to do with the information it gave out as it was spoken to by the security net. It wasn't going very well and the level of descriptive swearing was beginning to make my eyes water.

I was just about to start eating a sandwich that Okan handed me, when a familiar sensation of unspeakable dizziness crept over me.

"Oh no!" I said, sitting down breaking the connection so that the power went off. My room was clear in the moment before I blinked and I saw Okan reaching for the fixer on my face. Then they were gone.

It was not a great feeling. My eyes ached with the nanosecond's memory of a huge dark space and the accretion disk I had seen before. There was very little whooshing.

Cecil looked up at me from the bed with resentful eyes. I got up and ran the bath water and he grumbled, reluctantly following me. I stripped off the smelly clothes and climbed into the bath, sinking into the bubbles, as my neck really hurt. I couldn't forget the expression on Okan's face, it had been one of desperation. I sighed, maybe I was misreading things; it could easily have been exasperation with having the only person who could power the ship disappear on you.

Cecil rubbed his whiskers on my damp cheek, leaving fur stuck to me, which was similar to trying to remove chewing gum and left behind a tickling feeling no matter how much I rubbed.

I turned the electric blanket on and got more rice pudding from the fridge, then made a large brandy with honey and hot water before I came back to bed. The clock ticked loudly and I realised that this time, time had passed, not much, but some. Cecil slurped the bottom of the rice pudding bowl. I picked up my mobile phone. Simon's voice was muffled as if the pillow was over his head. At two in the morning, he was entitled to sound as he liked. "Simon," I whispered.

"Millie!" His voice was firm, worried and surprisingly strong. That's the mistake people could make with gay men, in thinking that their sexual preference made them vulnerable. In fact, most of them have had to fight for everything from recognition to sometimes, their lives. There's no such thing as weak and gay. "Millie?" He said again. I could hear him shuffling around and the click of what was probably a light switch.

"I was having a really bad night and got into a panic." I could feel the edge to my voice. Actually, I didn't really know how 1 felt. Something akin to the slow slide into madness that being in two places at one time can do to you. There was a short silence, which was punctuated by the steady breathing of thinking when not awake.

"Is this about that man?" Simon was definitely in command of some serious ESP.

"If I go mad, will you make sure there's no drool and cackling?" I whispered.

He said, with the reassurance of someone who understood the finer points of the existential crisis that was going on, "All drool will be wiped, all cackling will be smothered. I promise."

I sighed, "Thanks Simon. Good night." We disconnected.

Early morning was cold and clear, one of those autumn days that made you think winter was months away. I looked out of the bedroom window, checking to see if the view had disappeared overnight. Cecil asked to be excused and I opened the patio doors. My neighbours down the valley had a fire going already. The lazy curl of smoke drifted into the blue and I could see the farmer out in the field checking his sheep. He looked up as if I had called him and waved.

I made coffee and drank two glasses of cold water. It felt as if the bones at the base of my neck were welded together. Cecil followed me around the house as I did the morning bathroom routine and tidied my already tidy house. My parents hadn't been much interested in things and I had only collected books, which meant there was more space than furniture in the rooms. The third bedroom was the study. The same shelves, but different books and an old desk which had belonged to my grandmother, as far as I knew. I turned on my laptop and opened my emails, checking the correspondence, which was mostly fellow geeks talking about the latest science website.

The doorbell rang and I wondered briefly who would come calling this early on a Saturday morning. Sometimes the farmer's wife would bring me fresh eggs and the most amazing yogurt and cheese, which I was absolutely *sure* would never have passed any pointless EU tests.

The door to the kitchen opened before I got downstairs and Simon's cheerful bellow reverberated around the house, competing with the radio and the cat for attention.

"You shouldn't leave your door unlocked!" He put a big bag of warm bagels on the kitchen table and helped himself to coffee. I gave him an unexpected hug, inasmuch as it took both of us by surprise.

"Okay, now I'm really worried."

I went over to the fridge and put the makings of breakfast on the table. "I'm out of my depth Simon," I said wearily.

He sat down and sighed, pulling apart a bagel as if it had a secret inside. "I don't think you're supposed to have one foot on the bottom, I think love is supposed to be a little bit about drowning." He slathered cream cheese over the massacred bagel. "Is he one of those guys who drives you up the wall and you don't know whether to kill him or jump him?"

I thought for a moment as I chewed. "Yes."

He sighed, "They're the best kind." He reached out a sticky hand and added, "There's other stuff isn't there?" I nodded, putting down the food, my appetite leaving me.

Morning sun lit the corners of the kitchen, no shadows. We took our coffee outside and sat on the swing seat, old friends who don't need to talk. "Is there really nothing I can do?" He was looking at the view and I could only see the side of his face, but he sounded really sad.

The 'other stuff' was so big that it was like having a conversation with an elephant standing between you. I just couldn't seem to find the best way to quantify it. We chatted about the shops and the thought that Christmas had no business being around the corner on such an amazing autumn day.

Simon was one of those people who liked to pretend that he was a pessimist, but actually he was the sort of optimist who, according to Quentin Crisp, 'would get out of the bath to answer the telephone.'

"You never talk about your parents?" He sipped coffee and leaned back into the chair tipping his head up to the sun.

I shrugged, curling my feet under me. "I don't really know what to say." The farmer in the next field was trying to get the sheep to move across to fresh grass. They were undecided and seemed to be holding a meeting about whether to comply. I thought that he probably needed 'Babe' for the job. "My folks were so much a part of each other; I always felt a little extra to requirements."

Simon reached for my hand and was about to say something when the landline phone rang. I got up and went into the kitchen to answer it. There was silence on the other end and yet my heart seemed to stop. I could hear someone listening to me saying, "Hello, hello." After a moment the phone was put carefully down and the sense of something dark and old that belonged to a place I had never been, crept over me. I checked the caller ID. It was of course withheld.

As I turned to go back outside Simon was standing in the door-way. I jumped and gave a pathetic scream. "How many of those have you had?" He asked angrily.

"That's the first." I didn't tell him about my meeting with the walking cobra in the park. But somehow in my mind the two occurrences were inextricably linked.

"At some point Millie, you are going to have to tell me what's going on." He put his coffee cup down and stretched. "Come on, let's go shopping. TK Maxx has cashmere sweaters in." That was one of the many really wonderful things about gay men; they do know how to shop.

I slept that night in restless dreams that had me crying and shaking. I could see Okan and he shouted something to me, a warning I think, but I couldn't reach him, it was as if I was sifting air through my fingers. I looked down to see the swirling mass below me, and fear crept into the cold in my bones. I woke up in the dark with an agonising headache and the certainty that someone was in my house.

Cecil was sitting on the chair by the window, a small crouching shadow of moonlight. He looked as though he had ballooned, I realised that all the fur on his body was standing on end. Nothing moved. The quiet was that threatening kind, the one where you take small shallow breaths so as not to be noticed by the predator. A sharp pinch of pain on the side of my face had me gasping. I touched the small bump of the fixer and my hand came away wet. It had the dark oily sheen of blood in the darkness that floated around me.

I listened. The threatening nothing listened back. I heard the small shuffle of completely silent feet and the click of the kitchen door as it closed. Cecil squatted further down in the chair, not yet ready to relinquish the role of guard dog. But every atavistic cell told me I was now alone. I waited. Then I got up and dressed as quietly as I could, putting on boots and a warm jumper.

Creeping around in the dark is not something I would recommend, but it was appropriate under the circumstances. I held a baseball bat that I kept under the bed, it had been a present from a man I had met in New York. I think he was giving me his prize possession, but I couldn't say I'd ever appreciated it up to that point. It felt warm in my hand as if the power of hitting something really hard was seeping up my arm and into my brain. I checked the door to the kitchen that led out to a narrow path on the side of the house. It was locked. Either the person had a key to my house, or they didn't need one.

There was this feeling that sometime somewhere I had taken a wrong turning. I always got it at those dark moments when I questioned myself. You don't need to graze in the self-help section to know that most people have felt this way at some point in their lives. At the moment when I was stood checking my kitchen door, holding a baseball bat from an old boyfriend gripped in my sweating fist, I realised that the wrong turning had found me.

Cecil having located his bravery was hinting at an additional meal. I didn't want to turn on any lights so I moved carefully, making the rounds of the windows. The wind was banging up against the side of the house and the trees were mad scientists describing an experiment for the unwary. In the occasional scrap of moonlight, nothing seemed to be out of place. I touched the fixer and reaching out for my dream place I pulled my thoughts to the clearing where I had landed the little craft. I fell forward onto my hands and knees in the grass.

It was dark. A fresh breeze filled the trees with the sound of ships in full sail. Not cold and rainy, but a clear mild night. The craft gleamed on the edge of my vision. I got up, shaking with the distance my head seemed to have travelled, and the feeling of something else at the point of the journey between one place and the other. I was so afraid. I banged on the door key and the opening appeared quietly. No sound inside. It looked as if they had been in the middle of some repairs. All the tools were scattered about.

I came outside and looked around; the ashes of the fire when I reached down were completely cold. As I stood up again, I could see through the woods to a glitter of light.

The Weldon's ranch. I went into the ship and took a gun from the rack by the doorway, picking up one of the self-lighting blue squares and flicked it a few times before I worked out how to get it to flame. I set off, tracking across the fields and stumbling in the long grass. The trees seemed to bend towards me as if they wanted to tell me a secret that I wasn't sure I needed to know.

I realised that the light from the house was misleading. It glittered enticingly, but was actually much further away than I remembered. I tried to put the feelings of fear back in my home place but they seemed to have followed me through the dreamwalk. A sense of being watched slowly crept up my nerve endings. I increased my speed, stumbling over the rough ground. At the edge of my vision where the shadows were, something moved out of context. Not the wind in the trees or the moonlight rippling through the tall grass. I felt a sharp pain in the corner of my eye and my hand went instinctively up to the fixer, it was bleeding again. I turned and I twisted back to the kitchen and the hissing cat and then reached in one upright movement for the smooth line of the baseball bat as I picked it up from the floor, I swung out behind me connecting with something solid, and then nothing. I turned around again, I could see the field and the shadows and the walls of my house at the same moment on the periphery and in the blurry centre that always gives you nothing definite in the dark, there seemed to be a room that was not in my home. An angry shape reeling away from me. I took a step back into the fields of my dream place.

There is that sense about being hunted that your brain remembers from movement, before your conscious thought has had time to tell you what's real. I began to jog, holding the gun carefully and every few feet turning to check behind me. I turned back and the shadow was crouched in front of me. It was huge. I stopped on the curve of a coin. A vildenbeast, it was more of a wild cat than a pig. Predator and prey and I knew which one I was. I held a gun but none of the cards. Strong jaws, black fur, orange eyes, no sign of anything but an efficient killing machine. A shark with paws and whiskers. I wondered fleetingly what the point of designing the creature had been. I aimed the gun steadily, thinking that the chances of it stopping this animal before it got to me was remote.

"Don't fire that!" A voice whispered, causing me to gasp. Weldon came out of the trees and crept slowly towards me. He held a huge weapon. Carefully he came and stood next to me, reaching for my arm and pushing the gun down gently. A blast of pure energy landed next to the creature, it hissed and spat and spun around and away, leaving the smell of singed fur and the silence that follows real fear.

Weldon sighed, "Tara saw a light through the trees near the borderer's craft. Figured it might be one of you. Then she saw it was heading our way." He shook me gently. "What is wrong with you Millie, you know the vildens are breeding?"

"I just forgot," I whispered.

"Yeah, well, a memory like that will get you killed." He was grumpy with unspoken worry. I felt a huge urge to give way to some suppressed emotion of my own but I thought that crying would have had a bad effect on Weldon, who was trying to move us quietly towards his ranch.

Tara was standing on the wide veranda with one of the blasters tucked under her arm. When she saw it was me, she ran out and put her arms around me and we did something emotional for a minute that had Weldon shuffling around us and up the steps. We followed, Tara with her arm still tight around my shoulder.

I sat at the kitchen table with a plate of hot food and a drink that was mostly alcohol with a dash of tea in it. My tongue felt like, felt. I was still shaking and the whole of one side of my face was stiff with pain and blood. Tara was dabbing at it with a cloth and a liquid that stung. "Have you seen Okan?" I asked. She shook her head, wincing with me against the sharp stab of disinfectant.

"They were here a few days ago. I guess they had to go home."

I couldn't say why that unsettled me, maybe because the three of them had always been here before me or maybe because I didn't think that the term 'home' fit whatever places they came from.

I jumped as Tara put a cold coating of jelly that hardened into a clear dressing on the now clean wound. It felt as if the fixer had been interfered with. I wondered how the man in my house had done it without waking me and then I realised that the wound had followed me *through* the dreamwalk. The fact that the damage existed in both places was understandable, if I didn't try too hard with the wormhole science.

"Come on, you need some rest." Tara helped me up the stairs and into a bedroom. I didn't even get under the covers, just kicked off my boots and lay down. Something about the boots bothered me but I was too tired to remember. I could hear Tara and Weldon talking quietly in the next room, through the open doors. Weldon said he was going out to check the cattle and make sure the barns were secure. I could feel the pull of my house and the empty dark kitchen. I saw Cecil washing his paws, curled up in the fruit bowl on the table, his furry bulges overlapping the edges. My eyes closed and I know I slept, because I dreamed of wild animals and being hunted by a man with no face.

Nothing can prepare you for waking up in a room you don't know. My muddled brain filtered sunlight and crazy thoughts in equal measure. I saw the collected history of a short life. Tara came in armed with a towel and some clothes which she put on the bed.

"So, you ready for breakfast?" I sat up, stunned that I was still here.

"This was your daughter's room." It wasn't a question. I stood carefully holding my head which felt as if a night out with Simon had ended in an ABBA karaoke bar.

"She was sixteen the last time I saw her," Tara whispered. I sat back down on the bed and put my arms around her. "I miss her." Finding some strength, the kind that keeps your fingers clinging to the edge of the window frame, she got up and left me to the bathroom routine.

I stood on the veranda looking at the trees that hid the borderer's craft from the house. The hot milky coffee tasted not quite like my own but had the inflection, if you closed your eyes, of something different. Really everything was. From the slightly green sky to the fluffy trees and rich glossy grass, the cows that were out in the fields were small and white with the horns of a goat. The house seemed part American ranch and something similar to the dwellings in the south of Italy. I held up the steaming cup, even the container was made of a substance I didn't recognise. A mixture of plastic and metal that retained the heat without burning your fingers.

Tara had given me some clothes that were dyed in the rich colours she wore. Material that was light but warm, trousers and a long-sleeved top. I had borrowed a pair of her daughter's boots as hers were too big. I looked as though I was a local. Something odd about the boots came back to me, I thought about the pair Rari had given me on the previous visit and couldn't remember if I had them on when I had returned home. It didn't make sense, I fingered the painful damaged fixer, then I dismissed the possibility as another puzzle coloured by fear.

The craft seemed to be asking me some questions and I sighed, not wanting to leave the curl of safety that was probably not any more real than the impression of me belonging here. I felt a real pain of loss, as in the day I had heard my parents had been killed in a car crash. The dark rainy night and the road onto the moor crept into my brain making my eyes water with the longing of things lost and that enduring wave of sadness as the people you love continue *not* to be there.

"You going back over to the dropdown?" Tara came out of the house carrying her own coffee. I nodded. "You want company?" She asked me with a smile.

We walked through the trees which were deceptively benign in the sunlight. Tara carried a blaster just in case we bumped into a sleeping vilden. The craft was quiet without the laughter and complaints of the three men and I missed them. I stood for a moment looking at the scattered tools, trying to work out what they had been up to.

Tara hovered outside for a while then eventually she sidled in the doorway. "I've never been inside one of these." She grew bolder and came over to me. I tapped the console keys and a steady stream of readable information scrolled across the holo-screen. I realised that the handheld computer Okan usually carried must have been successfully attached to the main system in the craft. It would have impressed the IT geeks in the shop, I could almost imagine the conversation, actually, I couldn't even have *begun* to.

"Do you want to go for a ride?" I asked Tara. She looked horrified and curious at the same time. "Don't think of it as a borderer's ship Tara, it's just a vehicle to get around in." She followed me outside as I did a visual check, running my hands over the craft's surface, feeling the fizz pass through my fingers. The painted symbol which was in the shape of an upside-down arrow was smooth and didn't interrupt the contact. I pointed to it. "I think Okan is hoping this will stop us getting shot at." She snorted in an unladylike fashion and I carried on with my checks.

I had travelled mostly on my own and never really felt the loneliness that lingers in the dreams of other lives. Those memories you think you have, about people and experiences that spring into being on rainy days and don't exist except in your imagination. I caught a glimpse of myself through those eyes. Connecting to a spaceship on a moon in another verse, was really just another lonely rainy day.

"Tara, do you see many people like me?" I tapped the small unit by the door as I remembered Joao doing and put my hand on the power supply. Small green jelly blocks winked hopefully back.

She looked wary. "You mean travellers?" She was following me around the ship and watching me checking the systems with undisguised interest.

"Well, it's not something we talk about." She contemplated for a few moments, dealing with those ghosts that hang around our thoughts when we are forced to talk about things that are really better left unspoken.

"I know that there have been people like you around for several hundred years." I think I must have looked stunned because she laughed. "This system was founded on the abilities of a small group of travellers who brought their technology with them two or three hundred years ago." She sighed, "It's difficult, because in the last few decades somehow it's become not acceptable to talk about it. We are creeping back in time to a place where small mindedness and super-stition were normal," she stopped. I turned to look at her. It seemed as if what she had to say next was the something you needed to have eye contact for. "People think the travellers are to blame for several of the bad things that have happened."

A small thought was beginning to edge into the corners of what I usually call my mind, but of late had become something akin to Grand Central Station. "Not from my place Tara. The technology, we don't have it," I added almost to myself, "Probably not from Okan's either." She shrugged.

"What does that feel like?" She pointed to the slight flash of elec-tromagnetic energy that was a flicking tongue from my fingers to the ship and back.

"As if colours were set to music." I held my hand out and the fizz moved up my arm. You don't get to choose your life and for most of us it goes in stages and sometimes you just have to go on to the next part, even if you're not ready.

We strapped in and I pushed the keys to get power and direction. The little craft shot forward, which was a significant improvement to my last take off from the clearing; Tara shrieked, but only in a very ladylike way and with a smile on her face.

I swooped up over the trees and we were soon far away from the ranch and the fields. The ship flew low over the mountains, clear and deceptively peaceful in the morning light, tracks of animals were visible in the high snow and I pointed. "Vildens," Tara answered, "They are capable of surviving in all sorts of harsh environments." As if to answer my next question she carried on. "They were designed as a food source, something that could deal with anything in the early days of the settlers. But we made too good a job on that and they did some unexpected evolving of their own into a vicious predator. Do you have bioengineering where you're from?"

Feeling as if I was breaking one of the 'Okan laws of dreamwalking,' I shrugged. "Not much, we've just started."

"Tell them what happened to us, maybe they'll be more careful than we were." She looked back out of the window at the coastline and the small fishing boats.

I considered with great seriousness about how such a conversation would go and couldn't think of a place to start.

"Do you want to go for a swim?" I stuck my tongue out for the landing. The angle of the craft was a bit steep but the touchdown was one of those you walk away from. I did all the shutdown procedures while Tara sprinted down the sand and stripped off at the water's edge.

We spent so long in the sea my skin looked squelchy. I sat on the beach warming up, my toes curled into small whirls of sand. One of life's great pleasures was sand in your toes, right up there with anything Martin Luther King said and chocolate. Tara was stretched out getting the sort of exposure to the sun's rays that would have earned her a short pithy lecture from my parents on skin cancer.

"Joao and I were friends for a long time when we were teenagers." Her eyes were closed so she couldn't see my expression.

I leaned back on my elbows and thought about Joao. He always seemed to have that hungry way with him. I realised that the hunger was about more than food. It made me feel such a sadness for a love lost in time. Then for some reason Okan came to mind and the feeling seemed to be different, more of the cold creeping sensation when you know that the shadows are not going to let go.

"You remind me of my daughter," Tara said quietly.

"The awkward teenage rebellious phase worked well for me so I thought I'd stick with it." I rolled over and coated myself with sand, watching the wind make rich patterns in the dunes. A small crawling creature was making heavy work out of a climb up one side of the nearest dune and I couldn't think of a single reason it was attempting such an Everest; except for the worn-out explanation of getting to the top. Maybe even ugly bugs needed to see the view sometimes.

"She's still out there. I know it." Tara said, as she turned to look at me and I held out a hand. I couldn't imagine losing a child. But then I couldn't have imagined losing my parents and they were gone. A stray thought flickered through as I watched the creepy crawly do a ski run down the other side of the dune.

"How old is your daughter now, Tara?"

"She'll be twenty-three in a few days." Tara laughed at my expression and patted my arm. "Bioengineering isn't only for the practical things, there's nothing wrong with some serious anti-ageing manipulation."

It was no wonder she didn't need to worry about sun damage.

Tara was probably the same age as Okan, Rari and Joao, who had been part of the older boy's gang when I had dreamwalked as a child. Teenagers to my childishness.

"Millie, have your friends taken you to the skydancing towers?" Tara asked.

"No." It sounded wonderful and dangerous.

"You're going to love it." She grinned. I didn't doubt it. I had always been attracted to the experiences you know with complete certainty you should leave alone.

We walked back to the craft, brushing sand off now-dry skin. I put my trousers back on and sat in the doorway using my socks to remove the gritty bits that get stuck between your toes, before I put my boots on.

I pulled up over the trees and we went back towards Gold Cliffs. "I don't think we should land outside the towers." Tara smiled. "I'm not sure the peace symbol will work and I really don't feel like being shot at."

"Give me a rough idea and I'll find a place to put down." The little ship behaved as if it was more a part of me. Every time I flew it, I seemed to be able to relate to the way it reacted and it may have been my imagination, but there was something of a personality in the sensation.

"Do you see the towers?" She pointed. We were partway between Twin Rivers and Gold Cliffs. Close to the actual river. In the distance three squat white towers were grouped together. As we got nearer, I could see that they were interconnecting. Small vehicles were scattered around the base. "It's quiet today, which is good. Sometimes in the evening you can't get on for hours."

I 'parked' the borderer's craft at a reasonable distance, under cover of the trees, and we walked through the fields to the dust road. The towers glittered in the sunlight and I could hear voices talking in excited tones as we got nearer. That thin high edge of the nerves that means difficult and dangerous. I could feel my own levels of adrenalin beginning to surge.

We walked into a light entryway that had a desk on one side and a group of lift doors on the other. A man, dressed in an all-in-one overall, was taking names. We joined the small queue. Tara signed us in and the man looked pleased to see her. He gave her a hug and she introduced me. "Millie, this is Ravit."

He patted my shoulder. "You'll need to borrow a suit." He reached down and produced one from behind the desk, which was something delightful in what looked to be, Lycra hell.

The doors opened onto the middle floor. The whole of the tower was built around an inner hollow, with a huge glass dome above. You could walk around the outer edge of the drop and it seemed to be a viewing platform and a stepping off point. There was a level above us and one below. Groups of people were talking and laughing. Every now and then someone would shout 'stepping off' and would launch themselves into the centre of the open space, about eighty feet above the ground.

I had the suit on so fast Tara couldn't stop laughing. She was standing right on the edge of the viewing platform, with a row of empty seats behind her. "Make sure you launch yourself well away from the side," she explained, "Don't leave a foot behind otherwise you'll flip over." The rest of what she was saying was lost as I threw myself outwards. I heard her shout, "Stepping off," as I went past at a run.

The feeling about skydiving is that you never really forget you're falling, even when you reach terminal velocity which is, I think, somewhere about one hundred and twenty-seven miles an hour. You can do some 'relative work' for maybe twenty or thirty seconds, depending on how high you are and how good you are. There were wind tunnels in my verse, that mimicked freefall, small units that were used for practice and competition, but nothing that compared to these towers.

It was as though I was resting on an updraft, but not so unforgiving. You could in effect really sky dance. Move with grace and certainty, as if gravity had been altered and you were floating. I flipped over in a back loop and twisted in a corkscrew ending upside down, which was amateur stuff when I looked around me. Tara was waving and I swam over to her. "Are you coming in?" I asked her. She shook her head and went to sit down. I turned back and began trying to copy the complex moves of a young boy in a brightly coloured suit. He watched me with youthful impatience for a moment and then came over and began to show me, with the undisguised irritation of the very young, just exactly how I was doing it wrong.

Hours later I was still skydancing. The dome was turning a dark blue-green and the afternoon sports people were replaced with a rowdier crowd. I could see the floor above us filling up.

There is this sense of 'something remembered' about flying. I have felt it before in the dreams of real sleep, not dreamwalking. Those moments when you know you can fly, some atavistic DNA left over from the pterosaurs of our past. You push off with your toes digging into the earth and your arms become outstretched in the upward flight of lost things.

I turned slowly into the feeling and then moved towards the viewing platform. I watched several people slide gracefully like swans coming in for landing and then did my own impression of a heavily pregnant duck, ending up in an undignified forward roll. Tara pulled me to my unsteady feet. The ground seemed wrong, as if I was taking the first steps on dry land after months at sea. My inner ear did a song and dance routine that would have made Fred and Ginger proud. I leaned down to stop the waves of nausea being a problem. "It will pass," Tara said and patted me on the back.

We sat for a while watching the other skydancers, some of whom looked as if they'd been practising for a very long time. People were eating and drinking from the various food stalls that had opened up. Tara went off to get something for us and I leaned back in my seat to ease my muscles which were still shaky. I noticed a group of young men coming towards me. Their faces were flushed with that mixture of alcohol and perceived challenge. Bullying is always and everywhere. For all the times I've stood and fought, I've run and hid. I can't say that one works better than the other. But you sometimes have to pick a good emotional moment and tell the bullies to push off and hope that when you walk away your skirt isn't tucked into your underwear. For those of us permanently on the list, these things come around with obvious frequency.

"You're one of 'them' aren't you?" The leader of the group looked around for the usual approval. It was odd that the language never changed; maybe someone should give classes in bullying grammar. I could see Tara returning with two plates of food and a look of alarm.

"Well?" He leaned forward and the smell of meanness was heavy on his breath.

I stood up and reached to the small of my back, where the gun Okan had told me to carry without fail was pushed into my trousers. "Do you think you could go away?" I asked politely. The nasty little smile was replaced by a stunned look of wary surprise as I held the gun discretely, point down, resting on the side of my leg. I didn't know if they were armed. It seemed to me that most people were. Out on the edge of my vision I could see a security guard, his antennae for trouble, making him look in our direction. The bully held up his hands and began backing away. By the time the guard got over to us they had disappeared into the crowd and Tara was sitting down, a little white around the eyes. She sprang up as the guard came over, the slightly protective expression on her face giving her the look of a cat with kittens.

"Everything okay here?" The guard was suspicious, but there was nothing left in the way of an altercation.

"Just a few drunks looking for some fun." I took the plates of food from Tara's shaky hands and we sat down again. The man nodded, still not quite happy, but he went off glancing to his left and right, as if he was an air hostess checking for empty cups before landing.

"You know," Tara said when she could speak, "If he had seen that gun, he would have shot you. They don't allow any weapons in here."

"Do you think they will be waiting for us when we leave?" I asked, through a mouthful of food.

"Count on it. Both of the taller men are part of the town gang that use the towers as a meeting place." She pointed at the security guard. "Not much they can do about it. Every now and then there's a shooting and the authorities make speeches about sorting it out. But it's difficult to make a difference." She chewed thoughtfully. "The early settlers were so sure they could stop all the mistakes being made over, all the things that seem to be part of a growing world. I guess it's just what happens when people come together."

"What's the gang called?" I watched the guard watching us.

"Red boys. Into all the usual stuff, stealing, stimulants and fighting. Mostly they stick to the larger settlements, Twin Rivers is about as far into the outback as they go. Young people get caught up in the need to belong; before you know it, they're beyond help." I looked carefully at her; the bitterness was a small cloud on the edge of her peaceful heart.

"Did your *daughter* join a gang?"

Tara nodded. "Ziggy was taken while she and a group of gangers were selling some stuff to a dealer in Great Port." I must have made a question mark with my eyes because she answered, "It's the main docking port for the planet, not as big as the ones on Earth but it's a city of sorts." She whispered, "I guess I lost her a long time ago."

I watched the skydancers for a while, the easy sliding of air and body and wondered about the possibility of changing the laws of aerodynamics. Or maybe particle physics. I wondered if CERN could be persuaded to set up something similar, I would, of course, have been happy to help. Little things whirled around with the dust of old thoughts and the painted memories of other times. "Tara, do the borderers only take females? I mean even the children."

"Yes, of course," she said, in a matter-of-fact tone.

I couldn't work out why the thought seemed to circle around like buzzards at a possible feast. Something about this universe and the travellers of the past and the man in my house and the cold disc at the centre of my journey made the feelings too difficult to deal with. I got up. "One more time, because I can't leave this alone."

I rushed at the edge of the platform and Tara, laughing, called, "Stepping off," as I pushed up and out, with my toes curled for flight.

———

"How are we going to do this?" I was limping a little from a rather bad exit, not at all my fault as some kids had decided to do a five-man star which slid over onto me just as I was getting to the critical bit between the updraft and nothing. Tara and I were headed for the elevator to go down to the lobby. A hand caught my arm and as I twisted around reaching for my gun, I ended up nose to chest with Okan, the weapon pointed directly at him.

He spoke into my hair, "The whole low-profile advice was not lost on you then?"

I pulled away and looked up at him. "Where the hell have you *been?*"

His expression seemed to be stunned but with a tired, amused twist. "If you're not going to shoot me maybe you should put that thing away." He pushed the barrel down towards the floor.

I started to explain, "I'm in a bit of trouble here *and* there, if you see what I mean." Even Tara was having difficulty following this. "There was a fight of sorts."

"You had a fight in the towers?" Okan pulled me over towards the lift doors.

"No, actually yes. I mean I pulled my gun out to frighten off some bullies, which Tara said were the local gangers. I think they are waiting for us outside. But there was someone in my house and I hit whoever it was with a baseball bat. A present I've never really appreciated up to now." I leaned for a moment against Tara as I removed the skydancing suit. It was like getting out of a banana skin and I ended up hopping in an undignified way, trying not to add to the bruises that were already beginning to show.

I smiled at Rari and Joao who were standing by the open doors. Both were looking around as if they expected something to happen.

"Nice exit on the last one Millie," Joao said. He grinned and then nodded to Okan, warning him. The same security guard was pushing his way over to us. Everyone stopped and the scene took on a tinge of wariness.

"You'd better use the emergency stairs," the guard said. He made eye contact with Okan. "I just got it from Ravit that the gangers are hanging around." He pointed at me. "He also said to tell you to come back and he'd give you some skydancing lessons." He leaned down towards me. "Bring that *thing* in here again and *I'll* be giving you lessons, understand?" I nodded my best compliant nod. But somehow, he didn't look convinced. I thought about adding something helpful, but the man had a 'now would not be a good time' expression on his face.

The lift left without us and we followed the guard over to a small door in the far wall, half hidden by a stall selling sweet sticky things. The door slid open after he unlocked it using a finger pad. "It will bring you out at the back of the tower. The gangers don't have much imagination so you should be okay." He and Okan nodded their acceptance of each other's place in the order of things. I found myself squashed into a very small space with four other adults. We were the teenagers at a bad party all deciding to hide in the same wardrobe, nose to nose and no one speaking.

The back of the towers was in darkness and slippery shadows slid across the curve of the buildings. We waited in silence as Joao skirted off to one side. He came back after a moment. "Half a dozen gangers mostly armed and drunk," he whispered, "Millie, what did you *say*?"

"They don't seem to like *us* much," I trailed off.

"You *know* what these men are Joao; they pick a fight for the sake of it," Tara sounded exasperated.

94

"Where's the ship?" Rari asked. He was holding a gun which seemed to have appeared when we left the lift. I felt that pointing out I wasn't the only one who had been breaking the rules wouldn't be appropriate, and I was having difficulty remembering in the dark from which direction we had walked to the towers.

"This way." I pointed over to the right.

"Can we get to the track without being seen?" Okan asked Joao. He shrugged. They all seemed tired and worried, as if the clock was ticking on some unseen test. It made me feel as if I should be looking over my shoulder.

"Too late." Joao pointed and I saw the shadows stretch along the ground as the men came around the side of the building. Some animal instinct telling them where to look for the juiciest prey.

We used natural instinct of our own and backed up to form a protective shield, all facing outwards as the men began to circle. I saw Rari hand Tara a gun and Joao move to defend her with his body.

"We should get some decent money from the borderers for these two." The largest of the gangers said quietly to the man standing next to him.

"*What* did you just say?" Tara's voice could have penetrated several layers of concrete, though she spoke barely above a whisper and anyone who has ever had a mother could remember what deep trouble sounded like. My own shoulders cringed involuntarily in memory of things found out. She moved quicker than Joao could stop her and reached the surprised ganger, smacking him so hard around the head that *I* could hear ringing in my own ears. "You pathetic, ignorant, small minded vilden rat! Do you think that having lost my daughter to the borderers anything *you* could say or do would matter!" She hit him again, hard and the silence that followed the crack of her hand on his stunned face was a pugilist's nightmare of canvas before a crowd.

"You're Ziggy's mother?" One of the men said. He pushed past the lead bully and shone a small torch onto the furious woman. I felt rather than saw Joao move and Okan hold him back. "It's Ziggy's mum." He pointed to Tara and looked at the rest of the gang and then said again to himself as if to make sure, "Ziggy's mum." Tara seemed to melt, all the anger flowed away in a river of pain and loss and Joao caught her gun before it hit the ground. "No one got that mad at me before or since." The young man grinned and patted Tara. He thought for a moment and hunted for words that hadn't been said for so long he had trouble remembering them. "I miss her."

I know *my* mouth dropped open.

We walked back to the ship with our weird entourage. It was similar, I imagine, to being escorted through Harlem by the local heroin dealers. The stand-off had been over after a brief pause which changed the power dynamic strangely from the large gang leader to an angular young man with dreadlocks and a beautiful angelic grin. He introduced himself to us as Marl, without mentioning the rest of the gang, and they stood quietly behind him. Their guns had been slipped out of sight even though Okan and Rari had theirs in view. The predator was still out there though, stalking on the periphery.

I heard Marl say to Tara, "She practically brought me up, ran away from my stepfather after my mum died. Got no one else but the gang."

Tara asked the question that all parents who have lost children ask, "What happened? All I knew was she was taken."

Marl curved his long body down towards her in a gentle movement and put a comforting arm around her shoulders. I saw Joao stiffen in response; his face closed up as if you could hear a thick door slamming. The young ganger tried to offer her comfort in his words in the only way he knew how. "She fought like a vilden, killed two borderers before they took her." I wanted to cringe with the inappropriateness of the information, but it seemed to help Tara, she patted his arm and nodded as if this was the very thing she needed to hear.

I turned to look at the gang leader who was walking next to me. Okan and Rari were vying for the tail-end Charlie slot with the other three men. They were silent, keeping a distance and shuffling across each other like a maharajah's chess game. As if giving up the prime position would lose them the advantage if the whole thing came to blows again. I thought that in a firefight we would probably all end up dead anyway because proximity can be something of a problem with really nasty guns.

The ganger was leering at me; he hadn't given up the idea of just where his next meal might be coming from. He pointed at his chest.

"Torin," he said.

"Millie." I also pointed. I thought we looked as though we were an anthropologist and the leader of a rainforest tribe; it's just that I wasn't sure who was whom. "Marl is your brains?"

"Yeah," he said, without irony, "He does all our thinking for us. Gang needs a smart man. Never been hungry with Marl around." I watched the two shadows in front of me; Tara looked even more vulnerable and I thought about the fact that some people are never what they appear to be and who exactly was more dangerous. I realised that Joao never took his eyes off Marl, completely ignoring the rest, therefore maybe he had worked it out.

I turned back to the obvious, readable Torin. "Do the borderers really pay you for anyone you kidnap?"

"I've never kidnapped anyone!" He looked horrified. "Always been a fair fight, spoils of war and all that."

"Right," I said, "Of course." I could just see the man they had sent out in front to light the way, reach the ship. He held the open flame up to see better and I watched as he moved around the vehicle stopping at the peace symbol painted on the side. It looked small and unsuspecting beneath his sharp gaze.

"Yes, sometimes we have sold people to the borderers," Torin said defiantly, "But it's not always a good idea. The other gangs started to do it too. Lost a lot of friends that way. Wanted to have an amnesty, but some of them don't like to talk."

I tried not to laugh. It was one of those conversations that required a serious response not a flippant reply, unfortunately nothing helpful came to mind. So, I went with the non-committal, "Hm."

I found myself wondering about Ziggy, if she had been part of a deal and I looked carefully at Torin, his face was impassive in the shadowed light of the flame and guileless, even in his drunken bully state he had been exactly what he was, nothing held back; the torches the others carried moved as if they were looking for hidden answers, not footfalls.

We stood about in an uncomfortable group. Only Tara looked reluctant to let go of Marl. His shiny dark face was kind as he patted her hand. I knew that Okan would not want me to start up the ship while the gang was watching, but I couldn't think of a way to avoid it, as if we were the last guests at a party for misfits.

"How did you get the ship to work?" One of the other men asked into the quiet.

"Just lucky with some computer equipment," Rari answered. No one looked at me. They all nodded as if this was explanation enough. But I didn't think any of them was that stupid.

Torin tapped Marl on the shoulder. "We should get going." Marl nodded, then he hugged Tara and she looked stunned. Apart from the drug selling and the violence, I thought, he might really be a very nice young man. For a second there was a silence and then Torin held out a closed fist to Rari who hesitated before raising his own hand in the same gesture. They made contact and then nodded to each other. I wondered if we had just joined a gang. The other men slid back into the darkness and in a moment, Marl had followed them.

Joao lit one of the little thermo blocks for some light and we moved towards each other. The stunned survivors of a wild storm, a collective sigh of relief and the feeling that you get when you realise something dangerous is over. "Do you think they bought the explanation for the ship?" Rari asked no one in particular.

"Not for a moment," I answered. Rari nodded.

"Marl is going to come to the house," Tara said.

"Is that a good idea?" Joao's face was expressionless and the effort he was making to appear so was standing out in the muscles of his throat and shoulders.

"I don't care." The woman shrugged. "I just need to ask some more questions and he has answers."

I kept the thought that some rival gang may have sold Ziggy to the borderers unspoken, or worse, she may have been sold by someone she knew. It was just a feeling; it wouldn't have made any difference to what had happened and some things are better left unsaid.

Okan was in brooding mode. He studied the ground for a moment. "I think we'd better have a look around before we start her up."

He and Joao moved off into the dark and Rari opened the door to the ship. I went over to the main console and did my start up checks with the main lights off and Rari standing close enough for anyone watching at a distance to be unsure of who was 'in the driver's seat.'

He looked at Tara sitting in one of the empty seats at the back. She had her head in her hands but was silent in her despair. I stopped what I was doing and went over to her, crouching down and touching her knee gently. "It's the not knowing that destroys you from the inside."

"I never stopped looking," she said into her hands. Then sat up, reaching out for me. "I don't care if he's a ganger and dangerous. He's got the answers." She added, "There's something good there; I just have to find it."

I nodded. I wasn't sure if Marl wanted his goodness to *be* found, but I would help her look if that's what she needed.

Okan and Joao came into the craft. Joao went straight over to Tara and hugged her, she hugged him back and for a moment they both looked as if they were drowning. Okan shook his head at Rari's unasked question. I went back to the start up systems and Rari leaned as close as convenience allowed. They were both nervous and it made my fingers slippery.

We took off quietly over the trees and as I moved away towards Gold Cliffs, I saw the shine of two faces looking up in the far trees. Okan was sitting next to me and I heard him swear. "Well," I said, "That secret's out." I turned to Rari behind me. "They were over by the river."

"Couldn't search all night Okan," he said, "I think they had worked it out anyway."

"Not about her," Okan answered.

I could feel the sensation in my vertebrae where you shiver in your nerve endings with suppressed fear. Okan patted me on the shoulder. "You'll have to be more careful when you move around the place Millie. Not so much wandering off."

"What about home? What do I do about that?" I asked. Okan looked puzzled, as all men from the beginning of time are because, like them, he hadn't been listening to most of what I said. I tried not to grind my teeth in frustration. For some reason the combination of suppressed fear and irritation made my contact with the ship feel sloppy. I took a few deep breaths.

"It's the middle of the night at home," I said quietly. "I was asleep and had some difficulty coming here. I was in pain and it woke me up. My fixer was bleeding and I realised someone was in the house." I said this as calmly as I could, but the ship began to wobble and I sat still for a moment until my mind connected to the controls. Because there is nothing worse than falling out of the sky.

"I hit someone with a baseball bat and I saw something, somewhere else, but not my home and not here."

No one spoke. The cabin was full of unhelpful thoughts, in the end it was Tara who said, "You don't live with anyone where you come from?" It was an odd question, but I knew what she meant.

"No, no one. I have a cat that comes in from my neighbour's house, but I wasn't imagining it. There was someone there."

"I'm not sure this is a good time to talk about this," Okan said carefully.

"Look," I said, "She's here, understands what's going on and is part of it."

There was another silence, then Tara said, "Thank you."

I tried again. "When I went downstairs, I found the doors locked. No one got in from outside." It sounded weird to *me* but then I was dreamwalking in another verse and flying a biomechanical ship, therefore weird had become relative.

Okan sighed, "Do you think that you saw a different verse to this one?"

"Is that even possible?"

Joao said, "I don't come from yours or Okan's verse Millie, so yes."

I thought carefully about this, trying several different ways to quantify my feelings and then sighed at the potential for sadness and fear. "Are you saying that people dreamwalk to my verse?"

"Did you think it was a one-way street?" Rari said, barely above a whisper.

I flew on into the dark night with the moon in its green glow and the huge shadow of Jupiter, a big brother forever keeping watch over the little world. The trees were a sweep of movement below us.

I kept close to the ground, following the river rather than looking at the dimly lit holo-screen in front of me. It was a tunnel of a journey; all I could hear were the faint murmurings of Tara and Joao in the back of the ship and my own thoughts tapping at unopened doors.

We reached Gold Cliffs and I curved around the early hills until I saw the lights of the Weldon's farm. Pushing the little craft into small turns as if we were a microlite, I landed back in a clearing Okan had pointed out that was nearer the farm, in a short bumpy slide.

"Nice one Millie," Rari patted my shoulder.

"Thanks, I thought so."

"You need to start learning to use the holo-screen Millie," Okan said, "All the technical information is there, navigation, meteorology, speed, altitude, you can't just steer forever using the river." I scowled. To exactly no effect, as he was looking the other way and I had just wound down the power.

The farm was a halo of light. I could see Weldon coming out of a barn closing the doors behind him; he waved and walked towards us.

"Thought I was going to have to start up a search party." Then he saw Tara's face and his turned to anger. "What happened?"

"It's okay, Weldon." Tara moved over to him. "We had some trouble at the towers."

Weldon looked carefully at all of us. "It sounds as if it could be a good story; you'd better come in and get some food. Just put the stew out to simmer and there's bread." I could hear Joao's stomach rumbling from the doorway of the craft.

Rari closed up the ship and we walked to the farmhouse.

The table was scattered with plates and the wandering crumbs of fresh bread. I felt as if I had been awake forever. Weldon made the hot drinks with a kettle that seemed to be part of the stove, it was just a spout that came out of the top like a tap and he filled the metal cups with some rich gold liquid, added the hot water and a spoonful of honey, and then passed them to each of us in turn. I sipped and the warm gentle fire made the idea of keeping my eyes open a slim possibility.

"So, what happened?" Weldon took Tara's hand and kissed it. I tried not to look at Joao. I'd never been loved by one man, how complicated it must have been to be loved by two.

"We were doing some skydancing," Tara said.

"You haven't been there for years." Weldon looked puzzled.

"I wanted to take Millie. We were having some problems with a bunch of red boys. I think they were just drunk and looking for an easy time." Weldon had that closed in expression that some men wear when they want to punch someone. "It just escalated," Tara explained, "Okan, Rari and Joao came to the rescue and we went back to the ship and came home."

The glaring absence of several facts was staring all but one of us in the face, but no one said anything. Weldon's demeanour was that of a man who knew he had been short changed. He got up and opened a cupboard. "Cake?" The silence was filled with eating and drinking.

"Am I not to be trusted with any of this?" Weldon sighed, "I mean, have I done anything that would make you think I *couldn't* be trusted?"

Okan reached over and touched the man on the shoulder. "You know where we come from and you've always been a good friend." He paused and looked at Tara, who gave an almost imperceptible nod of her head. "We ran into more than trouble. The gang gave us some information about Ziggy. They were part of the group she belonged to. I don't know if they are anything more than a heartache, but I guess that's up to you and Tara."

Weldon nodded his head slowly; the dark eyes were full of the pain of suppressed memories. He looked at me. "You're a bit special, aren't you? You and that ship I mean."

"No, just different." I shrugged.

Rari smiled. He put his arm around me. "Well, *I* think you are Millie. Strange, but special."

"Are we in any danger?" Weldon drank a gulp of the fiery brew. No one spoke for a moment. I would have thought that it would have been obvious that everyone at the table was in deep trouble in a collective, intertwined way.

"I don't know," Okan said, "It's complicated."

Which was the understatement of the year. I wondered what I would find when I got back to my own verse. Cecil, a baseball bat and a door into yet another place. The failure of all common sense on a cosmic scale.

The dawn was a late era Turner painting of orange light in pale undefined streaks. I had staggered up to Ziggy's old room, with patches of my kitchen at home appearing on the stairs and the landing. As if I was wading through old memories played on a squeaky black and white projector.

Okan had said to try and hold onto 'here' until we could have a conversation about what to do. He and Rari had easily found themselves a bedroom each in the large family sized house, crashing out fully clothed and Joao had curled up on the couch in the kitchen, asleep before I got up to go. I saw Tara pull the rug from the back of a chair and tuck it around the sleeping man, as though he were her lost child, he was surely someone's. Weldon didn't seem to notice, but then we had all underestimated him before. I think most of us have the relationship that we know is possible, not the one that appears in the last three pages of a gothic novel.

I did sleep, but in the few hours that I was, I woke several times to find that my fixer was painful and I could feel the inside of the spray-on dressing was wet with blood again. The sensation of someone prowling around outside the door and a shrivel of fear brought me to my feet several times, almost feeling the bat in my hand and the shadow of the kitchen table with Cecil curled up in the fruit bowl, his curious face upturned in the moonlight.

The bathroom off Ziggy's room had a shower stall similar to the one in the ship. The water seemed to glide frictionless into the drain; you couldn't see the drops caught on the tiled surface of the walls. I played with the laws of physics for a while, finding little things pleasing, then dried off. I dressed in the clothes from the cupboard and hoped Tara wouldn't mind. Fishing under the bed I found Ziggy's boots alongside the ones that Rari had given me on the previous visit. I held them up, trying to remember what it was that bothered me about this stupid pair of boots. I gave up and put Ziggy's on because they were a better fit. Smelling hot food, I wandered down the stairs running my fingers through my damp hair in the hope of curl rather than frizz.

Weldon was alone in front of the stove. There were several dirty plates on the table. He handed me a cup of coffee. It had the rich deep aroma of fresh ground beans and cream that had known a cow in the not-too-distant past. He pointed at the table. "Sit yourself down. The others have gone over to the ship and Tara will be down in a minute." He began dishing up a mixture of fried rice and vegetables and fish.

"Kedgeree!" I said, delighted. I don't know why it had surprised me; there was a sense of the Scot about Weldon.

"Is that okay? I can make something else if you'd like."

I was unable to speak as my mouth was full, but I waved my fork around in the air and made noises of appreciation.

He smiled. Then frowned. Picking up a spoon, he stirred his coffee with enough honey to have had my parents find the address for the local dentist. "I wanted to ask you." I nearly choked on my rice. "Do you think," he sighed, "I'm worried about Tara. This ganger?"

I had no experience with the kind of advice that would make

anything okay for either of them, Simon had been my only confidant in the past few years and I didn't think a shopping trip and an ABBA tribute band would be of any help to Weldon. But I did understand grief and loss, the type that lasts a lifetime and shapes the person you are from the inside out. I put a hand across the table and touched Weldon's open palm. "Whatever it takes." He nodded. "Weldon; whatever I can do to help."

He squeezed my hand. "I was right the first time. You are special."

Tara came in at that moment. "Well, you two are cosy." She smiled the painful smile of someone who has had a brush with agony and not quite survived.

"We bonded over food," I said.

I watched as they did the ritual morning routine that reminded me of my parents, a little dance with coffee, eggs and kisses. It looked complicated, but when I had asked my mother about it once, she just smiled and said it was easy if you listened to the music inside your head.

I finished the whole plateful of food and drank another cup of coffee. The sun was almost fully up and Weldon stretched. "I'd better check the stock in the far fields today." He went over to the rack on the kitchen wall and pulled off the large blaster he was carrying the night he found me with the vildenbeast. He saw me looking at the gun.

"Mostly the stock sees off the creatures by surrounding them and using those heavy horns to slash. I've seen a vilden gutted by a large cow defending her calf. Never a good idea to go about unarmed though."

I stood up. "Well, I'd better," I saw Tara shake her head behind Weldon's back, "Have another cup of coffee," I finished lamely, sitting down again. He gave me a puzzled look and Tara gave me a grateful one. I sighed; subterfuge had not been one of my better subjects; in fact, I think I failed it.

We watched as Weldon set off on the runabout, the back of the vehicle was packed with medical supplies for the stock and the para-phernalia that people who work the land use every day when it takes too long to get home for something you might need. He looked as though he was one of my farming neighbours on Exmoor, except for the lack of actual wheels.

"Thanks," Tara said after he had gone, "He was so worried about me and I don't think I could have had another conversation about Ziggy."

The sun was warm in a green and slightly distant way. "How is it possible that the weather so good here? You're what, four hundred and eighty-three million miles away from the sun as opposed to Earth's ninety-three million?"

"There's a mirror system strung around Jupiter and back towards the central planets." She shrugged. "It was put there by the same travellers who moved the moons."

The ship was a buzz of activity and even though they had eaten a big breakfast Rari and Joao greeted the food as if they hadn't had anything for weeks. Eating sandwiches, they resumed the gentle arguments that go with technical geeks when they have a good idea. Okan was upside down inside the control panel on the front console. He waved a hand when I came in to see what he was doing and then stuck his head out. "Pass me that screwdriver." I handed it over. Little sparks of light and a smell of burning sock followed. "That should do it." He crawled crabwise out of the tiny gap and wiped the sweat off his face.

I handed him a sandwich and pointed at his handiwork. "Do what?"

"I just attached the handheld with the virus to the main computer. Hopefully it will make things easier."

I wondered *whom* exactly it would make things easier for and thought the days of following the river would be over soon. I was not usually a lazy person, but doing four things at once, which is what flying is about, was never high on my list of essential experiences. It was one of the many things I had tried in my life, that hadn't held my attention for very long. I had slightly preferred jumping out of aircraft.

"So, tell me again about what's happening in your verse?" He chewed bread and cheese and leaned against the back of the pilot's chair and I wanted to hit him really hard for being so calm about it.

"I don't understand why it doesn't bother you." I tried for a more reasonable tone. "What is this all about?" I pointed to the fixer, which was not covered by the dressing anymore, you could see the redness and bruising as if someone had been trying to take it off.

"Did you try and remove it?" Okan asked, looking closer, so close that I could feel his breath on the side of my face. I shifted slightly.

"No!" I gave in and thumped him.

He looked stunned. "What was that for?"

"For not taking me seriously and for not saying nice things about my landing last night."

If it was possible, he looked even more stunned. Then sat down tiredly in the pilot's chair; rubbing his chin which looked slightly stubbly. "I don't know what's going on Millie. I don't have any answers."

I sat down next to him. "Are you saying that you don't know anything, or you don't know anything about *this*? Because we both know that you know a lot about something." He began to snigger and then to laugh and I joined him because it was funny and my face hurt and I was really tired.

Joao stuck his head in the door. "You two having a private party?" He joined us. "Can you do me some juice Millie, I want to see if we can get the ship to respond to a different frequency so we don't look like a borderer."

I put my hand on the main power buttons and the shimmer of connection danced up my arm. "I sure wish I knew how you did that," Okan said.

"For what it's worth I think it's similar to a type of synaesthesia, you know when you see colours and sounds together. It just feels as if I can see it speaking."

Both men looked as if they had a slight case of explanation overdose, but Joao nodded. "I think I get it," then he shook his head. "Actually no, I have no idea."

He pulled off a panel as Rari and Tara came in, they had been talking outside and Tara's eyes were red. I guessed he had told her what he thought of Marl and the possibility of hearing the truth from the ganger and in turn I am sure she had told him she didn't care.

"I'd better go Millie, are you coming back to the house tonight?" She asked me.

It looked as if it was important that I did. "Of course, if that's okay? Though I don't always have a choice about when I go home."

She smiled. "I understand, don't worry. But if you can, that would be great."

Joao gave her a hug before she left and Rari stood up, looking embarrassed for a moment he said, "I didn't mean to hurt your feelings Tara, I," he stopped, it seemed to be the day for unfinished business.

"It's okay," she said quietly, "I think you're right; I just don't know what else to do."

Joao walked a little way towards the farmhouse with her and I watched for a moment as they disappeared into the trees. The halo of light around them from the patches of sun that spilled through the branches seemed to make them *both* look as if they were about to disappear off into the other verses. I wondered if Tara had ever thought about it, if they'd ever discussed the possibilities. I realised that they must have talked about nothing else for a while, such is the way of hopeless relationships. They stopped for a second and I looked away, something raw was being exposed, that possibly should have remained buried in the past.

I turned back into the ship and the quizzical stares of Okan and Rari.

"How about those flying lessons?" I asked Okan.

"How about learning the ship's systems first?"

I tried to think up a good retort, but couldn't come up with anything that wasn't rude.

The morning turned into a golden afternoon, Rari and Joao argued about the internal workings of the ship and I studied the information that marched across the holo-screen. It gave out speed, height, a variety of meteorological statistics and some helpful advice of the 'push here for take off' variety. The technical specifications to do with air content inside the ship and air pressure outside was displayed on a separate set of small holo-units off to the right of the main console. I thought whoever had sat in the co-pilot seat had dealt with it, though it could easily have been handled by one very large person with long arms.

Okan produced another small handheld computer and began scrolling down the tightly packed script. He showed me the jelly-like screen. It was as if the information seemed to spill over the edges of the actual shape if you looked at it directly, and appeared as a squashed hologram. I realised that it was not the same as the com that we had brought back to Weldon after he had left it in the bar. The holo-screen was different. "It doesn't come from here, does it?" I said, as several things slid into place.

I looked down at my boots, the ones I had borrowed from Ziggy, and then realised that the boots Rari had given me on a previous trip were under the bed in the farmhouse. They were there because I had put them on when I had dressed in my home on the moor and hit the intruder in the kitchen. A dreamwalking set of boots. I sighed. If I had looked around it was obvious that they had brought things with them and in fact they all seemed to be able to cross the barrier with more than the 'information' of themselves. "How do you do that?" I asked. He looked up, puzzled. "Bring things with you?" I pointed to the handheld.

He sat down. I could see the other two men were listening with the ability of half an ear that sleeping cats and careful people seem to have. "It takes practice." He thought for a second or two and then added, "The skills you use to find your way here are the same, you have to 'remember' you have something in your hand or the exact contents of a pack. It gets easier."

"Does it work with really big things?"

"If you can't lift it there, you can't have it here." He smiled, one of those tired, world-weary smiles. I wondered which world had made him so weary. "Reality exists in both places," he added.

"Okan?" I asked with a sudden flash of recognition that shocked me for a moment. "When I'm here, I'm not there anymore am I? Not even a little part of me."

He watched me carefully for my reaction. "No," he said, "Not asleep, not dreaming, not there."

All the things about time and space get pushed into a wave of epic size and motion when you added multiple universe theory. It was as if the possibilities had just become more endless.

I fingered the fixer on the side of my face as if l were searching for more answers. Okan looked almost relieved when I asked, "What are we going to do about the man in my house?"

"Joao is going to go back with you," he said.

I shook my head, just when I thought I was getting a handle on the complications there was one more stunned silence to add to the list.

"Okay," I said, "How is *that* possible?"

"It consists of using the same skills as finding your way here; it's just that you have to bring Joao with you. Make him fit into the place you come from." Okan tapped the handheld computer and the screen went flat. He put it down and leaned back in the seat with his hands on his knees. Joao and Rari had stopped what they were doing.

"This is down to me to get right." I tried to imagine if I even thought it was possible. "What happens if I can't do it?"

"He doesn't go." Okan fiddled with the top of the console.

"Is it that simple?" I asked, really knowing the answer.

"No."

We all sat in silence, listening to the wind in the trees and I could feel my fears creeping quietly into the corners of all the things not said.

"I want you to know that I am working really hard at not losing it," I said carefully.

Okan smiled. "I can see that and I am, of course, very grateful."

I was about to say something when a sharp pain in my head had me gasping and grabbing the edge of the seat. Okan reached for my hands. "What?" He shouted. The pain in my head was accompanied by a series of snapshots. A man's face, though I couldn't see his features, and sharp twists of light. "Stay here Millie, concentrate!" I pushed past the pain and squeezed Okan's hands as if I were hanging onto a life raft. It eased gradually and I leaned back my eyes full of the tears of pain.

Rari was leaning over me. "What was that?"

"I don't think someone wants me here." I put my hand on my face as the familiar trickle of blood flowed down to my chin. Joao handed me a wipe that he had pulled out of a medical pack. I pushed it up against the fixer and then leaned forward as the nausea took over.

"If you know who this is, please tell me," I whispered. There was silence.

"He isn't from our verse Millie," Okan spoke softly, "At least I don't think so."

"Can't be from mine," Joao added.

The afternoon was a different type of practice session. I spent hours describing the kitchen in minute detail, exactly where I was standing, how far I was from the table, each morsel of information tucked away as though I were a squirrel storing nuts for the winter. Several times I felt myself back in the room with the bat in my hand and I could see Cecil, his orange eyes glowing in puzzled surprise. Okan would shake me and shout, "Millie, get some control!" Until I could have hit him with the bat I didn't have in my hand and then for a moment, it was there. The bat, warm moulded wood, heavy and real and just there. Then it melted into a shadow and was gone.

I sat down abruptly. "Do I appear to be dissolving when I go back to my verse?"

"Well yes," Rari said, "But you're really amazing when you do."

I closed my eyes. "Somewhere between verse hopping and people trying to murder me, there should at least be doughnuts."

Joao patted my shoulder in what felt as if it could be sympathy. "Doughnuts *and* coffee," he added, "Lots of coffee."

We walked back from the barns to the Weldon's farmhouse in the twilight. I was too tired to speak and stumbled several times until Okan put his arm around me and pulled me along with him. He felt strong and real and somehow right. I wondered what Simon would say; he'd probably ask for a group hug.

"Do you have any idea what this man looks like, Millie?" Rari asked me.

"No, I can't see his face clearly." I shuddered.

"What is it?" Okan squeezed me to him.

"He has eyes, like a night without stars," I whispered.

The three of them seemed to move in an unspoken unison of trust, the wordless thread of those who have fought a war together. Some things are based on years of experience and memories and some exist when trust is forced on you through circumstances. I wondered how they saw me and then decided not to ask.

The lights were on around the outside of the house and I could see Tara coming out of the near barn. She swung the heavy doors and Joao went over to give her a hand. He took the gun she was juggling with and pushed at the doors with her, they laughed when they got tangled up together trying to get out of each other's way. I caught a look on Okan's face that seemed to be worry, but it disappeared as soon as it had come and I wasn't sure I had really seen anything. I knew how he felt; nothing about lost love can come to any good. It was as if we were watching an old film where you know the ending is going to be sad but you can't look away.

Weldon came up on the com in the kitchen while we were making supper, he was staying out with the cattle as there was a particularly aggressive vilden which had killed two of the young inexperienced calves. Okan asked him if he wanted company. "Come out tomorrow if you can and bring the large trailer, I need to remove the carcases; they're making the herd nervous."

"We'll be there at daylight." Okan broke the contact on the kitchen screen as Weldon nodded his goodbye.

I fell asleep in the food again, drifting in and out of the conversation.

"Millie!" Rari pulled me to my feet. "Go to bed, it's not very social to snore into the potato dish."

"Hey," I protested feebly, "I can be sophisticated, just not for long periods at a time."

Tara followed me upstairs and sat on the bed talking about the day until I came out of the shower. She was quiet for a moment as I wandered around covering myself with the long t-shirt that she handed me. It smelt of sunshine and wind-dried warmth. My mother had always line dried the clothes, saying it made her feel good to smell the sun on the things that she wore.

"Do you think there are barriers between this verse and the next?" Tara's question was one of those that require plenty of thought and careful consideration, but tiredness meant I was completely out of both.

"The Native Americans where I'm from used to say that this world is part of the next, I think they understood something about other verses."

"Should I stop looking for Ziggy?"

I put my hand on hers and squeezed. "Children are attached to you for life, they breathe the air you breathe in the beginning; when the cord is cut it doesn't mean you're not connected anymore." She looked stunned and I said gently, "Do you think I shouldn't know this because I don't have children? It is because I understand, that's *why* I don't have any and no, I don't think you should stop looking for her."

That silence of everything followed, where you look back over your words and realise that maybe you should have put it differently, or better, or in fact, not at all. She pulled at a locket that had been hidden by her shirt; it was a smooth metallic colour similar to platinum, and it contained a small holo-picture of a smiling girl in her teens. Pretty toffee coloured skin and thick hair tied up with bright strips of ribbon in plaits. She was the image her mother in every way but one. I looked closer just to make sure. One green eye and one blue. Joao's eyes. I leaned back on the bed and tried not to groan. "Please tell me heterochromia runs in the family."

"As far as I know it does, just not my family." Tara smiled at the picture and closed the locket, tucking it away under her thick shirt.

"Is Weldon aware?" I sat up and pushed pillows around me for support. I pointed to the space next to me and she shuffled off her shoes and grabbed the rest of the pillows, we both stared at the ceiling for a moment.

"Yes. I was on my own for a while; both my parents had been killed in an accident at Great Port. I came out to the settlements hoping to start a new life. I was working in Til Duster's place when I met Joao." She paused and plucked at the edge of a pillow until I poked her on the arm winding my hand around in the air until she laughed and carried on. "We were very young and I thought it was romantic and exciting to love a traveller. Weldon would come into the bar sometimes and just sit, making a drink last all evening. Then one day Joao was just gone, for months."

It sounded as if it was the kind of story that wouldn't be out of place with a box of popcorn and three hankies. I have always loved those films, I just never wanted to live through one.

"My mum used to say, 'sometimes we need to look for windows not mirrors,'" Tara whispered.

I thought for a bit and nodded. "That sounds really profound but I have no idea what it means."

Tara laughed, "I think she meant you have to look for solutions and not dwell on yourself."

"My mum was really very wise too." I looked at her carefully. "Does Joao know?"

She shrugged, in the way that people do when they find themselves in the safety net and not on the high wire and said, "I was living with Weldon by the time he came back. He never said anything so I just carried on. He saw Ziggy a few times but he never asked." I sighed, the chances of Joao *not* knowing was about the same as me winning a singing contest. Simon had said I sounded like a camel in distress, though I think it was not that easy to get through all of 'Dancing Queen' after four tequila slammers and a plateful of macaroni cheese. I wondered if Okan had worked out Ziggy's DNA potential and then thought it was probably a stupid question. I also mulled over *how* it was possible. I sighed. If you could bring a hand-held computer with you then a few sperm and the ability to fertilize would be no problem.

"I can hear you thinking." Tara smiled. The night stars and the curve of Jupiter were full in the window. I could see Leda bright on the horizon. The dark was busy with the space of out there and it made me feel hopeful in the way that only those who love science can be.

"Do you have any of that amazing cake left, the one with all the icing?"

We went downstairs, the light was still on in the kitchen and Joao was sleeping quietly on the sofa, stretched out with one arm above his head. With at least four bedrooms in the house spread over the upper two floors, I couldn't understand the attraction.

He breathed deeply and we walked around him to get to the kettle and the cake. I cut a large piece as Tara poured the rich brandy-like liquid into the steaming mugs of tea. We both jumped guiltily as he said without opening his eyes, "Cut me a large slice, Millie." I poked him with my foot and settled on the end of the sofa, pulling the edge of the rug around me. He sat up. His hair was stuck in bad peaks and he was wearing no shirt, just underwear. I could see what Tara had fallen for, the half-warrior, half-boyish-man would get you into trouble every time.

"When are we going to practice you coming home with me." I scraped the icing off the top of the cake and ate it first, as there was no point in waiting for the best part. Stretching my feet out and resting them on his lap, he moved his cup out of the way, settling himself with the cushions at his back. Tara was curled up in the chair by the stove. The half-light of the lamp cast gentle kind shadows and for a moment I felt as if I was somewhere I belonged.

Joao cleared his throat, "Well," he said.

"Oh my, you're not going to turn into one of those people who spends the same amount of time describing something as it actually takes to happen," Tara said, laughing at the expression on his face.

"I think you're ganging up on me," Joao grumbled.

The stove made that humming noise which was better than sleeping pills for knocking you out and I felt my head begin to loll forward. Before it ended with me asleep on the sofa, I stood up and staggered towards the stairs.

"Save it for the morning Joao. Goodnight."

I could hear their murmured conversation as I slumped onto the bed and pulled the covers over me. In my mind I reached out to the cat in the fruit basket on the kitchen table and scratched under his chin. He purred and butted my hand, his warm fur crackling under the influence of whatever electromagnetic field I seemed to carry about with me like an unwanted handbag.

At some point in the night, I woke to feel the cat curled behind my legs and as I moved, he did too. I looked out of the window at the false dawn edging up over the horizon and the comforting curve of Jupiter. Something seemed not quite right about the view, but I couldn't think what it was and I sank back down into the deep sleep of muddled thoughts and too much brandy.

The sharp hot blast of the shower did very little to wake me up. I was sure my tongue had been used as a floor cloth during the night. I cleaned my teeth and tried to remember what it was that had been bothering me. It was disconcerting, as if I were watching people dancing and not actually able to hear the music. I pulled on clothes and used some of the makeup in the bathroom that must have belonged to Ziggy. It might have been antique but it worked. We all need the barrier of mascara some days. I went over to make the bed and pulled the thick downie up over the pillows. As I straightened the cover my hand came away with a few strands of tabby cat hair.

The kitchen was busy with people eating and the lamplight made the dawn outside seem further away. Okan swallowed his food before he spoke, something that endeared him to me no end. I have never understood why some men think all women find the contents of their mouths attractive. "More practice today, Millie. Rari and I are going to take some things out to Weldon."

"Great, can't think of anything else I'd rather do except," I said thoughtfully, "Try and push a pig up a greasy pole maybe."

"Did we get up on the wrong side of the universe today?" Rari asked sympathetically.

"Oh, very droll, Rari." I thumped him on the arm and he pretended to be severely wounded; then swept up the last of the toast with the thick, rich honey dripping spectacularly down onto his shirt. He was still scooping it up with a finger as they went out of the door. Okan had his coffee cup in his hand as he walked over to the runabout to start it up.

I followed them out, wanting to say something, but not really knowing where to start. The coffee cup was held in my direction but Okan didn't look up from checking the contents of the storage bin on the back of the vehicle. I took it from the outstretched hand.

"Millie, I can hear your brain cells doing some serious thinking and it's making me nervous."

Rari was over by the barn hefting cattle feed. He appeared suddenly to be very un-professor like. I wondered if the 'teaching' involved unarmed combat.

"Have you ever brought anything live with you?" I asked hopefully. "I mean a not 'us' thing?" I pointed to him and then myself as if he was a bit dim.

Okan stopped what he was doing and gave me his full attention, something that made me feel even more uncomfortable. "Could you be more specific?"

"I think I brought my cat over for a few hours in the night."

"Your cat?" Okan was whispering, it sent shivers through my muscles and I clutched the coffee cup to me as if it was a barrier from all the bad that I could feel coming my way in the very near future.

"Actually," I explained, "It's not my cat, it belongs to my neighbours down the valley, but they don't look after it very well and they've gone on holiday."

Rari came up and heaved the bag of feed onto the back of the runabout, making it rock in protest. He wiped his sweating forehead and then looked at both of us. He sighed, "What now?"

"Are you sure?" Okan asked me with that edge of worry some parents have when their children turn out to have a real skill for some seriously dangerous hobby.

I shrugged. "I think so. I can't be sure about anything these days but Cecil has tabby fur and Tara doesn't have a cat." I held up a hand in the light from the security lamps in the yard. It was full of tabby hair; Cecil was something of a shedder.

"You need a licence for a cat on this world Millie," Rari said, getting the drift of the conversation in spookily fast timing. He turned to Okan. "We knew it might happen Oak,' nothing we can do about it now except try and keep it out of the grid." He shook his head as if reminding himself of the impossibility. "Are you sure?" I shrugged, filing 'the grid' under something to ask about when the team freaking out had reached nominal levels.

They say, or Jung does, that we genetically inherit our primeval fears. The buried alive, being eaten by animals' fear. I must have had something in my DNA from somewhere because hearing the words 'the grid' definitely fell into the category of primeval fear.

The two men climbed onto the precariously loaded vehicle and Okan revved the engine. He sighed and got off again, making it wobble dangerously and Rari swore, hanging onto the bar at the back. He came over to me and gave me a hug, then got back on the runabout. Rari gave me an exasperated smile and then a wave. They barely made the corner of the farm lane, tipping alarmingly onto one side. I realised Joao was standing on the steps of the house watching.

"Not bad, usually Rari ends up in the road when Oak's driving." He came over to me. "Are you okay?" He put an arm around my shoulders. "Let's get another layer of breakfast in us before we start with the crazy stuff."

Tara was filling the coffee pot from the tap on the stove and she added thick chewy brown gloop from a big metal container. It had that fresh ground smell but looked like something you'd have to scrape off your shoe. I accepted a cup and added enough creamy milk and sugar to have made my mother wince. I stirred thoughtfully. "Why do you have to have a licence for a cat here, Tara?"

She looked surprised. "All animals require a special licence; it stops abuse and prevents viral infection crossing the species barrier. I would love to have a cat," she looked wistful. "They're not easy to come by on the settler moons. Very expensive."

I thought about the tatty moggy at home who was sitting in my fruit bowl on the kitchen table and wondered if he would like a permanent change of address. I reached for toast and the cheese and made a sort of triple sandwich by adding a layer of honey. Joao looked carefully at the procedure and then stole half the completed masterpiece.

He nodded. "Good," he mumbled, through a full mouth.

We sat in comfortable silence listening to the chatter on the holo-screen that Tara had turned on. It was their version of the BBC world service, but solar-system-wide. Tara tutted at the market prices for beef and began putting dirty plates into the sink. I watched as she scraped them and put them into a rather odd-looking dish washer. It didn't so much whoosh as glow and rattle.

Joao leaned over to me. "No water, it blasts them then shakes them clean."

The best place for trying to send both of us back to my verse turned out to be the slightly dim corridor in-between the kitchen and the hall stairs. "You need to reproduce the surroundings you're going back to. No good trying to get the hang of this with a spectacular view of the mountains."

"Surely I'm going to have to learn to do this from anywhere?" I asked.

"Don't want to be making things too difficult at this point." Joao stood very close to me and patted his hand on my shoulder; then rather oddly he pressed a finger on my face over the fixer and put his other hand on his own fixer. It *felt* weird; it must have looked as if two crazy people were trying to learn a barn dance routine completely stone cold sober, which was *never* a good idea.

I closed my eyes and went through the verbal description of where everything was relative to where I had been standing when I dreamwalked into Tara's verse. We worked out that Joao would appear in the middle of the table if we went back in our current positions. More shuffling occurred with the music-less dance. I tried again. Worse; this time it would be the fridge.

"This must be a really small kitchen!" Joao was getting exasperated.

"It's a perfectly adequate size," I said defensively, "It's just not designed for people whizzing in and out."

"Well then you've got too much furniture." He ended up standing behind me and slightly to one side, but it was going to be very close to the back door. I was sweating with the strain of not returning, for some reason the lure of my own verse seemed to be incredibly strong. It made my head spin and for a moment I could see the swirl of light and the dark funnel at the centre, my breath caught in my throat and I strained not to be swallowed by the maw.

"Concentrate!" Joao warned as the flash and shadows of my kitchen caught both of us by surprise.

I pulled away from him and struggled to stay in the corridor. "Millie." Tara came into view. "Do you want to take a break?"

Joao looked at me as I was hyperventilating and sweating, my hair was all over the place and I leaned down to stop the dizziness, resting my hands on my knees. "Maybe a break would be good," he said. I nodded. Speaking was not an option.

We stood in the back garden drinking coffee and admiring the flowers that Tara had planted in huge tubs and boxes along the porch. The mountains were clear and bright, vast swathes of snow looped around the peaks in dangerous alluring beauty.

A small hedge marked the border between the domestic domain and the farm's fields. The herd of something that looked as though it was a very hairy goat cropped grass in slightly stroppy contentment. I pointed.

"Cashmere goats," Tara explained, "It's a good, high return business. Not much input from us, just food and care."

As if they knew they were being talked about, several of the creatures came to the edge of the boundary and raised their heads. Tara and I went over and I found myself scratching the space between some scary looking horns. The grumpy faces rubbed against my fingers as Cecil the cat did, looking for the perfect place. They were not quite the same as the creatures in my verse; more sheep-like. "We crossed them genetically with a breed of sheep," Tara said, as if she had heard my question. "A tough mountain species, they're good mothers as well."

Joao waved from the rocking chair on the wrap-around porch.

"Come on Millie. More practice."

I made a face, but not one he could see and Tara laughed and said, "The wind will change and you'll stay that way." I stopped. Of all the things that had made it through the different verses, that was the strangest. Little sayings handed down; the origins lost in the memories of people no one living had ever met. "What?" Tara asked.

"Nothing. The torture will be good for me." I handed the cup to her outstretched fingers and I went back into the shadowed hallway with all the other ghosts.

Rari and Okan arrived back coated in a cloud of red dust and the laughter of hard work as the green sunset crept close to the horizon. I stood out on the front steps feeling as if I was an extra in some cowboy film, Tara's hand knitted cashmere shawl wrapped around my shoulders. "How's Weldon? Is everything okay?"

Okan ran up the steps and put his arms around me in a not entirely unpleasant sweaty hug. It completed the picture of domestic home on the range bliss that was as uncertain as the goats out in the back fields. "He's well; we managed to get plenty done. Not easy working a spread as big as this on your own." He looked as if nothing would please him more than to be doing just that himself.

Rari staggered up carrying a huge bag of kit. "Don't worry, Okan, I'll get it, no problem." He dropped the stuff and stretched his back. "I'm not used to this." The smell of Tara's homemade stew reached his nose and I definitely saw it twitch. "Okay, last one in the shower gets the leftovers." I moved quickly out of the way as they both ran for the door.

I had never experienced the large family supper; the closest I ever came were reruns of The Waltons. My parents had snatched meals prepared by someone else, usually Margery, or occasionally Marks and Spencer, in-between fixing people. But here there was lots of laughter and noisy talk about the day and the tiredness that goes with doing something satisfying.

"How did the practice go?" Okan asked Joao. He didn't look in my direction.

"We're ready." Joao pulled the bread rolls towards him and took two.

"You do know that I'm actually sitting here and I can hear you?" I suddenly didn't feel hungry any more. The thought of returning to whoever was in my house was one fear, the other much bigger stealer of appetite was trying to bring someone back to my verse without leaving them in the quantum singularity along the way.

"Have you noticed the accretion disk when you travel back to your verse from this one?" I started buttering a roll, pulling apart the rich doughy bread and smelling the warm yeast that reminded me of the safe places in my past. I have always thought that smells bring more memories with them than any other sense. I didn't notice the silence until I had taken a large bite. Everyone was looking at me. "What?" I managed after some Olympic swallowing.

"You can see the wormhole when you dreamwalk?" Okan's voice was flat calm. I nodded, hoping that this wasn't something else that made me 'interesting.'

"You don't?" They all shook their heads, including Tara who, taken up with the collective suppressed emotion of the moment, had forgotten that she didn't actually do any verse hopping of her own.

"Right," I said.

Rari was pink with a mass of barely conceived questions forming a disorderly queue on his tongue. It came out as a jumble and Joao patted him on the back. "Steady now professor, take a nice deep breath."

"Can you be a bit more specific Millie?" He sounded pleading and hopeful, and I imagined a little boy who had just been promised a trip to the follies in Las Vegas.

"Well." I closed my eyes and tried not to go anywhere. The silent spin started slowly creeping into the shadows at the edge of my fingers. I opened my eyes. "I can see a black hole, I don't know how big it is, my feet seem to hover over the centre, so it's not much bigger than me. There is a swirl of colour for want of a better word, but it's more a rainbow of light." Rari nodded as if to encourage me.

"I can feel energy moving from the outer rim to the dark centre and it seems to include me. It frightens me," I added, "But I feel as though I belong there as well. Does that make sense? There is no sound. It looks as if it should be as noisy as a waterfall, but there's nothing, just my breathing."

I leaned back in my chair and took a bite of the bread. There was a small sigh from all of them, a release of tension. I tried not to mind about the brick wall that now separated them from me.

"I guess it *could* be possible because the dreamwalk through the singularity isn't instantaneous," Joao said. Okan nodded.

"How long does it take?" I asked, curiously.

"We think about point three of a second," Okan said. "But of course, time changes as you travel." He shrugged.

I sighed the way you do when an exam is just too difficult to pass. That 'not quite making it' feeling. "Are we going back to my verse tonight?" I looked at my plate, crumbling bits of bread in my fingers, and not wanting to hear the answer.

"We really need to know who this man is Millie," Rari said kindly.

I nodded my understanding but the instinct to run away and hide, as if I was still a child in the schoolyard full of bullies, was making my hands shake. Tara picked up plates and shuffled around behind me putting her arms across my body in a sort of backward hug. "You'll be with Joao; he won't let anyone hurt you."

"Yes, if I manage to get us both through the wormhole, otherwise I'll be facing the bad people alone and he'll be swimming in the wake of the accretion disk!"

A stunned silence followed. "Way to inspire confidence, Millie," Joao said.

We shuffled around for the evening, Okan and Rari talking quietly with Joao about the different possibilities of dealing with someone who could be from another verse, and Tara and I taking it in turns to make snide remarks about men who talked over the top of your head.

I patted her hand. "You won't go looking for Marl at Great Port until I come back, will you?" The expression on her face told me she had been thinking of doing exactly that, but I managed to extract a reluctant promise from her.

I stood in the hallway with Joao in the rather awkward positions we had practised all through the day. It made me snigger with nerves and the shadows seemed to be dancing in the corners of the wood floor, as if the little demons of doubt were waiting. I pushed the thoughts away from me and concentrated on the kitchen at home and the view of the valley in the moonlight. Okan moved his hand gently across my neck and then stood back with Tara and Rari; a collective cloud of anxiety hovering over them with the possibility of morning rain.

My head began to spin and I could see the disk and the black hole below my feet and I could still feel Joao and my breath was a thunderstorm in my ears and I reached out and touched the table, falling onto my knees with Joao banging into the back door.

The baseball bat curved in my fingers as I grabbed it instinctively from the floor and Cecil growled his warning. I swung out around behind me, contact shuddering through my arm to my body, knocking me sideways. A sharp cry and a sting of something against my back made me turn. The man was half in and half out of what seemed to be a tunnel into another room that didn't exist in my house.

He pulled at me, dragging me towards his verse. Joao snatched the bat from me and threw it hard. It made a sickening noise as it hit the man on the head. He fell backwards, but raised a small weapon and fired. Joao crumbled and I screamed.

The dark tunnel spun away and I dropped to the floor, exhausted and frightened, adrenaline making me shake and my teeth chatter. I turned to Joao and then back to where the tunnel had been, fearful of it reappearing.

Joao groaned, clutching his shoulder, the blood seeping out through his fingers. I pulled a small towel off the rail by the kitchen sink and pressed it to the wound. My hand came away covered in a sticky slimy mess. The phone clattered to the floor as I snatched it towards me with slippery shaking hands. I tapped in a number.

A sleepy voice answered, "Yes?"

"Can you come over, Simon? I need your help," I stuttered through my shock.

"I'm on my way." He didn't even ask why.

Joao was pale with the loss of blood seeping through my makeshift pressure bandage. My parents had left an emergency room size kit in the study, complete with a small rechargeable defibrillator. I raced up the stairs and hauled the box down including the AED, which was the size of my laptop. I found Joao slightly conscious and cringing with the pain. "If that's what I think it is, we don't need it yet," he whispered.

I was crying with relief. "I could hardly find a pulse Joao. I thought I'd lost you." I pulled out a bandage and made a better job of trying to stop the bleeding.

The back door was pounded and then pushed open and Simon appeared, his hair stuck up in punk-like peaks and there were some severe pillow burns down one side of his face. I had put the light on over the cooker and I could see the pool of blood on the floor reflected in his stunned eyes and the sickeningly sticky smell seemed to hang in the air around us like broken promises.

He picked up the landline phone without speaking to me and tapped in a number. "I need a favour." I couldn't hear the voice on the other end but Simon squatted down by Joao and then added, "Gunshot wound to the shoulder." This was followed by another short silence which must have been filled with questions. Simon looked at me and back down at Joao. "I think you'd better come here." I sagged with relief.

We put Joao in a more comfortable position on the kitchen floor and I fetched a cushion from the sofa by the window, placing it carefully under his head. Simon introduced himself and Joao replied. It was as if they were both attending a boring cocktail party. Cecil had gone back to the relative safety of the fruit bowl and looked on with undisguised interest. All cats love a drama.

The back door was tapped so quietly that I hardly realised

anyone was there. Simon got up from the half squat and went over to peer through the glass panel. He made me really nervous by asking who it was before he unlocked and opened it. I stayed on the floor by Joao, holding his hand. Then a thought made me lean close to him.

"There's no possibility of you going back to your verse is there?" I whispered urgently.

"No," he whispered back, "But it would be better if I stayed conscious right now. I didn't get a chance to ask why, as a small, neat, dark-haired woman came over to both of us and took Simon's place squatting down next to Joao. She looked at me and smiled and then did some reassuringly competent things with the contents of her bag. Syringes and sutures and a rather nasty pair of forceps later, Joao was sitting up, a heavy bandage around his arm and chest.

She went over to the light and held the tiny projectile in her fingers, examining it carefully. "I think you'd better keep this." She handed it to Simon together with a large pot of antibiotics and left as quietly as she came.

Simon looked at the object in the palm of his hand and then looked at me. "Go and have a bath, Millie. I will get Joao into the spare bedroom." He reached down and the two men came to some arrangement about pain and walking and mutual respect without saying a word, and I went upstairs and left them to follow at a snail's pace.

I lay back in the hot water and tried not to squeal as an agonising moment caught me by surprise. The sore area just below my shoulder blade revealed the smear of partly dried blood on my hand and reminded me of the sharp sting I had felt before I had hit out at the man with my baseball bat. It wasn't a cut, more of a small, round puncture wound.

It was difficult to see in the mirror, I wiped the steam off the surface and tried looking over my shoulder again. Wrapping the towel around me I came out onto the landing.

"Are you okay?" Simon asked and I jumped spectacularly.

"Simon! Sneaking around in the dark is not such a good idea right now." I leaned on the wall for support. "Can you get me a plaster from the emergency kit? I left it downstairs."

He sighed and went quietly along the corridor; none of the lights were on except a small faint line under the door of the spare room and he crept down the stars into the puddles of moonlight, as if there was a very real potential for someone to be in the kitchen. I could feel a trickle of bloody fluid ruining down my back along with the fear. It was odd that Simon, who hadn't been around, recognised the possibility of a return visit.

I pushed open the door to my childhood room and Joao turned painfully in my direction. Sitting down on the bed with my back to him, I whispered, "What does this look like to you?"

"As if someone tried to take a DNA sample. It's almost to the bone; you're bleeding all over the towel."

I turned round. "Wouldn't a few skin cells do? You can get DNA from a hair follicle; he didn't need to dig a hole in me."

"I think that's good enough for identification, you need other tissue samples for more complicated procedures." The quiet footsteps on the landing filtered through the potential questions.

Simon came in and we stopped talking as if we were all back in the school playground and no one was sure who the geeks were.

"Let me see," he said. I stood up and he swiped the wound with something appropriately stingy and then pressed a plaster carefully to my skin. "Well, it's been quite a night." He stood back and scrubbed at his face and hair and I went to get a dressing gown and my slippers. Joao was trying to sit up when I got back, sliding up the pillows using one arm. It must have really hurt, because his face was pale and sweating and he leaned back looking as if he'd just lost a fight with the darkness.

The silence was punctuated with the soft tapping of sheathed claws on the wood floor and Cecil slithered in through the barely open door, leaping onto the bed and curling around in a cushion of warm tabby fur. Joao looked stunned. He reached out and gently touched the paw nearest to him. "He's beautiful."

With creepy prescience Simon said sarcastically, "Not many cats where you come from, I'm guessing." Cecil purred his contentment. For a cat nothing compared to being the centre of attention; even if you didn't know where the centre was.

"What are we talking about here, some sort of hit job?" Simon yawned and flopped into the only chair, stretching out his long legs. I sat down on the bed again.

"You do know Simon that 'The Sopranos' is not actually a documentary?"

My back was stinging, so I might have sounded a little grumpy. The thought of trying to explain anything made me feel dizzy. It was closely followed by the 'not really knowing enough' feeling and then the 'need for a few explanations myself' sensation.

Simon looked at both of us and sighed, "I'll sleep on the sofa downstairs." He stood up and raided the wardrobe for blankets and pillows. "Don't stay up all night talking, kids."

"Thank you." Joao reached out a hand in an old-fashioned gesture and Simon shook it solemnly, a pair of misfits in the wrong Broadway play, waiting for the last rush of faint applause.

He closed the door after him and I sat back down on the bed, pulling my dressing gown around me against the cold and the pale fear of possibilities. "Is it safe to sleep?"

Joao shrugged; he reached out his fingers to the soft fur of Cecil's ears and gently scratched. The cat stretched out a paw and yawned, his pink tongue and sharp teeth taking over his face for a moment. "I think he might have to deal with a sore head and he can't run the risk of being stuck here. That wormhole was different." He looked at my confused expression. "Not like ours."

"I'm not an expert in these matters Joao, but I think a one quantum singularity is pretty much the same as any another. Give or take an accretion disk."

He stroked the cat carefully, thus earning himself vast amounts of cat points. Cecil rolled over onto his back so that his fat tummy could be equally appreciated. Joao obliged. "I think it was man-made."

I know I must have looked really stupid sitting there with my mouth open because Joao smiled. I said, "What you're saying is, we've found Rari's missing type three civilisation."

"I think *they* found us," Joao added, making my skin crawl.

We sat in silence and I could hear the old clock in the hallway downstairs chime the hour. Small shadows chased the moonlight across the floor and the half light of the bedside lamp gave the corners of the room the old night time powers of my childhood.

"The bigger question," I whispered, "Is what do we have that they could possibly want?"

"Millie, it's probably not a whole verse of people who are doing this. You don't represent everyone who lives in your verse and I don't suppose this man is working for more than one small group."

I thought about this carefully. "Why do you think that?"

"Because," Joao sounded exasperated, "The chances are, a larger organisation would have succeeded in getting you into that worm-hole by now!"

"Are you saying that *I* have something they might want?" I tried not to sound as if I was the coward that I actually felt I could be.

"I think," Joao was nearly shouting and he took a painful breath and began again. "That we're *all* interesting to them and up to now I've managed to stay under the radar, but not for much longer."

More quietness followed interspersed with Joao's painful breathing and my stunned silence. "I still don't understand the part where I used to go to sleep as a child in my pyjamas and dreamwalk around Tara's verse in my jeans and t-shirt. Therefore, I don't stand much of a chance with the needs of a psychopath from a type three civilization!"

"You caught onto the fixer really quickly," Joao said wickedly, "Rari and I were taking bets that you'd arrive at least once in your skin!" I laughed and thumped him on his good arm, very gently.

"What about you, did you ever travel in the nude?" I asked, checking the bandages on his shoulder for any bleed through.

"Where I grew up you slept in your clothes," he said bitterly.

"This DNA, Joao?" I crept carefully around the question. "I'm just wondering how complicated a procedure we are taking about. Molecular biology is still rather in its early stages here, we have some genetic engineering for inherited diseases; the usual drug and vaccination research and there is investigative scientific forensics." I shrugged, not sure how to continue.

He sighed a big sigh. "You know about subatomic particles?"

"Of course," I said, "A particle smaller than an atom, the electron, neutron and proton are supposed to be the most important." I studied the ceiling. "The electron is an elementary particle and the neutron and the proton are composed of quarks."

"If you were dealing with people who dreamwalked through a wormhole wouldn't you be studying them at the subatomic level?"

"We *definitely* can't do that here." I breathed my own tired painful breath and tried not to think what someone was doing to my quarks in another verse.

I stood up and stretched carefully. "Are you going to be alright?"

"People from my verse are tough, we heal quickly."

My bed felt cool and rumpled. I couldn't remember the days here or there for a moment and I pushed against my muddled brain for the normal answers to my life. Was it a work day tomorrow, would Tara wait for me or go looking for answers of her own in places that could only mean more trouble? I fell asleep mid-thought.

The early autumn sun of a bright cold day filtered through my closed lids and I realised someone was standing over me in the painful instant of waking. I shot up in bed, nearly upending the cup of coffee in Simon's hand.

"Look out!" He moved quickly back, shielding the hot drink from my defensive fingers.

"Ah!" I struggled for my voice, starting a jumble of words that had nothing to do with speech and everything to do with not much sleep.

"We *could* try for a conversation that consisted of complete sentences. But I think it's a bit too early for some people." He held the drink out for me.

I pulled the pillows up and leaned back, taking the steaming cup and sipping the hot milky liquid. Simon sat on the end of the bed. I looked at the clock and tried not to make the fact that I didn't know what day it was filter through. "It's Sunday, Millie. Don't panic, you're not late for work. Though having the boss as your best friend must count for something if it had been Monday morning."

Yesterday we had gone shopping together and ended up arguing over a cashmere sweater in the bargain section of TK Maxx, and he'd won. The time passing in the other verse added layers of memories that didn't fit, as if I were a puzzle with too many pieces.

"Are we really best friends?" I asked, the loneliness of the school-yard was always just around the corner of the next moment.

"Of course. Always and forever; no matter what." Simon spoke the words in the even unemotional way that made crying without dignity a real possibility.

"Well now," he said, after a while when I'd gulped hot coffee and he had tidied the books on the floor into neat stacks in size order. "I checked on your acquaintance just now. He looks as if he won't be needing the doctor again this morning. In fact, he was up and about. Not dressed though." Simon grinned cheerfully.

Joao walked in wearing one of my old dressing gowns which hung in floral splendour to just below his dignity. He carried a cup of coffee and yawned in-between slurps.

"Millie, this is the sort of place you could experiment with nuclear fusion and no one would notice until their teeth started falling out."

"You're more of a town type of guy then?" Simon asked.

The morning got away from us in the race for the only bathroom, you do *not* want to be last after two men, even if one of them *is* gay, and the sort of breakfast which consists of toast and laughter. It surprised me that Joao and Simon got on so well, but the middle of the night with blood on the floor could have been a bonding experience.

"If you need me just call." Simon was sitting in his car with the engine running. I reached in and hugged him with all my arms and heart and he patted my back the way you would a small child.

"He's not the man, I mean, it's not him." I couldn't finish the sentence.

"No, Joao is in love with someone else." Simon nodded wistfully.

"Now you read minds." I poked him gently in the face.

"Of course I can read minds, I'm gay. We have special powers. It's the karmic equivalent of sorry about the rest of the world."

I laughed and turned around as Joao came out of the front door and along the path. The small road led up the hill into the next valley and the lone farm. Down towards the village my parents had worked in, which was the way Simon was facing, the road wove around, stopping at the small houses tucked into the frame of the hills and the farm that belonged to my nearest neighbours. I could just see the house that Cecil came from. To get to me he had to pass the farm, but I thought the feral cats in the barns and outbuildings had made me a better proposition. All cats know a weak-willed person.

Simon and Joao shook hands. "Millie." Simon looked serious. "I think you should take some leave." He saw that I was about to argue and a flash of recognition passed between the two men. There was nothing worse than being 'discussed.' I wondered how the conversation had gone. "Just until this thing is sorted out."

I sighed, "Okay."

"Bloody hell that went well," Simon laughed, "I thought I was going to have to fight a bit harder than that. I had all sorts of relevant points to put forward."

"You might still need them." I scowled.

"Don't spoil a good thing Millie," Simon said pompously. He put the car into gear. "Call me if you require my further assistance!" This was said to both of us, it made me think for a moment, about those things I didn't understand, which I added to the long list of all the *other* things I couldn't comprehend. Simon swept off down the winding road going too fast for the safety of the sheep, tractors and trees, and I turned to go into the house.

"Nice vehicle." Joao watched it until it disappeared around the bend in the road. You could still hear the engine revving as Simon missed a few gears.

"It's a Boxster, I think it looks like Noddy's car."

"I mean the fact that it doesn't hover." Joao was looking at the view up the valley and his head turned at the sound of the buzzards wheeling away from the crows, who were always on the lookout for a fight.

"Do you have anything in your verse with wheels?"

"Not in my time." He stretched up and groaned, pulling at his arm. I wondered how it was possible he could have healed well enough in the night to be able to move at all. I studied his face. "Did you go back to the other verse?"

He grinned. "Just for a day. Got some stuff from Tara that worked on the wound. I don't think I can take your tablets for infection. I have too much pollution in my system, that and growing up in a verse with hardly any ozone layer." He saw my expression and added helpfully, "She sends her love, by the way."

"How can you come here without me?" I asked, puzzled.

"Only needed you for the first trip." He shrugged.

I felt as if I had opened a door and let in something that was supposed to stay outside. As though the ghosts of the trees and the night shadows that lived on the grassy hill slopes were crowded into my living room waiting for answers.

We walked slowly back up to the house, my little old Mini was still out on the driveway next to the path and Joao leaned down and looked into the windows. He studied the dashboard and the green and white stripes in the faded red paintwork, then looked at me.

"Her name is Mabel, she belonged to my mother. The garage manager who looks after her says she's a mechanical miracle; he's never had to change a spark plug in twenty years." Joao looked completely blank. "You know," I said, "The mysteries of the internal combustion engine is not really my subject either."

"Mabel," he said. "It figures." He looked back inside the car. "How fast does it go?"

I shrugged. "Sixty-five on a straight road with a following wind."

"Sixty-five what?" He frowned.

"Miles an hour," I added, heading for my front door.

He did some mental calculations and shook his head. "Let's hope we don't have to make a quick getaway in it."

I stopped, one foot on the step, my heart in my mouth. "Do you think there's *any* possibility we might have to do that?"

He didn't say anything and the night before became just the last few hours of something unfinished instead of the nightmare from another life. I finished my journey up the steps and through the door.

"The baseball bat Joao, did it have any blood on it?" We were standing in the kitchen and I made coffee, boiling milk in the microwave and adding it to the cups of frothy liquid from the complicated coffee machine that had been a present from Simon.

"I took a sample with me and gave it to Okan. He also sent his love by the way." I thumped his arm and then gasped as he winced and clutched his shoulder.

"Sorry!" I held the coffee out as a peace offering, drinking my own and reaching for the biscuit tin. Cecil appeared suddenly as if able to dreamwalk through his own personal verse. He climbed onto the table and looked hopefully at the opened tin. "Here you go old friend." I proffered the biscuit and Cecil took it and proceeded to make a phenomenal mess.

We sipped the hot liquid as the sun slid across the cold blue sky, filling the kitchen with bright autumn light through the double windows.

"The DNA you gave to Okan, what are you hoping to find? He must be someone like us if he can dreamwalk."

"Not necessarily." Joao was filtering information again; it made me think about grinding my teeth, but I remembered all the money my parents had spent on straightening them and I held off. "He seems to be able to make a wormhole, and that's really big technology."

"I agree," I said dryly.

"Millie, have you ever wondered how the physics works for us? That the quantum singularity goes where we are." I must have looked puzzled. "I mean exactly *how* we dreamwalk?"

I shook my head. "Up until this last trip I was just going to sleep in one verse and waking up in another. I'm still sore from last night and I'm frightened." I thought about it for a while. Cecil belly crawled nearer to the tin and delicately stole another biscuit. "I always thought a wormhole was fixed. An entrance and exit in one place. I imagine it doesn't work like that, otherwise we wouldn't be able to arrive in Tara's verse in different locations." I added quietly, "Do you know?"

He shrugged. "No, but I think the necessity for finding out has just become our first priority."

I tried to look innocent. "What do the people from Okan and Rari's verse think?"

Joao huffed a laugh, "You'll have to talk to Okan about that." He took pity on my grumpy face. "Okan and Rari don't have much say in where they go or what they do. They can be yanked back at will. It's complicated," he said half to himself, "Okan's playing a dangerous game."

It made me shiver with fear, as if we were all on borrowed time, whatever that meant when you were verse hopping. If infinity was multidirectional then so should hope be. I sighed with the, literally, endless possibilities of the trouble I was in. "Joao, do they know about me?"

He tried to look strong and positive but the things he had to deal with were real inside his own head and I never had the impression that Joao had ever held back with complex problems. Maybe growing up in a verse where the ozone layer was so thin, people were permanently polluted, and you didn't really know where your next meal was coming from, made the parameters for what was easy and what was difficult grow in different ways.

"I think Okan has managed to keep you a secret up to now."

Joao wandered off when I started the domestic tasks with cups and crumbs; Cecil looked longingly at the tin as it went back into the cupboard and then padded over to curl up in the fruit bowl for a wash and a sleep. I removed two apples and a pear which looked uncomfortable and reminded him that he was going to have to go home as soon as his family came back. He gave me the cat equivalent of 'I don't think so' and closed his eyes.

I found Joao in the study attempting things with my computer that I wasn't sure was actually possible. The mass of information on the screen was the type of jumble that computer programmers see when they're designing a new way to hack into the Pentagon for nuclear secrets. He had a copy of my electricity bill next to him. "Millie Rushcroft." He smiled at me. "Nice name."

"Thanks," I said, looking over his shoulder, "What's yours?" He looked puzzled. "Your last name."

"We don't go in for that in my verse; you usually have your father's name. My mother wasn't sure who it was." He looked at me. "Lots of gangs roaming around, so I'm Joao son of Matthew." He added sadly, "I think she had a brother growing up with the name and she just liked it." I tried to cover the desperation I felt, but it's difficult not to feel open sympathy for a woman who's been raped. I think it showed on my face because he said, "We found a safe place when I was thirteen or so, not so much violence as the cities and more food. My mother still lives there."

I nodded, as if I could understand, which I couldn't. I lived on Exmoor in mostly peaceful comfort and never went to bed without supper.

"What are you doing?" I pointed at the computer. It was as far off the beaten track as a walk in Nepal is to shopping in the local supermarket for eggs on a Saturday.

"Okan wanted to know how difficult it would be to get you off the grid if we needed to."

My stomach threatened to relinquish breakfast and most of my internal organs. "Why would we need to do that?"

Joao turned around in my office chair and struggled with the truth and lies and all the other possibilities in-between. "You've got to know it might be necessary, Millie?"

"I suppose I didn't really think things were that bad." He was silent and then he turned back to some unintelligible computer code and began tapping keys. It was the creepiest sound I had ever heard, next to footsteps in the dark.

I sat quietly in the chair by the bookshelves and watched Joao tread carefully through my existence. Cecil came clomping up the stairs and leapt onto my lap, washing a paw and curling around in a tabby cushion, tucking his paws into his nose so the purring reverberated in one solid sound. Joao muttered to himself and made a series of interesting expressions that followed the path of his explorations.

"Okay, I think that's theoretically feasible." He leaned back in the chair and looked at me. I had been daydreaming for a few hours and my back was stiff where the wound had been pressed against the chair. I jumped a bit at the sound of his voice and Cecil growled his concern. Joao flexed his fingers and closed down the system. "I would really like Okan to take a look. How would you feel about him coming here?" I shrugged.

The sun had travelled across the valley and I was beginning to think about evening and the possibility of unwanted visitors. "Joao, are we going to stay here tonight?"

"Do you want to?"

I hated it when people answered a question with a question. "Do you?" I tried to look confident and in charge of my emotions but the house where I had felt safe had become just another place of shadows.

"Maybe we'd be better to go."

I know my relief must have showed on my face because he smiled.

"Why do you think he's only visited at night? I asked, "Some theatrical creeping around in the dark?"

Joao shrugged. "I guess because most people sleep at night and we're more vulnerable." I nodded. A good sensible answer that made the skin crawl and parts of me want to hide in a very small place. He added quite unnecessarily, "He must have been wandering about for a while before you realised that he was here." Joao noticed the expression on my face and stopped talking.

We tidied up the house, or rather I did. Joao followed me around complaining. "I don't know how long I'm going to be away." I put the books in the study on the shelf and made the beds. In the kitchen I left food out and the small window open for Cecil, who was also following me. I crafted a careful note for Simon and put the rest of my incredibly neat house in order; turning off the lights and extra heating and making a cosy nest for the cat in a basket by the Aga.

"Millie, you're not going to be away for as long as if you were here! There's a temporal differential between all the verses." Joao expressed nuclear levels of exasperation.

"Exactly," I said, wondering if it would ever make any sense, "That's my point." His eyebrow raising and sighing would have done credit to a nine-year-old who was being made to eat broccoli.

I put some personal things in a backpack and had a quick shower. I think Joao was about to blow a fuse as I hung the damp towel in the airing cupboard. "Millie!"

"I'm a woman," I explained. Amazingly that seemed to work.

We stood in the kitchen watched by a contented Cecil who had settled obligingly in the basket, his purring competing with the comforting buzz of the Aga. I was nervously fiddling with the layers of clothing I had chosen post shower. Good jeans, a thin cashmere sweater, one that Simon hadn't managed to get his hands on first and my own boots. "I've never done this before," I explained. Joao looked stunned. "I mean, travel without sleep. The last trip doesn't count," I added, for the benefit of his puzzled expression.

Standing close together I watched as he settled himself for the other verse, and then I closed my own eyes and reached out for whatever it was inside me that brought the wormhole into my head. It took a moment for me to realise the shape of the disk below me and a realisation that something was not quite right, then, "Damn!" I was standing outside the barn in the middle of Gold Cliffs. I could imagine that Joao had turned up at the farmhouse without me. Okan was going to be *really* grumpy.

———

The lights of the bar were a welcome relief in the evening gloom. A green sun was slipping slowly below the hills as I walked up the steps. The chairs on the wide veranda were empty in the slight cool of the evening. I pushed open the doors and went in, feeling like a new girl at the end of term party.

Til Duster was standing behind the bar serving drinks and taking orders for food, which he then called back through the hatch to the kitchen behind him. No one was drunk, they were just having supper, talking through their day to each other in quiet voices, a mixture of people getting on with their evening. Several customers were waiting patiently at the bar as Til listened to a short man with a familiar stance, asking questions. I knew they were questions because Til kept shaking his head. Finally, he gestured to his other customers and apologised with a shrug of his shoulders. Something about the conversation that they were having bothered me, then I realised that Til didn't like him, which was odd because Til liked everybody except the borderers. The look on the bar owner's face had been one of distaste. I couldn't place the stranger, who took his food and drink over to a table in the corner of the room, until a wall mounted down light outlined his features. There was something familiar about the expression, though I couldn't see him clearly. My feet stopped walking. The gentle early noise of the bar seemed to recede.

I could feel my breath begin to hitch and my eyes slid across to meet Til's, he slowly and almost imperceptibly shook his head. Backing away from the room I sidled out of the doorway without the man, who was still sitting chewing his food in contemplation, becoming aware of me. I stood for a moment, thinking. How could the intruder from my house be in the bar in Gold Cliffs?

The alley to the side of the building was full of creeping memories. I could see the shadows of borderers with every step. A small flight of stairs at the back of the bar led up to the apartment that Til and his son Solly lived in. I slinked towards them stopping every time I heard the doors of the bar swing open, until the sound of the footfalls went down the road past the alley.

The base of the open stairs was in complete darkness, a well of unhelpful possibilities, with a small pool of light at the top over the apartment door. I couldn't think of anything else to do, I had no access to a personal com and though Okan would have worked out by now where I was, that I had returned to my original point of entry to this verse, it would still take some time by runabout to get to the town.

Trying *not* to think too much about what sort of rats they had here, I moved slowly towards the base of the stairs. One of the shadows seemed to have shifted slightly and I stopped, trying to look with the side of my eye to compensate for the blind spot. I was literally holding my breath and listening in the dark for ghosts.

A gritty noise behind me had me spinning on my feet trying to catch the dangerous movement; the hand over my mouth was a complete giveaway. Right in the moment before I bit and shoved and grabbed, the feeling of safety made me sag against the arm and body behind me. "Please tell me you're not going to scream?" A quiet voice said. He removed his hand.

"A simple hello would have done!" I whispered crossly.

Okan grinned. "I'll remember that next time." He took a step away from me still holding my arms and I took a step forward and he seemed puzzled for a moment until I put my hand up to his face and pulled him close enough to kiss him. His surprise lasted for no more than a second and then his fingers were in my hair.

The door at the top of the stairs opened and we pulled apart looking as casual as two people could do who had been kissing in a dark alley with the bad man the other side of a wall. "Up here!" Til whispered, as if he was a deaf theatregoer. I went up the stairs as quickly as I could. Okan stayed at the foot with a gun in his hand, watching the entrance to the side of the building until I was through the door, and then he ran up two at a time.

"Appreciate it Til." Okan patted him on the back.

"I knew that man was trouble as soon as he came in," Til muttered to himself as he went over to the kitchen unit and began making coffee. "I called Okan as soon as he started asking about you, Millie."

I nodded my thanks.

"Is there any way I can get a look at him?" Okan asked.

Til looked back over his shoulder. "Sure, over there, the room scanners are always on."

A small unit of screens in the corner almost hidden by a pot plant gave a continuous view of the bar from several angles. I could imagine Til's partner Ginnie insisting on the plants so she wouldn't have to look at the bar when she was in her own space.

I gave Til a hug in exchange for the coffee he offered me. He held on for a moment too long, like the sense of me was too difficult to let go. "Sorry," he said quietly.

"I understand." I patted his face. I really did; I knew that loss had felt to me as if no one would ever touch you again. You had empty arms *and* an empty heart.

"Is this the man?" Okan was studying the screen. He tapped the curved gel surface with a finger and it rippled slightly.

"Yeah, that's him." Til handed Okan his coffee.

The cameras were sharp and well defined. I took a gulp of scalding hot coffee and choked. It was the first time I had seen the man's face in clear light, rather than the shadows of my night time house. I realised I had met him before his nocturnal visit. Or technically I had bumped into him. He was the cobra in the park and he had been looking for me then.

Okan patted my back and Til took the cup out of my shaking hand, they both looked puzzled, my fear must have shown in my eyes, speech was impossible. I sat down and stretched out my wobbly legs.

"You okay Millie?" Til sat down next to me and patted my back. Okan leaned down towards me, his hands on his knees. I said nothing.

"He doesn't know you're here Millie," Til explained carefully as if he was quieting a restless horse. "Okan won't let him get near you." I nodded. "Who is this guy anyway?" Til asked. "Doesn't look like security. Did you piss off some gangers Millie?"

"Something like that," I said, watching Okan watching Til.

"Hey!" Til pointed at the screen. "He's going. What do you want me to do?" He asked Okan.

"See if you can find out where he's headed," Okan replied. Then he went to the door to the steps outside and Til hurried down to the bar by the main stairs.

Til paused, looking everywhere but directly at us. "I realise I don't know what's going on and that's okay. I've got your back. You're family." He disappeared, his face red with a momentary overload of emotion.

"Where are you off to?" I stood and went over to Okan, who was watching the alley through the glass top of the door.

"Stay here, I'm going to try and follow him."

"One more thing before you go, this man was in the park near where I work, he's been verse hopping my way for some time."

Okan tutted with exasperation. "Those are the sort of details that I need to know about, why didn't you say anything before?"

"Because *I* didn't know. I've never seen his face, in the house I thought he was just trying to kill me, not introduce himself!"

Okan paused before making a smart reply and then grinned. He leaned down and kissed me hard on the mouth. "It was my turn," he said.

"I didn't know we were keeping score!" I backed away, trying not to let the sudden embarrassment show on my face. "I would offer to come with you, but I've had enough creeping around in the dark for the moment." Is Joao cross with me?" I asked to Okan's preoccupied back.

"No, but Tara was *furious* with *him*." He grinned. "I could hear her shouting when he was on the com warning me." He turned off the outside light and opened the door, pausing to let his eyes adjust to the dark and then he slipped quietly down the stairs.

I sat down on the long sofa and began sipping coffee. A herd of buffaloes in the shape of two boys came charging up the main stairs from the bar and threw themselves at me in a heap of grubby small humanity. "Dad *said* you were here!" Solly shouted. Lu squeezed his arms around my neck and hugged me as if his life depended on it. They began telling me about their day at school which had been 'ugh' and the basketball game against Twin Rivers school, which had been 'mag.' Lu was sitting on my lap and Solly was jammed up next to me and the conversation would have been clearly heard across a national football stadium after a home win. I didn't mind.

Til followed them up the stairs at a more sedate pace and grinned at the sight. "Give the poor woman a bit of room, guys." They moved about a nanometre and carried on with the last and vital details of the game.

Til began to prepare supper and the smell of food caught the attention of the feral DNA that all children have in large quantities. "Go wash up you two." Til pointed at the back corridor and they went off grumbling with small boy humour.

Lu looked round. "Will you be here when I get back?"

I tried not to sound as sad as I felt. "Yes. I'm staying for supper." The expression of relief on the little boy's face made my eyes water, but luckily, he was too far away to see. "Is that okay?" I asked Til.

"You're always welcome here Millie," he replied gruffly.

We relived the basketball game again with fresh bread and home-made soup. Lu's eyes kept coming back to me over the top of a huge glass of milk and when they had yawned for the fortieth time, I chivvied them off to bed with the promise of a story which Solly said he was too old for, but he would sit with Lu just to keep him company. Til was stacking the dirty bowls into the same type of unit that I had seen at the farmhouse.

Both boys were curled up under the covers when I went into the bedroom. It was full of the clutter of small male things. I picked up sports clothes and equipment and put them away in the cupboards and straightened the bedcovers on both beds. Solly looked at me with the solemn expression of the truly hurt. "My mum used to do that," he said quietly. I sat on the end of his bed with my back to the wall and read the evening's request. It was a bloodthirsty tale of robots with lots of 'vanquishing,' the kind of story that children love. I did my best with the different voices and looked up every now and then until I could see that both of them were asleep.

Til was standing in the doorway as I crept out, pulling the door nearly closed behind me. "Fast asleep," I said quietly.

"There's no need to whisper," he said in a conversational tone, "They could both sleep through a hurricane." He looked sad. "My wife used to do that." He shrugged off the pain. "Okan's back."

"How did it go?" I reached for the bread that Til had left out for Okan and put it on the table as the bar owner ladled soup into a bowl for him.

"I lost him out near the stables." Okan looked carefully at me. The hidden message was the man had verse hopped. It made sense in a spooky multiple universe way.

"Isn't that the place you guys usually come and go?" Til said, matter-of-fact as he brought extra soup to the table and sat down. I tried really hard not to smile at the expression on Okan's face, but didn't succeed. I got a scowl for my levity. Til shrugged.

"Had a traveller friend when I was a child, got curious one day." He realised that Okan was *really* bothered. "You have to remember this system was advanced by the science of a group of travellers. It's an important part of our history. Though I think that's not always seen as a good thing these days."

These were similar to the words Tara had used. I thought about the fact that the passage of time always seemed to change all the positive stuff into something to be mistrusted eventually. We lived in cycles, reinventing the wheel over and over again instead of learning from the past.

"Are you going back to the farm tonight?" Til made more coffee and put it on the table together with the milk and sugar and some small creamy cakes that looked delicious. Okan drank his usual scalding hot black brew and I sipped my very milky version.

"I think we should. Can you let me know if you see him again?" Okan reached for a cake and swallowed it in two bites.

"Sure, no problem." Til began clearing plates for the second time that evening and I got up to help, feeling guilty as I'd got out of it the first time by reading a story to the boys. "Don't worry, nothing much to do here." Til waved me away. "Finish your coffee."

The com buzzed and Okan picked up the small jell-unit from the table and pressed a black square on the corner. A holograph of Joao appeared. "Everything okay?" He sounded anxious. I was too busy being impressed by the clarity of the three-dimensional screen to concentrate on what he was saying.

But Okan answered, "We're all fine here."

Joao looked relieved. "Tara's been giving me 'advice,'" he added, "You two coming back tonight?" When Okan replied that we were setting off right now, Joao said, "I'll meet you halfway with the other runabout. The vildens are still breeding." The hologram disappeared.

"Don't think they're that much of a danger anymore," Til said, "But I guess that's code for something he doesn't want to say out loud." I laughed. Til came from a background that didn't practice subterfuge or deception. I thought if you settled a moon, you'd have had to be up front about most things, because not saying what you meant could probably get you killed.

I set off down the steps after Okan had been out to look around for a moment. He called quietly up to where I was waiting with Til. I hugged the bar owner again for all he had done that evening and he looked carefully at me before saying, "Remember you are family."

I walked blindly down the dark stairs, feeling my way with my hand on the rail for each step. Okan was waiting on the runabout with the hover-jets already going. It made it difficult to get onto the seat behind him and he leaned over, pulling me up with one arm, as if I was getting onto the back of a horse. It seemed appropriate somehow, a quick getaway from the bad guys on a trusty steed, but possibly my imagination was getting away from me.

The sky was full of the endless stars of out there, a map of the universe of home with each spark of light from distant suns. I tipped my head back and drank in the magic with the wind, as the dusty black road passed beneath the runabout.

Joao was on the edge of the track with a small torch, flicking the light in our direction. We stopped briefly; Okan asked him what was happening.

"Saw one of the gangers out by the dropdown craft. They didn't see me, but they had a good look around."

"Does Tara know?" I asked Joao. He hesitated for a moment, then shook his head.

We travelled back to the farm in tandem, Joao behind us. Okan moved the weapon he carried tucked under the back of his shirt into a more accessible place by the handlebar of the runabout. The stars rushed away from us and the magic dissipated into the dust along the road. I hung on as we shimmied down the turning to the farm and stopped on a coin near the door.

Tara was on the veranda waiting. She came down the steps to greet me and I saw Weldon and Rari outlined in the lighted entryway. She didn't actually say 'where have you been' but it was engraved in every fibre of her being. Joao answered as if she had spoken.

"Got back as quickly as we could."

I could feel my eyes drooping with the late-night talk and the strain of seeing someone who didn't seem to wish me anything but harm, in the only other place I had ever felt relatively safe. What *was* interesting was the fact that the other dreamwalkers now talked freely in front of Weldon. He made brandy and honey with hot water and passed around the thick mugs, sitting down with us and listening to the new information that Okan gave them about the man.

"Did you get a good look at him?" Weldon asked me. I nodded. "You're sure?"

I nodded again. "I was scuba diving in the Coral Sea years ago, I had just finished my advanced open water diving course and we were really deep, my instructor was busy with some photography and I felt this shadow hovering over me. When I looked up it was a huge shark." I stopped, the breath, or lack of it blocking my throat.

"What happened?" Tara asked, with the fascination we all have for scary memories.

"Nothing. The shark went off after a while; it must have been fifteen feet long." I shook my head. "The dangerous part is the swim back up to the boat. I just knew it was there watching me, every now and then I caught a glimpse, almost beyond visibility. I was no more than the possibility of easy food for the creature and we both knew it." I drank a big gulp of brandy and tried not to let my hand shake as I put the mug down. "This man has the same genetic makeup."

Weldon leaned over and patted my arm. "Not while I'm here," he said. He thought a moment and looked at Okan. "Could he be from the same verse as you and Rari?"

"I don't think so," Okan answered, with something that sounded as if it could be bitterness. "He has more technology than we do. The unit I work for is not likely to have kept it to themselves." I reached out a hand and touched his. He curled his fingers around mine and we tried not to let the things better left unsaid make it into the room.

"So, what you're saying is there's another verse." Weldon got up and grabbed the brandy bottle adding extra everything to all the partly-drunk mugs.

Rari spoke, "We don't know anything for sure, but I'm very worried that he's now got a good sample of Millie's DNA." He looked at me.

"The advanced science of studying our subatomic coding is still in the early stages in our verse," I said

"Here too," Weldon spoke. "I know some experimentation has been done on a few unfortunate travellers on Earth." The casual statement made me shiver; it was the word 'experimentation' which was similar to the way some awful people had tested shampoo on rabbits, when it didn't matter about the 'subject.' I didn't want to be a rabbit.

"Millie, what do you know about your parents?" Rari asked carefully, making small circles in a patch of spilt liquid on the table with one gentle finger. I felt chilled, wrapping my hands around the mug of brandy.

"I've reached a point in my life where I can't spend any more time trying to understand my mother and father."

He nodded. "Do you think they were able to dreamwalk themselves?"

I couldn't say I had ever thought about it before. "You don't have dreamwalking parents, do you?" I asked the table in general. Though it really only affected the three men from other verses, both Tara and Weldon shook their heads along with the others. It made me smile for a moment. "Why do you think my parents might be different?" Rari shrugged, his thoughts very much his own.

"So, what now?" Weldon asked after a pause which included me yawning and Tara getting up to make a snack with bread and fruit and cake. Eating punctuated every waking moment and some of the sleeping ones, it was food for uneasy thoughts. He added, "We've lived with travellers for so long no one's ever spent much time on the how or why."

Weldon took some cake and offered me the icing which I took. This man saw so much more than the big picture. All the little things were clear in his mind, as in the fact that I always ate the icing and not the cake. "You know," he said, "There's a Native American saying that goes something along the lines of 'transformation happens as the spirit moves between the realms of the universe.' Seems to me that this has been around a lot longer than the last few hundred years. Whoever knows about the dreamwalking must be part of something really much older than what's happening now. My mother had a good friend when she was young who was a traveller. Maybe we should look into some of the history?"

"We'd have to be careful," Okan said, "I don't want to set off any traps."

"We could talk to some of the people we know who had 'friends?'" Joao added.

I nodded. "One of the women in the caves we rescued said she had a traveller friend and so did Til."

"I think we need to go back much further than that," Rari said. "Is there anyone you know that could help us?" He asked Weldon. Weldon had a speechless conversation with Tara and they agreed on something or someone. "There's a professor of anthropology at the university in Twin Rivers who might be useful, he's the type of person who gets a nosebleed if they haven't mentioned someone important and influential in the last sentence. But he knows more about the travellers than anyone I've ever met."

"Is he safe?" Okan asked, filling the room with the tension that usually happens before a winning shot in the last few seconds of a game. On this occasion the silence wasn't exciting, it was the creeping shadows on a dark night.

"I don't know," Weldon replied, "There was some talk about him in the past giving up the whereabouts of dreamwalkers on Earth. They say that's why he came to the colonies. He wasn't forgiven for that."

"People are always afraid of what's different," I said. "Did you have a pogrom?"

"Something of the like, it was nearly fifty years ago now; some religious groups hated the idea of the travellers." Weldon shrugged. "We like to think we're wiser now."

"They always blame their bad behaviour on religion," I added, feeling woozy with so much brandy messing up my brain cells. I reached for the bread and butter and pinched the rest of the icing from Weldon's plate. He moved it so that it was more accessible and earned himself vast amounts of gratitude.

He looked stunned. "Do you believe in a religion Millie?"

"Science, *not* religion. It was good enough for Einstein, it's good enough for me." The brandy was into even my speech patterns and I could feel my tongue fuzzing up in happy foggy company with my brain. Okan must have noticed because he cut me a large piece of cheese and put it on my plate.

I chewed and the talk began to move onto cattle and the farm, and the gentle hopeful things of life lived on a spread far away from the thoughts that made you wonder whether it was worth giving humanity a second chance.

"What about the borderers Okan?" Rari asked, bringing me back to the empty plate and the darkness outside the windows. Okan shrugged.

"What about them?" I asked.

"Well," Okan said carefully, "They might have information we need."

"Rari thinks they are looking for something every time they raid," Joao said. "Therefore, *we* might have something to bargain with."

"What could we have that they could *possibly* want?" I just couldn't see that a group of murderous thieves would be of any use in the grand scheme of things. In fact, they looked as if they could be a downright liability.

Okan studied the table. "They may have some connection to the type three civilisation that made this verse a type two."

That was it, a complete brain overload. I tried not to hyperventilate but the probability of not having a crisis was slim. "What are you saying exactly, we go on a data gathering trip with the people who kidnap and maim." I paused for a moment of thought. "What makes you think the borderers have a connection?"

Okan shrugged, which made me want to hit him really hard. "We've been at this for a long time Millie, some things just don't add up. They have technology that doesn't come from the central planets; they seem to be stealing to order. I think the killing is down to them alone, a necessary side effect of the attacks as they see it."

"Tell that to Lu's mother," I whispered.

The hardest thing to hear is a reasoned argument from an intelligent man about terrorism. It was as if all the laws of humanity had gone out of the room.

We went our separate ways after that, Weldon to check the stock with Rari and Okan as company, Joao moved quietly around the house making sure the back door was locked and each downstairs window secure. Tara and I stood in the kitchen and I passed her the various plates and cups to fill the little unit. She closed the front and set the sequence. A barely perceptible vibration meant the cycle had started.

I could tell she wanted to speak to me but when I asked her, she put her finger to her lips in the age-old gesture for secrecy. She had deep sleepless rings around her eyes and her back was ramrod straight with tension. We went upstairs together and I pushed the familiar door of Ziggy's room open and went over to the bed, grateful with weariness. A long t-shirt was draped comfortingly over a chair and I used the toothbrush from my backpack for a quick scrape before crawling underneath the downie.

In the half-conscious state of nearly asleep I could hear Okan, Weldon and Rari talking in the hall below. Shattered whispers of sound filtered through, as if my ears were awake but not the rest of me. I couldn't think what it was they were talking about. Something close to 'they won't let this go.' I drifted off into the not quite here, or there, place. Cecil was asleep as usual in the fruit bowl and he lifted his face for my outstretched hand. I wondered if it would always be like this, in one verse dreaming of another, until where you really were and where you should be, became all one inside your head.

The shoulder shake was gentle and the barely breathed word near my face whispered, "Millie," in the gentle urgency of the middle of the night. I groaned. Tara's voice. I opened my eyes. There was no light from inside the house, just the moon Leda, low in the sky and the huge form of Jupiter, a looming ghost casting its reflected light over everything. I sat up. She was fully dressed, as if for a journey.

I sighed and pushed back the warm covers. Grabbing my clothes, I dressed in the dark bathroom and crept downstairs after her carrying my boots. I realised the ones I had borrowed from Ziggy were in the bedroom on the moor in my verse, I wondered if they were having trouble existing there without my feet in them. My head spun a little at the thought.

The house was full of sleeping men, not one of them seemed to sense the possibilities of potential trouble. Tara unlatched the back door with an experienced and well-oiled silence and we slithered out into the cool night. She grabbed two coats from rack before closing it carefully behind her. We waited in the quiet and then put our boots on, and I followed her over to the barn.

"I need to speak to the gangers," Tara whispered, as she opened the big doors. "I must know about Ziggy."

"Of course, why else would we be sneaking around in the middle of the night?" I pulled the coat around me and then hugged her. "I would never let you go on your own." It was as if all the despair she had put off in the intervening years had come back to haunt her and her body was full of the pain and fear of unanswered questions.

"Did you know they'd been around looking at the borderer's craft?" I helped her drag the runabout away from the wall and push it over to the door.

"I saw Torin; he brought a message from Marl. I didn't tell anyone." She sighed, "It just didn't seem a good idea."

"Neither is this, Tara." We began pushing the vehicle down the road so as not to make too much noise when we started it up.

"I know," she answered.

The dark rose up to meet us at the edge of every turn in the road away from the farm. Puffing with the effort of pushing a vehicle that was supposed to be hovering, I was weakly relieved when eventually Tara started the runabout. I got up behind her, my legs shaking from the effort and the nerves of being discovered, though what I thought would happen I didn't know; a stinging lecture from Okan might actually be preferable to flying off into the night on a desperate quest. Then I felt guilty for a moment as if I had betrayed Tara the possibility of some hope. I was aware of the neat gun she always carried, tucked safely in the small of her back, as I put my arms around her waist to hold on. I thought, she's not totally without common sense and I patted my own gun. We were all dressed up, and ready, both of us.

"About an hour to Twin Rivers and then maybe another two for Great Port." Tara lifted the runabout to its highest setting, which felt very high, at least ten feet off the ground, and pushed forward. I had been in cars that were driven by people who thought the laws of physics were for the average idiot, but I had never been in a vehicle that actually defied the laws of physics.

The runabout shimmied through the miles. It made me feel sick for a while until I worked out to look only in front and not to the side. I could feel the cool night becoming colder and was glad of the thick, wool coat that Tara had given me. It was obvious that it was made from the cashmere the goats produced and was light and soft, with a waterproof outer layer.

We stopped by a field of curious cows just outside Twin Rivers and Tara pulled a flask out of the back pannier. I gulped the hot milky coffee with lots of sugar as I uncurled my cramped back and legs and walked up and down while I drank the smooth liquid.

We didn't speak, but she put a grateful hand on my arm and I held her cold fingers for a moment. "Do you think anyone will have noticed we've gone yet?"

She shook her head, then confessed. "I did a terrible thing."

"What?" I couldn't imagine her doing anything that was worse than swearing when she stubbed a toe.

"I put some sleeping tincture in their brandy." She looked at me, her face in the moonlight was suffused with shame, she bit her lip and I could hear a tremble in her voice as she spoke.

I laughed. "Okan is going to be *so* angry when he wakes up and realises that he's been drugged; I'm almost sorry I'm going to miss it." I started to laugh again. It was the expression on her face and the dark night and the craziness and the fact that I still had a hole in my back put there by someone who was trying to do something, but I didn't know what. Eventually she joined in and the cows looked on in long-lashed astonishment at these two mad women rocking with laughter on the edge of nowhere in the middle of the night.

We kept the sleeping town to one side and followed the tracks that led to the farms and mining camps. We didn't see anyone until we had left Twin Rivers an hour behind. Tara patted my arm which was around her waist and pointed ahead. I could just see a small group of people on the side of the rough road. They were walking towards us. Tara moved the runabout over to avoid them and I saw a brief flash of pale faces in the dark, looming caricatures of expressions, none of which looked very friendly. I was glad we were travelling at such speed.

Tara moved over the hedge and into the field and we went across country for a few miles, dancing with trees and small ponds and the herds of disapproving cattle. She leaned back. "Sometimes the vagrants string wires across the road." She slid her finger along her neck. I didn't know which was more off putting; that even this more 'advanced' verse had vagrants or that I could add them to the list of people who seemed to want to kill me.

The back of my neck was freezing and my hands and knees were cramped into a permanent sitting position when we reached the edge of Great Port. The lights were zigzags of colours as we settled to the ground. I pushed myself off the runabout and tried to stand up, achieving a kind of hunchback of Notre Dame effect. There was plenty of groaning from both of us.

The space terminal was really a city. From our vantage point on top of one of the hills that surrounded the flat basin, it was a grid of buildings and roads. The original port was in the centre and a spiral of business and pleasure had whirled in, creating a vast complex metropolis. The type of place I usually avoided. I am one of those people who get into trouble in cities. It reminded me of New York and I had found plenty of trouble there, not all of it bad. You could hear the steady hum of life being lived that exists when somewhere never sleeps.

"Tara," I said, into the quiet that we had brought with us, "What are we going to do?" I looked at her. "Is there a plan?"

"I haven't had time to think of one, I was too busy working out how to get away without the usual testosterone escort." She sounded waspish and I laughed. Her humour was one of the many things that made her a good friend. We looked carefully down at the city and then back at each other. "There is a bar where Marl said he can be reached." She pulled out the handheld com and pressed two keys. A small hologram of the city wavered about in the breeze. She then tapped in a name and the map dizzyingly plotted a route to the building from where we stood.

"I think that qualifies," I said helpfully.

The streets were full of people with a purpose, out for a good time, out to make money, out to rob the unwary. I think we might have looked as if we came with a sign. A big arrow would not have been a surprise for all the interest we were attracting. I hunched further down in my seat and tried to look mean and worldly, which fooled exactly nobody. Tara skilfully wove her way through the crowds and other vehicles, some of which seemed to be driven by those who had already had much too good a time and were happy to share their fortune. After the tenth near miss I suggested we get off and walk but Tara just laughed.

The area where the bar was had fewer drunks and more of the rough element. We scouted around for a place to leave the runabout and decided on a small hotel incongruously called The Wellington, which had a secure compound at the back. It also had a separate stairway to the rooms for sneaking in and out. Tara went through the door marked 'office' to see about a room and I parked the runabout, locked the steering column and pulled the bags we had brought with us out of the back pannier.

I joined her in the reception area which consisted of one very small oriental looking woman, a hologram computer and a potted plant. She was watching a video of some seriously bad-tempered men beating up another man; it was accompanied by stirring music and lots of grunts and groans. The language sounded similar to Cantonese.

Tara negotiated what seemed to be astronomical rates from the pantomime going on between them. After protracted dealing, the woman indicated that we were going to bankrupt her but she would do it out of the goodness of her heart. It felt as if it could have been a Saturday night in Shanghai. I could guess from the expression on Tara's face that the woman would be sending all her children to private school from now on.

The room was a surprise. More than just clean and quiet, it had its own bathroom and a huge window that looked out over one area of the port. The two beds were semi circles in opposite corners of the room and a large expanse of floor was filled by a low table and chairs with a small computer unit. One cupboard revealed a cooking area and storage space.

"How long do you think we've got before Okan finds us?" I said, making coffee and bringing it over to the table. Tara was stretched out with her bare feet resting on the other chair. She moved them to let me sit down.

"Two days maybe." She looked at my face. "At the most." She unpacked the bag I had dropped by her chair earlier, bringing out bread and cheese and cake and we had a breakfast picnic, talking and laughing, more truants from a really difficult history test and not adults on an important quest.

I started yawning first and it went back and forth between us as if we were infected with viral sleep deprivation. I pointed to the bed and went over, shedding clothes and reaching for the covers. It was still dark outside and although you couldn't see the stars as well as you could out in the countryside, you could still see Leda and the paling curve of Jupiter. "You won't go home while you're asleep, will you?" Tara asked from the other bed.

"No, I'm here for the duration."

"Thanks," she whispered.

It felt as if it had been a moment, the way it does when you fall asleep in the early hours and wake up when you've reached the deep sleep cycle. My brain fought with my eyes for a while until I remembered where I was. I pulled the downie and sheet up over my head and worried about how angry Okan was going to be with me.

Somehow the thought of his reaction made me feel as if I'd got one over on him. I couldn't imagine why that was so important. Pushing the psycho-analysis aside with the covers, I staggered to the window.

A bright clear day was busy with the people who work for a living. Cargo pods were being shifted and stacked. A large cone-shaped ship slid carefully down towards the terminal, where I could see minute figures waiting to swarm over it. Maintenance, fuel and passengers, all the things about travel remained the same wherever you were.

Tara joined me, she was holding more coffee and I took a cup gratefully, we stood for a while watching the business of the port and trying to keep back the creeping worry of what happened next. I knew she was winging it, which seemed appropriate considering where we were. "Who gets the shower first?" I asked. We ran for the door at the same time, giggling as we both got jammed trying to get in together. The laughter was as good as toothpaste and shampoo for dusty hearts.

The street was quiet in the way of mornings in night-time places. We walked towards the sound of a market and the smells that go with cooking outside on rusty stoves. I watched a woman strip something that looked as though it could be the skin, from a creature that might have been a rabbit and decided that I would do my best not to throw up, as it might bring us some more unwanted attention. It wasn't as if anyone noticed us, it was more that they were *not* noticing us. It made you want to look over your shoulder all the time.

We decided on a rice and vegetables breakfast with strong aromatic tea. Small bowls of food were set out on a makeshift counter in front of the stall on the side of the road. The market was jammed with shoppers arguing over produce and the walking hangovers you only saw in my verse on a Sunday morning in Cardiff, after Wales had been playing England and won.

I ate and watched the buzz of crowded people all talking, eating, buying and watching back. Tara was quiet, picking at her food and nervously tapping the fork as if an out of key tune was playing in her mind. I held the timpani down with my hand. "We can't do anything about it until tonight," I whispered. She nodded, but when I released her fingers, she began tapping again.

The disgusted look on the man's face as we handed back our breakfast bowls nearly full, made me remember my mother and her 'half the world is starving' lecture played in my memory chip, as if a car was stuck in second gear. I offered profuse apologies and a big tip. He still looked insulted.

"Hey ladies! Looking for a good time tonight?" A short man with the unshaven, shaved head and the bad teeth of the permanent sleazebag blocked our way. He danced around for a moment. "Can offer you a really good time, for of course, a small fee." He smiled winningly, his grey, green dental problem on full display. A waft of halitosis that could have scraped the barnacles from a transatlantic steam ship found its way to us. I thought Tara was going to hit him, so I stepped between the two of them. He pushed me away and as he did, I felt his fingers inside my jacket. He must have been disappointed because not only did I not carry a wallet but I am no more than adequately endowed.

He backed off when he felt the short barrel of Tara's gun in the vulnerable part of his body between the hip and shoulder. "Sorry 'bout that lady. Got to go," he said, as he hurried off into the crowd. I shrugged.

"Where is your wallet?" Tara asked me. She had given me a handful of cash and a combined identity prepaid credit card before we left the hotel. I had pushed some of the money in the front pocket of my jeans and put the card in my backpack and left it in the room. She tutted when I explained. "That card can be used as identification if we get stopped. You should carry it with you all the time."

"Who does it say I am?" I asked curiously.

"Weldon's sister. We had it made for you, just in case anyone came asking. His real sister died when she was seven, but that was way back and no one really checks."

I was touched and surprised that they'd even thought about it. My mind wandered off for a moment and I put some things together.

"Do Rari, Okan and Joao have false cards?"

"Of course," she said. "Not from us, I don't know where they got them."

We walked for a while taking in more sights and smells and trying not to bump into anyone who was doing their best *not* to avoid us. It was similar to the first morning at an inner-city school in the bad old days in my verse, with wall-to-wall gangs. The type of people who think there are no innocent victims, just those who are not as well armed as they should be.

"Do you know what Okan's other name is?" I asked Tara. She looked really surprised. I shrugged. "I just never thought to ask this time and it didn't seem to matter when we were children."

"D'Ferrino." She dodged a particularly aggressive version of the ganger species, who would have quite happily walked over her. "Rari is a McDonald and Joao doesn't have a last name."

"He's called son of Matthew," I said. She stopped. I added, "He told me when we were in my verse. I think it's just whoever the father is supposed to be. But I got the impression his mum was raped and she used an uncle's name." I shook my head. "I think Joao comes from a verse that you and I would be grateful never to have experienced."

"It was rough on Earth for a while after the global wars, but that was in my parent's time and they brought me out here to get away from it."

"You said both of your parents died in an accident?" I inched up beside her and hooked an arm through hers, it made us less easy to knock over, but not impossible.

"Yeah, my dad was an engineer; there was a spaceship full of settlers." She stopped for a moment and then began to explain. "In those days they came in any vehicle they could find, lots of smugglers loaded the ships to the gunnels, set it on automatic pilot and then left them to it. Some didn't make it and were just found adrift months later. Some of them died trying to land the damn things. I was only small, but I can remember my parents talking about it over supper. My mum was a doctor and I think the hospital was full of the people who actually got here."

We were quiet for a while, then she continued. "The ship was in a really bad state, venting air and the man who was piloting it had very little experience. He banged it down at the end of the runway and it broke in two. My dad went to help and my mum was called in to treat the survivors. A fire got out of control and ignited what was left of the fuel." She sat down on a convenient bench which had a view of the main terminal. "They saw my dad go in after her; she was trying to rescue some children who were trapped in one of the sleeping quarters."

I suddenly realised how difficult it must have been for her to come back, having lost so much. I looked out over the busy port, with its mindless hum of activity. Not only were there the memories of the death of her parents, but she could now add the thought of her child to the pain. "You've got courage," I said. "I've never been anywhere near where my mum and dad were killed."

It had seemed an odd thing to need to do, wander out onto the lonely stretch of road on the moor where the car had skidded. Even Simon had suggested it might give me closure. A word I have always hated. Who needs to close a door, when what you want really is a wall, between you and all the loneliness.

She said, "Not courage, just desperation."

We sat there for a while and watched the world go by, the sounds and smells of a busy day in someone else's life pushing past the collective thoughts and memories. Somehow the fact that I was actually sitting by a space port in the main city on Europa, with Jupiter high in the sky and the wormhole of another verse quite literally in the back of my mind, didn't seem as abnormal as trying to find out where Ziggy had gone. But then what was usual and unusual is relative and I probably had a viral dose of it.

I found myself listening to a painful wail, which could have been that of a small animal or a child in pain. The crates from the last transport had been unloaded quite close to the perimeter fence and some of them smelt ripe enough to make me realise that there were livestock in them.

I had pitied the poor chickens and sheep moved from one field to another at home, you could see their confusion at trying to find the familiar places of a few days ago. The hooting wail began again and I watched a grey unit rock with unsuppressed misery.

Tara was looking worried. "I think there is contraband cargo in those crates." She leaned forward and studied the logo on the side of the narrow bars. "They must have forgotten them because they usually offload this stuff at night and they get picked up by whoever has bought the contract. It's the black market," she explained, "High end bioengineered creatures." I must have looked puzzled. "I used to live here remember, after my parents died, I stayed on for a while and tried to survive on the streets. You see a lot of the other side of the system that way."

The rest of what I was thinking of asking ended when a large hovercraft pulled up to the gate in the perimeter. A group of three men clambered out and unlocked it using an audio key code. It sounded similar to the first five notes of ABBA's dancing queen which made me laugh. They scowled in our direction and I tried to make myself look harmless.

The men began loading up their contraband, stacking it haphazardly on the back of the vehicle, tying the larger boxes on and putting the smaller ones into the gaps. None of it was done with any furtive moves and the people on the street walked by as if the boxes and men were completely invisible.

"That's brash," Tara whispered. "The perimeter is supposed to be policed day and night. They don't seem bothered."

"I haven't seen anyone while we've been here and that camera isn't moving so maybe it's not working." I pointed carefully to the small security unit that was covering the area of the fence we were in. It was a larger version of the handheld com most of the people used for a phone, a square of jelly with various coloured buttons and a holographic screen, and it was blank.

A particularly plaintive hoot accompanied the last box as it was jammed into a ridged space. The men took great delight in bashing the side of the box to get a reaction. Silent fear accompanied the aggression, although I had difficulty keeping my own response to a minimum. Grinding my teeth helped, and Tara's hand on my arm.

They sped off and the small crate slid gracefully to the ground at my feet. No one looked, though everyone saw. I picked it up; it was light, a scuffle inside and a snuffle made me hug whatever it was to my chest. Tara and I walked back down to the hotel. After the first five hundred yards we seemed to blend in, as if we were recognised as one of them. Stealing someone else's contraband had made us family.

"I hope this isn't a rat or a snake," Tara said. I stopped hugging it to me for a moment until we got to the room via the stairs and put it down on the floor.

"I don't think a snake would give a rat's arse about being in a box," I punned, opening the top warily.

"Be careful, lots of these things can bite. People pay a massive amount of money for exotic species."

The crate lid slid back. We stared. "What is that?" I asked.

Tara looked horrified. "We are in so much trouble!"

It was love at first sight for all of us. I could feel my heart squeeze and my fingers folded around the little creature as it gave one more hopeless sigh. Its tiny trunk curled over my arm and I held it to me with tears in my eyes. "What kind of evil bastard does this?" I whispered. The miniature elephant was about half the size of Cecil the tabby cat. It was in a pitiful state, seriously dehydrated, so much so that skin hung in places on its frail body and there were sore patches where it had rubbed against the bars of the cruel cage. I tried not to cry but sadness is catching and the vulnerable and lost make their way straight to the painful memories of the past.

Tara went over to her pack and began mixing up something from her medical kit; the little creature was sucking on my hair having found a suitable place to be safe, which was somewhere up by my left ear.

"Try this." Tara held out a syringe with an opaque liquid in it. "We use it for the premature livestock; it's a really rich mixture and is supposed to be species universal, you could give it to a child."

"What's it doing in your medical kit?" I held the tube up to the elephant and it sniffed hopefully. No coaxing was necessary and it sucked hungrily on the food, some of which ended up over my cashmere sweater.

"It's also good for any illness when you can't get solid food down. I always carry some." She shrugged; leaning down to the chair I was sitting in and stroking the bit of the little body that wasn't hidden by my hair. "They won't let this go. These creatures are worth a fortune. I've actually never seen one. They get sold to the rich and stupid, anyone who will pay for the process."

"Did it come from Earth?" I was talking quietly as the sucking had been replaced by a contented sigh and then something that sounded as if it could be gentle snoring. It still had a death grip on a chunk of my hair.

"I think they are produced on Mars, less chance of discovery there and made to order. This creature is highly illegal. It would be destroyed if the police found it before the smugglers." I gripped the small warm body to me and looked carefully at Tara.

"That's not going to happen though, is it?"

She sighed and patted my arm, much as you would a child with its first difficult hurdle to overcome in the vast complicated game that is the reality of life. "Not if I can help it."

A knock at the door made both of us leap up guiltily and I stuffed the elephant down the front of my sweater. It gave a small hoot of surprise, but settled somewhere around my stomach and I put my arms casually over the lump. Tara kicked the empty box over towards the bed and opened the door. We both projected an air of polite innocence.

The hotel proprietor stood outside. "Will you need clean laundry for tomorrow?" She asked. Her eyes travelled straight to my lump and the expression on her face went from narrow curiosity to puzzlement as the 'lump' decided to wake up and explore the new environment. It must have looked as if my intestines were doing a tango. I kept a facial expression of ambiguity worthy of an international poker player. Hers fell back on several thousand years of oriental inscrutability. Neither side noticed that my stomach was now making the odd puzzled snuffle. "I hope you enjoy your stay," she said carefully, as she closed the door behind her. I slid down to the chair, overcome with greasy nerves.

"Do you think she'll tell anyone?" I hauled the creature out from under my sweater. It blinked and burped, looking around with intelligent eyes. Fear had been replaced with the endless curiosity of the young. I put it down on the floor and it tottered around exploring the dusty space under the bed and coming back every now and then to check that we hadn't both disappeared.

"I think if someone paid her enough, she would sell her children," Tara answered, making up more of the mixture and holding the tube out. The tiny trunk pulled the recognised object to its mouth and began sucking again. It huddled against Tara's leg and finished the food in serious speed. "Little and often," Tara explained to its small enquiring face. She added, "I wonder if you're still dehydrated?" The question was answered by a small stream of urine. "Okay, that would be no." She moved her foot out of the way and I went to get a cloth from the bathroom.

When I came over to her, she was holding the elephant on her lap. It was on its back and it waited patiently while she examined the area between its hind legs. "What are you doing?" I wiped up the puddle.

"Trying to see if it's male or female."

I looked over her shoulder. "Is that a willy?" I pointed out a small wrinkle.

"I don't think so." Tara looked exasperated.

"Are you sure?" I peered closer.

"I'm a farmer; I'm supposed to know about these things." We all contemplated the thought for a moment. "Right," she said, talking to the elephant, "It's unanimous, you're one of us." The creature looked pleased and we set about the vital mission of a name. You needed a good one for an elephant.

Tara went out and bought the makings of a meal from the market while I played with Flora. She charged up and down herd-less and I hoped the rooms were soundproofed. After a while I put the shower on cool and put her in the stall, the spray made her crazy with joy and when Tara came back in, I was wet with the splashing. I dried the elephant's little body on a towel and put some of the cream from Tara' bottomless medical pack on the sore areas. Tara made an amazing supper out of a few bags of vegetables, pasta and some cheese.

We sat on the floor eating; Flora was asleep on Tara's lap. "What's the plan?" I asked as Tara got quieter, her face pale with nerves.

"The bar is just around the corner. I suppose we could go and see if Marl can be contacted." She stroked a silky ear as the elephant sighed with new-found safety. "They don't take into consideration that some things are not meant to be so small." I looked at her. "Often those creatures that have been bioengineered don't live that long," Tara said, as quietly as she could so as not to come to the notice of whatever deities were listening, and we both tried not to choke on the food.

"How old do you think she is?" I got up and took the nearly full plates back to the sink. I scraped the rubbish into the recycler and put the plates into the cleaning unit, then started making the coffee.

"I am guessing around six months. Not old enough to be away from her mother, not that she had one. She would have been made in an incubator from an embryo that had been biogenetically altered. Who knows what they mixed her with to get her this size." The tiny trunk swirled around Tara's wrist without Flora waking. A small sigh, barely a whisper on the still air, escaped her and for a moment it looked as if she wouldn't take another breath, we both held ours. Then everyone breathed again.

I made a nest in my cashmere sweater and Flora turned around several times before settling into the folds, suggesting cat in the bio-mix somewhere. I had fitted myself out with a t-shirt I had brought with me and a sweater that Tara had in her Mary Poppins of a pack. It was cool so we took our coats and both of us, without verbal consultation, put the guns in the appropriate places. The little crea-ture gave a plaintive hoot but was so tired and full of food that her tummy bulged and her eyes drooped. We left a light on in the bath-room and went out quietly, like careful parents on a night out.

"I have a bad feeling about this," I said as the door to the bar swung open on the sight you usually got with a Victorian cartoon of the Soho streets. Dickens would have felt at home. Tara gave me a sharp shove and pushed me inside. I watched a young woman help herself to the ID/credit card of the man who had his hand on her leg. She saw me watching and winked. Hormones counted for almost everything and I smiled back.

"Do you want a drink?" Tara asked.

"What are the chances it won't be spiked?" I tried for a table and lost to three very large men who had the logo of the port emblazoned on their jackets. They didn't offer to share, which was a huge relief. I followed Tara to the bar and we grabbed a couple of stools. She ordered beer in bottles and made sure the tops were sealed before she paid for them. "I see living on the streets stays with you," I said, taking the beer from her.

She shrugged, looking around the room and then leaned in to catch the bartender's attention. A small amount of money passed quickly between them and then he nodded his head towards a man playing pool over by the back rooms. I thought I recognised him from the night at the skydancing towers, but I wasn't sure. Tara looked at me, I didn't think either of us was in any doubt about the high wire act we were performing but sometimes life was about choices, not right and wrong. She slipped off the stool and went over to the ganger and spoke a few words. He pretended for a moment that he didn't know who she was, but I could see by his face and the way he moved his hands that he had been waiting for us. It made me feel cold and I looked warily around the room. No one else was recognisable, but nothing felt right either.

What was odd was the reaction of the port workers. They watched carefully like crocodiles with migrating herds. Their table was over by the door and my head went back and forward trying to keep an eye on both Tara and the port workers simultaneously, it was just the same as being at a Wimbledon final. Tara played on her femininity but I knew that she knew and I could see that she had transferred her gun from the back of her trousers to a holster under her arm. The ganger was leaning down to talk to her and I looked back just in time to see one of the port workers get up and leave.

It felt as if it was a set up. Tara came back, bringing the ganger with her. He smiled his reptile smile and I shook the outstretched hand and hoped mine wasn't cold and trembling.

"Millie, it's good to meet you, my name is Gasat." He nodded at the bartender who slid a beer across the greasy surface of the bar towards his open hand. The ganger tipped his head back and took a great gulp. I wondered if betrayal made you thirsty.

"Gasat and Torin are brothers," Tara said helpfully, as she could see that I had no idea who he really was, never mind a name. It made sense as he had the same feral air of life lived in a constant search for the next meal.

" Do you know those port workers Gasat?" I asked him, drinking some of my beer. He shrugged.

"Seen them around, can't say I know them," he lied.

"That's odd, they seem to know you." I tried not to look like the fish out of water that I so gaspingly was.

He spoke, ignoring me, "You need to find Marl?" The bartender shoved another bottle towards him and he opened the top, throwing the old one in a large container in the corner where it clanked against a thousand others.

"He told me he comes in here and it would be a good place to contact him," Tara said.

"Yeah, he's here from time to time." He finished his drink and pushed away from us pretending drunkenness. I couldn't work out what he was up to. "I'll get a message to him." He paused and then asked carefully, "Where are you staying?"

There it was. The missing piece.

"We'll be in here tomorrow at the same time," Tara answered.

"Okay." He didn't look disappointed, which probably meant just changing from plan A to plan B. He said goodnight and weaved his way theatrically over towards the door.

The bartender brought us some soup and bread which was hot and tasty. I thanked him.

"My mother is the cook, I'll tell her you liked it," he said smiling.

"You can tell her she can be my mum if she wants to, her cooking is wonderful," I said.

He laughed and went over to see to some drunk who only cared about the quality of the beer, not the food.

Tara and I sat at the bar while we ate, feeling safer for some reason. The curtain behind the bar moved aside at one point and a small, round woman came over to us.

"You want pie?" She asked, in an accent that could have given Okan a run for his money in its grating proximity to Central Park.

"I would love pie!" I said, feeling warm towards her and missing Okan at the same time. She gave me the equivalent of a huge hug in nonverbal communication and went out through the curtain.

'Pie' was a symphony of lemon meringue and I ate two pieces, astounding several punters who had probably never seen anyone consume food in the same way they usually consumed alcohol. I scraped up the crumbs, making the bartender laugh out loud. "My mother is your new best friend." He took the plate from my reluctant hands and leaned in as if wiping the surface of the bar. "Come through to the back; don't leave by the front door." I nodded.

Tara and I slid carefully out towards the loos doing a girly impression with our packs, as if looking for the right lipstick in a sea of unnecessary contents. The back rooms of the building were rough but clean and there was a line of stairs off to one side where a steady stream of 'staff' and clients disappeared after quiet, mutually acceptable negotiations. The door to the kitchen opened in a thoughtful moment and 'mother' stuck her head around and beckoned us towards her. I felt as if the backstage pass was going to get us more than the autograph of the aged rock star.

The kitchen was reassuringly clean with the scrubbed look of the truly fanatical. Pans were hung over the stove in a comforting, shiny size order. The coffee pot crouched grumbling in one corner, spreading the positive aroma of early mornings and late nights.

"Perhaps you'd better sit for a bit," mother said without explanation. We sat. She poured out huge cups from the percolator and pushed a jug of thick cream and the sugar bowl towards us. I drowned my coffee in both and she grunted, as if confirming something.

"You're from New York, aren't you?" I asked.

"Not for many years, I came out here after the first food riots and the pogroms." She sat down and tapped her fingers on my wrist. "I'm a dreamwalker like you."

My mouth must have opened but unusually for me nothing came out. She smiled and got up, retrieving the lemon meringue pie from a cupboard. "You'd better put something in that hole if you can't think of anything to say." She cut more for both of us and we waited while nothing happened.

"Which verse do you come from?" I asked hopefully. It was odd that the only dreamwalkers I had met up to that point were the ones that were part of the original Gold Cliffs gang. I suppose I had thought that we were a specific group. But this woman was much older, a piece of something I didn't understand.

"I come from the type three verse. When I began to dreamwalk it was something of an experiment, to try and get scientific development to other verses. Share what we had." She looked sad.

"As if you were taking food and medicine to earthquake sufferers, or bibles to natives?" I asked unhelpfully.

"We didn't push our views on anyone." She smiled. "I know; it's a difficult concept. People who have everything always seem to want a change in opinion from those who have nothing. But we never went in great numbers and never with any ulterior motive except to share. We just tried to give their science and technology a shove in the right direction, nothing more."

"What went wrong?" Tara asked with great prescience. She sipped her coffee black, thereby earning herself points from the ex-New Yorker.

"Things shift. Not everyone wanted the dreamwalking to continue. Not everyone could go, so conspiracy theories grew. For a technically advanced race, we were disgustingly parochial."

She held out her hand again. "Nancy Lawson. My son is called Theo." I shook hers and so did Tara and then we sat for a moment in companionable silence, all thinking about the unlikelihood of lemon meringue pie.

Theo stuck his head into the kitchen from the bar, letting in the noise and a strong smell of unwashed beer bottles. "Now would be a good time." He nodded towards the door into the alley at the back of the building.

"Thank you," I said, giving her a hug. We slid through the doorway and out into the alley. I could see Theo beckoning us from the shadows at the end of the next building.

"You look just like your mother," Nancy whispered to me as she closed the door.

I stopped, causing a complicated traffic jam of confused feet. Tara grabbed me by the arm ignoring my incoherent mumbling and walked us towards Theo. "Millie, what is wrong with you?" She pushed me in front of her and we rounded the corner.

Theo was checking the street. It was full of people but he seemed to be looking for a particular face. "The gangers have watchers; can't see their usual guy. Go this way!" He pointed down a dark back street when Tara made to go off down the road. "It will get you back onto the main drag near the security fence to the port." He looked down at his feet. "Don't tell me where you're staying, just in case someone offers me more than I can resist for the information. I have a gambling problem and everyone around here knows."

"Thank you," Tara said. I was still speechless with information overload and could only nod.

We made our way down the narrow unlit street; it was mainly warehousing and storage and shadowed steps. Tara moved her gun from the holster into her hand and because she did, so did I. As I looked back, I could see Theo watching us from a dark doorway, he raised a hand and I waved back and then the curve in the road hid him from view.

The port boundary fence was glowing a bright green, like phosphorescence on a lake. It rippled as if it were a living thing, making me think of silent creatures from the deep sea that caught their unwary prey by using their bioluminescence to make themselves look appetizing. The fence led us back to the main road and we ended up on the busy street, full of the revellers of the night before. It was a paradox that we felt safer with the people instead of the shadows considering the circumstances. Tara put her gun back in the holster under her arm and I unhinged my sweaty fingers from around the smooth feral metal and put mine away too.

It was as though we were walking against a strong tide, one step forward two steps sideways. The door to the hotel was a gift of Christmas morning proportions. Our landlady grunted an oriental greeting as we went through to the back stairs. Although it was possible to reach the rooms from the stairs outside, we'd both had enough of dark corners.

As I opened the door using the four-digit code we had programmed when we had booked in, the sound of squeaking greeted us. The miniature pachyderm equivalent of 'where have you been?' I threw myself into a chair, unprepared for the onslaught. The small cuddly thing launched itself from a great distance landing with the desired effect on my stomach. Tara looked on like an indulgent parent as some squeezing and kissing ended in the sort of noise you usually saw in Heathrow airport arrivals.

"What was all that about?" Tara asked. She had just come out of the bathroom and her hair was wet and curly from the shower. I was folded up around the now sleeping Flora in borrowed pyjamas and a blanket. "Back in the alley?" She said. "You looked as if you'd seen a ghost. It frightened the life out of me." She rubbed the towel over the damp curls.

I shrugged. "Nancy said I looked like my mother." I was beginning to wonder if I had misheard her, or maybe was suffering from lemon meringue overload.

"What?" Tara was suitably monosyllabic.

It was an appropriate response under the circumstances, but not helpful. Exasperated I said, "I think my head is going to explode."

"Well let me know, because I don't want to get any brain matter on me," Tara answered, rubbing the towel over her hair again.

I laughed, "It's not possible to forget that you're a doctor's daughter."

I stroked the elephant's silky ears and Flora gave a contented sigh. I was glad she could feel safe, because my idea of safety had just upended me into the cold water of open sea, with no hope of a boat for miles. I could get a handle on the verse hopping because I had never done anything else. As if I had been going to the same place for the summer holiday every year, it was just a part of my life, maybe the best part.

But you needed your parents to be what you thought they were. The water closed over my head for a moment and I groaned, making Flora hoot with intuitive concern. She sat up and stared, her little body trembling. Tara took her from me and cuddled her into wet hair where she began sucking on a large curl in anxious sympathy.

"Okay." Tara moved up and down making a drink with brandy and honey and hot water that would knock one of Flora's larger relatives out. "I am guessing that this changes things?"

"I would think so." I said unhelpfully. I leaned forward in the chair and took the drink gratefully.

"Let's see what we have here." Tara settled in the other chair and curled her feet under her. Flora slid comfortably down into the folds of Tara's dressing gown. "You start dreamwalking with Okan and Joao and Rari as a child. Then have a break while you grow up. They don't and carry on coming here."

I nodded. "Do you know anything about the people Okan and Rari work for?"

"It sounds as if it's government run and something about it makes Okan very unhappy."

I took a gulp of the drink and tried to choke discreetly, as it was very strong. "What do you mean?"

Tara swigged her own drink like a port worker. "I get the feeling that he's running out of time. But I don't know why."

I looked at her and she shrugged at her own lack of knowledge and asked, "Do you think it has something to do with you?"

It was my turn to shrug.

"I think you're going to have to get some answers about that," she added.

We sat in silence for a while listening to a steady rain that had begun pattering on the windows and the quiet peaceful breathing of the sleeping Flora.

"What about the man who has been following you from verse to verse?" Tara looked tired. It wasn't as if she didn't have her own nightmares to fight in the early hours.

"I can't think why he could be interested in me. I'm a nobody. I don't *have* anything." The brandy was making my words slide together and my lips were slightly numb.

"You can make the dropdown ship work. Okan and the others can't do that."

"I was able to bring Cecil my cat with me the other night," I said, "I don't think any of them can do that either, verse hop with someone that doesn't usually dreamwalk on their own." I had forgotten about it until we'd started to plot things out between us.

"Really?" Tara looked stunned. "A cat; how does that work?"

I shook my head. "I have *no* idea. Until someone gives me an explanation for the ability to jump through a wormhole at will, I think the things that make me different from the others will just be one more mystery in quantum physics I can't solve!"

I leaned forward and put my head in my hands and squeezed my fingers against my eyes until bright spots swirled and a strange vision of the kitchen at home with the moonlight dusting the shadows came into focus. A tap on my shoulder brought me back to the hotel room. Tara looked anxious. "You looked as if you were leaving me for a moment."

"I'm sorry," I said quietly, "It's just that wherever I look are unanswered questions. I thought I knew where I came from and now I don't."

We drank in silence for a while and then Tara made up another nutritional mixture for Flora, who joined in the contented slurping.

"Do you think we're safe here?" I asked.

Tara shook her head, which made my stomach lurch. She said, "If we don't find Marl tomorrow night we'd better get out, I don't want to think what Gasat has arranged with those port workers."

"I suppose if you live on the streets for long enough, you lose sight of what's right and wrong, people are just your next meal."

"I think the cost of feelings becomes too high to hold onto," she said bitterly, "You stop caring if you live or die so other people's lives don't matter that much either."

I reached across and took her hand. "We'll get something before we have to leave."

I took Flora to the bathroom and encouraged her to use the facilities, she inspected the plughole in the shower and obligingly did her business. My mother would have had a fit, so I swished the cleaning fluid around in her honour.

Tara was double checking the door lock when I came out to the main room. Flora had joined me as I had a bath and she was now padding about leaving small, round, curly footprints on the wood floor. I swept her up and rubbed a towel over her wriggling form.

"Did you change the code?" I slathered cream on the disappearing sores on Flora's skin. She was healing well.

"I don't know how much good it will do, but I put one of my own alarm locks on the door." Tara pointed out the small unit with a flashing green key. "It might give us a head start if someone tries to get in."

"What about the hotel owner, doesn't she have a master code to all the rooms?"

"This will stop anyone just walking in, but it won't stop anyone breaking the door down." Tara came over and helped Flora who was trying to scramble up onto my bed. "Unless they have a gadget that neutralises the alarm."

"Is there such a thing?" I got into the bed, moving Flora with my foot as I used to do with Cecil, and for a moment I felt guilty, as if I had abandoned the cat. Poor Cecil who was caught in the space in-between just like me.

"Without a doubt," she said, adding, "We should sleep on the floor away from the beds, it might give us a few more seconds if they did get in."

"Do you think there's any point? If they're that organised, they would have someone out the back by the windows to cut off our escape anyway and I wouldn't give us much of a chance in a firefight." I tried not to sound as frightened as I felt.

"I don't think they want to kill us." Tara pulled the covers up to her chin and dimmed the lamp by the bed, tapping the metal edge.

"Tara, do we have any tracking devices on us, a GPS or something similar?" I was puzzling the fact that Okan hadn't come crashing through the door with a fifteen-minute lecture about responsibility and a serious scowl.

"I disabled them. We have a tracking system attached to the identity credit cards. You can buy a gadget to interfere with the signal. Of course," she added, "You can buy something that will get around that too. But it all takes time."

The light from the port flickered across the dark windows as we lay in our beds thinking. The rain was now heavy and the wind battered the windows, reminding me of the moor and winter nights and for a second or two I was homesick, whatever that meant in the scheme of things, home becoming progressively more difficult to define. Flora made a nest and curled up, adding to the sense of guilt for the creature I had left behind.

"Do you realise that, unlike the rest of us, your dreams carry on without you after you wake up?" Tara whispered.

Sleep was the usual confused passage of time and shadows with those sounds in strange places that make it difficult to be restful. Flora woke me up once to go to the bathroom. Her little trunk and sweet breath tickled my eyes and nose until I picked her up and went like a somnambulist without turning on the lights or opening my eyes. I put her on Tara's bed when I got back, working out that there might be another visit to the bathroom scheduled and Tara should have a share in the duties. Flora wriggled under the covers until only a small amount of ear and one bright eye were exposed and Tara grumbled at the cold pads coming into contact with her warm body, without really waking up.

I got back into my own bed and stretched out, twisted thoughts making dropping back to sleep impossible. I tried to remember the faces of my parents. They had seemed so much a part of the work that they did. Continuous with the healing and frustration, that made up the average country practice. My mother had had a slight Scottish accent and had trained at Edinburgh Royal Infirmary. Her family were 'estranged' and I accepted the lack of grandparents the way that you do when you don't know any different. Dad had been from Canada and had never gone home after he met my mother; we had sent Christmas cards to his parents and brother every year. I tried to think if I remembered any phone calls, emails, or letters coming to us and realised that I didn't. That was the mystery of a hidden life.

Tara made me jump by whispering into the dark, "She could have been lying."

"How did you know what I was thinking about?" I settled back in the bed.

"It's possible that Nancy lied," Tara persisted.

"You don't really believe that do you?" I sighed.

"No. She couldn't take her eyes off you the moment she came through from the kitchen that first time." Tara must have moved the elephant because there was an indignant hoot. "You take up a lot of room for such a small thing! Do you look like your mother?" Tara asked.

"Are you talking to me or the elephant?" I said and Tara laughed. We were quiet again for a while. "No," I answered. "My mum was tall and blonde with blue eyes and my dad was tall and blonde too, though he had brown eyes like me. "Actually, I can't seem to remember what my parents really looked like," I said.

"I get that with Ziggy. I think it's the way the mind deals with the loss."

A long silence followed and Flora began to snore. "Maybe we should go back to the bar tomorrow morning and ask some questions," Tara said.

"Don't you think that would be putting us in unnecessary danger? It's going to be tricky enough trying to make contact with Marl later on." Her lack of an answer was answer enough. I added silently to myself, 'even if he didn't know what was going on,' which I very much doubted.

I let my thoughts spin around in my head and came back to something I had not been able to quantify before. "Rari asked me if either of my parents had dreamwalked." Tara shuffled in the dark.

"Yes, when we were having supper."

"I didn't realise he was suggesting that they might be from another verse."

Tara was stunned and so was I really. It had just clicked, as if a series of cogs and wheels were at last all turning in the same direction. "What are you saying?" She sat up in bed, earning herself black marks from a hooting Flora for letting the cold in. "That Rari knew about your parents?"

"I don't know, maybe he just guessed," I finished lamely.

"Do you think the others know?" Tara asked, ignoring my get out clause.

I sighed. More than anything I didn't want to be in this alone, but it was beginning to feel as if 'on my own' was looking for me. "I don't know, Tara." I reached for a blanket and as if I was a walking tepee, I went over to the small kitchen area and began making a milky drink, the kind my mother would prescribe for nightmares with lots of honey. I settled on the end of Tara's bed and handed her one of the mugs. She sat up and balanced it carefully on the covers in-between sipping.

"Do any of the other planets have settled moons?" I asked, filling the dark with words to chase away unwanted thoughts.

"The central planets, Earth and Mars, both have colonies on their moons. Earth's moon is a smallish one, but Phobos and Deimos have very large populations. There are terraformed colonies on Saturn's moon Titan which has Atlas as its own moon and there are biospheres on Uranus's moons Titania and Oberon. Then there's Ganymede."

I tried not to choke but it was difficult. I could see Tara's teeth gleaming in the port's security lights reflected through the rain on the window. She was laughing. "There's another colony around Jupiter?" I managed.

"Sure, why have one when you can have two!"

It was odd but I felt proud, as if I was part of something special, we were out there, which is where I had always thought we belonged anyway. The books on my desk at work slipped to the floor in my mind, never to be restacked. "Don't forget we didn't do it alone Millie," Tara whispered, as if telling an old story to a child, "The travellers gave us the technology and it was a long time ago."

I drifted back to my bed and curled up against the things I didn't want to think about. "Of course, I haven't told you about the space stations yet. Or the mining colonies on the Kuiper belt," Tara said.

"Now you're just showing off," I laughed.

I know I slept because I dreamed about Cecil and the view from the kitchen windows of the house on the moor and the farm in the curve of the road. It felt as though it was somewhere I once knew but couldn't quite remember and the thoughts made me sad.

Sleeping in guarantees a thick head and that sensation of being late for an appointment, even if you actually have nowhere to go. I staggered to the kitchen to make coffee and then the bathroom, while Tara grumbled into her dressing gown and grabbed a cup before the machine had finished its task. Even Flora squeaked and hooted her feelings, following me into the shower and flicking water over her back until we both had a grudging smile.

I made the usual breakfast of fruit and cheese and bread with honey, adding more coffee to the cups. Tara came back in from her visit to the bathroom and sat down into the vacant chair, scooping up Flora and feeding her the nutrient solution. I spread thick honey on my piece of bread and chewed. "We have *got* to stop the dorm room conversations," Tara said, "I'm getting too old for existing on four hours sleep a night."

I mumbled through my food, then swallowed and pointed as Flora stole a half a peach and stuffed it into her mouth. "Do you think that's okay?" I managed without choking.

"I think she's feeling better," Tara said, "Most small things exist on their mother's milk. I'm not sure how this creature has been adapted to cope with the world around it." Flora sucked contentedly on the fruit and then asked politely with her trunk for more. Tara gave her another slice. "We'd better call it quits at that, we don't want an upset stomach, do we?" Tara spoke directly to the elephant so I didn't bother to reply.

"Are you sure you want to go and talk to Nancy?" I asked, looking at my plate and trying to make the question light of any need.

Tara wasn't fooled. "It's important." She finished her coffee and then took Flora for her visit to the bathroom while I collected my thoughts and the gun from under my pillow. I fitted it carefully into the neat harness Tara had lent me, so that it sat in the small of my back and was invisible under my shirt and jacket. I wondered what sort of a meltdown my mother would have had if she could have seen me.

It's a little-known fact that there are more guns on Exmoor than on a street in Baghdad. My parents were always called out several times during the hunting season to gunshot wounds either stupidly self-inflicted, or stupidly inflicted on other people when they were supposed to be killing birds or animals. I remembered the grumpy disapproval about the need to kill anything. Then there were the suicides, it was a short walk to the locked gun cabinet from debt or depression, usually via a bottle of whiskey.

Tara tucked the sleepy elephant into a curl of bedcovers and we double locked the door with the alarm on the inside activated using one more gadget from Tara's vast supply.

The hotel manager was waiting for us in the lobby as we came down the stairs. She wasn't looking at us or hovering near the stairs but stood quietly behind her desk. Without raising her eyes or her voice she said, "Some men from the port are asking around about a missing crate and a miniature pachyderm." We both stopped like rabbits in the inevitable headlights. She added, "Not seen, not heard anything." We both nodded. Fully warned.

As we got to the door, I turned. "Thank you." I hunted for her name and realised I didn't know it.

Her face held the usual calm, noncommittal expression, and after a careful pause she said, "Elsie Wang." I nodded and so did she. There was an undefined silent crossing of boundaries. I wondered how she had ended up working in a hotel called The Wellington, on a recycled moon within spitting distance of Jupiter. We all had our stories. I imagined hers was impressive. Then I wondered if she was related to Jarry Wang, Lu's mother and what that would mean.

Somehow the streets were the same level of drunken noisy people as the night before, as if we had just walked out of and then back into a painting. One of those busy Victorian impressionist paintings with an imaginative title like 'Backstreets' or

'Revellers.' I tripped over a man sleeping peacefully on the side of the road, his face pillowed on a large pizza. The street stalls were doing a great trade and even though I had just eaten the smell of fried rice made my mouth water. There was fresh warm bread and fruit I didn't recognise, soups and stews and the odd crawling thing destined for someone's plate. A stall full of sweets and cakes drew me like a magnet and Tara laughed and steered me towards the port's back fence and the narrow road away from the main thoroughfare.

We approached the bar from the same alley that Theo had seen us into the night before and after looking carefully about I tapped on the kitchen door. Tara was facing down towards the road and she had removed her gun from its holster and was holding it point down by the side of her leg. It was as if we were waiting for the first clap of thunder that preceded the inevitable storm.

A tousled head popped out of the doorway. Theo's bleary eyes looked unfocused, then puzzled, and eventually he smiled. "Can't stay away? Mum said you would be back." He moved from the door and we slid inside. The kitchen was humming with cooking about to start. Food in all states of preparation lay around in the sort of organised order that I could never aspire to. Theo wandered off to the coffee pot and I realised he was still in his dressing gown. Both Tara and I averted our eyes from the slightly see-through floaty, green garment he had hopefully borrowed from his much shorter partner, to answer the door. "Mum will be back in a moment. Help yourself to coffee and cake." He disappeared into the darkened bar and we sat down at the table. Tara got up after a moment and checked the bar for people, it was empty, then she went over to the back door and made sure it was locked. I did my part and poured us two cups of coffee.

"You're back early." Nancy bustled in, clearly, she had not been worrying all night about life smacking her on the nose with impossible questions, she brought the coffee pot to the table with the large icing-filled cake. It looked as if it had come from the stall in the main street. I took the offered slice with the hope that it might be accompanied by a few helpful explanations. "I can't tell you much,"

Nancy said, with the sort of prescience that made me choke on the crumbs in the back of my throat.

"What time do you open?" Tara asked, nodding at the door to the bar.

"In half an hour." Nancy began chopping up vegetables for a stew and throwing them into a pot full of stock. It smelt good before she'd done anything. Some people had the gift of making food special, I had always thought it must have something to do with love and sharp knives.

"My mother?" I asked, before my head exploded. I found myself tapping the fork on the table in an untidy tympanic accompaniment to the silence that followed the question. Nancy sighed and wiped her greasy fingers on a cloth; she sat down and poured herself coffee. Which I hoped was a good sign.

"This is the little that I know." My face must have been full of the suppressed exasperation that was making me feel as if spontaneous combustion was more than a myth. "Your mother was part of the scientific elite; I came forward when they realised that a small group of the population had developed the ability to dreamwalk. At first it was accepted as part of the natural progression of an advanced civilisation. Then, things changed. There are always people who want to use their power for evil." She paused, deep in thought.

"I fled to the verse we had spent the most time in and the one that had benefited from our shared technology. I don't know what happened to your mother." Nancy's face was clouded with sadness and she sipped her coffee nervously adding, "But I do know she was in trouble. I never met your father; he was part of a different scientific team, something to do with medical research I think."

"Can't you go back?" Tara asked.

Nancy looked sad. "Even if I was able to, I'm not sure what would happen. I don't have a fixer." She leaned forward and touched the small mole on the side of my face. "It's been a long time since I dreamwalked, I get flashes in my sleep of the house I used to live in, but someone else lives in it now. I feel like a ghost. As I got older it became more difficult to move through the wormhole. The more time you spend in another verse the more difficult it is to go back."

My face must have betrayed my horror. "Don't worry, you have plenty of time," she said patting my hand. "Also, *you* have a fixer."

"In my verse, my parents were GP's," I stuttered, "Just country doctors. I never knew them as anything else."

"It must be a shock," Nancy said sympathetically. She added, "I'm glad they got away."

"They both died in a car crash when I was a teenager," I whispered.

Nancy paled visibly. "Maybe they didn't get away after all."

I must have looked as though I was going to be sick, I certainly felt as if I was, I rested my head on the table until the blue and red flashing lights subsided. Tara stroked my hair and Nancy said soothing unintelligible things. My face stopped sweating after a moment. I sat up and brushed away tears. "I can't believe someone would want to kill them. Why would anyone want to do that?"

"I'm not sure," Nancy tried again, "I think they made you."

A small click penetrated the clogged silence. Tara was up on her feet and reaching for a gun. I couldn't say that my reactions were as fluid, but Nancy had moved like a pit viper sideways across the room and retrieved a wicked looking weapon from a large pot on the kitchen shelf. She also pressed a small hidden green key on the wall above the work surface, and it flashed red. I could hear the sort of quiet that contains creeping footsteps. I moved over to the door into the bar and leaned against the wall behind it. Tara slid down by the large table and rested the gun on the top for a better aim. Nancy watched the back door from behind the cold storage and out of the line of fire from the bar.

I'm sure if there was a manual listed as 'what to do in the event of a firefight in a small room,' the first piece of advice would be, 'don't.' Shortly followed by, 'leave.' I looked over to the back door and then pointedly at Tara. She shook her head. Anyone who was smart enough to come in through the front door without smashing it to pieces would have thought about the back exit with some care.

The footfalls were the careful practiced sounds of more than one person. I was trying to keep myself calm, and I glanced at Nancy who was doing some deep breathing of her own. The large cold storage unit rumbled noisily when the power came on as it fell below its temperature requirement. The movement in the bar stopped for a moment. There was no crack in the doorway for me to worry about being seen through and I flattened myself further into the unrelenting wall, gripping the gun and hoping for a minor miracle.

Nancy must have been able to see something because she looked pointedly at both of us in turn and lifted three fingers slowly to her chest. I felt as if I was an extra in a western film and the sudden urge to laugh surprised me. I wiped a trickle of sweat from one eye and waited. The shadow crept into the room and a large hand gripped the edge of the door. They were not sure what to expect, but three armed women had probably not featured high on the list. I saw Tara's face and the look of controlled fear and realised that the minor miracle would have to wait. The gun in my hand was loud in the small space and so was the scream of angry pain as I fired point blank at the man's curled fingers. Blood spurted onto the floor in a bright flow and the sound of Tara's gun made a sharp whoomph sound as the narrow beam and projectile hit soft flesh. The shadow without a face fell backwards into the man behind him and the swearing was accompanied by multiple bursts of sharp light into the room. The cold storage unit gave up without a fight.

Nancy made a strange sight as she fired back at the unseen men. Her lips were curved back against her teeth in a feral grin and I could hear her saying to herself, "Bastards," over and over, as if it was a mantra. Stuck behind the door I couldn't see the men, but something told me to stay where I was. A loud bang made me look away from Tara's angry, shocked expression as she continued firing at the dark doorway. The back door seemed to bulge on its hinges. It buckled and then spun, crashing down on the floor in a cloud of dust and noise. I fired into the lighted square of the outside and kept on firing. It seemed important but I couldn't remember why.

A short blast hit Tara in the back and she flew forward in a heart stopping crunch against the table. I fired at nothing, again and again into the space where the back door had been, and didn't notice the shadow from the bar now had a face and was reaching like a spider in my direction for its next meal, until a steady light pulse of projectiles and an unbelievable racket cut into his flesh and he slipped in the blood and severed fingers on the floor. Nancy shouted something to me but I couldn't hear her, the combination of small spaces and loud noises making it impossible. I tried to reach Tara but something pinged against my side and I looked down to see my own blood against the background of fear.

I don't think they were trying to kill us, but when you were angry, bad things happened. My feet became something interesting and I staggered towards the table and Tara, who was now a broken doll a fractious child had thrown away. My fingers slipped into clumsy fists as I grabbed a handful of her clothing and pulled. She groaned when I moved her and the sound of gunfire and the light splitting flashes didn't disguise the pain.

Nancy was still crouched in the corner between the shattered storage unit and the edge of a cupboard, firing at the back entrance.

Whoever had been coming in that way had given up and pulled back. A smattering of noise from the darkened bar preceded a silence so deafening that I put my hands to my ears for a moment. Theo shouted, "All clear here!" He came into the kitchen and moved carefully towards the back door using the edges of the room, as if he were a child who doesn't dare step on the cracks for fear of the bears. His gun pointed up one side of the street and then he dodged over to check the other side. "It's okay," he added.

Nancy came over to me and we moved Tara into a more hopeful position. Her breathing was laboured and her face a sweaty luminous dial that usually meant internal bleeding. I gasped at the pool of blood that seemed to be collecting around my hand, which was pressed against my own side. "Sonic weapon," Nancy said, looking at Tara, "It causes internal impact injuries. Similar to a car accident," she explained to the one person in the room who hadn't had much experience with weapons training. I nodded. She noticed my own injury and grabbed a towel from the now-shredded work surface. "That, on the other hand, is a good old-fashioned projectile wound." I nodded again because speaking had become a lost art inside my head.

Theo came back into the kitchen from the alley. "Two dead out there and three in the bar. Impressive." He looked around him at the mess; pieces of the storage unit's power crystals were scattered across the floor and the door was hanging out at the side. The table Tara had been behind was kneeling on two legs and the stew puddled around our feet and mixed with the blood in an objectionable swirl. I realised Theo was still wearing the green voile dressing gown over nothing. He tucked it tidily around him and went over to Tara, gently kneeling in the muck on the floor. Pulling a com from a unit on his wrist he began speaking quietly into the glowing square.

I found myself leaning against a cupboard door and sliding down it to get to the floor which seemed a long distance away. Nancy's face was suddenly all I could see down a long dark tunnel. "Millie, stay with me!" She shouted. I reached out for Tara and in that moment a figure came in through the back doorway. Theo leapt up and grabbed the gun he had put down. I heard Nancy yell, "No!" Then there was someone else at the end of the tunnel shaking me back into now and mouthing words I couldn't hear. I knew the face, but I didn't know why.

My thoughts tumbled around like the washing on spin dry. I pulled at the threads, remembering the fear and the noise. I opened my eyes to see Okan; he was pressing a spray syringe to my arm and talking over his shoulder. He turned to see me watching him. "Good, you're back." His face was crumpled with worry.

"Tara?" I whispered.

"We're going to get you to the doctor. Tara's already gone with Joao and Nancy."

I heard Theo's voice say, "Don't worry about the bodies. I will deal with it."

Okan nodded and turned. "Rari?"

I grabbed his arm. "You must go back to the rooms and get Flora!"

"Who's Flora?" He asked, puzzled.

"Promise me?" I shouted in the loudest whisper I could manage and then began to hyperventilate which made my eyes spin and that made Okan panic.

"I'll go! Don't worry Millie," I heard Rari say, "Anyway if I have to rescue a woman in distress, she might feel she owes me something."

Ha, I thought, does he have a surprise coming. I staggered to my feet with Okan half lifting me. I put the key with the code for the room into Rari's hand and found myself reaching for the kitchen table, only it wasn't the one in Nancy's kitchen. Okan had his arms around my waist and we fell in a spectacular circle around the event horizon of the wormhole. My whole body was shielded from the floor by Okan.

Cecil's bright eyes looked down on us from the fruit bowl, his furry cat brows peaked in irritation and then I passed out.

The pain woke me. I watched Simon move from the window to the bed as if he knew my eyes were open. His outline seemed to shimmer, indicating that the focus button in my head wasn't tuned in properly. A woman I vaguely recognised got up from the chair and stood beside him. My brain filtered through her features as if I was checking the flickering pages from a screen of mug shots in the police station. The doctor who had treated Joao smiled at me. "You people sure know how to have a good time!" She checked my pulse and blood pressure and then looked at Simon. The same nod of agreement passed between them and she closed the door quietly as she left.

A moment of a thought process trickled through my mind, as if I was pulling on the end of a loose thread, which may have been given a serious push from the high levels of pain medication, and I asked Simon in a barely discernible voice, "You're a dreamwalker, aren't you?"

"When did you work it out?" He sat on the end of the bed and patted my feet in a worried way, as if touching me might make the bad things disappear.

"When Nancy told me about my parents." I tried to sit up and then changed my mind as the room took on the glowing proportions of a volcano, complete with eruption noises.

"Ah, the delectable Nancy." He nodded. "She was very fond of your mother."

Okan came in carrying a full tray of tea and toast. "I guess the doctor will be back tomorrow. She doesn't talk much, does she?" He offered the mug to Simon and they exchanged milk and sugar in the irritating familiarity of people who have gone through a crisis together. I realised that had been me and felt left out and grumpy.

"Do you know each other too?" I asked, reaching unsuccessfully for some toast.

"No, actually we don't," Okan said, "But Joao told me what he thought when he and Simon met and I found the number in your phone while you were bleeding all over the kitchen floor." He passed me a tiny square of toast and I leaned back on the pillows and tried to eat lying down which was not that easy with buttered toast. The feeling of hunger wore off as soon as I started chewing, and I passed the toast back. Okan looked at it for a moment and then put it in his mouth. It was very disturbing when someone you haven't actually slept with and who isn't your mother, finished your food. I tried not to let the spinning room in for a moment. Both the men put out steadying hands, which was also disconcerting.

I waited until all the furniture was back in the right place. "I can't believe you dreamwalk!" I said to Simon.

"What. A gay guy can't be a traveller? Who do you think invented matching luggage?" Simon helped himself to a large plate of food and began covering the toast with thick layers of jam. He and Okan did the irritating routine again and passed the jar back and forward, sharing a knife until I wanted to scream. I lifted the downie and examined the bandage around my waist.

"It looks much worse than it is," Simon said, "Plus you will have a small sexy scar, a warrior queen type of thing." He and Okan nodded as if it was something only men appreciated.

"This must be bad, if you're making a joke out of my being shot." Simon moved the toast around on his plate and his face seemed to be full of shadows. "I think from what Okan said that the port workers were trying to get you for a buyer. The firefight must have surprised them."

"Yes," I said, "It really surprised me too." I sat up suddenly, causing the room to erupt again and both of the men to discard their food in an unnaturally fast way, as if they were the juggler who spins plates on the end of the poles of wood, and then keeps running up and down to keep them spinning. "Tara?" I gasped eventually when the world had finally come to a complete stop.

"She's okay, Millie. Joao took her to the doctor, he was able to stop the internal bleeding, and there was just a broken wrist from the collision with the table." Okan was holding onto my arms as if he expected me to leap out of bed and jump to the other verse.

Simon had ended up with custody of both plates and was looking on with exasperation. "Stop this right now! Or I will bring back the doctor and get her to sedate you for the next week."

I watched the sunset through the windows of the bedroom. Cecil was sleeping, curled up in the downie in reverberating contentment having found his way from the fruit bowl to the end of the bed. My feeble attempts at moving across the room had given me an idea of how stupid most films were when the newly shot get up and walk around the next day.

Okan came in quietly through the doorway. "Simon will be back tomorrow. How are you feeling?"

He sat on the bed and I reached for his hand. "I need to understand some things?" He nodded.

"How did you know we were at Nancy's bar?" I asked, starting with what I thought was an easy one.

"Joao knew that Tara was thinking about seeing the gangers again. It made sense that you would go with her. We tracked you with the runabout and then followed you both to the port. I met Nancy way back when I first came here. I said if she heard anything about you both to let us know. She contacted me when she recognised you."

"Do you know who this man is? The one who is following me from verse to verse."

"No, but I guess that he comes from Nancy's verse," he added, "The one your parents left."

"Did you know about Nancy and my parents, that they were dreamwalkers?"

"Not for sure," Okan answered evasively.

"What about you, Okan?"

"It's complicated," he said, getting up and going over to the window, "I don't have the freedom to do what I want."

I couldn't think what that really meant but it didn't sound good. Actually, none of it did.

"What do we do now?" I shifted in the bed, making Cecil grumble.

"Now? We cover our tracks." Okan turned around and I couldn't see his face, but the sound of his voice made my heart bounce around in my chest. In the firefight in Nancy's bar there hadn't been time to be frightened, but now there was.

"Do you mean all of us or just me?"

He sighed, "Those port workers were serious about their business. I'm not sure if we could fight them off again."

"You were fighting in the alley?" I asked.

"Why do you think it took us so long to get to you after Nancy set off the alarm?"

It explained the button pushing on the kitchen wall. "I thought she was alerting Theo of the green negligee," I laughed.

"I'm thinking of getting myself one of those," Okan said with a smile.

We both paused at the edge of the conversation, a place that seemed strange and yet familiar. I changed tack. "What do you make of the temporal differential between the verses?" Okan sat down on the bed.

"You're full of surprises," he said.

I stuttered on, "I don't know much about temporal compression theory, but even I know the tidal forces at the edge of an event horizon should pull you apart. What I think I mean is, at some point your body would be in different times and the temporal differential when we were children, didn't seem to be so specific."

"I am not a scientist Millie, I'm a dreamwalker like you but I've always thought that the dreamwalk gene creates our ability to pass through the energy barrier of the different verses, it seems pretty instant. When we were children dreamwalking without the fixer, I think we experienced time dilation as opposed to the temporal differential, the fixer changes us to *include* temporal differential."

I thought about what he had said. "What are you if you're not a scientist?" Then much faster as the thoughts came tumbling through. "A dreamwalk gene?"

He laughed, "What did you think it was about?"

"I'm not sure." I really wasn't. I had gone from dreaming into another world to being part of an experiment. I leaned back into the pillows. "Sleep," I whispered, "Is the one place you should feel safe."

Okan got up and moved me over on the bed, leaning back against the headboard, he put his arm around me and I put my head on his chest. "We can be safe for a while," he said.

"Those port workers," I said, "I don't think they cared if they killed me or not."

"Some men hunt in packs," Okan spoke quietly, "They lose sight of the goal when the group mentality takes over." It was chilling in its simplicity. Sometimes what connected us were the unanswered questions or pain or both. We are usually separated by our thinking and our beliefs, but it ought to be the other way around. I sighed.

"The fixer is going to be a problem, isn't it?" I said, with a prescience I didn't think I owned.

"There are people from my verse who want you for the same reason as the people from the type three verse." I looked up at him and he tried not to be worried, but his face was that combination of shadows that make up the thoughts of people who have spent their lives staying one step ahead.

I tried for some balance. "For real objects with real mass, nothing goes faster than the speed of light."

"Don't be so parochial," he answered.

I thought about the combination of scholar/warrior that was Okan and realised, that if you didn't have the scholar, all that you would end up with was a killing machine.

The morning after the night before was even more awkward when there hadn't been a night before.

I tried to do something with my hair by pulling at it with my fingers, even though this had never worked. Okan fared no better, having slept sitting up with me curled against him. His back must have felt as if it was a war zone after heavy bombing. We scrambled for our much- needed dignity without success. I used the bathroom first and Okan headed for the kitchen with a loudly complaining Cecil in tow.

I took off the bandages and was pleasantly surprised by a small neat scar that looked red and raised and was stiff and sore but wasn't agony, and it was healing. I had never been shot before, but I thought the enthusiastic gene therapy from my over indulgent parents clearly must have included something helpful.

The smell of coffee and fresh bread and the low deep voices meant that Simon was in the house. I dressed and went downstairs. They were sitting at the kitchen table leaning in like conspirators in a gunpowder plot.

"Excellent, you look better." Simon got up and gave me a hug and a kiss. I hugged him back feeling as if I was the drowning person and he was the life raft, and he didn't let go until I did, which is the test of true friendship.

"I'm running out of coping strategies," I said, sitting down and helping myself to toasted bagels and cream cheese. I suddenly realised I was starving.

"I've got several you can borrow." Simon shrugged. "I particularly like the one with Ben Browder and a jar of maple syrup," he added helpfully.

Okan looked stunned and then pointed upstairs. "I think I'll leave you to it." He headed off to the bathroom.

I chewed for a while, enjoying the feeling of food in my stomach and the contentment that only breakfast can bring. "It must be as it is now for journalists; once, in the past there was only ever bad luck, now even the people who take the photographs and tell the story are fair game."

"I think that maybe *you* were always fair game," Simon said, stuffing in a large mouthful of bagel. I probably looked grumpy because he added, "Oh no here comes the hormone walkabout!" For Simon being politically correct was not exactly high on his list.

"Simon!"

"What? I can be tactful," he said. "Okay, maybe not tactful *exactly*." I laughed and then had to hold my side where the scar was, because even though the outside looked good the inside still really hurt, which was a metaphor for my life.

Cecil followed us out into the garden and we sat in the sunshine on the seat overlooking the valley and watched the tractor doing some lazy autumn work in the fields. "Are you going to tell me about my parents?" I leaned my head against the wall behind me, which was radiating a gentle warmth, and I closed my eyes.

"She had the same mad need for periodic tables," he said sadly, his voice barely a whisper.

"I imagine *hers* didn't have ninety-four naturally occurring elements on it," I said bitterly, as an unwelcome tear found its way down the side of my face.

"No," he said.

"The gene manipulation." I turned to look at him, my eyes blinking back the tears in the sunlight. I could see rainbows on my lashes. "Would I understand it if you explained it to me?"

"I'm not a scientist, Millie. I was just one of the original dreamwalkers. I met your parents when I went into the programme. It was," he added, "A very exciting time. We thought we were on the threshold of a new evolution."

"What happened?" I asked.

"Some people were not ready for the possibilities." He looked desperately sad.

We sat quietly for a while, drinking coffee and listening to the silence of the countryside, which comes with the sound of the wind in the trees and birdsong and the distant rumble of farm life going on as it should.

"Okan says there's a dreamwalk gene. Is that similar to a travel gene? I remember reading an article in the paper about D47 causing an effect on the brain."

"I'll just bet you do," Simon said dryly. He finished his coffee and sat back on the seat. "The travel gene acts at the molecular level, the dreamwalk gene works at the subatomic level. It's about particle physics. I didn't understand it then and I don't now though," he added, "Your mother tried. She said once after an exasperating conversation 'the more intricate the pattern the simpler the theory.'"

"I think that it has a connection with chaos theory," I mused.

"You sound just like her," Simon said wistfully, "She and your dad were part of something special."

More time was spent watching the drifting clouds as we both dealt with memories, and the broken stories of no happy ending. Okan came out to join us looking appropriately scrubbed. He was carrying a tray with more coffee and some cake that Simon had obviously brought with him that morning. I knew this because anything sweet was not usually safe in my house; it calls to me until I have eaten it all.

He had a 'how's it going?' expression which Simon returned. "If you give each other one more significant look I am going to do something violent!" The coffee was poured and the cake passed around without speaking and Okan sat down.

Cecil became everyone's best friend until he had succeeded in acquiring cake rights.

"We were talking about the dreamwalk gene," I said. Neither of the two men spoke. "What I want to know is," I paused, not for effect but because I was trying to get the everything into perspective, "What's different about me?"

Both of the men looked surprised, but Okan got there first. "I thought you realised. I mean didn't Nancy say something?" He glanced at Simon, who shrugged.

I tried not to be exasperated but it was impossible to avoid grinding my teeth in frustration. It was difficult to be the only one in the room, or in this case the garden, who didn't get the joke. "I realise we all have the dreamwalk gene and that the people from the type three verse don't want us wandering about at will and I imagine the people from your verse," I looked at Okan, "Are interested in us too, but what makes me different?"

They were quiet and then Okan spoke, "All of us," he pointed at himself and then Simon, "Rari, Joao even Nancy, were born with the gene, we're just the spin of a dice and there aren't many of us. Maybe a quirk of evolution maybe an aberration depending on who you talk to." He sounded angry. I thought the people in his verse leaned more towards the latter. "You Millie, your parents *made* you." I must have looked puzzled or stunned or both because he said it again, "They made you with the gene, you're the key to creating the dreamwalk gene in people who don't have it."

Simon moved forward because I think my blood pressure must have dropped visibly and the sky began to spin, my memories and the clouds spun too. Okan reached for me as well, touching the fixer on my face and keeping me in the verse that had the coffee and the cat, but didn't seem to be home anymore. I longed for something to hold onto, but you can build whole cities out of longing. "Hang on Millie," he said.

After a moment I realised that up and down had returned to their respective places. "How do you do that? Stay where you want to be, I can't seem to do that," I grumbled, "As soon as something gets tricky, I zoom off somewhere else. It's very disconcerting."

"I've had more practice," Okan answered, with more than a touch of bitterness.

"I just thought, actually, I don't really know what I thought. I expected some gene therapy manipulation which gave me an edge, but," I trailed off remembering something Nancy had said in the kitchen before the firefight. Her exact words were, 'they made you.' "What you're saying is they started from the beginning with me. *How* is it even *possible?*" I asked.

"Ah well, *that's* the question," Simon said dryly.

"The other stuff, the fact that I can fly the borderer's craft and the fast healing," I showed them my scar, "Is that part of it?" Okan shrugged and Simon said nothing. I sighed. "You really need to do something about the ship; I can't be the only one able to fly it."

"We're working on it," Okan said.

I watched as the two men did a little dance with the dirty cups and the debris of cake. I sat without moving, I am not one of those people who always felt the need to do things because it *is* their home. Besides when you've been shot at and lied to and bounced around several universes you really need to sit still and be on your own for a while.

Cecil came over and curled up on my lap. He washed a paw and then settled and I scooped my arms around his furry warmth. His owners had never contacted me about picking him up. Some people just don't understand that cats *are* family.

Time passed and I realised that I had been sitting for too long, my scar ached and my back was wooden bench shaped. I let Cecil slip to the ground and we wandered back in through the kitchen, looking for company and answers.

The house was waiting and so it seemed was Okan. I found him working on my computer, Simon had gone. I leaned over his shoulder and he touched my hand in a gesture that made me think of beginnings.

"What are you doing?" I asked. The screen was full of the computer information Joao had been trawling through on his last visit. I realised I missed both him and Rari, Tara and Weldon, the verse with the skydancing towers and interesting cows. It made me dizzy to think of them and I pushed at the fixer on my face.

Okan spoke, without turning around, "You're getting the hang of that." He then pointed at the screen. "I need to get you off the grid in this verse."

"Is that possible?" I pulled up the chair from the corner of the study and sat down next to him.

"Yeah, I think so, but it's going to take some time. You're stitched into everything," he said, with exasperation. The screen bubbled and Okan swore. It seemed to object to the language because it threw him out of whatever he was doing and returned calmly to the usual desktop symbols. Okan banged his head gently on the study work surface, which was liberally scattered with my usual layers of science paperwork, so I didn't worry too much about him doing himself untold damage.

"It's not going to well then," I said helpfully.

"Simon is going to have to take your car and put it in his name."

Okan tried again with the computer and I didn't answer. I began thinking about all of the information that made up a life, from registration at birth, to the voting forms that asked for all your personal details. There was my over-used credit card and the endless subscriptions to every magazine that had ever run a series on quantum mechanics. I patted Okan on the back in sympathy for his efforts thus far.

The walk down the road was by way of a diversion. I thought that if Okan did one more venture into the wilder side of exotic language, the ghosts of all the Edwardians who had lived there would be moving out under protest. You should never upset a house's previous occupants.

"You're going to ask Cecil's owners if they would be happy if he moved in with you permanently?" Okan asked, puzzled. "I don't actually think there's any doubt who he lives with." Okan's New York accent seemed to be stronger in the lanes of Exmoor than on a terraformed moon around Jupiter. It made me realise how far from home he was.

"Do you miss your verse?" I asked him with curiosity.

"Not really." He picked a length of grass out of a hedgerow and stuck the end in his mouth as if he was a part of the countryside around him, instead of a city boy with coffee instead of blood.

"What about your family?" I tried again, resisting the temptation to kiss him, because you don't get answers if you start along that path with someone. His eyes smiled a little as if he could read my mind and he stopped and reached for my face and tangled his fingers in my hair. His eyes had a dark ring around the inner brown colour of the iris and he leaned down.

I tried to remember what I had been saying before we stopped. "Your family?"

"Simon said you don't give up once you get on the track of something." Okan stretched up and then put an arm around me. "They gave me up to the organisation once they realised that I had the gene. I haven't seen them more than twice since I was thirteen."

I stood very still. "Is 'the organisation' as creepy as it sounds?"

He looked philosophical, which I thought came with the experience. "Yeah, I think that they very well might be."

"Is that how you met Rari?"

"Rari and I were part of the same group as you; we didn't meet in our own verse until much later. He works for the same organisation, but in a different capacity."

"Does everything have to be in code," I said, exasperated, "Is the world going to come to an end if I know what Rari does for a living?"

"Okay." Okan thought about it for a moment. "You have to understand, I've been keeping secrets for a long time and so has Rari. His job is very sensitive. If the people we work for knew I was talking about it," he trailed off.

"I'm sorry Okan. I understand, I really do. It's just that up until a few weeks ago I didn't have to hide from anyone and I worked in a bookshop with my best friend who's gay."

"Sounds like a nice life," he said, without any trace of irony.

The house that belonged to Cecil's neglectful owners, was the other side of the farm and we walked into the watchful, curious and incredibly kind farmer's wife who was standing in the lane doing something totally unnecessary with her front doorstep. "Millie! How nice to see you, this must be your young man?"

Okan's eyebrows shot up and I elbowed him in the ribs. "It's nice to see you too, Mrs Payne."

"Oh, I've told you before, call me Edwina." She came over to us and smiled up at Okan who was at least a foot taller than she was.

He shook her hand and introduced himself, "Okan D'Ferrino, Mrs Payne, it's very good to meet you."

"Well," she said, smiling with delight, "He's not from around here, is he?"

"No." I smiled back. "Not really." Okan elbowed me in return, forgetting the newly healed wound and I gasped slightly.

She didn't notice. "I've got some fresh eggs and some cheese. I'll go and get them."

We hovered around as the farm dog came out to inspect us and a group of piglets grew curious, pushing their snouts through the narrow gaps in the hedge on the side of the road. Okan bent down to fuss the dog and I realised that I missed the Weldon's farm. "How are we *ever* going to hide from these people?" I asked, with the fear catching in my throat, "It's not as if we're even managing to stay one step ahead."

Okan looked at me. "I hadn't planned on them finding you so quickly. I thought I could buy us some time." He stopped as Mrs Payne came out, a huge basket of provisions over one arm.

"Here," she said, "This should fill up that big man of yours."

The 'big man' blushed slightly which made me smile, and then took the basket from her. "You're very kind," he said.

I realised that hopeful feelings were still all around us and we could find goodness in the usual places, as in the heart and open face of Edwina Payne. I hugged her and she hugged me back. "Well," she said."

I knocked on the door of the house further down the road. It had been a pretty bungalow once, but the lines were blurred by an unfortunate second floor addition and some seriously bad decorative brickwork. A yappy dog scrabbled at the other side of the door giving me a clue as to why Cecil had moved in with me. No one answered, so I pulled the pre-prepared note from my jeans pocket and pushed it into the letter box.

"You're going to take that cat through the wormhole, aren't you?" Okan asked, as we walked back up to my house on the side of the hill. Mr Payne had waved to us from the perch of his tractor in the top field and we waved back as if we were children on an adventure.

"Yes. I'm not leaving him here and I think Tara will love him."

Okan sighed, "You can't save everything and everyone, Millie."

"I'm going to have a good try." I went through the gate, opened the door to my house and watched as Cecil shot out past me hissing and spitting, his fur up in a ridge on his back. I stopped, causing a traffic jam.

Okan had a gun in his hand before I could turn to warn him.

"Get behind me," he said quietly, pushing at the same time as handing me a small weapon that he had strapped to his ankle. A walking arsenal. I wondered if he had any grenades tucked into his underwear.

We must have made enough noise outside to have alerted whoever was lurking, and the sudden silence would have been a complete giveaway that we were aware of them. The stillness inside the house held deep feelings in waves of emotion, which were nearly all mine and mostly of fear. I was not one of those people who felt the need to assert themselves whenever someone offers protection. The fact that a large armed man was standing between me and whoever, was absolutely fine.

Okan crept towards the stairs; he stood at the bottom and leaned carefully around the newel post, staring up to the landing above. He looked back at me and shrugged. I turned to see Cecil hovering in the doorway, his fur a halo of light around him and his teeth bared in a vicious smile of loathing. He didn't come back in but growled quietly until it was lost in the sound of careful breathing.

The door to the kitchen was nearly closed and I saw a shadow pass across the tiled floor, as the sun shone in the windows and someone took up a better position. I heard a click. It sounded as if it was the back door which was odd, or seemed it to me, those people with access to a wormhole really shouldn't have needed the old-fashioned exits.

I pointed. Okan crept forward doing the 'get behind me' sign again. I found myself wishing that Rari and Joao were here, and Tara, who was much better at being a warrior queen than I would ever be. My hand shook with the pressure of my fingers on the gun.

A sound erupted near my face as part of the careful Edwardian plastering flew in fragments around me, splintering into lethal missiles. I fired and ran, aiming for the place on the upper landing where the shots of light had come from. Okan rammed himself at the kitchen door making it bounce against whoever was using it as a shield. He squatted down, firing up and around and a screech of pain seemed inappropriately gratifying. Something snatched at my shoulder and I clutched the scrap of material with the seeping edge of blood underneath. I fired continuously, suddenly angry at the fact that they were in my house. I heard and then felt the thump of impact as my haphazard spatter with the gun hit someone.

I saw a bloodied face through the banister and the sight made me gasp and my shout of stunned surprise made Okan look away from his contact for a moment, long enough for whomever to get in an accurate burst of fire. Okan went down like a freshly felled tree.

Everything was quiet for a second. As if the visual part of the film was waiting to catch up with the soundtrack. I went over to Okan, who seemed stunned rather than bloody. He lifted one hand with great difficulty and gripped my arm. I pulled with all my strength and managed to get him sitting upright. I checked carefully through the crack in the door. The kitchen was empty.

The stairs however contained the still, blood-dripping body of a borderer.

I phoned Simon. "Oh, what now? Enough already!" He sighed and was silent for a moment. "Do I need to bring the doctor?" He asked.

I looked at Okan. "Do you need a doctor?"

He shook his head. "It was a sonic weapon and I didn't take a direct hit. You?"

"Just a scratch," I laughed, "I have always wanted to say that!" Okan looked puzzled, as he obviously hadn't grown up on an inappropriate diet of action films.

Simon snorted, "I'm on my way."

I slid down the wall and ended up on the floor in the hall next to Okan. "How badly do you think they want to get hold of me?" Okan just looked at me, his body still slumped. "Enough to enlist the help of the borderers," I answered myself. I settled back, leaning against him and he struggled for a moment until he could put his arm around me. "I don't know anything about this but isn't giving type three verse wormhole technology to a group of borderers a bit stupid?"

"Desperate and stupid," Okan said.

I looked up at him. "I suppose this *is* the type three verse? Not your people."

He shook his head. "We don't have the ability and anyway *I'm* supposed to be the one getting hold of you."

"How's that working out?" I leaned back against him.

"It's much more difficult than I thought it would be."

Simon found us still on the floor; he pushed open the front door and followed a now complaining Cecil into the house. He helped Okan get to his feet. I couldn't have moved a twig on my own at that moment.

Okan pointed to the upper landing and we went into the kitchen as Simon went over to the stairs. The sound I heard was the rattle of the wind in the trees when the weather came from the north east. The cat did another backflip with his fur spiked and shot under the sofa.

"Simon," I called, "Is everything okay?"

"No problem. I was able to send him back to his point of origin." He came into the kitchen looking pleased. "Though you'll need some bleach to get the stains out of the wood floor and you've made a *terrible* mess of the banisters." I looked at him. My arm was still seeping blood and the kitchen looked as if a small war had been lost in the space between the door and the sink. Okan had taken refuge on the sofa with the growling Cecil. "Okay," he said. "I *really* am going to work on the tact."

"What do you mean 'sent him back?'" I picked up the kettle from the floor and put it back on the long-suffering Aga. The work surface was covered in debris from broken things, but I found a few mugs in the cupboard that were relatively untouched.

"He had the same type of fixer as you and Okan, I just gave it a little shove. Someone's going to get a bit of a shock when he turns up."

"A fixer?" I looked at Okan. "Do you have any ideas as to how that's happened?"

"One or two," Okan answered, "None of them good."

"Let's be clear about this," I said, making tea and reaching for the patterned tin which had my emergency stash of double chocolate biscuits. "The borderers have access to the type three verse's wormhole technology and your verse's fixers. Is it possible that this could get any worse?"

Simon knew his way around a vacuum and he began clearing up after six biscuits and a gallon of tea. He did some more cleaning with bleach and hot water and even if the house still felt as if it was a war zone it didn't look so much like one.

Okan's face was pale and he went quiet for a while, resting back with his eyes closed. I had seen Tara take a blast from a sonic weapon and it amazed me that he was even conscious. I could hear him thinking. He was angry and worried and was working that process where you run scenarios through your mind to see what you've missed.

"Is there any way that the scientist from the type three verse could be communicating or collaborating with your verse?"

Okan shook his head. "My people are very paranoid and not likely to make a bargain with someone, even to hand over the very technology they've been searching for. I can't see that any scientist from the type three verse, could be making a deal with the people they want to restrict to their own verse. It just doesn't make sense." He shifted in painful, frustrated tiredness.

"Are you okay?" I asked, coming over and sitting down next to him. He nodded. "You have a theory, don't you?" I said gently, not really wanting to know the answer.

He sat up and his expression was a combination of a wry smile and disappearing into the shadows. "Do you remember the other kids that we used to play with? The boy with the red hair and that girl who used to laugh all the time?"

I remembered that there were at least fifteen or twenty of us at one point. We got on in groups as all children do, squabbling and making up. A school playground in an event horizon of possibilities. "What are you saying?" I whispered.

"Well," Okan said quietly, "Where did they all go?" I looked at him, horrified.

Simon came in whistling a tune that sounded as if it came from a night out with a tribute band. He stopped. "What now?"

I didn't answer Simon, but said to Okan, "I didn't return until I was an adult and even then, it was probably because of the trauma. Maybe some people just don't dreamwalk into adulthood." Okan didn't say anything. He just looked at me. "It wasn't an accident I went back to dreamwalking," I sighed, and put my head in my hands, pressing my fingers against my eyes until the orange swirls of light made me invisible to the darkness. Eventually I spoke, "What do *you* think happened to them, Okan?"

"I think someone collected their fixers."

Simon emptied the bucket of bloody water into the sink, rinsed, bleaching the dregs, and tidying up as he went. He poured more tea and sat down at the table picking up more biscuits and handing at least half to Cecil, who was happy to help.

"How difficult would it be to remove the fixer without damaging or killing the host?" I asked. Okan was silent. "Right. Stupid question."

My side ached and the scrape of the wound on my shoulder stung.

"I'm going to have a bath." Both men nodded. I left without saying any more. With the hot water up to my neck and the bubbles in my hair, I finally found myself wondering when did nowhere fast become a destination.

Simon came in, gay guy friends, of course, having bathroom privi-leges. He sat down on the closed loo seat and sniffed unhelpfully. "That whole stunned speechless expression, is a good look for you." I threw a handful of bubbles which hit him squarely in the face.

"Do you have any idea who this scientist might be?" I asked him, "The one who is using Darth Vader as a role model." I sunk further down into the bath as if the water was a barrier from the inevitability of the truth.

"Maybe." Simon studied his fingernails and then finding something unacceptable under one, he swished it in the water by my feet. I hoped it wasn't blood from the borderer. Something about sharing my bathwater with any of it made me cringe with disgust.

Simon was thinking about what to say. "It's just that, from your description, if it's who I think it is. I'm surprised. He never did anything even a little *interesting* in all the years I knew him." He snorted with derision. I laughed. There was nothing like a few condescending words from a good friend to see the darkness in a different light.

He got up to go and pushed the towel into a more convenient place so that I could reach it without getting water all over the floor. "Millie, what gives life meaning is not the big things; it's the journey you take looking for them."

"Great, Simon, philosophy and bathwater in equal measure." I winced at the sting on my shoulder as I moved to get out of the bath.

"Are you bleeding again? I'll go and get the first aid box from the study." He pulled the door to behind him and I wrapped a towel around me and wandered into the bedroom. "Here we go," he said, coming into the room after me. I sat down and he examined the wound, smothering it in antiseptic ointment, and putting a waterproof dressing over it. He sighed, "You're getting a battering, girl."

I could hear Okan moving around in the study next door. Clearly removing the information from the computer couldn't wait and I realised we were going on a dreamwalk in the next few hours.

"What about my home, Simon and my parent's things?" I had never really thought about it much before, but now it seemed that the house was full of belongings empowered with memories.

"What would you save if the place was on fire?" Simon asked me.

"That's a trick question," I said grumpily.

"It's only furniture," he said. I nodded my reluctant agreement. "Also, books," he added.

"That's just sacrilege," I snapped, pulling my dressing gown on carefully over the sore spots, of which there seemed to be many.

"Make me a brandy, will you Simon?" I asked, "My body feels as if it's been through the spin dryer."

I also felt sad and tired and without the hope that is supposed to be free for all of us. Okan was grumpy and just grunted a response when I asked him how the grid search was going. I sat down in the study and watched him trying to construct a sentence that didn't have swear words in it. In the end he smiled. "Not well. But I think I might have to leave it for now and get Simon to do the basics with your house and car. He told me he has power of attorney over your legal matters."

The man being talked about came in with a tray of steaming mugs filled with brandy and honey, lemon and hot water; a certainty for getting rid of the muscle pain, actually a sure way to remove any sensation at all. I sipped gratefully and spoke thinking aloud, "With the temporal differential between the verses, we're talking about Einstein's theory of special relativity, not general relativity?" Okan looked thoughtful.

"Is this a private geek moment or can anyone join in?" Simon settled himself comfortably on the floor, as the only person in the room who hadn't been shot, he was the only one who would be able to get up without help.

I tried to explain, "In special relativity the time dilation is reciprocal, that is, as observed from the point of view of each verse it is the other verse that is time dilated. Of course, in general relativity it is *not* reciprocal."

"You know it's funny the words are going in but nothing seems to be," Simon paused dramatically, "No, nothing happening there either." I thumped him and he smiled.

"I know, information overload." I sipped more brandy.

"Aah!" Okan said, "This is stronger than Weldon's brew." He tapped a few more keys and sat back, checking the data as it scrawled across the screen. He made a face, as if grudgingly admitting the possibility of success.

I watched him for a while and then realised Simon was watching me. He grinned and I tutted, there's nothing worse than being caught with your feelings all over your face.

"Are you coming with us?" I asked Simon.

He was surprised by the question. But he could see my barely concealed panic at the thought of something or someone getting to him. "I should be okay, Millie. I don't have a fixer, so it's not as straight forward for me to verse hop. But it means I'm not that easy to trace either."

"Couldn't he just look you up on the Internet or something?" I shuffled my cup from hand to hand in worry.

Simon laughed, "I'm not using the name he knows me by and I don't look the same. I've had a lot of practice at this Millie." He patted my hand.

I wasn't so confident. It seemed to me that Simon was too sure of his own life to be worried, even after scrubbing blood off the upper landing. "What?" I said, just catching up with him, "Is Simon not your real name?" I was stunned and for some reason a little hurt, but that may have been the brandy.

"I left it all Millie, my home, my family *and* my name, if you just escaped why would you bring it with you?" He asked quietly. Okan harrumphed, still intent with the results of the computer. Giving the important things up made more sense to him than it did to me and he'd had more experience of it.

I tried to sleep, but the bed was full of places I couldn't lie on. Cecil grumbled and then went over to the chair and began washing again, as if I had made his fur rumpled with my restless movements. I went out onto the landing and opened the door to my old room. Okan was a quiet, straight line in the bed. His eyes opened and he sat up.

"Is everything alright?" The 'eyes open, brain working' made me wonder what kind of programming he had had to live with from the age of thirteen.

"Yes," I whispered, even though we were alone in the house, if you didn't count the cat. It was as if the shadows had listening rights. Simon had gone for the night. "I just can't sleep," I said, curling up next to him, he curved carefully around me, trying to avoid the wounds on my body with the damage on his. Simon had treated

Okan earlier that evening and told me he was one large, dark bruise from his shoulder to his hip.

"Great," he said quietly, "I finally get you into bed and I can't do anything about it." He sounded as if he was laughing.

I turned slightly and kissed him. "This is some sort of test, isn't it?" He said with exasperation.

I put his arm under and around me and cuddled in. "If it is," I said, "You passed." I slid into real sleep and dreamed of being adrift on wild seas in a boat with no oars.

―――――――

"Do you think the best place for us right now is in the other verse?" I was putting butter on my bagel and feeding Cecil at the same time. He must have ended up a little buttery because he stopped to wash before he ate.

"I can't protect you here. I have a better chance of keeping you from Zatar if we are at the Weldon's farm." Okan was trying to get comfortable in the kitchen chair and was drinking coffee that would have made my eyes water but was considered normal for the average New Yorker. I thought if there was any left over, I could probably do the rust spots on the Mini Cooper.

"Zatar, is that the name of the scientist?" I hadn't heard it before, but Simon and Okan had been talking quietly in the kitchen when I came down. Somehow it suited him.

"That's who we think it is," Simon added, "It's odd, I didn't think he'd have the cranial capacity to pull off anything much above ordering soup and his fashion sense was positively foetal." Okan was looking puzzled, I don't think he completely understood Simon's idea of a put down. But it was doing wonders for *my* blood pressure.

"When are we off?" I asked carefully. Okan had been up early working on the computer and seemed to be much happier with what he'd been able to achieve. It just looked as if it was 'geek speak' to me when I had checked over his shoulder. A language in which I was usually fluent, though there are dialects that I don't comprehend and computer was one of them.

Simon handed me a small bag over the marmalade and coffee.

"What's this?" I asked.

"As I understand from Okan this is good currency in the other verse. As far as I know we still use them in my old verse too."

I opened the bag and a slither of small clear bright stones fell out. Diamonds. "Why would I need these? I pushed them around with my finger; they looked very white and sparkly, and were therefore good quality."

"You can't take the money we use here and you're going to need something to fund your life with." Simon was matter of fact about the details but it made me sigh. My *life* was being taken over by circumstances beyond my control and I felt as if all the important decisions were being made for me. Simon patted my hand. "Whatever you want to do is okay by me. Wherever you want to be. It's the money your parents left you and until we get this sorted out, you're going to need some safe money in that verse."

"I understand, Simon." I stroked Cecil's head as he got up onto the table eyeing the possibility for seconds, having finished his own food. Neither Okan nor Simon seemed to have a cat problem. I thought about the fact that Margery would have had a fit to see the animal accepting an offer of buttered bagel from Simon and curling up in the fruit bowl to eat it.

"We need to leave as soon as possible," Okan said, "I imagine they will try again soon and we don't have much of an advantage due to the temporal differential between the verses."

Simon shook his head like a wet dog. "I swear all that geek stuff affects my brain!"

Suddenly, I realised something. "Simon, have you ever been to the type two verse?"

"Of course," he said. "I was there for several years before I came here. Give my love to Nancy when you see her."

I leaned down and banged my forehead gently on the table several times. Okan rubbed my back in sympathy. "Why is it," I said, in muffled impatience, "That all the things I *actually* know are outweighed by all the stuff I don't know?" I stared carefully at the table. "You'd both better not be smiling when I look up."

We gathered up the belongings I couldn't leave home without and I tidied up, again. Cecil was stunned to be included in the preparations. A small pack was filled with the essentials, including my stash of diamonds. "Okan thinks Weldon knows someone who can convert them into currency for you," Simon said.

"I'll just bet he does," I answered unhelpfully.

"I need to close up the house Millie." Simon didn't look at me. "When you return it may look a little different."

"Do you think I'm going to be able to come back this time?" I was incredulous.

"Yes," Simon answered, "Whether you'll want to stay, well, that's another matter."

I stood in the hall while Okan had a quiet word with my friend. They were obviously in agreement because there was much nodding of heads and shaking of hands. Simon came over and kissed me. Then I grabbed the stunned Cecil and reached for Okan and we dreamwalked through the wheel of an accretion disk and the silent rumble of the singularity, into the hall at the Weldon's farmhouse.

Tara shrieked, "Where have you been?" She was coming out of the kitchen as my brain lifted the web of the universe from my fogged thoughts.

Rari stuck his head through the doorway. "About time. Thought we were going to have to send out a search party."

"That would be me," Joao said, joining him.

It was good to see them and I put my arms around Tara. "I'm sorry I left you in all that mess." I put Cecil on the floor between us where he turned around a few times and staggered a bit. Tara shrieked again, picking him up and squeezing him to her. Cecil looked stunned but he recognised a minion when he saw one, so he put up with the kissing for the appropriate amount of time.

"Flora, come and meet?"

"Cecil," I finished for her.

A small proboscis curled its way around the door, sniffing for potential friend or foe. It stopped probing the air for a moment and then a bright eye and an ear followed. They say elephants never forget. The launch was interstellar and the noise loud enough to have included several of her family members. I caught her up and did some kissing and hugging of my own. Okan looked on for a moment, his face the complete blank of the incredulous male.

"Any coffee in there?" He asked the two men. They nodded in collective testosterone understanding and retired to avoid all things female. As he passed Tara, he helped himself to Cecil who was looking horrified as only a cat can when faced with the unknown. "You don't want any part of that mate," he said to Cecil, "It's emotional stuff."

"What are we saying here?" Tara was sitting down handing out plates of scrambled eggs and hot buttered bread. Okan began eating as if he hadn't just had a full breakfast a matter of minutes ago. "The borderers were in your house! How is that possible?"

Weldon came in through the back door from checking the goats in the barn and shook a light rain from his jacket. I got up and gave him a hug; he hugged me for a moment and then stood back still holding my arms. "You had us worried, Millie." He sat down next to Okan and pinched a piece of hot bread from Okan's plate. "Are you okay?" He patted him on the shoulder and Okan winced and gasped a little. "Right," Weldon said, "That would be no then."

Rari and Joao had paused with food halfway to their mouths, as if they were from an old photograph in freeze frame, forever part of the past. "Please tell me they don't have fixers?" Rari whispered. No one replied. He put the fork down on his plate and his face became glassy pale. "We really are in trouble!"

"I'm hoping not," I added cheerfully, drowning my coffee in cream and sugar and stirring it with a vigorous movement, "One of them was dead when we sent him back. I imagine that might give them something to worry about."

"Not so much as you'd think," Okan said, looking at my coffee with the sort of horror only reserved for a deeply criminal beverage offence.

"A *dead* borderer!" Tara made a face.

Weldon was watching the different expressions on each of us, reading and interpreting people's real feelings. "You're really frightened about this Millie?" My hand shook. I was not used to my defences being transparent. "You know Okan would stand between you and anything. Then there is the rest of us." I wanted to put my head down on the table and cry; it was simply the only thing I really needed to hear. I nodded, because speaking was impossible.

Rari was hoping for more details, but Okan made eye contact with him and his expression clearly said 'later.'

"How is Nancy?" I asked, after a suitable pause when everyone made an effort to return the destructive worms to the metaphorical can. I pinched the other bit of buttered bread from Okan's plate, the fact that he didn't stab me with his knife made me think that our relationship had potential. Tara got up and put more food together with the magic of long practice.

"She asked us to contact her as soon as you got back." Weldon was fishing for more scrambled eggs, then he added three large pieces of bread with honey and ate them in a messy sandwich.

"We can use the farm com and have a chat after breakfast," Tara suggested.

"Is that a good idea," Joao asked Okan, "Do you think it would be better to keep a low profile?"

"I think we're way beyond that." Okan shrugged. "I just don't know. He looked tired and in pain and it frightened me more than the blood dripping down my stairs and the hollow feline features of the draining corpse on my landing. We were all silent. It was as if someone had turned off the lights for a moment. Okan sighed, "I'm okay, I just feel as if I took on the entire NFL by myself in a grudge match."

"I think I'd better take a look at that sonic blast damage," Weldon said, "It's been a while and it should be healed by now."

"Actually, it's not been that long," Okan said, "Don't forget the temporal differential between the verses."

"I don't understand." Weldon looked puzzled. "Are we not running on the same time?"

Okan pointed at me. "That's all the geek I do, ask her for the complete technical explanation."

"Don't put yourself down," I said smiling, "I think you do excellent nerd on several levels."

"Thanks," Okan said to me. He asked Weldon, "Have you got anything for soft tissue regeneration?"

"Just had some new gadget delivered for the livestock, I was hoping for an opportunity to try it."

They got up to go and my attempt to explain the important parts of Einstein's theory of relativity and time dilation drifted off, as they seemed to be preoccupied with crop rotations and the latest gossip from the town. Tara spoke, "You haven't been gone as long in your verse as you have here?" I shook my head. "Well," she said, "That must feel weird?"

Rari and Joao went off to put the herd out into the fields and I could hear Okan and Weldon in the distillery talking quietly. "How is your arm?" I asked Tara. Her wrist had a thin, clear jelly-like tube on it that went up to her elbow. It looked nearly healed.

"It's fine, thanks. I can remove the cast next week. The sonic blast was painful but the doctor at the port was able to stop the internal bleeding without much problem."

Flora and Cecil were eyeing each other from their different vantage points. Flora in a basket by the stove and Cecil curled up on the work surface. Tara reached over for him and put him on her lap. She pulled at his ears and stroked him until he began to purr. "We'll have to get a licence for Cecil *and* come up with an imaginative explanation for how he ended up here."

"Has anyone found out about Flora?" I sat back and tried to find a comfortable position that didn't make me hurt.

"Rari went to the rooms and had to argue with Elsie about taking her. I understand the woman was rather fierce about defending our little friend. In the end she spoke to Nancy who guaranteed that Rari wasn't a port worker or any other evil fiend out to get us! It took a bit of convincing. Rari said he used all his charm but couldn't get around her. I think he was stunned that his usual moves needed some practice!"

"What about the port workers and the gangers, did they come back?" I reached out a hand for the sniffing Flora who was vying for attention, having noticed Cecil's move to Tara's lap.

"Joao said he saw some of the gangers hanging around when he left to take me to the doctor. It's all such a mess, Millie." Tara sounded desperate. I put my hand out over the kitchen table and she took it. "I have missed you," she said, "I mean I love the guys. But it's not the same as us," she trailed off.

"I know," I said, "Sometimes the only way you don't have to explain what you mean is when you talk to another woman."

We got up, abandoning our lap creatures to the basket by the stove. Cecil looked horrified at first at the possibility of sharing a sleeping place with something so obviously beneath him, but Flora began stroking him with her trunk, in a misplaced sense of comfort, much as a child would suck its thumb and rub a blanket, he settled and eventually the steady rumble of contentment emanated from him.

Tara was still struggling with her arm in a cast, so I followed her about the house trying to help by getting in the way. We chatted and laughed about the things that didn't matter and avoided all the subjects that did.

The path of the working day took us outside and the clear, blue-green sky was a warm hopeful treat for the nerve endings. The barn doors were open and we took various mixtures from the bins stacked neatly against one wall inside and went over to feed the nursing mother goats. Tiny dancing kids were making more noise than a school playground full of children overdosed on E numbers.

Between us we made sure that all the creatures were fed, which consisted mostly of Tara pointing and me tipping the mixture into the appropriate feeding trough. Tara checked that all the kids were getting their own adequate supply of food 'on tap' which meant some patient pushing and shoving on our part to get the right parent with the right offspring. "They're good mothers, this particular breed," Tara said, "Patient and uncomplicated," she added. I nodded my agreement as if I actually knew what she was talking about, although there was not usually much on goat breeding in the pages of Science Focus.

Eventually the sun and fresh air called us outside again and we sat for a while on the porch drinking coffee and eating the kind of cake I dream about in other verses. Rari and Joao arrived back from the fields looking slightly muddy, some of the herd had not liked the field that had been chosen for them and had staged a jail break for a more interesting spot. Okan and Weldon came outside, still talking about marketing and stock and something that sounded as if it could have been football results.

They joined us for a while, making the space on the porch seem small with their voices and laughter. Weldon fetched more coffee and they finished the cake between them as if the siege was nearly over and fresh supplies would be coming through the lines at any moment. "Okay," Okan said eventually, "Weldon and I are going out to the check on the cows, can you stay near the house Millie? Rari and Joao will be around." I nodded. Here it was; all the clear bright parts of the day were suddenly overcome with the shadows. I sighed. It wasn't over, just suspended for an unknown length of time to be decided by someone else.

"Weldon," I asked, "This professor you talked about who might know something about the other dreamwalkers. Do you think it would be possible to meet him?"

"What are you thinking, Millie?" Joao looked puzzled.

"I'm thinking I don't want to wait around until Zatar decides to have another go, I want to do something and find out about what's going on."

"I'm not sure there's any doubt about what's happening," Okan said. He looked thoughtful. "But I get your point. It would be nice to stop just reacting to whatever they do."

"Hey," Rari said, half joking, half nervous, "That's fighting talk."

"Yeah well, the thought of getting the first punch in sounds good," Okan growled. He looked as though he was a warrior who had just remembered where he'd left his sword.

"Do you think this professor could help us in any way?" Joao asked Weldon.

"I think," Weldon said, after careful thought, "That it can't hurt to try. It seems we have a big problem if the borderers are now getting involved, and Okan says the fixers are going to make it more complicated," he added, after a pause in which everyone listened to the space of no words, "It's going to escalate into a full-blown war if this goes on much longer."

The day seemed to pass with the usual chores that concern all farmers. Animals and crops, the feed stores and medical problems the vet might need to be called on for. Maintenance of the buildings and the tasks that I didn't understand, but had to be done anyway.

Tara asked me to help her with the bales of cashmere that were going to be delivered to the local spinners and knitters. It felt as if I was plunging my hands into a cloud. I packed up boxes until my sneezing made a drink a necessity. The small light boxes intrigued me; they seemed to be made of a smooth dry substance that looked similar to the coating on my cooking pans. "Teflon," Tara explained, when she saw me looking at them, "We use it for all sorts of things. Do you have it at home?"

"Yes." I nodded. "But it's not used in so many ways."

I thought carefully as I stacked the boxes. Tara was counting and her face was furrowed in concentration. She saw me looking at her.

"What?"

"Do you think Weldon trusts this professor?"

"No." She shook her head. "But he might be able to fill in a few of the blanks." She stopped what she was doing. "I don't know Millie; I guess we're all walking a tightrope." I think the expression on my face must have betrayed my feelings, because she came over and sat down on the nearest box and began rubbing her arm around the edge of the cast where it must have been aching. "Look, I don't think this is just about you anymore. I think that Okan and Rari and Joao will all disappear the way the other dreamwalkers did. I remember them when I was growing up, they went away one by one as if a pogrom was happening and no one knew, and what about Nancy?" I must have looked devastated because she added, "It's not your fault. If you weren't here, it would still be happening."

I sat down next to her and we watched as the afternoon began to turn into evening and we could hear Okan and Weldon coming back from the far fields on the runabout. They were laughing and trading stories about falling off fast moving objects, it sounded as if Okan had won on points, because I heard Weldon say, "I can't *believe* you survived that!" I made a mental note to tell him about my flying attempts off the roof of the barn in Gold Cliffs and Okan's part in it.

"Do you think your parents stopped you dreamwalking to protect you?" Tara asked. I was stunned, she seemed to have the ability to see things that would never have occurred to me. "I'm a parent," she said, laughing at my expression. "If it were me dealing with it, that's what I would have done. Tried to make you look more ordinary, to keep you safe."

"I didn't dreamwalk for several years. You could be right. Maybe they were able to stop me, though I don't know how. I've never been able to control it, until Okan gave me the fixer."

We thought about things for a moment and then Tara did it again, the circus caravan clairvoyance. "It's difficult, the fixer. Do you feel angry with Okan?"

"I think," I said carefully, "That he had no choice; that he did it to keep me close and hoped that he could stay one step ahead of whoever is pulling the strings in his verse."

"I don't think he or Rari are safe from their own people, never mind Zatar," Tara said.

The evening moved carefully over the dusk of the gold and green sunset and we still sat, listening to the unanswered questions and the swirls of impossible fear, I wondered if everyone on the edge of great darkness felt as if they were being pulled in, as though we were waiting for the moment before the guns of war. I closed my eyes and reached for Tara's hand and I watched the massive shape of the wormhole creep towards me. Somehow it was comforting, as if my blood was full of the swirl of star matter and I was part of the event horizon of everywhere. I sat up. "What was *that*?" Tara whispered, "Is that what you see every time you dreamwalk?"

"You could *see* it?" I asked her. She nodded, stunned. I shrugged. "What I am able to do seems to be getting more complicated."

"You *think*!" Tara laughed.

A shout came from the porch. Joao sounded anxious as he called both of us. I sighed, "We'd better go, or we won't be allowed out to play at all tomorrow." Tara snorted.

The kitchen was full of noisy bodies; Flora and Cecil were trying to cause fatal injury by getting underfoot. Weldon was cooking and Joao was doing something dreadful to a loaf of bread. Rari winced and took over, reshaping the slices so that they were edible. Okan came in fresh from the shower and he gave me a hug and a kiss, much to the interest of Weldon and Tara who said nothing, but watched loudly.

"Are you feeling better?" I asked him. I was still dusty, with bits of cashmere stuck to my clothes and hair. A shower sounded wonderful. He smiled at me and nodded, lifting up the edge of his t-shirt and showing me the yellowing bruises that had replaced the painful black ones.

"Nice," Tara said, pointedly admiring the muscles rather than the healing. The rest of the room laughed and Okan blushed, which made my heart jump. Something I hoped no one had noticed.

I went upstairs to Ziggy's room and stripped off. The water was hot and it affected me in the way that makes your DNA remember that once there were gills. I pulled out the type two verse equivalent of jeans and a t-shirt. The material was similar but lighter and somehow the weave was smoother. The black top was tight fitting but not tight, it moved with your body. I turned up the jeans, Ziggy must have been two inches taller than me, or she wore high heels. The slippers were my own, brought with me on the last trip.

Supper was well underway when I got back. A vegetable stew and some rich herb dumplings. It was served with thick cheese on toast and a dark red wine.

The conversation was full of possibilities and a layer of unspoken fears, mainly mine. It was hard to not be sure of where you were, but what was the alternative, buying time in a place I couldn't breathe, in a verse that had no time for me. I felt incredibly bitter for a moment and my face must have given something away, because Tara smiled at me and patted my arm as she poured more wine into my glass.

"Okan?" Weldon asked into another pause when everyone was thinking about something they didn't want to say, "If they can pull you back to your verse anytime they want, why don't they?" Both Rari and Joao were looking to see if all the doors were going to be opened at once.

Okan answered, "They are used to us being away for months," he stopped, "If they don't suspect us of anything," he stopped again, you could hear the goats in the barn and Flora breathing hopefully by the table. He sighed, struggling with what must have been years of programming, "I guess the fact that they haven't pulled us back means we still have some control."

It felt as if someone had let the air out of all the tyres at once. A relief all round. Not exactly an end to the secrets but maybe the beginning of the end. I just caught the fleeting expression on Rari's face as he tried to hide behind a mouthful of stew but he saw me watching him and he smiled and shrugged. He couldn't erase the feelings though and I could see that he was scared. It was as if what frightened him was too ingrained for him to think he could win. Weldon noticed too but he was quicker at making it not seem intrusive. I wondered if the men who fought in the trenches had sat below a night full of stars and talked and laughed with the same sense of loss and longing of what will be. I realised that of course they had.

"Are we going to make an appointment to see Professor Theadus tomorrow?" Weldon asked. A small silence again as we all thought about how dangerous this might be.

"I know you think I'm a stupid woman but I would like to go," I added my bit.

"Actually, what I think is that stupidity is pretty much gender neutral," Rari said thoughtfully, "I also think we should go as soon as possible," he finished.

Flora was making a climbing expedition of getting onto my lap, so I gave up my attempt at getting food past the lump of fear that had taken up permanent residence in my throat and pulled her up. She hooted her gratitude and sat patiently until I gave her a small piece of toast which made Cecil, sitting at his vantage point by the stove, furious.

"You think we're going to lose, don't you Rari?" I said quietly, breaking all the rules. I stroked Flora's beautiful rough skin and she hooted again with anxiety as my eyes filled with tears. No one insulted me by asking what I was talking about. That was the feeling of the men in the trenches; they knew some of them would not be there when they searched for the stars of home again. Rari looked stunned. I got up and went outside the kitchen onto the back veranda, closing the door quietly behind me. Flora cuddled into my neck, sucking a curl of my hair.

I found an old rocker to sit on and breathed in the dark and cool of the evening and watched the goats and cattle in the fields until the feeling of utter despair was not so bad that I couldn't control it. The kitchen door opened and a large shadow moved through the dark towards me. "You'd better wrap this around you," Okan said. He handed me one of Tara's rich, thick shawls and I pulled it over my shoulders and smothered Flora in cashmere, who was delighted at the extra comfort.

Okan sat down on the steps, he put a hand on my leg and I could feel his fingers warm on my skin through the fabric. I whispered, "Don't you feel this is impossible, as if we're all outside trying to get in?"

He said, in a matter-of-fact way as if it meant something to him, "Some of us are born outsiders."

"Yes," I said, "You're right. I wonder if there's a club we can join."

The quiet followed the words and I leaned back onto the rocker and looked up at the night sky that looked the same as the one from my back garden on the moor, but different. The moon, Leda, was reflecting light onto the edge of Jupiter and it was a myriad of coloured layers, a half-sucked gob stopper from my childhood. I pondered on the fact that my mother would ignore the lilac colour of my tongue after one of the forbidden sweets of my history. I realised that I was no good with the past, it held me to a promise I could no longer keep.

"I can hear you thinking," Okan said, his voice smiling. He got up and pulled me to my feet. Flora was scrabbling at the security blanket and I wrapped her in it and put her on the rocker behind me. We went down the steps and out into the moonlight, walking slowly towards the hedge that separated Tara's flower and herb garden from the fields of cattle. He put an arm around me and held me close to him, trying to give me some of his strength.

"Rari has had a more difficult time with all this. He was taken from his family as a small child and the system can be very cruel to someone like him."

"What do you mean?" We had stopped by the hedge and I was leaning on Okan's chest, he had his chin resting on my head. I looked up.

The moonlight was bright enough to see his expression. He looked surprised. "He's like Simon."

"Rari's gay?" I shouted.

Okan's face was a study in not laughing. "He usually likes to keep it to himself, but I guess that's not possible now, as they must have heard you in Gold Cliffs."

He leaned down still laughing and kissed me, his hands were on my face and then in my hair and pulling me into him and I reached around him and curled my fingers in his shirt.

"You two want some coffee and cake?" Joao said from the veranda. His eyes were slightly averted as if he knew what we were doing. "Tara sent me," he said by way of an explanation. Absolving himself from all blame in interrupting.

"Tara is better than the borderers for keeping us apart," Okan grumbled.

"Yes, that and the fact that one of us keeps getting shot," I added helpfully.

"Coffee sounds good," I said to Joao, who was almost through the door back into the kitchen. He waved an embarrassed hand by way of a response.

I scooped Flora up as we passed the rocker; she was asleep and hooted her irritation at being disturbed. "You'll get eaten if you stay out here," I told her. Okan kissed the back of my neck just before we got to the open door and reached around me for another hug. It mattered, that one more demonstration of affection.

Supper was over in the kitchen, but we lingered over coffee and brandy and cake. Weldon handed me a large mug filled with hot water and honey and enough alcohol to kill a horse. He pushed over a plate as I went to sit down. It was a large slice of Tara's homemade cake with the icing already cut off and the cake neatly laid over to the side. Okan began eating the bits of sponge that I never usually bothered with.

It was complicated when people knew you so well. I was used to living with the privacy of loneliness. Being alone is seductive; it sucks you in with the promise of no more pain and loss and just the quiet of your life passing by in moments.

"I have spoken to Professor Theadus, he will see us tomorrow," Weldon said. He reached for his own slice of cake and carefully cut off the top layer. He pushed it over onto my plate and I smiled my thanks.

"Not in *any* way are you getting your hands on mine." Joao guarded his with sticky fingers. I thought about the fact that he'd probably had an icing free childhood and offered him some from my plate. He looked stunned, which made me even sadder. Whatever else my life had been, there had always been the icing on the cake.

The men went out to check the stock. If they checked for other things, they didn't make a song and dance about it, though I would have forgiven a two-step considering the circumstances. Tara and I did the goats in the barn again, feeding and watering the mothers and counting babies to see if anyone had been busy in our absence. Two tiny little twins were being washed and fed by their overindulgent parent, their little bleat lost in the evening noise of the barn.

An unidentifiable sound made both of us look up from what we were doing and Tara produced a small gun from the ankle of her loose trousers with alarming speed and dexterity. I backed towards her and we made it over to the door without taking our eyes from the origin of the noise. Rari came out of the shadows. He was carrying a bag of feed and smiling. He stopped suddenly, seeing the gun in Tara's hand and his grin faded. "I'm so sorry. I thought you saw me. I should have said something when I came in, but you were both busy with the kids." He looked really upset. I realised that Tara was nearly in tears and I must have had an expression on my face that would have been close to terrified.

We sat down outside in the dark and tried the breathing slowly method of calming down, but it took a while. There is only so much shooting a person can take before seeing evil curled waiting in every corner. The surface normality was spread so thin a creak of a floorboard could crack it.

Okan came over and sat down next to me, putting an arm around me. Tara was leaning back against the barn wall with her eyes closed. "Do you think there's even a chance of us getting away with this?" I asked Okan.

"Yes," he said, without a pause for thought.

Rari was carrying the half-emptied feed bag back into the barn. I could see he was trying for another way to apologise. "It's okay Rari," I said, "Just make more noise next time, or Tara's going to shoot you."

"I'll try and remember that," he said, sitting down and patting Tara on the shoulder, as if he was an older brother who had borrowed her phone and lost it.

"You'd better," Tara whispered.

Weldon and Joao were sitting on the veranda in the dark, drinking more brandy and talking quietly about things that sounded as though I wouldn't want to hear them. The odd word drifted over and I recognised the sensation of tension returning with the words, 'dropdown' and 'landing area' and 'borderers.' I sighed, "Nothing about this is okay." Tara nodded but didn't open her eyes.

The drinking outside must have gone on long after I was asleep because the steps outside my door woke me and I couldn't see a clock or my watch, just the familiar face of Jupiter, full and rich in the dark of the night sky. I slipped back into sleep and dreamed of worlds I knew I had never been, in verses that were back through the wormhole.

I showered, playing with the water flow trying to make it stick to the antistatic walls. It was not possible, but fun if you had the time which I didn't. I pondered the fact that had been puzzling me in the night after the dreamwalking had taken me to another verse empty of people. "Okan," I said, as I came down the stairs raising a questioning finger.

"Is this going to be *really* boring?" He asked, exasperated, with the dust of the feed bins about him and the lingering aura of a slight hangover.

"Don't be mean; you know I have this deep-seated fear of not knowing something." We were in the kitchen and I sat down.

"Couldn't you just deal with your fear like the rest of us do by sitting under the table, sticking your fingers in your ears and singing?" He said, with a groan and a grin.

He made for the coffee pot and poured several mugs just as the rest of the men came in through the back door. They filled up the room with maleness and the laughter that goes with early morning and too much night before alcohol.

"Millie's got a question," Okan said to the room. Rari sat down as Joao began breaking eggs into a pan on the stove. Weldon washed his hands and began chopping onions and some fresh mushrooms.

"Oh no, is it really boring," Rari said.

"You were listening at the door. You heard Okan say that!" I whinged.

Tara came into the kitchen from the hall, her hair was wet and she looked desperately tired. I could see Weldon noticing and then Joao, who did his best not to show it. Life was still, after all, more complicated than just being shot at.

"Yeah, I did, actually," Rari admitted. He drank a mug full of coffee and leaned back, holding it out so that Joao could fill it again for him. He looked at me. "Go on then, I can't wait."

I pondered on sulking for a while but Okan raised his eyebrows and poked me in the undamaged side of my ribs. "Okay. Why do we always come here when we dreamwalk, why not the other verses?"

"Good question," Rari said. "If you want a personal opinion, I think it's the quantum singularity equivalent of a downward slope.

Haven't you noticed how much easier it is to get here than it is to get home?"

I thought for a moment. "No, I can't say I have." I let the silence fill the unanswered questions before I asked, "You said something a while ago about the possibility of other verses. Does that mean you've been somewhere else but here?"

Rari put down his coffee mug. "Yes," he said, "But not without help and it was difficult." He drank more coffee. "Have you?" He asked quietly.

"Last night," I said. The room exchanged the inevitable glances of things I didn't understand. "One more significant look is what we all *really* need right now!"

"Sorry Millie, old habits die hard," Okan said. "Where did you go?"

I thought about not answering, but it would have been pointless and I needed to know what they knew. "A verse completely empty of anyone. Very strange, but somehow not threatening. I walked about for hours."

"Do you know what planet you were on?" Okan asked gently, as if coaxing a witness in a difficult trial.

"No." I closed my eyes and reached out for the grass cliffs near the sea, birds were wheeling and diving into the water and I could see a lone bear wandering along the shoreline looking for food. It was cold and clear.

"Millie!" A hand squeezed my arm. I opened my eyes. "Don't do that." Okan said.

"Sorry. Did I verse hop?"

"Nearly," Rari sighed. He looked at Okan. "Could be useful?"

"Why would it be?" I asked, reaching for the plate of eggs that Weldon was passing to me. I smiled at him and he kissed the top of my head the way my dad used to do after one of my flying lessons from a tree had taken a turn for the worse.

"We might need a place to hide," Joao said. Making the world spin into that place of shadows I longed to get away from.

We decided to take the borderer's craft, so as to get everyone in on the trip. It was still in the clearing near the far barn where Weldon kept the runabout vehicles. I ran my hands around the outside, reconnecting with the biomechanical feel. The surface crackled with blue energy and I sensed the waking up of some large and sleepy creature.

Weldon and Okan came back from the far fields, looking slightly dusty from checking the stock and went into the house to clean up a little before they joined us. Joao and Rari were on guard duty, though they tried to make it look as if they were just hanging around. Tara had removed the cast and was flexing her fingers and wrist. The expression on her face made me realise that it must still be painful. I put my arms around her and she hugged me back and smiled. "Your parents must have taught you the benefits of that."

"My mum taught me to take a moment and my dad taught me to take chances," I said, "It was the emotional equivalent of a 'push me pull you.'" She looked puzzled. "Cultural reference to a mythical creature," I explained.

"I *think* I get it," she said.

I leaned towards her and whispered, "I haven't given up on Ziggy and neither should you." She wasn't able to answer because Rari and Joao joined us at the ship with Okan and Weldon just behind them.

"Have you done the preflight checks?" Okan asked.

"Not yet," I said, "I've been doing some deep meaningful shit with the biomechanical interface." They all looked stunned except Tara, who giggled.

"Right," Okan said, "Well, that's not the least bit creepy." He pointed to the open door and smiled at me. I walked through in front of him.

The ship was setting up its process of getting the different systems running. All the little gismos that Rari and Joao had added to make it easier for them to fly it were still attached, as if they were the hopeful science project of a dedicated geek.

"Does any of this work?" I asked Rari.

"Sort of." He shrugged.

"It would be a good idea to make it more efficient. You might need to be able to fly it when I'm not around."

"We're working on it, Millie," Okan said.

I sat in the pilot's chair, getting my back as far into it as I could and still be able to have my feet on the floor. It felt as if it had been built for the giant in Jack and the Beanstalk. I shuddered a bit thinking of the body in my house and the dead feral eyes of the giant, angry even in their blankness.

"Okay Buddy, how are you?" I asked the ship, tapping lighted keys and getting a stream of information on the holo-screen and the head-up display. It made very little sense to me but I tried not to mind. "What are you saying old chap, is everything ready to go?" The holographic screen spun a little, showing a small section in red and some numbers that looked as if they could be weight levels and the air supply. "He says we don't have enough air for a long trip with all of you onboard, but I think he's fine to do a short trip." I turned round to see them all looking at me. "What?" I said.

"That was not right on so many levels," Okan said, shaking his head slowly.

"You just don't know how to treat Buddy."

"Oh no, she's given it a name now!" Joao whispered in a loud voice.

The take off was not smooth, more like a hasty duck on an icy river. Okan was gritting his teeth and trying not to grab the controls. I levelled out and you could hear the sigh of relief as a collective noise. "That was interesting," Okan said.

"That's not the word I would have used," Rari muttered.

"You know you could do this yourself," I grumbled.

"Unfortunately, the connection with any of us lacks a certain consistency," Okan said despondently.

I swung out over the far fields and Weldon leaned out to observe his stock. "They seem to be avoiding one area of grazing." He pointed. "What do you think, Okan?"

Okan got up and went over to the window to see where Weldon was indicating. "You might have a vildenbeast problem." They both nodded in agreement.

"We'd better go and take a look when we get back," Weldon said.

Rari was leaning over my shoulder checking the readouts on the head-up display.

"Is everything okay?" I asked him.

"It seems to be. I don't know how long our program will work though," he said. I must have looked puzzled because he added, "The ship has the ability to regenerate, it might feel the additions we made were a type of illness and heal itself."

"That wouldn't be very good for me," I said, worried. "I can scarcely understand what I'm doing as it is."

"Hopefully Buddy hasn't noticed," Rari said.

The fields of the farm were left behind and Okan came and sat down next to me again. We passed over the mining colony and a few curious faces looked up at us, people scattered in alarm until they saw the international peace sign painted in big letters on the base and sides of the craft. Then their curiosity got the better of them and they stood outside and pointed. I hoped no one had a missile launcher in their lunch box.

I swept around as many of the other settlements as I could, taking the odd direction from Okan, who just pointed every now and then to the left or the right. He seemed more relaxed in the borderer's craft than he had been for days. "It's easier when you're in the air," I said quietly to him. He nodded his agreement, a man of few words for the moment.

I felt my own vertebrae unstitching from the convoluted curves that combined pain and tension. There was something about flying that could give you a sense of freedom and isolation. As if you had left all the difficult things on the ground. Maybe the atavistic memory disappeared as soon as you touched down, but there was definitely something in it that made me sure about the genetics of dinosaur, bird, us, evolutionary connection, even if we did all start out as cyanobacteria.

I watched as Okan tapped a few keys on his jury-rigged attachment and the head-up display and the holo-screen, after careful thought, spat out some helpful suggestions about landing. Twin Rivers was nearly a mile away and the craft wanted us to get nearer and merge us in with the official air traffic. "Listen Buddy, we're not doing that." I added, for the benefit of the cynics in the back, "He seems disappointed." Tara laughed, which put her forever on my list of people to be stranded on a desert island with.

"How about the slip road for the mining colony?" Joao suggested, "It's close and no one uses it unless the weather's bad."

Okan stood up and looked out of the front windows as I did a lazy turn to confirm the possibilities. "Yeah, let's go there." He shrugged in my direction and I set up carefully making the appropriate facial expressions for the best possible landing, which as everyone knows makes an important difference.

We 'parked' close to a scattering of trees and the group got up and out collecting all the personal paraphernalia that people don't leave home without. My backpack was on the floor by my feet and I scrambled around looking for the notepad that had fallen out. Weldon stood next to me and as I straightened up, he passed me a card of the same jelly-like substance all the technical equipment seemed to be made of. "It's your identity card and account." I went to put it in my pack with the com Okan handed me. The card looked as if it was the same one that Tara had given me on our last trip to Great Port. It had been in my pocket when I had been shot and I ran my finger over the damaged area: the raised numbers and a name appeared in a small holographic dance of coloured light. It said, Nole Weldon. "My sister," Weldon explained. "You left it behind in the kitchen of the bar at Great Port. Nancy got it back to us."

Okan had taken several of the diamonds that Simon had given me and disappeared off into Gold Cliffs one morning for several hours. He came back and gave the information to Weldon who then spent the rest of the day in front of the computer in the study. I didn't ask any questions and they didn't give me an explanation. Rules were broken that day in such vast quantities; I think all of the good people in that house, who had come before, must have been spinning in their graves.

We set off from the craft towards the town. I patted the surface of the ship before we left and received an aggressive fizz of static in return. "Is Buddy, okay?" Rari asked considerately, standing next to me.

"He doesn't like being left alone," I said, "This place makes him apprehensive."

"Yeah well, I'm with Buddy," Joao said, "It makes *me* nervous too."

Okan tried not to shake his head, but there was a slight raising of the eyes in amused exasperation. He ran his hand down the small of my back checking to make sure the gun he had given me was still there. It was disconcerting and reassuring at the same time. "Don't go wandering off; we haven't managed any more than a basic connection with the ship, which makes flying it a challenge," Okan said.

"Yeah, that's not the word I'd use," Rari snorted.

It must have looked from a distance as if we were a group of friends out on some local safari to see the wildlife. Okan and Rari were deep in a discussion about setting a trap for the possible vilden-beast that might be back in the far grazing on the farm. Tara was collecting small flowers and leaves that seemed to have medicinal properties from what I could hear of her explanation to Joao, who put all the different samples she gave him into small hessian bags for her.

Weldon and I sauntered at the back enjoying the sunshine and the fact that no one was shooting at us. He handed me a bar of the local artisan chocolate which was delicious. I broke a piece off and gave the bar back to him. "How did your sister die?" I asked gently. It seemed to be important for me to know if I was going to be using her name, anything else felt impolite.

"We had just come out to Ganymede. Some of my past relatives had bought the land from the government in one of the resettlement schemes. But it was all very new and exciting for us. I was a young man, still a teenager really and I decided to come with them. My parents had been lucky enough to be allowed two children and my sister was seven when we came." He paused, his eyes a shadow of remembering, gone back to the faraway places of the past. The sun was warm on my back and I linked arms with Weldon as we walked. He patted my hand. "She was like you, full of life and very curious."

He sighed, "That winter was freezing, the weather net wasn't as efficient as it is now and the seasons were extreme. Nole caught a fever that wouldn't lift. She lasted for a few weeks and then she died." The memory was still fresh in his mind as all loss is even after the years have made grey fools of us all. Grief is the one thing we carry with us wherever we go. Whenever we are.

"I am proud that you think I can use her name for a while," I said.

He focused on my face and then stopped walking for a moment and kissed the top of my head. "You remind me of what is most important to me, family," he said.

The edge of the town was deceptively close and we moved into streets full of people in a moment, as if someone had marked a line on the ground and labelled the two sides, 'country' and 'town' and forgotten the word periphery. I found myself looking over my shoulder every few minutes until Okan leaned over to me and whispered, "Don't keep doing that, you're making the locals nervous."

I knew that all of us had weapons concealed somewhere about. I could feel the gun that Okan had given me at the farmhouse, tucked in the back of my jeans in the small holster that Tara had provided. Rari and Joao favoured the underarm approach and Tara had hers strapped to her ankle. We were a walking army of barely concealed, suppressed aggression. I found myself having to concentrate on breathing, it felt as if there were just too many people too close.

Okan took my arm and did his best warrior impression, trying to make me understand that I was protected. It worked.

The hospital was almost central in the town and came as an unwelcome reminder of past battles. Geographically the university was next door in a sprawling complex of white buildings and stunning artwork. As we turned into the grounds a guard came forward and asked us for 'idents.' He said 'please' and smiled, which was reassuring as was the careless glance he gave our cards. Weldon thanked him in return and then explained that we had an appointment with Professor Theadus. The guard gave us simple directions which involved a lot of pointing and another smile. He turned back to check the cards of the next group of visitors, who looked as if they were shiny faced, hopeful, prospective students on a familiarisation day.

The university was the usual puzzling organisation of lecture rooms and laboratories and offices, with the noise getting lower as we walked further from the centre of the hub. Up some stairs and along a dark corridor was where they kept the dusty professors. Each door had a name on it, some of them with a speciality attached. Okan pointed to a turning on the left and we kept on walking, the sounds of people learning at the tops of their voices had almost completely disappeared.

We were quiet along with the sense of the place, I felt as if I were walking back in time, to the day I went to see my tutor to tell her I was not returning after the summer break. She had been disappointed but not surprised, which had made me even sadder.

Joao seemed nervous, he checked up and down the rows of doors and then looked at Okan. "Couldn't do much here if we got into trouble," he said in a whisper.

It summed us all up, always defending ourselves against the unknown. I wondered from the expressions on each of the dreamwalker's faces, if they had been doing it forever. I realised it was a question that didn't need an answer.

Weldon knocked at the door that said 'Professor Donald Theadus' and underneath the word, Anthropology. Tara was standing next to me. "He's a bit intimidating," she said, "Don't let him get to you."

"Just what I need right now." I jumped back as the door swung aggressively open. "Hi," I said, as everyone else seemed to be at a loss for words.

Okan, Rari and Joao because the man in front of us was no more than four feet tall, and Weldon and Tara because they were in awe of him.

He looked me up and down, and then the people behind me and grunted. Standing back, he let the door bang against the hinges and we followed him in like a bunch of football hooligans who had met their match.

The study was full of books and papers. I think I would have been disappointed if it hadn't been; it also had a vast collection of tribal masks on the walls. They looked on with benign evil, as we tried to settle ourselves into sitting positions in the meagre offerings scattered around. I ended up perched on the side of a wobbly chair with Okan's large frame squashed into it, Rari and Joao sat on the window ledge after removing nearly a lifetime's worth of flies with the books. Tara and Weldon fared better with a chair each. Tara's had a high back and something that could have been ankle and wrist restraints.

The professor saw me looking at the detail carved above Tara's head and said, "It was used to sacrifice the usual ignorant, unsuspecting virgin by a tribe bothered by their local volcanic eruptions." He then gave Tara a narrow, appraising look, as if he were measuring her up for a possible ceremony.

"Is there any other sort of virgin?" I said, "Unsuspecting I mean," I trailed off under the shiny stare of the professor.

I hoped Weldon was going to say something but the silence stretched into epic proportions. "What do you want?" The professor asked, looking from one to the other of us.

"Answers," Okan said quietly, after a moment, when it was obvious that no one else was going to speak.

The professor was silent too after that, then he sighed. "Are you all travellers?" He asked, adding, "Dreamwalkers." As if it was a word he had only just discovered. His chair had a stool in front of it and he leaned forward trying to reach it without getting up. I pushed it with my foot so that it slid in his direction; he didn't smile or say thank you, but pulled it the rest of the way until he could put his feet on it.

His hair and clothes were as cluttered as the rooms and his voice grated as if his throat had been damaged from shouting at disinterested students for too many years. He looked up at me and smiled.

"When does a tragedy become a statistic I wonder?" Then he went into the professorial torpor that usually leads to great thinking in the academic world.

"When enough people die," I said, recognising the similarity to Stalin's thoughts on the subject.

He looked up again as if surprised to see us still there. I suppose it had been a long time since anyone had actually listened to anything he said in the university. Teachers were used to being invisible.

Eventually he spoke, "The internal terrorist wars were reaching a peak and people were seeing evil everywhere. I was working for the central planet's scientist guild. We needed volunteers for the programme we were running. It was exciting for us. Travellers from other verses had always been around, and there was maybe two hundred years of shared technology." He shrugged, looking very sad and said quietly, "We were young."

The silence filled up the shifting shadows with unsolved mysteries and I wanted to reach across and pat the knotted hands of the man as he suffered in his memories. It looked as if the pseudoachondroplasia had caused osteoarthritis in his joints, which meant he would have been in pain all the time. I wondered why, in the obviously superior type two verse, he had not been treated.

"What happened?" I asked. Though from the expression on his face and the little that Weldon and Tara had already told me it was obvious that something terrible had occurred.

He shrugged. "The tests were going well. All the different groups were in the building at the same time, we were having a conference about the results we were getting and it was a chance for people to meet someone from a different verse."

Okan interrupted, "How many different verses were there?" It was a sharp question and loaded with unspoken importance.

Professor Theadus smiled. "Five."

I know it stunned me and I could see the rest of them counting it off, my verse, Okan and Rari's verse, Joao's verse, the type three verse that the technology and my parents came from and the one we were in now. "You mean including this one?" Okan asked.

The professor smiled again and then with great deliberation, slowly shook his head. "I mean five *not* including this one."

We all took a moment and tried to think about the possibilities. The professor was a fisherman casting his net over and over, patiently waiting. I didn't know why it was a shock, why should it have been, if *we* were all here why not someone else. I thought back, trying to remember if anyone from the original gang might have been from the other verse; then gave it up. Children don't talk about quantum mechanics, or maybe some of them did, me for example.

"What happened?" Rari said, bringing us back to the study and the past and the problems.

The professor tried to push the memories away but you could see they were fresh, as if it had happened yesterday. We all had those thoughts that brought with them new pain. "There was a bomb and a suicide bomber and an end to all the hopes and dreams of people like me." He spoke in that blank matter of fact way that denotes an unhealed wound and the truly damaged. "We were young and naive," he said again, as if it explained everything, "We didn't *understand* people's fear. They believed you had a sort of swarm technology; that you could communicate over large distances with each other."

I snorted, "I can't communicate over very *short* distances with this lot!" I pointed at the men and Tara laughed her appreciation. But we were all sad. The silence stretched again into uncomfortable places.

"This other verse, what do you know about it?" I asked curiously.

"Type two like this one, helped along with their technology by the type three verse. They felt no threat from their own people and were in the process of opening a negotiation for 'a greater understanding.'" Professor Theadus made quote marks with his painful fingers. He sighed, "We lost everything that day. It was as if we spun back towards the Dark Ages."

I thought about this for a while, the fact that they had had a time called the Dark Ages was interesting and that our paths had only diverged when the type three verse had helped the other type two verses along with their technology; but not Joao's verse or Okan and Rari's, or mine. I wondered who had made the rules and why. Possibly it had just been a matter of star matter. I didn't think it was difficult to get to my verse, but Okan and Rari had both said it was an 'uphill' journey to some destinations. Then maybe I'd got it wrong. I fingered the fixer on my face and tried not to add up numbers I couldn't identify to start with.

"What do you know about the borderers?" Okan asked the professor.

He laughed, "Their motto is 'when we fight, we know our dead do not abandon us.' What else is there to say?" He sighed, "They have a hidden society based on the hive structure. A leader, usually male, an upper hierarchy that consists mostly of scientists and strategists and a group of expendable foot soldiers. Each unit works in complete autonomy, they have factions and alliances and they fight amongst themselves sometimes. Hate the takeover of their territory as they see it. They were made and abandoned by a callous government for a war no one remembers. Their reproduction process was interfered with at the genetic level so they have very few females naturally and they compensate by taking women from the colonies." He paused. "I have interviewed the occasional survivor of a kidnapping. It often involves the psychological connection syndrome, of post-traumatic stress." He shrugged at the end of the information trail.

I could see that he hadn't told Okan anything that he didn't already know. He wasn't disappointed, more reassured as if it confirmed the possibilities.

Okan leaned forward in his wobbly chair. "What do you think the borderers want?"

"A future," the professor said simply. "Any future. As all tribes that live on the periphery, they face extinction. Them more than most I think." He sagged into his bent shoulders. Tired with all the questions and the feelings they must have engendered.

"Have you met anyone from the type three verse recently?" Rari asked casually.

Professor Theadus looked stunned. "Are they here again? Why would they come to see me?" He studied our faces. "No," he said. "You are the first travellers I have seen for a long time."

As we got up to go, I leaned down and gave the professor a hug. He looked as if no one had touched him for a long time, as if the hugging mechanism in his body was rusty from lack of use.

"Thank you," I said.

He looked up at me. "Be careful," he said, then he added as an afterthought, "All of you."

The sunshine was a warm welcome to the outside world. A place where people were not forgotten and the memories of the young students were so fresh, they had no power to cause pain yet. All experience being tinged with the hope of new things.

A strange, quiet group of outsiders made no impression on the town in amongst the rest of the dwellers getting on with their collective lives. We walked along in silence for a while and struggled with the various bits of information that had sparked a different thread of thought in each of us.

"Do you think he was lying," Rari asked Okan, "About seeing people from the type three verse?"

"Yes," I said, as Okan had just shrugged in a preoccupied way that was making me wonder what was going on, "He was also very nervous."

"Understandably so," Weldon said, checking carefully behind him by using the technique of stopping to look at something on a stall as if buying supplies. I realised it was for the third or fourth time since we had left the university. Joao fell back and disappeared down a side street and our pace picked up a notch.

The next time we stopped at a stall I bought a bag of the local small cakes, sweet and round with a type of marshmallow cheese in the centre. Okan was tucking the fold of his trouser into his boot and in a moment, he had transferred another weapon into the palm of his hand, hidden by his sleeve. "I can't believe you're buying food," he said, smiling as we started off again. Rari was close in front and Weldon had dropped behind a pace.

"I always get hungry when I'm frightened and anyway," I added, eating a cake, "If someone is watching it will look more natural if we have actually bought something."

Tara held out a hand. "Give me one of those, maybe it will work for *my* fear."

People were getting sparser as the edge of the town drew nearer. Fewer stalls and shops and fewer crowds to hide in. I saw Joao at the junction to a side street; he had been running and was out of breath. He signalled Okan with a slight hand movement and I could feel the tension building between the men. "Are we going to get hit?" I asked.

"I think the professor made a call as soon as we left the room," Rari said.

"I don't think he had a choice," Okan answered.

We were nearly running. I could feel the pressure of Okan's hand on my arm. I tucked the bag of cakes into a pocket of my backpack and then reached carefully for the gun in the holster at the small of my back. I clutched it to me thinking its proximity might make me feel more confident. Then smiled to myself, remembering the fact that it hadn't made any difference the last time I had to use it. The places where I had got shot before began to tingle with the memories of nerve endings not quite healed.

Tara was having trouble keeping up and so was I, the pace Okan and Weldon were setting made it look as if something was about to happen. "Okan," I said, exasperated, "Who is chasing us?"

"I don't know." Okan didn't look back, he just got hold of my arm and made me move faster. "Joao says it's more than six people moving fast. If I had to guess I'd say whoever Zatar was able to hire."

"Either port workers or borderers or both," I huffed, out of breath.

"I think they'd probably notice a few borderers in town so I suppose *I'd* go with the port workers," Weldon said, through well-paced gasps.

The track to where we had left the ship was a blur of grass verges. Rari dropped behind and disappeared through the trees and I hadn't seen Joao since the side road in town. I was hoping a small ambush had been planned for this sort of occasion in one of my many absences. I could hear running feet, certain in their strength and numbers and we increased our pace again until my lungs felt as if they had been stuffed with cotton wool. I saw the edge of the craft appear in the curve of the road and tried not to look around. Too late, one glance. The running feet were gaining, faces full of the glee of pursuit and the image of capture.

A small spurt of earth erupted close to me, catching the top of my shoe and making me stumble, Okan gripped my arm again and dragged me back upright, but it nearly tipped Tara over trying to avoid me. "Sorry," I said, in pointless politeness.

"No problem," she gasped back. Fear and good manners running neck and neck.

Someone shot back, Rari, on a parallel course and half hidden, had caught one of the men and he spun in a vicious circle and fell causing a murderous traffic jam on the narrow track. The rest of the men howled like a pack of dogs after a bear. Unreasoned feelings older than time for all of us; pursuers and pursued playing a part.

I could feel the thought of locking myself into the ship and into safety creeping up on me, right up to the moment when I saw the men guarding the craft, each in the firing position he felt comfortable with, lying, kneeling or standing edge on to the figures coming fast up the road. Us. Okan dropped to one knee and pulled out his gun. The shots were vicious and accurate and Weldon shoved me out to the side and fired in the squat half crouch that most people use when they want to make themselves as small as possible a target, but still keep moving.

We were trapped between the two groups; our only advantage was that these men had been told to keep us alive. How long that would have lasted when their friends were dropping around them would have been anyone's guess. At some point you stop fighting for money or motive and start fighting for the man next to you and you don't care who's paying.

Tara and I went for different trees and took up opposite positions, firing up and down the track. A flicker of movement caught at the bark next to my face and a sting of a chipping slashed my forehead causing me to shout out, more in surprise than pain. Okan was distracted for a second and the thud of the bullet was a sickening sound into the meat of his shoulder, throwing him backwards onto the ground. He got up, grabbing at the blood as it pooled on his clothing.

I went to move towards him and Tara snatched at a handful of my clothing, preventing me. Her face showed the tiredness of the feelings I couldn't seem to quantify. I wanted to sleep for a week. Okan had moved out of the line of sight and shoved a wad of torn shirt against the wound. He waved me back to the tree line and I found myself taking careful and considered aim at the shapes that had stopped being people.

I had this 'gift,' one that I discovered at a clay shoot on Exmoor. When I was angry, I could hit anything I aimed at. It was a wicked blessing and I didn't remember it most of the time because it required a level of commitment for a piece of me that I was not sure I wanted to own. The gun melded inwards and I forgot the measured breathing in and out and 'aimed for the centre of everything.' Which was the only bit of advice my father had ever given me on the subject, as he watched in bemused interest while I demolished the competition and went off with the much-coveted winner's trophy. It had happened because one of the school bullies had told me I was a pathetic idiot and it had made me furious.

I was angry now. The gun filled the horizon and the thought that each object was a living person became something to remember later. I kept firing and I kept hitting the centre of the target. The consequence was, those men who were still standing and firing back at us, were madder than hornets.

Someone touched my shoulder. Careful not to get between me and the anger, but insistent. "Millie! Hold your fire for a moment." The hand was shaking me, trying to reach through the inner voices, the ones that said, 'keep firing until they're all dead.' Joao's face loomed and then reached an outline of focus. "I think they're backing off," he tried to say as I lowered the gun.

"Is Okan okay?" I asked, not recognising my own voice, which sounded as if I had swallowed everything above the Arctic Circle. "Because if he's not." My gun came up again.

"He's fine," Joao said gently, pushing the weapon down. "Or he will be once we get him to a doctor."

The noise had stopped and I looked around. Weldon was still on the ground behind a large rock, Rari was close to Tara and both had trees as cover. Okan was half sitting with his back against a stump; he waved us further away from the road. The shooting was over in everyone's head except for the bodies that were lying scattered around in the impossible, careless positions of death. Each angle of head and arm an indication of how they had died; as if they had been washed up by the river of life for the last time.

I slumped back and squatted down, the gun resting on my knee. Joao removed it from my paralysed fingers with care. He leaned down and patted my head. "I hope you're never mad at me," he laughed. The end of the sound was cut off by an absurd slap of movement and I looked up. He was falling towards me, his mouth still smiling, but his eyes nearly blank. Tara screamed and staggered towards us and I caught Joao as he fell and we slipped towards the empty space of in-between. The mass of the quantum singularity swirled towards me and I pushed back for the first time in my life but it felt as if I was fighting a cloud of wire mesh, impossible.

The cave floor came up to meet me and I banged down with Joao in my arms and the weight of him knocked me back and my head hit the ground hard and all the anger dissipated in one moment of stunned silence.

I could feel the damp from the stone seeping into my soul and the hard rocky surface sticking into the unprotected areas of my back.

I shivered; it was much colder here. Joao was unconscious and bleeding. I pushed him gently off me and pulled at the pack that was half off my shoulder, glad that it hadn't gone missing on the way. A small, stray thought about a lost and found depot somewhere on the edge of the singularity, manned by the grumpy universal counterpart of the British Rail worker, crept into my mind and I sniggered. The sound echoed through the cave making me start.

The two extra layers I never left home without, were rolled into the top of the pack and I put them on, a thin cashmere sweater and a waterproof jacket, it was not much but they helped with the bone aching cold. I shuffled around for the first aid kit Tara had given me. Joao groaned and I touched his shoulder gently trying to keep him still, but he came fully around and then made an effort to sit up. He decided against it as the pain hit with a force that shook both of us. We agreed silently that he wouldn't do that again.

I pulled at his bloody shirt and we both looked at the wound site. Nasty, but not pumping. The bullet had gone all the way through the meaty part of his side, leaving a shocking hole but not much damage. He nearly passed out again as I began washing the area with some of the antiseptic. I sprayed the substance they used as an antibiotic in Tara's verse, before I poured the jelly-like protection onto both the entry and exit wound and let it set. We were both sweating with shock by the time I had finished. Having doctors as parents didn't prepare you for the messy painful process.

I leaned back against the side of the cave wall and tried to get my breath back. My head felt as if hot needles were being pounded into the base of my neck and my eyes seemed to be a bit blurry.

Joao indicated with one weak finger. "Did you hit your head?"

I nodded. "Where are we?"

"My verse," he whispered.

"I worked that out. Where exactly?" I touched the place on my skull where the pain was worst and came back with slightly bloody fingers. Great, both of us were bleeding. My head felt stuffed with feathers and I was beginning to feel sick. It didn't take a great medical leap to remember what the symptoms for concussion were.

"This is the point where the wormhole picked me up and spit me out when I was a child. I used to come here to sleep, it was a safe place." Joao was in pain and he gritted his teeth on the last part.

"Sorry. I forgot the most important thing." I reached for the pack again and got out a pressure syringe of analgesic. I pushed it against his arm and he smiled his thanks. "Just don't go to sleep."

He took a deep breath in as the pain receded and slid carefully upright into a slight sitting position. "Watch it," I said, "I have no idea if you're bleeding internally." He smiled and his eyes closed. "Joao! Stay with me," I shouted, but he didn't hear me.

I pulled him carefully back down and put him on his side. Then checked around and picked up my gun which Joao had dropped when we arrived. It still had plenty of charge in the laser part and I topped up the squat, deceptively benign looking bullets from my pack. Tucking the weapon into the holster in the small of my back I felt inappropriately reassured, as if I now lived a life that required being armed along with the other necessities of appropriate dress, as in my underwear and trainers.

Joao was breathing deeply and his skin was a good colour. Sleep was the best cure for shock and pain and sometimes our body's healing mechanism takes over and gives us what we need despite ourselves.

The entrance to the cave was misted, but bright. I walked towards it, touching the cave walls as they sparkled with something that could have been pyrite. The spray came from a waterfall that was just to one side, it spluttered and rippled in the sunshine, not so much of a thunder of water, more a good hefty trickle. The drop below into the pool was vertiginous and I moved my feet back from the narrow ledge with care. No wonder Joao had felt safe, no self-respecting gazelle would traverse the path up without a stiff drink for courage.

The rustle behind me and Joao's whisper made me turn, it was a moment before my eyes adjusted to the gloom, as the sunlight didn't reach into the back of the cave.

"Sorry, I passed out again." He moved carefully, fiddling to get something from his pocket. I went to help and smiled as the contents spilled over the ground. It was a small boy's hoard of odds and ends, only older and somehow sadder. I noticed a bag of specimens that he'd been collecting for Tara and had obviously forgotten to give back. "This is a signalling device that I use to contact the settlement where my mother is." He held it out to me.

It was similar to the com units that Tara and Weldon had. I wondered if there had been any crossover. "Did you bring this here Joao? From the other verse I mean." I fingered the jelly-like back. A small hologram sprang out from the surface.

"No. Before the war we had a reasonably sophisticated technology. There's still some left, but not much infrastructure. It's basically a hand to mouth existence, though people have banded together in groups now. Built back up on what was there." He shrugged, making what must have been a terrifying childhood into something possible to live with. We all needed a manageable past. I wondered again about where the type three verse people had dreamwalked to, if they had in fact come to Joao's verse.

The red dot in one corner of the com began to wink in a steady rhythm. "If I pass out again don't leave the cave, it's still not safe, lots of gangs find it's easier to take from those who have, rather than work to get something." His warning was light and clear and full of the unspoken menace of his childhood. He pointed. "Over there are some stores I keep for emergencies."

I went to look. The back of the cave was a series of several smaller curves, as if a long-ago dweller had decided that he needed to create a few bedrooms. In reality it must have been a natural event, maybe water from the look of the smooth walls, but I much preferred my original idea of some cave dweller with a Neanderthal architect and a practical partner.

The tidy storage stacked in the 'back bedroom' made me smile even more, as it was everything you might need for a siege. I picked up a handy torch and made some effort to find something to eat. One bag held a variety of energy bars that were a mixture of sweet and savoury. Not exactly macaroni cheese, but it would do.

Joao was trying to look as if he didn't need more pain relief when I got back. "Is there any chance you could do a trip through the wormhole?" I asked hopefully.

He shook his head. "No, not yet." He tried to fill in the gaps. "I'd rather you didn't go back on your own, I mean you could go to your verse or Tara's, but it might be a problem."

"I understand, so could the borderers and Zatar and I think we all need a break and the easiest way is for me to be somewhere the type three scientist doesn't usually go." I settled back down on the cold floor working out the details.

"I can see you thinking," Joao said, smiling.

"Have any of the type three dreamwalkers been here to your knowledge; or anyone else from another verse?" I asked him.

"I don't think it's likely that there's only the one place in each verse where the wormhole is closest to this doorway, or crossing place; Okan calls it an energy barrier and it seems *unlikely* that we're the only ones with the dreamwalk gene." He shuffled around on his back trying to get into a pain-free position. "I don't know Millie, Rari's the one who knows all this. He says that the gene makes us 'attractive' to the quantum mechanics of the universe." He added, "Whatever *that* means."

"I think I know," I said, "It's as if we have the key and can unlock the doorway."

"You would," he said, with a smile and a great deal of affection, "You and Rari 'the professor' are the biggest geeks I've ever met."

"Do you think we're safe here?" I asked, leaning on the wall next to him, my head was still hurting and my eyes blurred every now and then making me feel sick. He pointed at the fixer on the side of his head and made a face instead of shrugging his shoulders, which was not possible when you were lying down.

It was easy to forget the fixer, the tracking device and aid to safe wormhole travel. I rubbed the side of my face and fiddled with the small bump. "Does it make a difference?"

"Again, you need to talk to Rari," Joao sounded really tired. "As far as I know it helps to get a neater connection between the quantum singularity and the subatomic changes in our bodies. Okan said it would be like learning to ski without an instructor if you didn't have it."

"Yes," I said, "I can imagine he would know!" We both laughed, which caused a momentary gasp of pain from Joao and me to clutch the ground as it spun. He grabbed my arm as I must have looked a bit hazy. "Don't worry I'm still here; anyway, can you picture it if I went back without you, Tara would go interstellar never mind ballistic."

The quiet was filled with the usual unanswered questions. I sighed, "What does Rari teach?" It seemed one of the easier things to talk about, but I could see Joao was troubled by it.

"He's with a group that 'instructs' people about the science and history of the dreamwalkers." He explained it carefully as if the word was a substitute for something much more sinister. I opened one eye and looked at him. "He always says it feels as if he's betraying his family every day, I know he hates it. I don't think he and Okan have worked out a way to keep us out of the organisation's line of sight." I pointed at myself. "Yeah, they're as interested in you as the type three verse is." We both paused for more pain-filled thoughts. So much for the easy questions.

I sat up eventually and checked his wound site watching the area closely for blood leaking, but it remained dry and I could see through the clear dressing that the bullet hole was angry but not inflamed. "It must really hurt," I said, reaching for the analgesics again.

"I need to stay awake, don't give me any more just yet." He held my hand with the pressure syringe away from him. "If they come, I need to talk to them. People are suspicious of strangers around here."

"I suppose a war will do that to a society," I said. The gun in my back holster suddenly felt more important than it should have been.

"If things look as if they're not going so well, if one of the gangs finds us, just verse hop, don't think about it, just go." He gripped my arm even harder, making sure I understood what he was not saying.

Joao was exhausted by all the talk and I put a hand on his arm to make the most of the unspoken contact that would stop me spinning away into another verse. We rested in our uncomfortable pain and the memories of things not right and didn't speak too much for a while. I closed my eyes and tried not to want the comfort of my friends and somewhere else apart from a cave in the side of a hill behind a waterfall, where gangs roamed around looking for an easy option and people were suspicious of strangers.

The small red light was still flickering on the com unit Joao had in his hand, but the evening was closing in and I was worried about us staying the night on the cave floor. I went to the back where the stores were and hunted around for more layers, finding musty sleeping bags and some blankets. They felt slightly damp but it was better than the bone cold of the stone. Joao shuffled around so that I could get something underneath him and I wrapped the blankets around his body. "I suppose a fire is out of the question?" I asked.

"It would be like a flare saying 'come and get me.'" He smiled. "The people at the camp should be here soon, it's not always possible to just leave the safe areas." He looked embarrassed as if the fact that the post apocalypse security, or lack of it, was his responsibility.

"It's not always a good idea to wander around Exmoor at night in my verse," I said.

"You're just trying to make me feel better," he replied sadly.

"Actually yes," I laughed, "Though you might just get mistaken for a rabbit and get a shotgun full of pellets in your back if the poachers are out 'lamping!'"

The cold was beginning to get to me and I pulled the blankets over the two of us and cuddled up to Joao for warmth. He sniggered as I put my arms around him. "I'd get Okan poking me in the nose if he could see us now."

"Yes, and I bet Tara would have something to say about it too."

He was silent for a while. "Tara has a partner and Weldon's a good man."

"He's also not stupid," I added, "He knows and he deals with it."

"Don't want to push it in the man's face though," Joao said gruffly.

The cuddling was having an interesting if awkward effect on Joao. "Sorry," he said, and then we both ended up with a fit of the giggles.

"Why is it so cold!" I got up and searched for more blankets in the back of the cave again, coming back and adding them to the pile around us.

"We're in British Colombia Millie, it's still spring; luckily we don't have snow."

I sat up. "Canada!" I didn't know why I was so surprised. "It's early autumn in my verse."

"Temporal differential," Joao said, "I know it's difficult to work out."

"It's spring in Tara's verse too," I sighed.

"That's more complicated as they have more than one spring season."

"Aah!" I said, adding, "You're from British Colombia?"

"Sure, I told you both Rari and me are from near Vancouver, but different verses."

"I suppose if I had ended up sharing a wormhole experience with an unconscious Okan we would have come out somewhere near Central Park."

I cuddled back down making us both part of an enormous cocoon of battered blankets and musty sleeping bags. "Is there a border between Canada and America in this verse?"

"Yeah, but not much of one," he sighed.

I watched the sun setting through the cave entrance and the rainbow of light that the mist from the waterfall created on the walls. A small sound that was not part of anything around us made Joao sit up gently. He pushed me away from him and untangled the arm that had been around me from the blankets. I pulled my gun from the holster and held it to my side, crouching on my heels and trying to blend into the pattern of shadows.

A small buzz of whispered voices metamorphosed into men creeping slowly up the twisted path. Joao sweated himself into a nearly standing position; it must have hurt, because his face was twisted in pain. He didn't have to put his finger to his lips; I understood that I needed to keep still at all costs. His gun was one of those that Okan used, similar to mine, a combination of laser and projectile. He held it close to his body and leaned on the wall for extra support. He figured that if he was standing, they might think twice about attacking us; although it wouldn't take a second glance to see that we were no match for anyone armed with pillows, never mind anything else. A cave is not a good place for a firefight, maybe better than a kitchen, but not by much.

I tried not to think about being anywhere else, a strong sense of needing to see Okan and check out his damage for myself was hard to fight and the edges of my vision blurred, making the cave walls shimmy and dance. I suppose I thought that we would be going back to Tara's verse on the turnaround, that Joao's ability to verse hop was better than mine and the physical damage would not be a mental barrier. I sighed and pulled back from the desire to run and hide somewhere different, it seemed important to start finding an ending to the journey that had begun with a child and a dreamwalk.

A face appeared around the side of the entrance and a small hand waved. "Joao it's me, Truda." Joao didn't just relax, he crumbled.

Curling down into a ball, I caught him before he hit the ground. A group of people came into the cave; they held torches that were partly concealed by bits of cloth to reduce the light. Truda helped me lie Joao down again and she smiled. The faces of the men standing behind her were watchful and hard, suspicious with layers of experience.

Joao pointed at me. "This is my friend Millie." Then he fainted again.

The trip to the 'enclave' as Truda called it started off as a serious slog. It began to rain, the really cold wet Canadian type, that doesn't leave an inch of you untouched. One man went out in front, followed by two men with Joao on a makeshift stretcher between them, followed by me and Joao's mother and then two heavily armed men. "We don't go anywhere with less than this," Truda explained, when I looked puzzled by the process of getting back to where they lived.

It was a special forces level of operation, creeping through the undergrowth at one point when one of the men did a recce, making us wait in the darkness while he moved on ahead and checked out the path. He came back scaring the skin off me by standing next to me before I realised that he was there. I could see his teeth as he grinned in the moonlight, displaying the sense of humour that is attached to a steep, aggressive learning curve. It reminded me of Okan and Rari and I resisted the temptation to thump him.

"Not that way," he whispered to the others, he pointed to his left and we moved off the path and went through the forest, Joao was bumped around but he never made a sound. I felt as if I could do some whimpering for him, but resisted the temptation. Truda moved forward at one point and patted him on the shoulder, I saw him touch her hand. They didn't speak. I wondered if now would be a good time to head off home and what Okan would say if I did. My house on the moor and the warm downie on my bed began to call me from all corners of my mind. I tried to remind myself of the dead borderer on the upper landing but it just didn't seem real. Nothing did.

Having a crisis was never a convenient thing at the best of times, but on a rainy night in British Colombia in a different verse it was suicidal. I stopped, causing a traffic jam of grumpy men. My breath came in ragged gasps and I tried to remind myself of how easy breathing used to be. The leaves on the trees lashed water down the back of my neck, making it feel as if I was standing in a power shower fully clothed.

The man who had been leading the group and had frightened me with his creeping around in the dark tactics, came back to see what the problem was. He whispered, "What's up?" Holding onto my arm as I was hyperventilating so much standing had become difficult. I shook my head. "We can't stay here," his whisper was urgent, "The gangs are roaming around looking for easy prey and right now that's us!" I nodded. The dark was folded into thick layers and he held a torch close to his body so that the light was a small pool against his chest. "Come on," he said not unkindly, pulling me towards him and giving me an unexpected hug, patting my back as if I was a child. "We're nearly there," he whispered into my ear, "Then you can get dry and sleep some."

It worked. I stood back and nodded. Speaking would have been out of the question, but walking was okay. He went back to the front of the line and we moved off. The man behind me leaned forward and said, "I'd have left you."

We travelled for what could have been another hour, but was probably only ten minutes. The rain seemed to have taken on a vindictive edge so that we were slipping and sliding in the wet leaves and mud. Every now and then it was necessary to manoeuvre Joao over a log or ditch, making the two men carrying him vulnerable to whatever danger was around us. The leader stood watching the forest and the last man moved back down the barely there, trail. Truda helped the men support Joao and I did my best to see footsteps in the dark.

Something at the corner of my eye moved in the close line of the trees. I turned my head to one side to get a better look without the interference of the blind spot. A ruffle of shadows had my attention. I pulled my gun from the holster in the wet layers of my clothing and held it pointed to the ground, listening. The forest was full of the patter of rain and the sway of wind in the upper branches. The careful feet of the men moving Joao were interspersed with suppressed grunts of effort. I watched the place where I had seen something. I tapped a ring on my finger against the barrel of the gun to get the attention of the leader and his head turned towards me, although I couldn't see his face. I pointed.

They were forest sharks. Silent and greedy, following us and waiting until we were accessible.

My gun came up and I fired as the first of the gang came in from the trees. A carefully aimed shot dropped the man just as he reached out to grab hold of me. He was close. I could feel his breath on my face when I fired. I leaped onto the log that Joao had been lifted over and then dropped to the ground behind it; raising my head sideways I sighted another figure pulling at Truda and trying to drag her toward the thicker foliage, I took careful aim as she punched him full in the lower regions of his body, he fell as I fired. Truda hopped over the log and landed awkwardly on her side next to me. We didn't speak. She moved snake-like over to Joao who had dragged himself up to a sitting position and was firing at moving targets with the tiredness of long practice.

I saw the man who had been watching our backs on the trail running to join us, it looked as if he had tripped on a root or hole in the ground, then he spun as he fell and I realised he had been hit. The noise of gunfire and shouting and the muddle of people trying to find the same cover spilled over into them and us. Using the log as a barrier I crawled as close to the injured man as I could. He was still, but for a small distressed movement in one of his hands, as he felt for the wound.

Slithering towards him I reached out an arm and grabbed a handful of clothing. He grunted. It must have hurt. I braced myself against the edge of the branches that fanned out in a tangle, giving the false illusion of protection. I pulled. He was heavy, but the mud acted in our favour and he slid towards me. The sputter of chipped wood hit my face as one of them shot directly at me. Truda shouted and the cover fire distracted them away from us for the moments it took to pull the injured man behind the log.

We gasped for breath as if we were landed fish and I could feel the sticky traces of blood on my skin mixed in with the mud and rain and the wet leaves that stuck to everything. He patted my arm as I reached to see if I could do anything about his injury. "There was me thinking you were a stupid woman," he said.

"The jury's still out on that." I ducked down as the smatter of bullets traced a pattern on the protective wood near my head, then fired a round at the irritating shadow leaning against a nearby tree; I was rewarded with a curse and the sound of a body falling. One more angry ghost to feed my night-time fears.

The noise ended as suddenly as it had begun. We stayed in our safe, dirty, wet rabbit holes for a few minutes savouring the silence and a return to the sound of rain on the leaves. I sighed, reaching for the emergency kit in my pack and hauling out a compression pad with the resignation of a trench veteran in the lull before the next wave. The wound was deep into the muscle of his shoulder and the puddle of blood welled into the rivulets of water coming off the log. I pressed hard enough to make him swear and hiss through clenched teeth, "My name's Carson."

"Pleased to meet you Carson," I said, pushing harder against the wound.

The leader of the group disappeared off into the undergrowth, he whispered to the other three men before slipping quietly into the shadows. "What's he doing?" I asked Truda, as the three men moved into a keeping watch stance in defensive positions. She was holding a torch so that I could work on the damage to Carson.

"He's gone to check for survivors and to see if the gang has really left us alone," Carson said through gritted teeth, as I put the packing gel into the ragged hole.

I heard a shot and we all paused to look in the direction of the sound, nothing came back but the wind rattling the branches of the trees. "I guess he found a survivor," Truda muttered.

Joao was reloading his gun with the deliberate painful movements of bitter experience. His face in the dark was a white circle with the mocking black eyes and mouth of a circus clown.

I shivered in the wet clothes that flapped around me and tried to remember the vital things about keeping people alive; then I remembered that I didn't actually have any training in treating injuries and sighed with frustration. If being a doctor's child had taught me one thing it was that sometimes you knew enough to know you didn't know anything. "Do you have medical training where you come from?" Truda asked, with excellent timing.

"No. I work in a bookshop," I said, making Carson groan. I still hadn't forgiven him for the crack about leaving me in the forest.

"How far are we from the settlement?" I tapped the gel dressing in place and watched for the giveaway signs of blood seepage.

"No more than twenty minutes' walk now." Truda turned the torchlight so that I could see the dressing on the exit wound as I gently helped Carson to roll onto his side.

"Both Joao and Carson are going to need to see a real doctor and they both must have antibiotics. I can't guarantee that there isn't anything nasty lurking in the tract dragged in by the bullet and I'm not sure that I was able to stop the bleeding. This gel can act as a pressure dressing, but still," I drifted off and shrugged my shoulders.

The leader of the group appeared, standing over us and making me jump again. I didn't resist the temptation this time and thumped him hard; it was like hitting a tidy wall. "*Don't* keep doing that!" He grinned.

"Can you walk?" He asked Carson.

"Sure Muglier." Carson staggered to his feet with help from Truda and me.

The battered little convoy set off in weary resignation. Two of the men carried Joao again and Truda and I helped Carson between us. Muglier moved back and forward checking the trail in front and behind us, with the fifth man dropped right back just in case.

It seemed more than twenty minutes but eventually I could see the pinpoint lights of a tower through the trees and after that the clearing became a path, which then became a road.

The rain had stopped and I remembered once hearing an

explorer say you could never really see the stars unless you were in the middle of the Pacific Ocean on a quiet night. There were still a few places on land that you could see them in my verse, not many, but I looked up and took in the magic of the Canadian night sky and the stars that are in the heart of each of us, down to the spinning atoms.

Carson was leaning heavily on me, his breath ragged with pain and I was glad to see some people coming down the road towards us. The two men carrying Joao relinquished their burden with shaking arms and grateful thanks and someone helped Carson away from Truda and me. I nearly dropped with the weariness of standing up on my own. All the injuries I had experienced over the last few weeks were creating a symphony of aches that stretched up my spine and into my mind, making shadow pictures on my nearly closing eyelids. It became difficult to remember why I was in this verse and not at home in bed.

"Millie!" Joao was speaking quietly and urgently. He touched my arm and I sighed, leaning down to give him a hug as I walked one side of his stretcher. I felt as though I was an old horse being led on the next journey into nowhere.

The boundary of the compound was a ditch, a fence and a watch-tower. Inside, small buildings stretched away, set out along several streets similar to a medieval town. It was well lit and surprisingly modern, as if a group of new age enthusiasts had decided to go organic but with the technological comforts thrown in. I could see solar panels on the roofs and street lighting outside each house.

A man walked down one of the roads towards us, his lopsided stride seemed familiar; he was at first partly in shadow and then out in the light of the house lamps, it looked to my tired eyes as if he carried his own zebra crossing with him.

"What's Joao done now?" He said before he came to a stop by the stretcher. I could now see his face clearly and I found myself looking from one to the other in stunned silence. Twins.

"This is my brother, Joris," Joao said to me, "He's the doctor here."

The stun grenade caught us in silhouette and I threw myself onto the ground as the low-pressure wave of light and sound rendered me blind and deaf for the appropriate amount of time. I felt someone land on top of me, knocking what breath I did have left, out of my lungs. Chaos. I grumpily pushed the body aside and pulled myself into a crouch. I said to no one, "It always looks so much easier when you see it in the films. All that flying through the air, then they get up and brush themselves down."

"They usually have something soft to land on." Muglier pulled me to my feet.

"Yes well, *you* did!"

I drew the gun from the damp holster under the soggy t-shirt and tried to see through my streaming eyes. The two men had dropped Joao's stretcher and were firing at the still open gate.

A shout came from the watchtower, "Incoming!"

"Damn, these gangs are not giving up tonight!" Muglier said. He ran towards the gate with a group of men and women and I ran too. The barrage from inside the compound far exceeded the firepower that was coming in from the other side of the ditch, but they just wouldn't go away.

"What do these people want?" I was sheltering close to the inner wall, crouched and firing when I could.

"Anything they can get without working for it," Muglier said grimly.

The stretcher and Joao were disappearing into the nearest building and I saw Carson trying to persuade someone to let him join us. A very determined woman was shaking her head and pushing him towards the doorway.

The silence of nothing appeared out of the dark as if it was an old friend. We all waited, breathing at the end of a difficult race that had caught us all by surprise.

"They've gone!" The disembodied voice called down from the watchtower.

I slid down the wall into a sitting position and my legs came out from under me and I realised that I was completely spent. "You, okay?" A face swam into view. Muglier was tired and dirty and his eyes were a surprising pale blue. I couldn't speak, just shook my head. He tutted and put one arm under my legs and one around my back. Lifting me up from the ground, he carried me towards the building. I put my head on his shoulder and tried not to cry.

The space around me was clean and bright and I smelled the fresh combination of sunshine and breakfast. Joris looked in through the door and seeing me awake, came into the room. "How do you feel? You were suffering from a bit of shock last night."

"I'm okay, how are the other patients?" I sat up in the bed and realised I was wearing a set of pyjamas; my clothes were on a chair and looked clean and ironed.

"Joao is whinging so he must be feeling better; you did a good job there."

"What about Carson?"

Joris sat on the end of the bed, something which made me feel a little uncomfortable, as I didn't have the history with him that I had with his brother. He was completely oblivious. "I operated on a blood vessel, but we got it in time. Do you have medical training?"

"No." I staggered up and wobbled to the window. The sun shone on a courtyard full of flowers in tubs. The kitchen door was open and a woman, Truda, came out and put some food onto the small wooden table. She looked up and waved at me. I turned around to find Joris standing right behind me. I jumped back and for a moment and he seemed to be angry, a flicker of something I couldn't define slipped into his expression, then was gone. "I think I'll get dressed," I said.

"Bathroom's the one at the end of the corridor," he said. He closed the bedroom door quietly behind him.

There's nothing different about washing wherever you are, I thought, as I put the clean clothes on. My pack was on the floor by the bed and I rummaged through the contents looking for makeup and moisturiser. I have always been a low maintenance person and I didn't need my own brand of shampoo to feel comfortable, but I did like to have a few things. I felt rather than realised that someone had gone carefully through my belongings. Even the tops on the bottles were on too tight, as if a man had closed them. It made me feel as if I needed to look over my shoulder and I indulged myself, checking the room, though for what, I wasn't sure.

I went out into the corridor and was about to go down the stairs when I heard Joao calling me from the bedroom next door. I tapped and entered. He looked terrible.

"Ugh!" I said, "Don't go in for any beauty competitions in the next few days."

"You just tell it like it is Millie, don't hold back on my account." He smiled.

I jumped onto the end of the bed, like a nine-year-old at a slumber party. He winced as I gave him a hug.

"What is wrong with your brother?" I whispered after listening for silent footsteps on the landing.

Joao's face took on the guarded expression I remembered he wore as a child. "It's complicated," he said.

"I'll just bet it is," I muttered, "Someone's been through my backpack."

He looked up, worried. "Are you sure?" I nodded. "Okay, maybe things are not as safe here as I thought."

"You mean apart from the roving gangs that did their best to kill us last night?"

He shrugged. "What can I say, it's home."

"When was the last time you were here?" I settled against the pillows next to him, leaning on the headboard.

"Months," he said. "Actually," he added after some thought, "Nearly a year, the temporal differential between Tara's verse and this one is the most extreme. Yours is somewhere in the middle I think."

I nodded and sighed, trying to work out the time between the different verses was a short walk to a big headache. "What do people think when you go away for so long?"

He smiled. "Not many people know that I dreamwalk. I managed, by luck to keep it to a small group, my brother, a few friends, my mother. The others just forgive what they see as a wanderer who gets into trouble, because I bring back technology that they can use. In the early days it was food. My mother thought I was stealing it when I was a child. Only Joris knew."

"Why doesn't he dreamwalk with you?" I asked, curious.

"He can't," Joao said quietly.

There it was; the reason for the division and bitter twisted edge that hung around them. One could, one couldn't, what was difficult between brothers, would be impossible between twins.

"He must hate you?" I said.

"He does. He hides it well as an adult, but it's there." Joao moved carefully in the prison of the bed covers and his own guilt. "When we were children, he was just jealous, the way you would be if one of you got music lessons and the other didn't, but as we grew up it got more and more complicated."

"I don't know much about genetics," I said, "But it seems odd that identical twins would have such a specific gene missing in one of them?"

Joao shrugged. He pointed out of the window. "Not that long ago this verse was a type one. Something to be proud of. People around here just thought I was stealing technology from the debris of the past. Joris knew the truth and he wanted some of that for himself." Joao shrugged again. A whole world of emotional meaning in the flicker of a moment.

"When did the change happen?" I stumbled over finding the polite way to put holocaust.

"My mother was a child. She remembers what it was like before."

I got up and went over to the window, the village was setting up for the morning and I could see people on the hill outside the enclave working in the fields. A small tractor with interesting hovering jets seemed to be making light of ploughing. My neighbours at home would have been impressed.

I fingered the fixer on my face and tried to rub out some of the stiffness. "How was it possible that all the children had fixers Joao? I mean they all came from different verses?"

Joao made a face that was half a head shake and half an eye raise. "Okan and Rari were children too, but they were given presents if they put the fixers on the other kids." I must have looked horrified. "I know. Rari says it's the one thing that makes him desperate."

"What we need," I said, deep in thought as I turned back to the window again, "Is one of the tracking devices that Okan's verse uses to keep tabs on them." Joao was silent but I could sense him thinking.

"I wonder how easy it would be for either of them to get hold of one." I turned back to look at him and I could see the expression on his face. "Yes, that's what I thought."

"You were in a bad way yourself last night Millie?" He said, sounding worried.

I sat back down on the end of the bed and thought about how I had felt. "All that killing, all that anger and fear, it's a lot for someone like me to deal with. We don't get much use for a semiautomatic weapon in the bookshop, except," I added with a grin, "During the buy one get one free week, those pensioners can be nasty!"

Any more conversation was interrupted by Truda coming in with a tray of food. She looked as if she were a mother hen with her chicks all safe in the nest. I'd never seen anyone bustle before, but she was really good at it. "Come and sit outside in the sun Millie, you're too pale. Joao you need to eat and rest."

The sun felt good, and warm on my skin in a bright clear blue sky. There was the smell of homemade bread and jam and the sounds of people getting on with their lives in the early morning. I sat in a corner of the little courtyard and wondered how long it had taken them to get this far from the utter chaos of a disintegrating civilisation; when it was, that they had stopped being stunned victims and started building again. Truda came out and brought something that smelled as if it could be coffee, but wasn't. "It's made from a type of nut, doesn't taste too bad."

"Do you remember real coffee?" I asked, sipping and treading carefully at the same time.

"Yes, I was young, but I remember the time before." She handed me the buttered bread and a bowl of jam. "Eat something, you look half-starved girl."

We talked about the flowers and her garden and tomato bugs and the dreaded slugs and she laughed when I said that I went out early every morning before work to shout at them and throw them into the farmer's field, but I couldn't quite bring myself to pour salt on them. The fact that I had killed men the previous night was not lost on either of us but we didn't mention it. Some things were better left unsaid. The thought that it was easier to kill someone who was shooting at you than a creature that eats your flowers was one of those things that must be left to the dark hours.

Her eyes were like Joao's, one blue and one green. I wondered if Joris had the same trait or if it was just something else, he didn't get when the genes were shared out. I remembered him standing behind me and realised that I had avoided eye contact. Truda lifted her head up to the sun and smiled at the warmth. "It feels as if the spring has been a long time coming this year." Her hair was dark and she had the creamy skin and slender shape of the truly lucky.

I ate the bread and drank the coffee, which actually tasted dreadful but I was a well-trained guest. The fact that it was still spring filtered through my consciousness. All the back and forward through the singularity had made for a difficult time in keeping up with the different seasons. On Europa in Tara's verse, it was late spring, in mine it was somewhere in the middle of autumn and here it seemed to be still early spring, even if you took into account the difference between a Jupiter's moon and a Canadian climate. I wondered where Okan and Rari's verse came in the temporal differential scale between the verses; then stopped as it made my head spin in an alarming fashion for a moment.

"So, you're up at last!" Joris said cheerfully, making it sound as if he hadn't been in my room earlier. He sat down and helped himself to breakfast, Truda poured coffee for him and I moved my chair slightly so that our legs wouldn't touch when he leaned forward. I could see that he had the family eyes, though on him it looked somehow less interesting and more off putting. "I just checked on

Joao, he's asleep." He added, "The more rest he gets the better. No wandering off for a while." This was said looking at me in a pointed fashion.

He made me realise why I still found the winged monkeys in the Wizard of Oz frightening. Joris looked angry for a moment as he picked up on my fear. Then the emotion was swallowed by a mask of easy-going joviality. That was even worse. I found myself preferring the outright hostility of the gangers in Tara's verse to the hidden agenda of the man in front of me. The fact was that I was sure he had one. I sighed, really tired for a second. Wherever I went, I was being hunted and it was *almost* too much to bear, as if being caught would finally end the game and I could stop being afraid. The subatomic equivalent of being a yoyo would have to go on until it didn't.

"Would you like a trip around the enclave?" A deep voice from the gate came as a welcome relief.

"Muglier!" Truda said, pleased, "Come in and have some coffee and breakfast?!"

"Don't mind if I do." He hopped over the courtyard gate and sat himself down at the table, pushing in-between a now furious Joris and me. He slopped coffee from the pot and covered a piece of bread in enough jam to make my mother reach for the dentist's phone number.

"How are you feeling today? You looked like something a cat threw up last night." Muglier grinned as Joris made a big thing out of getting up and leaving. He kissed Truda on the top of her head and nodded to me. I did my best not to shudder again. Really, it was as if I were looking at the mirror image of Joao, just not quite right. Truda seemed oblivious to the fact that one of her sons was an evil creep and the other one verse hopped.

I took some of the dried fruit and nuts out of the bowl in the middle of the table and chewed thoughtfully. "I feel *slightly* better than cat sick this morning." Muglier laughed and the sound crinkled the corners of his eyes in the way that a laugh is supposed to. "Is Joao awake?" He asked casually, making me look up from trying to work out just exactly what type of dried fruit I was eating. I took a sip of the hot drink and cringed involuntarily.

"Okay," Truda sighed, "So it's not coffee." It was as if I had made her memories of the things that had been, more clearly defined. There was nothing worse than looking back and seeing just the good parts.

"Maybe not," I said, "But this jam is the best I have ever tasted and the bread is amazing, do you mind if I have another piece?" Truda handed me the plate with the pleased expression of someone who has a pathological need to feed people and I ate one slice too many just to see her smile.

"That was good of you," Muglier said when we were alone, "You don't strike me as a breakfast person." He swilled more coffee into his cup and drank it down, he was not someone who remembered 'before,' I thought. "Come on let's have that walk, you can work off some of the bread." He pulled me to my feet and I waddled to the gate.

The village was more of a town. It covered one side of the hill; in the past it would have been spread out in typical settler fashion. There would have been long lazy streets with a boardwalk on each side, as it drifted out towards the edges of the centre. The need to be safe inside a claustrophobic wall had chopped it down to size and given it the changed look of a place that had once been something else. So many towns in England had grown up that way; it was more similar to home than the Canada of my verse. We'd fought a few civil war and insurrection in England and it had seeped into our architecture. Always defending ourselves against the neighbours, most of the bigger towns had the remainder of a wall around them leftover from the 'good old days.'

Muglier waited until we were a fair distance from the house before he said, "Seems while we were picking you up there were strangers in the town." He smiled and waved to a woman coming out of her front door with a little child in tow. She waved back and went up the street to what looked as if it was a school, a small group of adults were gathering by the gate, saying goodbye to a variety of different sizes of child.

"Is that unusual? Strangers, I mean."

"Yep." He walked on up the street and I followed. "School," he said, pointing rather unnecessarily, as the noise level couldn't have been anything else except a fight between rival monkey colonies. "Medical centre. Meeting house. Store." He carried on up the hill and carried on pointing until we got to a seat placed at a vantage. It was close to the brow of the hill and behind it was a small over-crowded graveyard. He sat and leaned back in the sunshine, looking at me. I sat down next to him and we were silent for a while.

"Joao says you're in love with someone from the other place?"

"Oh yes, he's the man of my dreams," I said dryly, then cracked up at my own joke. Muglier didn't get it which made me laugh even more.

The view was all hills and somewhere not too distant there would be the sea, although I couldn't see it, the smell of sea on the wind and the tell-tale gulls following the tractor was a complete giveaway.

"Which way is Vancouver?" I asked.

"What's left of it is just to the south of here."

"The sea?"

He pointed to the west. "The strangers were not so 'strange' to Joris," he said, after a short pause. He leaned forward resting his elbows on his knees. Then he looked over at me. "You know anything about what's going on?"

I shook my head in frustration. Really it would have been too difficult to say who they were; the possibilities were endless.

"It's a pity; we could use someone with your skills around the enclave."

"Do you have a bookshop that needs organising?" I said sarcastically.

He laughed and leaned back again; his arm slipped around the length of the seat resting close to my shoulders. He smiled; the easy warm expression of the type of man who fits comfortably into the near outback. He reminded me of mountains, horses and wide-open spaces and the attractive intelligence that means rules needed bending to make things work. I reminded myself of Okan and moved a little further away from the interested gaze.

"The warrior queen impression," I said, "It's not real. I really *do* work in a bookshop where I come from."

"I was there in that forest and you did some serious damage for someone who's *only* a bookseller." He smiled, not quite giving up on the physical attraction.

"Most of the booksellers I know are mean fighters, it's an occupational hazard." I shrugged. "You have no idea how useful a submachine gun would be during the sales."

"For real?" He asked me, puzzled, "I mean I know books were scarce here for a while but usually it didn't end in bloodshed."

"No," I smiled. "I'm being ironic."

He made a face, one that looked both exasperated and charmed at the same time. I turned back to the fields and thought about semolina, the only food that caused me to shudder, which was much more effective than a cold shower. The smile and the humour were making it difficult to concentrate on the important things, as in how close the bad people were getting each time I dreamwalked. They must have been right behind us as we verse hopped. The thought that a fixer tracking device would come in handy filtered through the grey matter again. How difficult could it be; surely Okan and Rari had access to the technical equipment in their verse?

"So, what are we saying here? Is this enclave in any danger?" Muglier was touching the back of my neck and I struggled to hear the question through the haze of murky possibilities, all of which included me getting myself into a mess. I am such an idiot, I thought with a sigh.

"I think the trouble is all mine, although I'm sure you've got your work cut out for you with Joris." I put my hands over my eyes and tried not to let the universe in. "Are you the town lawman?" I asked, curious about the questions and the general sense of authority.

He laughed, "We still use the word sheriff here, haven't quite gone back to the days of the border wars, and you're right about Joris." He leaned towards me and pushed a stray hair away from my eyes.

"You're a complete flirt," I said.

"Yep," he smiled. "Do you think Joao is okay to go back with you?" I shrugged. "I just don't want something I can't deal with inside this place. Taken us long time to feel safe again."

I nodded. "I'll do my best." It felt as if nowhere was going to be safe anymore anyway. One place, one verse, all the claustrophobic feelings of being pursued through space and time filling in the beautiful blue cloudless sky with doubts and wishes.

"How long have you known about Joao?" I asked.

"We grew up together; eventually the fact that he would just disappear was not a childish game anymore." Muglier fished around in his pocket and came out with a small bag of what looked to be sweets, he offered me one. "Truda makes them for the kids. I always steal some." He carried on. "Didn't bother me much. I like the fact that science is still a part of our lives, so much opportunity for small minded prejudice in a world that went through what we did. Joao talked about exotic matter and bending space/time and traversable wormholes." He shrugged again. "My mother was a physicist before the change."

I tried not to look impressed, but it was difficult, the trip to the semolina mound was becoming an imminent necessity. There is nothing sexier than intelligence, nothing more attractive than humour, it was a deadly combination. "We should go!" I got to my feet. He didn't look puzzled. I was much easier to read than a book.

Muglier put a hand on my face sliding it around the back of my neck and leaned in, kissing my forehead in a most unbrotherly fashion. "If the relationship with the dream guy doesn't work out," He left the sentence unfinished and I tried not to let my blood pressure pop any important arteries in my brain.

We walked down the hill as the school went into their classes, the whoop of children's voices stilled as the rooms closed around them in an envelope of learning, armour against an uncertain future.

I felt rather than saw a door opening on one side of the road. The houses were bigger and more spread out further up the hill and most of the commercial businesses and community buildings were interspersed with the dwellings in the lower part of the town.

It was if a small wave of energy moved out towards me. I gasped. Muglier pushed me behind him and took a full blast of something in the chest. He went down like a felled tree. "Run!" He shouted, pulling out a gun into his nearly useless hand. I held him for a moment pressing my shaking fingers down on the gaping wound. Then looked up at the figures emerging from the house, there were two of them, determined in their approach. I wondered why they had tried to kill me, maybe they didn't need me alive anymore or the troops were just fighting back. They'd lost a few men to my irritating inability to be captured and it could make people careless.

I grabbed a handful of Muglier's blood-soaked jacket and pulled. He shouted at me again, angry, "Get *out* of here!" But his voice was thin and weak with pain. I took the gun from him and fired, curving down over him in a futile gesture, but it was too late, the damage had been done. He whispered into my hair, "It's okay Millie, go." The two figures were moving carefully towards me, guns out, watching for the next move, the town hid behind their doors and there was no cover. I fired. They dived towards the ground at the edge of a building.

"Hey!" A voice behind me made me spin with the gun extended in my hand. "Don't shoot!" I recognised one of the men who had carried Joao the previous night. He came out of the doorway and knelt down on one knee beside me providing covering fire, spraying shots at the two now pinned down attackers, while I struggled with Muglier.

I pulled at the injured man and he managed to scoot his feet along the ground to help me and we got into the temporary shelter of the house. "You're a stubborn woman," he whispered, as I yanked a cloth from one of the nearby wooden chairs and pushed it hard against the wound. Muglier strained to sit up, pressing his hand over mine for a moment. "I've got it," he said.

"Out the back!" Our rescuer looked over his shoulder for a second, leaving himself open and vulnerable, a sonic shot kicked into him spinning him into the wall. He grunted and sighed and slipped down. He had saved my life and I didn't know his name.

The back door was already open, I hitched Muglier to his feet and we staggered towards it. "Where is everyone?" I asked him, "Why is there no help?"

"Most people are in the fields and the deputies are further down the street at the office," he whispered, "It's on its way." He held up a small disc, covered in blood but visibly bleeping a series of colours.

"What was his name?" I asked sadly, "The man who died."

"Guimund," he said, as we hobbled down the path to the back gate, "His name was Guimund," he whispered to himself. I nodded. When there was time, we would remember him.

The men in the street were careful in their pursuit, worried about another rescue. What had probably been sold as an easy take was turning into a trap for them. The longer they hung around the more likely it would be that help would show up for us.

Muglier was struggling to move his feet and the blood had seeped through the cloth, catching in the pattern of embroidery that had been lovingly hand stitched. It looked obscene, as if someone had splashed red paint across a Picasso. He sat down despite me trying to hold him up. "Muglier!" I half sobbed.

"Time to go Millie," he said quietly, "Give me the gun." His voice came in short gasps and a small bubble of blood appeared at the corner of his mouth.

"No," I whispered, squatting down next to him. He was a big strong man, full of life and hope and laughter and my face crumpled with the things I couldn't say.

"Go find Joao as quick as you can and get back to, wherever." He propped himself against the back fence of the garden, out of line of sight of the door. A warrior with a heart, the same as those men who came before him, who knew how they were going to die and didn't fight the possibilities.

I handed him the gun and went to move away then turned and reached over to him pulling his face to mine and kissing him full on the mouth. My tears mixed with his blood. He didn't speak but wiped the smear from my lips with shaking fingers. Then pointed. I went. The sound of gunfire followed me over the wall, to the alley behind the houses, down the hill and into every bad dream I would ever have for the rest of my life.

The back of Truda's house was quiet, but I stopped and counted to ten before going in. Nothing, no sound. Either the men further up the hill were all there was, or there was more waiting. My own gun had been in the pack I had left in the bedroom. The one that had been searched. I hadn't checked to see if it still had bullets in it, just the pressure laser charge that fired the weapon. Okan used a larger version of the weapon with the laser as an effective deterrent but I had no idea if mine worked just on the one setting.

I crept up the stairs. Quiet voices were coming from Joao's room. Two male voices. Not arguing, just discussing something. I went through the door like a missile; it banged against the wall and sprang back nearly hitting me. "Muglier is lying in a pool of his own blood because of you and Guimund's dead!" I hit Joris full in the face with my closed fist, almost guaranteeing a broken knuckle, and the pain in my hand made my eyes water, he staggered back looking horrified and his nose seemed satisfyingly bloody and crooked.

But he didn't say 'I don't know what you're talking about.' He said, "No one was supposed to get hurt except you."

"Can you move?" I asked Joao; he was watching the proceedings from the bed and his mouth had dropped open.

He turned to Joris. "What did you *do*?"

I pulled at the covers and helped Joao to his feet. He staggered. "Can you dreamwalk with my help?"

"I think so," he said weakly. The bandage around his middle was tight and clean, with no blood coming through and he looked a better colour than he had done that morning.

Joris was standing by the door. I went over to him and he backed up a fraction. "If you want to live, I suggest you go and see if you can do anything for Muglier." He was still for a moment and his eyes were beads of pure hate. It was not the '*woman* scorned' you had to worry about, I thought, it was 'the love to hatred turned' and there was no greater love than that of a brother. He spun on one heel and was gone, whether to warn the attackers or actually do something about Muglier I didn't know. But I knew we didn't have much time. I ran to get my backpack from the other bedroom.

Joao was slowly getting dressed when I returned. I tipped the contents of the pack on the bed and checked the gun that was at the bottom. "Does this thing work without the projectiles?" They were gone.

"Yes," Joao answered, doing something pitiful with his trousers. "It's a concentrated light beam, a laser, just change the setting."

"I'm guessing the person who searched my pack didn't know that," I muttered, "Actually," I added thoughtfully, "*I* didn't know that."

Joao harrumphed and managed his other trouser leg. He looked at me. "Is Muglier dead?" I shrugged and tried not to sob. "Shit!" He said, "What a mess I've bought to my family." He sat down as he tried to do up the buttons on his trousers and I picked up his shirt.

"I've brought Joao. Don't you mean me? I did this!" I was trying not to cry but I could still taste Muglier's blood on my mouth and it was making me crazy, in several shades of messy despair. Joao pulled the shirt down over his head with a pain filled grunt and his face appeared with his hair all stuck up in a peak. He put his arms around me, still tangled in the clothing.

"None of this is your fault, Millie! The universe spat you out and now we've got to deal with it." It was not very profound but I understood.

A pounding on the stairs made us both reach for the gun that I had put down on the bed. Truda began shouting a second before she came into the room. "There are men coming down the street, I don't know them and it seems there was a fight in the settlement. I think Muglier is down and one other, Joris has gone to see if he can help with the injured!"

I looked carefully at Joao and he shook his head in an almost imperceptible way; more a denial of the eyes than a movement. No sense in causing any more grief, his expression said. I didn't agree with him but it wasn't my family and it wasn't my evil twin who had done the betraying, or really my pain.

She was out of breath and she took in the state of Joao's dress and the gun in my hand and then her face shone with the pale light of loss that only a mother can feel, when she knows there's a good chance, she might never see her child again.

I dragged Joao to his feet and we stood close together in a sort of untidy embrace. Truda put her hand on his face and her tears flowed for both of us, different tears but for the same reason, the wave of loneliness pierced the sunshine and clouded a clear blue sky. It was time to run away again.

My eyes held Joao's and I pulled him in with me. The room swirled around us and Truda's agonised cry followed me down the path of the wormhole and into the silent rumble of the negative energy in every atom of my body. I watched through Joao's mind as we tumbled out into the main street of Gold Cliffs and the door to the stable banged in the wind making me jump. He fell to the ground in a spectacular faint and I sat down in the dirt and rested my head for a moment.

Til Duster looked astonished as I hobbled in through the back door of his apartment half carrying a now almost walking Joao. I was covered in the dust and blood of nightmares and Joao looked as if he had been hit by a train. "Well," Til said, "You two look as if you could do with a cup of tea."

Joao said, "Tea would be good right now." I tried not to be exasperated, but it was difficult, and I don't think I managed it. The trip through the wormhole had been an experience of epic proportions. I could still fell the sensation of Joao slipping through my fingers as we arrived into the comforting smell of straw and sweaty horse by the stable.

I used Til's com as mine had been through the singularity one too many times, the dust and dirt were thick on the gel-screen. The dive over the wall into the alley in Joao's verse hadn't helped and it was losing its ability to make a clear hologram. It hopped about and shivered like an amateur belly dancer.

Tara answered Okan's com, "Oh my, where are you?" Her voice was an agonised whisper, as if anything louder would make the possibilities disappear. "Is Joao with you?"

"In body if not in spirit," I said. Joao grunted; leaning back into the sofa cushions that Til had thoughtfully packed around the injured man's aching back.

Tara sobbed, "I've been so worried. Okan tried to explain the difference in time between the verses, but it doesn't help when you're worried to know that you've only been away, what is it, two days in Joao's verse?"

"Is Okan there?" I asked hopefully. Tara crying was one painful moment more than I could bear at that point.

"I'll get him. Can I speak to Joao?" She asked, equally hopeful.

I handed over the com and watched the fizz as Tara moved to the stairs in the house while still questioning Joao about his wounds and listening to the things he didn't say. She was amazing it was like watching a speeded-up conversation with a clairvoyant. Joao barely had to open his mouth and she got it all out of him. I saw her turn her head and she shouted up the stairs, "Okan, they're back!" It made all of us wince; someone should have invented a volume switch on the com so that it compensated for raised levels of anxiety.

Okan's face took over from Tara's, it was a mess of worry and relief in equal measure. I took the com back from Joao before he had time to speak, it was my turn anyway.

"Come and get us," I said, before Okan could open his mouth. "I think that we're just one step ahead right now."

He nodded. "I'm on my way." The com went dark and the little hologram swirled into a mini vortex of its own in rainbow colours. Which was somehow interesting.

"Anyone I should know about?" Til asked, hovering about with a teapot in one hand, looking as if he was just about to morph into warrior mode at any moment if the need arose.

"Same people as before Til," I answered.

"Okay, cup of tea, Millie?" Til said, warrior mode having been switched off for the time being. He poured out a large mug and added several spoons of honey and a plate with cake on it. I sighed my gratitude. Every nerve ending felt as if it were sticking out sideways, and I was one of those creatures you see in zoos, where the notice on the bars says 'don't put your hands through.' Anyone putting their hands inside *my* 'enclosure' right now would be in for a nasty shock, I thought.

Okan must have used the boost on the runabout, because he arrived in the sort of timeframe that usually involved quantum physics. He came in through the door to the living room as if he wasn't sure that we would still be there. I stood up, my hand on my weapon as soon as I heard the sound of feet on the outside stairway, and went to the vantage point close to the doorway that was hidden from the entrance. Til looked surprised for a moment and then removed a gun from the storage container on the kitchen wall, using a thumbprint to open it. He threw a smaller version to Joao sitting on the sofa.

I stood for a moment with my fingers on the trigger. "You're always trying to shoot me," Okan said quietly. I nodded. He held out his arms and I went over to him, he managed to remove the weapon from my hand before he folded me in.

The space on the runabout was mostly taken up with Joao and the support structure Til and Okan had rigged to prevent any more damage. Til gave me the basic instructions needed to use the vehicle he kept at the bar. It was smaller than the farm version, but fast and nippy. I could keep up with Okan and watch out for Joao as we sped back to Weldon's.

I gave Til a hug before we left and some advice. "Be careful, these people seem to have changed the rules. I don't think they care any more about who they hurt."

Til hugged me too. "Not many people do," he said wryly. "But I get it," he added when I tried to explain what I really meant. I noticed that he had put the gun in a harness on his hip, rather than back in the locker.

I looked back a couple of times before the bend in the road out of town and I could still see Til waving until the curve of the hills separated him from us. Something about it made me sad.

Weldon was waiting at the end of the road to the farm. I paused long enough for him to hop up behind me and we followed Okan down the track. Tara stood up from the rocker on the veranda, walking quickly down the steps. Okan curved the runabout around in a neat semicircle to stop in just the right place. I skidded to a halt, nearly unseating myself and pitching Weldon into the ground in a heap. "Millie!" He shook himself off like a shaggy dog in a rainstorm.

"Sorry! Til didn't cover stopping in the instruction guide." I turned everything off and waited for the vehicle to settle on its stand before I hopped down. My legs were like water and I sat down suddenly beside Weldon.

"Are you okay?" He asked me gently. I looked at him; layers of panic must have shown in my face because he put his arm around me. We sat in the dust of the road by the front of the house and he patted my shaking shoulders.

Rari came around the side of the barn; he dropped the feed bag he was carrying and ran over to help Okan and Tara with Joao, who looked as though he was barely conscious. I stood up sighing and pulled Weldon to his feet. "Thanks," I said, "It's been a difficult day."

Joao was curled up on his side in the bed when I went in to see if he could manage any food. Weldon had prepared a soup with most of the main food groups in it and a few I didn't recognise, he'd added some powder and a dropper full of brown liquid to the bowl I had put on a tray for Joao. Water and a mixture of honey and a local flower juice with a straw completed the meal.

Tara was sitting by the bed with her hand on Joao's shoulder, the lines of worry smoothed out on her forehead if not in her heart. They were talking quietly and I felt as if I were the unexpected guest at an invitation-only party for a moment, then Tara smiled and came over to me, taking the tray and managing to hug me at the same time. "Has this got Weldon's magic potion in it?" She asked, positioning the food so that Joao could feed himself without too much pain or movement.

"I hope so, only magic is going to get me back on my feet." Joao began spooning up the soup.

"How long do you think we've got?" I asked after a moment when the sense of being hunted filtered through the thought of safe places that the farm usually gave me.

"Not more than a few days if the past record is anything to go by." Joao finished up the scrapings with the edge of the spoon in the way of people who have experienced real hunger growing up. He reached for the drink and winced a little. Tara pushed it closer, sitting back on the chair by the bed.

The door opened and Weldon came in carrying lunch for a small army helped by Okan and a slightly grubby Rari. "Thought we'd have the meal up here if you're up to company?" Weldon asked Joao. Joao looked pleased and the picnic was laid out on the floor. There were thick slices of bread and butter with the soup, fruit and cheese with some small sweet cakes and more of the juice in tall cups.

I realised I was hungry. It had been a long time since breakfast and a lot of blood had passed under the bridge instead of water. I reached for one of the cakes and bit into the rich mixture of icing and sponge. "Did you always eat your pudding first as a child?" Okan asked me, sitting with his back against the wall of the room and favouring the one shoulder, I remembered the shot that I thought had killed him and reached out a hand which he took. "It's fine Millie, nearly healed, thanks to Weldon's treatment and the local nanobots." I nodded, but I took another cake, which is of course a recognised antidote for pain and fear.

"Okay," said Weldon, after a suitable time when he had handed me a bowl of soup and some bread, looking hopefully into my face. I spooned the hot food and wondered if he had spiked mine with the herbs and tinctures he and Tara collected and prepared. "What next?" he added.

"I think we need to get one of the devices from Okan's verse that can track all the dreamwalkers." I finished the soup by scraping the bowl the way Joao had, with no further doubt in my mind that it had been embellished with the Weldon magic.

"Well," said Okan. He looked stunned, patting my back as if he thought I might bolt like a restless horse.

I looked up from my bowl scraping. "What?"

"You don't think that's going to be a mite dangerous," Rari said, a wry smile on his dusty face. He chewed the bread thoughtfully and stretched his long legs out in front of him to get comfortable.

"More dangerous than verse hopping followed by a gang of psychopaths?" I asked helpfully.

"Yeah," Rari said, shrugging, "You've got a point." He looked at Okan.

"Actually," Okan said, "We've been trying to work out a plan."

I nodded, you could call it ESP or intuition, or just one too many digits on my wormhole gene, but I had guessed that they might have been thinking about it, which was one more piece in the Okan puzzle. I looked carefully at Joao's face; there was no surprise there, just resignation as if it was part of the hidden plan. "What will you do?" I asked, not really expecting much of an answer.

Okan settled back against the wall with a handful of cakes that he popped in one after the other, swallowing then without much chewing. A small enquiring squeak from the vicinity of the doorway was followed by Flora, who was looking annoyed about being left out of the picnic. She hooted her frustration and came over to me. I scooped her up and rubbed my face against her rough skin. More hoots and squeaks and forgiveness in the shape of a piece of buttered bread and a slice of peach. She settled in my lap, leaving a trail of juice on my jeans.

"There are two tracking devices," Okan said. No one stopped eating or drinking but everyone was paying full attention. It was the last part of the story, the bit where all the chips settle where they may and not everyone gets a happy ending and we all knew it. "Once we have one and the other is disabled, we have to do something about these." He pointed to the fixer on his face. "Rari and I can be removed while they still function fully, and when we steal the tracker there's no going back for either of us." He looked at Rari.

The curl of fear was thick within the shaft of sunlight on the floor, and the smell of rain on the wind coming into the bedroom through the half open window, fought with the shadows between us all.

Then Rari shrugged. "What do I have to go back for except more of the same? More 'deprogramming' because I'm not 'normal,'" he said bitterly, "Betrayal of the only thing that makes sense, this place, these people." He shrugged again. "This is where we belong; we decided a long time ago that we would do it if we could Oak. I think we should just get on with it." The shadows fell into untidy heaps and we all breathed in the possibilities of the future.

"Okay," I said again. "What's the plan?" Cecil swept in through the open doorway and hopped onto the bed, settling himself down next to a grateful Joao and began to wash. All cats love a good plan.

"We go back," Okan said. He looked bleak. "Rari and I, we take something with us, some interesting technology that we can use as a distraction. But we have to deal with the fixers first."

"Maybe Simon can help," I said. Hugging the cuddly Flora to me for warmth in the sudden chill I could feel from the thought of what we could lose. She grumbled, but allowed herself to be engulfed in the embrace, just extending her trunk to test the fear on my breath; her sensitive snout tapping gently at my lips like a child's sleepy kiss.

"How? What makes you think that Simon has any answers?" Okan looked puzzled.

"He comes from the type three verse and we both know he knows more than he's saying." I stroked Flora who went back to snoring her approval in gentle waves.

"Do you think he would come here?" Joao asked, looking worried.

I nodded. "If I asked him to, he would."

There was quiet for a while as the rest of the food disappeared and the debris was collected up by Weldon. He sat back down on the end of the bed and reached for Joao's empty bowl and cup. "I might have a solution for the 'something interesting,'" he said. "One of my friends at the university is working on the final details for an unlimited energy source based on the sunlight conversion of marine microbes."

Tara looked up. "What about the men who chased us from Professor Theadus's office, won't they be watching the place?"

"I don't think so Tara," Okan said, "They don't need to have people waiting around, don't forget they have a tracking device too."

"Of course," I said, "I'd forgotten about that one!"

"We're not going to get out in front by stealing the one from my verse, but we should be able to even the odds, they won't have an advantage anymore." Okan stood up and stretched, his joints popped and he groaned from the many nearly-healed wounds and old bruises. He perched on the window sill, the afternoon sun made an outline of his shape on the floor and I put my foot into the Okan shadow for some connection. "What are you thinking?" He asked me.

"I've just worked out that someone from the type three verse must have made the fixers and the tracking device at some point in the past. I don't really think that your verse has the ability?" I looked up at Okan. "Otherwise, they would have made more."

He shrugged. "You're right. I think it was one of those items of technology that the type three verse scattered around, before the bomb went off at the conference Professor Theadus says ended it all." I tried not to feel irritated that he hadn't mentioned it before and I had been left to work out one more piece of the puzzle.

I struggled to quantify my thoughts. "I can't work out how Zatar has managed to use the fixers to get a team of mercenaries into the dreamwalking verses?"

Joao looked bleak and Rari sighed his deepest sigh yet. "Millie," Rari said, "The fixer is keyed into the DNA of the individual dreamwalker; it bonds with him or her at a very basic level. We think if the DNA was used in gene therapy treatment it would be possible to fool the fixer into thinking *you're* the dreamwalker." He huffed at my horrified face. "I bet they lost a few when they first started experimenting. I can't imagine it would last very long before the person's own DNA started to take control again, but I think that's how they're doing it." He paused, looking at Okan.

"What are you not saying?" I asked, not really wanting to know the answer; the things that I didn't know having become more comforting somehow.

"The crossover gene that you carry, the one your parents made, would solve their problem of the rejection of the fixer," Rari said carefully.

"Why don't they just make more fixers?" I asked, ignoring the previous statement.

"I think because they don't have any more dreamwalkers to go with them, it doesn't work without the wormhole gene we carry.

They got rid of all their dreamwalkers, Millie. You have to start with the person and then the fixer, it doesn't work the other way around." He added, "I think the dreamwalking gene 'wakes up' the fixer technology."

We all sat for a while in our different worlds and contemplated the fact that a fixer and a dreamwalker existed at all, never mind the crazy people who had put the two together, both of whom were probably related to me. "I wonder how they worked it out," I whispered to myself, "What a leap of understanding."

Okan nodded. "Yep," he said. He was closest to me and heard me clearly, but the quiet was that 'still of the night' sound and everyone nodded, as if the sense of it had passed from one to the other of us using osmosis.

Weldon banged more dishes together and Tara moved out of her chair to help with the overspill from the loaded tray. I reached up for a hand to get to my feet; Okan pulled me to him and then held onto my hand. "I can hear you thinking and it scares the life out of me." His face was smiling but there was something dark in the expression as well.

"I don't understand how Zatar can make a wormhole and just walk into my house. You remember Joao, that's what you said when we were in my kitchen. You said it looked different, as if it was man-made."

"You mean the first time I got shot," Joao said dryly, wincing at the previous pain and the current agony.

Rari shrugged. "We just don't know Millie. I mean we've discussed it." Not when I was around, they hadn't. "But we can't come up with anything. Unless," he managed to look embarrassed and enthusiastic at the same time, "He has the dreamwalk gene and he's adapted the ability to include an artificial singularity. It may have been the next step as far as the type three verse was concerned. Just because they don't want us doing it doesn't mean they don't have plans for the ability themselves."

The room was quiet again and Tara put the extra bowls she had been carrying down on the table by the bed, she stood very still. "What plans do you think they have? When you were discussing it, you must have come up with a theory." She spoke with that low even tone that suggested temper control just barely on the red line. We all looked at Rari, who looked at Okan, who shrugged again. I resisted the temptation to punch someone or something because this almost never worked.

"I suppose we thought that he might be thinking about setting up a group of dreamwalkers under his command, as in infiltration of the different verses."

"What we're suggesting here is a multiverse army?" Weldon said. The tray was still held in his hands and the door open for a trip down to the kitchen, mundane and earth shattering in equal measure.

"If he can solve the problem of the genetic rejection of the fixers," Rari said, "That is what I'm saying."

All eyes turned to me. I leaned in towards Okan and felt his arm go around my shoulders and the room became a rush of swirling anti-noise and the feeling of running away was pulsing in my head. I put my feet firmly on the floor again and tried to think of the fact that everyone in the house was on my side. Flora wound her way around my legs, making falling over a distinct possibility. I picked her up and her little snorts and squeaks of anxiety formed a direct pathway to my brain. The sense of being hunted as if I was an animal dissipated in her tickly breath and unconditional love. "Shit!" I said.

"Yeah." Weldon carried on out the door. "I'm with you Millie."

Joao looked as if he had had as much in the way of visitors and truth that anyone who's come close to dying can take. He lay back on the pillows and tried unsuccessfully to lose the grey tinge around the edges. I left along with Rari and Tara, Okan stayed behind and closed the door and the echo of a small quiet buzz of conversation followed us down the stairs. "I hate it when he does that," Tara muttered. "I mean what is there left to hide?"

"Okan suffers from the paranoia of most of us from our verse." Rari stretched up tapping the carved curl of wood that decorated the middle of the arch above the corridor. It represented a bunch of flowers with a bee in the blossom and was just before the doorway into the kitchen. "He has had to live with the possibility of betrayal since he was a child." Rari smiled. "It makes you careful."

"Is that the same as saying he doesn't trust us?" Tara asked. She began loading dirty dishes into the machine. I still wondered how it worked with no water. I remembered something about sonics and shaking things clean but couldn't remember the details. I passed her a wayward bowl.

"He would give his life for you Tara," Rari said quietly, "Let him have some time with the other stuff." Tara stood still for a moment, the bowl held forgotten in her hand, then she nodded slowly and the film rewound and picked up speed and we all breathed again.

Rari went out of the back door heading off to the barns and the afternoon feed for the goats. He hugged me before he went. "Come and give me a hand when you get a moment."

Tara began a detailed program of the farm's accounts on the kitchen computer, groaning at the impossibility of the required information. It seemed as if the necessary bureaucratic paper trail whispered its bad breath through the different verses.

I went back to the other end of the house and listened at the foot of the stairs; the steady noise of conversation continued from Joao's bedroom. Sunshine cast a dusty light through the open front door and I could see Rari dragging the big feed sacks into the barn on the side of the track.

The door to the left of me opened and Weldon looked out. "You can't possibly hear what they're saying." He smiled. "I tried."

I followed him into the large study. More computer equipment and stacks of files were piled high on one side of an old desk and the walls were lined with books and discs. Holo-pictures of the farm as it was being built gave an eerie sense of déjà vu, as they slowly grew in size only to start again as the program reran. One wall was given over to a chart with holographic representations of the farm's timetable. I could see the months and days plotted out but it was difficult to understand with the many different seasons the moon had. There were at least six that I could see, with two growing seasons back-to-back.

"Do you still have my sister's ID on you?" Weldon asked, after sitting down in one of the fireside chairs. He leaned forward and flicked a switch on the base of the stove and a small flame sprang up, it wasn't cold in the house, but somehow in a primitive memory it was comforting. I sat in the corresponding chair and leaned my aching back into the cushions.

"Yes," I said, "It's in my backpack. Along with a gun that's out of bullets and a bloodstained cashmere sweater."

"It's good to travel light," he said straight faced, then added, "You'd better put the cashmere in cold water."

"Are you sure you've never met Simon before?" I asked.

We studied the fire for a while in the sort of companionable silence that usually goes with long friendship and alcohol. "I remember Joao saying once that he had known of experiments being done with fixers on non-dreamwalkers. Was that something that happened here or in Okan's verse, do you know?"

Weldon had not grown-up understanding that his secrets were his strength the way that Okan had, so he answered immediately, "I have read the details of the scientific trials that were done here, a while ago, Professor Theadus was part of the team. It was abandoned as soon as they realised the implications. But not before several volunteers had died in a spectacular mess." He added after some thought, "I guess we all long for the chance of somewhere else. Maybe they thought with all that junk DNA, who's to say we don't all have the wormhole gene lying dormant somewhere?"

"Do you think Okan and Rari's verse tried it too?"

He snorted, "I don't doubt it, but not for the same reasons."

"The original dreamwalkers must have gone everywhere, every verse, seeding their technology, like a farmer sowing fertile soil." I leaned back in my chair. I could see that Weldon liked the analogy, as he was smiling. "I suppose when the bomb went off the technology scattered with the dreamwalkers, it would have been difficult to find a place of safety. Zatar must be making good use of several people."

"Sometimes progress is not made by people thinking of endless possibilities but the fact that someone has a gun to your head."

More silence followed, filled with the hissing fire and the

thoughts of two people trying not to let the difficult feelings get away from them.

"How did you start working with plants for herbal medicine?" I asked, a change of subject being necessary for my emotional welfare. "Both you and Tara have a real gift."

He seemed pleased with the compliment as I hoped he would be, it felt comforting to say nice things to good people. "My mother was a herbalist on Earth before they 'settled.' I grew up with things in jars all over the house. Tara's mother was a doctor so she inherited her love of healing people."

"Are the plants here the same as the ones on Earth?"

"Ah, now that's a good question." Weldon settled himself into his chair with the enthusiasm of the true fanatic. I hoped my ears weren't going to fall off with the forthcoming explanation. "When the moon was first terraformed, it affected the developing plant life, several subspecies of which, have the genetic code for self-repair. Of course," he made a face, "Some of them are extremely toxic to humans, but this one," he held up a grubby root that looked similar to ginger, "Has tissue regenerative properties. I put it in the soup. I think all of you are in need of some repair at the cellular level. It's good for bruising as well as an effective anti-inflammatory."

"My cells and bruises thank you," I said politely.

"They're very welcome," he replied formally.

He held it out to me and I sniffed it, smelling nothing but warm earth and great potential. "Do you treat the people in the town?"

"I am famous for my hangover cure," he said wryly. "Though most people rely on a more clinical approach for their needs." He explained helpfully, when I raised my eyebrows, "I mean we can grow a kidney if you need one, things like organ replacement, limb reattachment, laser surgery, it's all effective and immediate, we have pre-birth genetic testing and an immunisation programme but," he trailed off looking into the fire with the expression of a man swimming against the tide.

"Don't stop, you had me with the hangover cure!" I laughed.

"Well, I think that sometimes it's good to let the body take care of its own healing, if there's time."

It sounded as if it was one of those lectures my mother used to give her patients when they asked for antibiotics. I moved my feet away from the warmth of the flames as my toes were cooking gently. "Is it the same all over the solar system, do people get a similar level of care? It sounds pretty impressive."

He snorted, "If you get out to the mining colonies on the Kuiper Belt, you'd see the type of medical support that should have gone out with bleeding and using dirty hair to pack wounds."

I winced.

We were interrupted by a tap on the door; Okan stuck his head around the edge. "Can anyone join this club?" Weldon got up and moved another chair closer to the fire and Okan came over, he kissed the top of my head as if he hadn't seen me for a while and sat down, stretching his long legs out with a groan. "I need some more of your soup, I think Weldon."

"Try this." Weldon got up again and removed an opaque brown bottle from the labelled collection on the shelves. He poured a small amount into a glass and handed it to Okan, who took it gratefully.

"Ugh!" Okan spluttered, making a face that was fit for a nine-year-old eating broccoli. He shook his head as if to clear it. "What *was* that?"

"One of my stronger preparations, it will boost your own immune system and help it to repair itself." Weldon studied the bottle. "Actually, I've been waiting for someone to try it on."

I laughed at the expression on Okan's face. "Well," I said, ruining the moment, "When are you and Rari going to go back to your verse and get the tracking device?"

"Do you think we should speak to Simon first?" He asked, answering a question with a question, which was borderline infuriating.

"I suppose that means I have to go and get him?" I shuffled in misplaced annoyance. I felt as if I was part of some insane hopscotch, each box representing a different verse.

Flora pushed against the not quite open door and Weldon got up and opened it, scooping her up and putting her on his lap as he sat down again. She circled as if she had been taking lessons from Cecil.

"Do you think you could go tomorrow morning?" Okan said, not really asking. I shrugged.

The feeling that the sand was running out of the egg timer filtered through my thoughts. "You'd better give me some of that mixture Weldon, in anticipation of the fact that someone is bound to shoot at me and I need all the help I can get." I sounded grumpy and tired, which just about covered it, except for the part about being afraid.

"Where are *you* going to be?" I asked, letting all my feelings out in one long resentful sentence. I wasn't really expecting an answer and I didn't get one. Okan had reverted to his terminally enigmatic state which in itself was truly nerve wracking.

I looked from one to the other of the two men; every non movement was pure alpha male. Okan made it look normal, but the sense of power rested uneasily on Weldon, he was the type of leader who was always surprised when he turned around and discovered other people following him. I wondered how he had ended up as a farmer on a distant moon and then realised that there were large gaps in what I did know about him.

Sighing I got up to leave, realising that Okan wanted to talk to Weldon alone. "I'll go and give Rari a hand in the barn."

"Take this with you and get Tara to put four drops in some water and honey for Joao." Weldon handed me the brown bottle of herbal mixture that he had used Okan as a test case for.

I slightly banged the door behind me, much as a teenager leaving the headmaster's study would. Tara was still making faces at the computer in the kitchen, mumbling the facts and figures as a mantra against the powers of small-minded bureaucracy. I handed her the bottle with the instructions and she paused for a myopic moment.

"Right, got it," she said, then sighed theatrically, "Do you have all this in your verse?"

"I know farmers who would rather have their arms up the backside of a pregnant cow than work out the latest regulations."

She thought about it for a moment. "I think I'm one of them."

"I'm going to give Rari a hand with the goats before he has a fit about having to do it all on his own." I took a cup of tea and some cake from the kitchen and went out into the yard at the front of the house.

The barn doors were open and the smell of livestock and feed were rich in the air, but not at an objectionable level. Filters high on the side of the building moved the tainted air away from the inside and gave the people working with the animals a much more pleasant environment. I was standing outside looking up at the mechanism, wondering how it worked. "Charcoal mainly," Rari said helpfully, taking the tea from me and helping himself to the cake leaving me holding an empty plate. He sat down on the seat outside the barn, groaning as his back was rested for a second. "They use the fan to move the air through the filters and the charcoal strips the smell. That," he pointed to a small metal hut with a furnace shaped door, "Is the microbe waste disposal unit. Very efficient."

"Do you like farming?" I asked curiously. Rari seemed of all of them to be the least suited to the great outdoors. He looked as if he was the history professor you wanted to please with your latest essay.

He sighed his contentment. "I love it here." Leaning back after gulping the tea down he polished off the cake with his eyes closed.

"My parents had a farm in Canada. I was very young when I joined the organisation, but I can still remember the way it felt to have the sun on my face and a wide sky, being surrounded by fields and the smell of fresh cut hay."

The sadness was so real that I reached out and took his hand. He didn't open his eyes but squeezed my fingers. "You're not sure you're going to get away with this and come back here, are you?" I asked quietly. The steady pressure on my hand was answer enough.

"I suppose that's why Okan has reverted to warrior mode," I added.

"Give him a chance, Millie, he's trying. It's difficult to overcome a lifetime of watching over your shoulder." He looked over to me with a grin that lit up the too serious face. "Plus, I think a little paranoia might do us all some good right now."

He stood up and pulled me to my feet. "Come on, let's go and finish feeding the goats, or did you just come out here to sulk?"

"Okay." I said, "But I reserve the right to go back to sulking if I feel like it."

The barn was a sea of creatures and the noise returned to rock festival levels as soon as we were spotted. Curiosity and hunger combined and the little new heads of the tiny kids butted each other as they got excited. I filled the feed bins and found myself stroking the warm fur and scratching the spot between the ears that drives most cats into a purring frenzy. It seemed to work on the goats too. Rari did the heavy work with the large sacks, lifting them into convenient places so that I could access as many of the pens as possible without having to carry the bins too far. He was singing a song I didn't recognise in a warm deep voice, I found myself humming along with the chorus, which was something about a lost love; wasn't it always.

My throat was full of dust and I realised, as I swiped my sweaty forehead that it was in my hair and on my face too. Tara appeared, a clean tidy angel in the doorway of the barn, waving with one hand and carrying a tray with the other. Rari and I swooped down on her as if we were parched travellers on a difficult journey. "I needed that!" Rari gasped after drinking down a large mug of juice. He took the tray from Tara, who was just standing there and smiling in the way of those people who love to look after everyone and we went outside to the seat. "It seems to me that I just finish one feed and have to start again on the next," Rari said, exasperated. He stretched his legs out and picked up a sandwich, ignoring the layer of dirt he had added to the bread. I took the damp cloth from Tara's outstretched hand and wiped my fingers and face. The cloth came away a disgusting colour.

"How's Joao?" I asked, after eating a cheese and pickle sandwich the size of a hardback book.

"Better." Tara was chewing her own doorstep of a sandwich and she handed me tea, stirring in a spoonful of honey while I held the mug. "The tincture that Weldon has been working on is very effective. The regenerative properties are better than anything else we've tried, except of course the medical nanobots. I'm not sure how, but I think that the fact that you dreamwalk also has an effect on your ability to heal."

I nodded my agreement, it seemed to me that the wound I'd got from the shooting in the bar had been almost magical in its speed to mend. When I was a child, I had broken my arm on a particular tree climb that had been something of a challenge for my six-year-old self. I remembered my mother putting my arm in a cast and the itching, but not really how long it had been on for. The speed of things was just not something I'd noticed as a child, but then we don't make those comparisons when we're young. "I think I'd better have some of that tincture," I said, "My back feels like a puzzle that's been done by someone in a bad-temper." She smiled a wicked smile.

I snorted, "It's already in the tea."

"What's stopping Zatar trying to get at us here?" Tara asked Rari who choked on the abrupt right angle in conversation. Rari put down the empty mug on the tray and finished his last mouthful chewing carefully.

"Nothing that I can see," he said

We all nodded as if this made perfect sense, which it didn't.

"If it looks as if we're losing Millie," Rari whispered, "Take Tara and get to the uninhabited verse. Gather what you can carry and go." He got up and stretched as if he hadn't just delivered the bombshell of a lifetime. "Come on you, three more pens and we're done." He went into the barn leaving Tara and I gaping.

I put down the half-eaten cake with shaking hands. "I wish," I said.

"Yeah, me too," Tara sighed. She closed her eyes for a moment, then said, "Do you remember when death was supposed to be about growing old?"

"I think you would have to be in a different place for that, really no one gets to live the life they hoped they would." I sighed my own sigh.

"I suppose making plans is a way of fooling ourselves that we do." Tara got up and collected the plates, shuffling them into a neat stack.

I staggered upright, thinking mean thoughts about the two men who were still discussing tactical possibilities in the study. "They'll be out in the field next week," Tara said.

"What?" I couldn't understand why Okan and Weldon would need to be.

"The goats, you idiot!" Tara laughed, "They are old enough to go out to the grazing pastures and the weather's mild enough." I must have looked puzzled still because she added, "No more feed bins."

"Great!" I brushed an impossible layer of sticky dust from my clothes and longed for the days when I didn't have a fixer and my mother washed everything that wasn't attached to a coat hanger.

"Well," she said, walking away, "Obviously they will still need extra feed, but at least it won't be in the barn."

"Huh!" I muttered the curses that got you absolutely nowhere with the spirits of these things.

"What are you saying?" The evening meal was accompanied by the usual impossible conversations, where I asked questions and Okan didn't answer them. He looked tired and closed in, as if the thoughts he had to think were too difficult to deal with, which was a lucky guess on my part.

"I'm *saying* that the only thing we have going for us is the fact that Rari's security clearance can get us just about unlimited access."

"*This* is your plan?" I reached for the bread and slathered butter across it in layers that would give someone who hadn't just done manual labour for seven hours a heart attack. "Oh, no, wait, that's right, no one here is supposed to know, just in case." Hunger was making me cranky.

"Millie!" Weldon said, "Lighten up!"

"Yes, papa bear," I replied through soup and bread. Tara gasped and Weldon stopped, his spoon halfway to his mouth. "What did I do wrong?" I said.

"Nolie, my sister used to call me that," he answered.

"Well," I said, thinking about it for a moment, "She was right, you are." I added without pause and in the wrong tone, "Sometime soon Rari, you're going to have to tell me just *exactly* what it is you do in your verse." We all looked at him and he shrugged, but not before the longest pause had flickered around the table.

"How does the power conversion occur between the oceanic micro-organisms and the sunlight?" Rari asked, breaking the not uncomfortable silence that followed.

"I don't know," Weldon answered, "But I will get the information from my friend at the university tomorrow, he's going to send it through a secure computer line." He addressed the last part to Okan who had stopped for a second and was about to ask a question. Okan nodded and resumed eating.

Rari and I were both trying not to groan at the unused muscles lodging serious protest. I saw him stretch his back as if the vertebrae had been rearranged in an inconvenient order. "Not in any pain are you professor?" Okan asked with a smile.

"I think you should do the feed bins tomorrow," Rari replied, "Millie will help."

"Thanks, what did I ever do to you?" I held out my bowl like Oliver for more soup as Weldon passed by with the pot from the stove.

We were in mid-bicker when the door opened and Joao staggered in. Tara began to scold him for getting out of bed but Rari got up and helped him into a chair and Okan reached for bread and butter to fill a plate that Weldon passed him. It was as if we were not complete without Joao and the table felt comfortably crowded; our elbows bumping in a song and dance of old favourites.

"Tomorrow Millie goes to fetch Simon," Joao said. "Then, you two are off soon after that?" He asked Okan. My stomach did a small yo-yo and I stopped eating. "What?" Joao looked around.

"Very subtle." Rari shook his head.

"It's okay," I said. "It makes it easier when someone says it the way it actually is." I took the pudding bowl from Tara, who had filled it with a creamy fruit mixture that looked delicious.

I stood up and began collecting the debris from the soup and bread and stacking the plates in the dish cleaning machine. It was cathartic, as if ordering crockery and spoons in neat rows would help with getting my life into the same straight lines. The door to the kitchen opened again and Flora swept through from whatever adventure she had been able to persuade Cecil to participate in. I lifted her up, noticing that she seemed to be getting heaver and had grown a little. "You are turning into a little fatty!" I said to her, kissing her on the top of her head.

"Yeah, you're right Millie, I keep telling Okan the same thing," Joao said, straight faced, "But he just won't listen!" Okan took aim with a pudding spoon and hit Joao in the eye with a perfect shot. "I can't believe you did that!" Joao looked suitably stunned and then made a big thing out of wiping the cream out of his eye and eating it. Tara tried to look cross but her face kept smiling.

"Are you saying you *really* don't know how this energy source works?" Rari asked hopefully to the collective groans from around the table.

"Sorry Rari, I *really* don't," Weldon answered. He held out his pudding bowl to me as I was still standing near the counter and I put three large spoons of the creamy mixture in, adding fruit from the bottom of the serving bowl and handing it back. I leaned down to give him a hug and a small pinging noise erupted from the com that was situated by the back door, it was the one that Weldon used to keep an eye, or really an ear, on the stock. Coded for the vildenbeast's higher body temperature and quicker movement, it wasn't a particularly accurate sensor system but it fulfilled a need. We all looked at it. I realised by the expressions on the faces of everyone in the room but me, that it had now been programmed for something else.

For a split second nothing happened. Then Weldon pointed his personal com at the main light unit. The room went dark at the same time as Okan pushed me to the ground. Rari was by the door to the house with a gun in his hand. I could see the gleam on the surface of the weapon in the moonlight from the window, which had been open to bring in a welcome breeze. Now it had welcomed in something else. Weldon tapped his personal com again and connected to the wall unit. A small holograph sprang up; two men were standing by the dropdown ship. They seemed to be waiting. "They better not be trying to steal Buddy," I whispered anxiously.

"It's Marl," Tara said, her voice was normal in volume and therefore loud in the dark.

We all moved from our defensive positions, as no one was actually shooting at us it seemed pointless to act out any battle tactics, though Weldon didn't turn the lights back on and Okan didn't let go of my arm.

"I'm going to go out and see what they want," Tara said. She was trying to keep the edge of hope from her words but I could feel it radiating from her in supernova proportions.

The small pinpoints of red light from the slim torches we carried made it possible not to trip over our feet. Rari, Tara and I were moving quietly through the trees at the side of the track to where the ship had been parked. I knew Okan and Weldon were armed and somewhere in the dark shadows. Joao was by the farmhouse front door, also armed but angry about being left behind.

"Hey!" Marl said, "We thought you'd be out soon. Better than ringing the doorbell," he pointed at the ship. He gave Tara a hug and shook my hand. Rari nodded his greeting and Marl returned it. The other man that I recognised from the night at the skydancing towers, waved at me. We all looked as if we were planning an afternoon tea at a good London hotel, but without the cucumber sandwiches.

"Don't suppose you can give us a tour of the ship," Marl asked Rari, who shook his head slowly. "No, I didn't think so," he laughed. He stretched. "I guess Okan's out there in the dark with a bead on me?" Rari said nothing. Marl shrugged. "It's what I'd do."

"Did you find out anything about Ziggy?" Tara asked.

"To the point," Marl said, "Yes, I did."

We stood for a moment, each thinking our separate thoughts. Tara sagged against me and I wanted to strangle Marl and hear his bones crack. I didn't know if your bones actually cracked when you snapped someone's neck, but if there was any justice, it would have been a good loud one. Tara was shaking with suppressed emotion of her own, it just didn't involve violence. Rari was leaning carefully against the ship with the hand that held the gun free and clear. He looked less like a professor than I had ever seen him. More like the type of men who earn a living by creeping up on you from behind. I imagined Marl was used to people wanting to kill him and I was positive I wasn't in his top ten of things to worry about, Rari I was not so sure. Marl hadn't fallen for the geeky professor profile for a second.

We stood in awkward silence for a moment and then Tara detached herself from my unwilling fingers and went for a short walk with Marl. They spoke quietly and no matter what listening tactics I tried, I couldn't hear what they said. Rari and Marl's associate eyed each other in the way that dogs who think they might have to fight someone else's battle do, it was unnerving.

I remembered a man I had met when I had been trying out skydiving. It had lasted, the skydiving, a few summers and featured some spectacular sunsets at ten thousand feet over the old military bases, that were dotted around England. He had decided when he left the army that he was good at only one thing, which was killing people. Either his partner was severely dense or she didn't seem to mind. He hired out to the countries and obscure places you have to find on a wall map and died in a stupid parachuting accident the summer I gave it up. It was odd the memories that sprung to mind when you were standing in the dark with armed people around you. What you remembered was not so much about death, but mainly the stupidity.

Tara returned and gave me a hug. "It was good of you to tell me Marl," she said, looking over her shoulder at him.

"That's okay," Marl replied, as if we were standing in a shop asking for the cheese counter. Though 'you owe me one' was clearly written in the spaces in-between each word.

The men turned to go and Rari straightened up. He watched as they got onto a small runabout. Marl gave a salute and they swept away into the dark, the whoosh of the machine bending the grass and filling the moonlight with mad shadows.

Our own shadows came out of the trees and Weldon went to Tara and put his arm around her. "I know," she said. "He's probably lying. But I had to hear it anyway."

I looked from Okan to Weldon to Rari and back again. "Right, for those of us without a listening device, what did he say?"

"That Ziggy was with a small, powerful borderers group called the Tar Dal. She has been seen by someone who escaped." Tara's voice seemed to shake with emotion.

"What are the chances that it *might* be true?" I asked no one.

"As in all credible lies it might have an element of truth to it," Okan said. "Someone took her and they're a good possible candidate."

"I didn't know they had names." I wasn't sure why it bothered me so much, but there was something about giving a family name to a group that was disconcerting.

"Come on, let's go before Joao has a fit and comes storming out here with a blaster," Weldon said, with great prescience as a moment later the sound of careful footsteps was accompanied by a few swearwords as Joao realised, we were alone.

"Damn! I was looking forward to meeting that guy again," he grumbled, still looking angry.

I walked off into the dark and tried to gather my own thoughts. A hand on my shoulder made me jump. "Are you okay?" Okan asked me. He put his arm around me and squeezed. It was the strength of hug that made you remember your bones aren't flexible, but was comforting on so many levels. I sighed. Okan said, "I can hear you thinking again, did I ever mention that it makes me really nervous?"

The others had joined us after Weldon and Rari had been on a short walkabout to check that Marl and his friend had left. "What is the possibility," I said, "Of anyone *actually* escaping from the borderers?"

"I don't imagine Marl was thinking we might fall for the information, he was maybe just hoping that he could get a bit closer," Okan said. His voice was careful but it was clear and I didn't ask closer to what, or to whom.

Tara was quiet and her feelings were the puzzled, hurt and angry that comes to anybody who has lost someone. "I know I'm being messed with but I can't give up," she whispered.

"No one expects you to," Okan said. "I will help you look until we find out where she is." It sounded as if it was the promise from a warrior just before he goes off on a quest and it felt as if the dragons were out there; old as time and not always on your side.

The house was a pool of calm sitting in the clouded fields, where someone had decided long ago, here was a good place to build a future. Weldon's ancestors had chosen well. I sat out on the veranda in the rocking chair, Cecil asleep on my lap. I could see the shadows of the cattle in the moonlight and feel Jupiter leaning down towards me, a curve of expectation full in the dark sky. "What do you think?" I whispered to the cat. His ears flicked my words away. "It feels as if it could be home doesn't it."

"For as long as you want." Weldon came and sat down next to me in the other rocker.

"Isn't it difficult to have us here?" I asked him, my voice still quiet with evening. "It's been nothing but trouble since we turned up," I added.

Weldon was silent for a moment, then, "I can't imagine my life without you. My family has all come back to me in you, all the brothers and sisters I never had. Tara is more alive than I've seen her since we lost Ziggy, and my parents would have been pleased to see the house full of life the way it's supposed to be. For the first time I have someone to share the heavy stuff with." I didn't think for a moment he was just talking about lifting feed.

He and I sat wordless for a long time after that, because anything I could think of would have been totally inadequate and Weldon was all talked out.

We were peaceful in our stillness, so I moved carefully around the kitchen trying not to disturb the ghosts and making a hot drink as I watched Weldon set the alarms and lock all the doors. He came over to the table and gave me a hug. "Don't stay up too late." Then he was gone.

I crept up the stairs not wanting to bother anyone, but I could see a light under Joao's door and I tapped on the wood hoping for some company. "Come on in," Joao's whisper was loud enough to wake up Flora who stuck her trunk out of the open, dark doorway to Tara and Weldon's room. I scooped her up as I went in to see Joao.

"What's up Millie, can't sleep?" Joao settled himself on the pillows shuffling to one side of the big bed so I could join him. I leaned back against the headboard and settled Flora into the space between us. She began the circling that predisposed sleep.

"I'm just feeling a bit," I didn't finish. He held out his hand and I took it.

Okan's head appeared around the slightly open door, his hair stuck up in restless midnight peaks. "Are you moving in on my date?" He asked Joao, yawning.

Joao nodded. "Yep, she was getting bored waiting for you to do the right thing." Okan made a face as if he agreed.

"You do know I'm still sitting here?" I smiled. It was as if the words were part of a puzzle where all the 'pieces' were here and under one roof where they belonged. Except of course for Simon.

"What's that about?" Okan touched my winkled forehead with a gentle finger. He then moved to squash me up against Flora and Joao who both grumbled in a tuneless harmony.

"Simon," I said. I pulled Flora onto my lap where she settled with her trunk twined around one of my fingers. Her puppy breathing was something you could have listened to all night.

"Are you worried he won't come over here?" Joao looked sideways at me and managed to catch Okan's eyes with the expression that hides years of communicating without speaking.

"I think I'm worried that he will," I said, without really understanding what I was talking about. However, it made perfect sense to Okan and Joao who both nodded wisely. I wished someone would explain it to me. Because the thought of what would happen next was making sleep impossible.

Rari yawned loudly and pushed open the door to the bedroom. He had a tray of brandy mugs which were my favourite and a plate of some large biscuits that Tara had managed to make in-between filling out pointless online forms. He sat the tray down on the small table by Joao's side of the bed and we passed the drinks and food around. Hot water and honey vied with the strong brandy making a potent mixture. Even the fumes made my head spin. I broke a biscuit and dunked it into the drink.

"That is *so* disgusting, I think I'm going to have to try it," Rari said. But his experience was woefully thin and a bit fell off into his drink causing a mini tidal wave.

"Don't you get brandy on my covers!" Tara said. She brought in her own mug and settled next to Rari on the other end of the bed.

We ate and talked, whispering until Weldon came in with another tray and more brandy. My head and eyes had stopped working in unison and every time I moved to look at someone it was a moment before my vision caught up. I laughed as I realised, we were all crammed onto the double bed, as if the chairs in the room were too far away for night-time conversation. The shadows started at the edge of the covers in the one single lamplight. Here was safety for a while in this ship in the sea of the dark night.

I got up to go to my room, or Ziggy's, staggering for a moment against the overwhelming odds of two brandies and several chocolate biscuits. "Night Millie!" Tara laughed, as I climbed over a grumbling Okan and slid out the door carrying Flora.

My bed was a haven of space, only Cecil curled in one corner spoiled the symmetry of emptiness. Flora settled on the pillow and pulled a curl of my hair carefully towards her to suck. I slept, but not peacefully. Somehow, I was tangled up with Professor Theadus in an argument, where I was tied to the sacrifice chair and he asked me questions I couldn't answer about my parents and the wormhole gene. It felt real enough to make me wake with fear.

Okan was stretched out on the other side of the bed, breathing quietly. Cecil curled up asleep against him. I watched the man's face in the half light of the moon that splashed across both of us. It seemed amazingly peaceful, as if he was able to push away all the things he didn't want to deal with. My night time was *full* of everything. I felt resentful for a moment, then grateful not to be alone. Flora squeaked in her sleep, curling my hair even tighter in her fist of a trunk. I moved carefully so that I could put a hand on Okan's chest and feel him breathing. I was the same as Flora, seeking comfort in contact.

I must have slept again because I dreamed of the verse that was empty of people and walking along the seashore with Cecil and Flora. The little elephant couldn't resist the waves and ran back and forth playing chase with the sand and tide. Cecil was content to be scooped up and carried. He purred his contentment on my shoulder and the sun was warm on my back.

I pushed back the covers and headed to the bathroom. There was no sign of Okan or the little creatures. Standing under the shower I let the water run over my hair and down my back. "You want some tea?" Tara shouted from the bedroom. She came in, bringing a large mug and some juice in a glass, which I gestured for her to pass through the shower door and drank in one go.

"What *is* all over the floor?" She muttered as she left me to it. "Sand!" I heard her say as she puzzled her way to the landing. I smiled and tipped my head back under the shower.

The kitchen was full of people with somewhere else to be. All the fresh food Weldon had prepared was being eaten as if another meal might not be possible for a while. Joao and Rari came in from the barns through the back door and settled down in the spaces, talking about feed bins to Tara and the next crop rotation to Weldon. I wanted to shout and scream; anything to stop the normal. My hand shook as I reached for bread and cheese and Weldon put down his forkful of eggs and passed me a plate.

It got very quiet quickly. Okan tried to say something but I got up to go before he could start. I went into the hall and watched as Rari came out to me. He gave me a hug and pulled a strand of my damp hair. "We'll be here when you get back, Millie. Try not to take too long, the time differential is not in our favour this way around."

Flora hooted from the doorway to the kitchen but Tara grabbed her before she could run to me. "For goodness' sake this girl is covered in sand too! Where have you been poppet?" She asked the surprised pachyderm.

Rari looked at me, speculating and I shrugged. "I'll be as quick as I can," I said.

Tara gave me a hug. "Be careful." She had squashed Flora between us and the sand trickled off her in little dusty curls into the sunlight, I watched the wood floor as it went away from me and shaped itself into a cloud of accreted particles, and the rush of shocking silence that was the wormhole.

My kitchen was suspiciously tidy and clean with no me and no cat. The fridge had been defrosted and turned off and the cupboards were empty. I wandered around the house checking the boxed books and the folded clothes. It was as if I had moved but didn't know it. I lifted the landline phone which was still connected, then I dialled Simon's number and got the busy signal.

I walked down the road towards the village. It was one of those late autumn mornings that make living on the moor a well-kept secret. Clear blue skies and warm enough to go without a coat. A fresh breeze caught the brown leaves and helped them to fall to the ground as if they couldn't make the decision for themselves.

The farm was autumn quiet in its peacefulness, Mr Payne had finished ploughing over the fields and they were beautiful in their furrowed symmetry. I thought about the spring fields in Joao's verse, looking almost the same, except for the hovering vehicle, which I was certain Mr Payne would have welcomed with the grateful lack of suspicion of farmers everywhere. Anything to get the ploughing done before the rain and frost. A flapping set of the whitest sheets in five verses hung on the washing line.

The stretched bungalow that belonged to Cecil's owners was really empty. They had talked several times about going to Spain for the winter and I supposed this year had seemed a good time to start.

The valley was sleepy in its absence of people and the sense of coming winter was full in the sparse trees and the few fat clouds on the horizon.

My heart ached for a moment and it took me by surprise, it is not easy to understand homesickness unless you have been *made* to leave. It's about choice and familiarity and the smell of winter on the wind and the need to belong somewhere.

I had never spent much time at Simon's house in the village. It was on the other hill overlooking the small river that ran through the edge of the fields. I spoke to no one as I went down the road, the shops were just beginning their day and as I passed by her, the girl in the deli waved to me and yawned and smiled at the same time.

Simon embraced the country look as if he had read the book first. The double fronted Georgian house was decorated to the required standards of a true obsessive. There were builders and carpenters in the area who would tremble if you even mentioned the words Bridge House.

I knocked on the front door, ignoring the traditional bell pull on one side; something that I knew drove Simon up the wall and into the garden. I arranged my smile as I heard his feet tapping on the immaculately polished hall floor. He flung open the door ready with a lecture of what looked as if it could be epic proportions and stopped. My grin got bigger. Then I realised his silence contained something that I had never seen on Simon's face before. Fear.

"What are you *doing* here?" He practically hissed, grabbing my arm and dragging me in. He checked the lane to the left and right and then signalled to someone on the hill behind the house that I couldn't see. He turned to look at me reaching to give me a hug even as he said, "They've been here. Trevor was here yesterday." I must have looked blank because he added, "Zatar." I felt my knees wobble and Simon helped me to a chair in the hall that was absolutely right for the period. Its spindly legs looked to be in a more precarious state than mine, but you should never underestimate the Georgians, it seemed to bear my weight with even tempered tolerance and the odd creak.

"Trevor?" I asked, puzzled.

"Yes." Simon looked back at me with that 'what is she thinking' expression on his face.

"It's not very intimidating." I began to smile.

"I don't think we can have a debate on exactly how many psychopaths in history were called Trevor or Colin. I mean someone must have thought Adolph was a cute name once," he snapped.

"Come on, we need to get out of here for now." He pulled me to my feet. "I'll make you coffee."

We went into the kitchen; an homage to the pages of all design catalogues everywhere. The coffee pot on the counter would have kept me in science books for a year. "I have asked Margery to look after things for a while and my friends will sort out any of the security details." He began the procedure for the coffee to brew and something that was similar to the dashboard of a 747 filtered, sluttered and poured out the perfect cup.

"Cake?" He asked me. "I smiled. "Okay, stupid question." He cut a huge portion of chocolate cake and then sat down to drink his own cup.

"What did Trevor want?" I asked through the thick icing that stuck to the roof of my mouth along with the fear.

"Don't underestimate this man, Millie." Simon studied the swirl of foam on the surface of the liquid in his cup. "He was always a mean bastard, even in the early days," he added thoughtfully.

"How did he know you were here? I thought you said you would be safe without the fixer." I drank the hot coffee and marvelled at the smooth taste of the beans that probably cost more than the average monthly mortgage.

"Apparently he's been watching us for some time," he said dryly.

"What did he want?" I asked, but knew the answer before he said it.

"You."

"So why didn't he kill you, he's been shooting at everyone else."

"He thinks I can get you for him, as the other attempts," Simon waved his hand around to describe the mayhem that had been following me around, "Haven't been too successful."

"Simon, do you know who made the fixers?" I looked carefully at the man's face. He was so dear to me that the ripple of concealment was a surprise. He was thinking about how much he should say. I realised for the first time that more than my own skin was at stake. More than Okan and Rari getting away from the organisation that had programmed them for hate and fear. Or Joao finding a place where he could live with his own past and stop paying for other people's. A sense of something bigger filtered through my conscious thought. He hadn't answered, but I groaned anyway.

"Where will this end?"

"Let's go, I need to get my travel things." Simon pulled me to my feet again. "I don't want to be here when Zatar gets back. He'll know you are here. It's easier to get a response from the fixers in this verse."

"How do you know that?"

"He told me," Simon said as he went up the stairs. I followed more slowly and found him in the oh so perfect bedroom, stuffing another cashmere jumper into a small leather designer label back-pack. "You never know when you'll need an extra layer."

"Are you sure you don't know Tara?" I asked suspiciously. It felt as if everyone I had met lately was interconnected on a level I couldn't yet understand. My life was a vast puzzle with clues that had been scattered to each of the verses over time and distance, waiting for someone to put the pieces back together again. "You're travelling a bit light for a gay guy," I said, "Where's the heated socks?"

"Sometimes darling you can be really spiteful," he smiled. "Come on, whiz me into neverwhere." He grabbed the neat pack and slung it over his shoulder and we went downstairs. I noticed with a sense of passing sadness that he scanned the rooms and the deep stairwell as if he were remembering it all for the future.

He tapped a security code into the box on the wall by the front door and we went into the kitchen. A small com unit rested on the counter by the sink and was flashing a red light. It looked suspiciously similar to the technology that Tara's verse used. Not something you could get on eBay. Simon spoke into the com after tapping the lighted key. "I'm off. Keep an eye out, I'll check in." A deep attractive voice answered him in the affirmative, using the type of language familiar to those who had probably spent several years in a special forces unit. I found myself making a face. Simon knew everyone; it was the who's who of off the wall people. A collection of misfits who fitted into their own world, wherever that was. I wondered just how many people who lived in the village had actually *really* earned the term 'incomers.'

"If this place was filled with dreamwalkers I wouldn't be surprised." I sat down while he put the coffee pot and the cups in the dishwasher.

"Don't be so suspicious," Simon drawled.

"Well, my money is on that woman who works in the post office," I grumbled.

"She comes from *Walthamstow*!" Simon made a face. "Actually, that might as well be another verse."

"Come on, time to go." He pulled me to my feet. "*Don't* get this wrong, it's a while since I did this and the spin gives my middle ear a bit of a do, now, give me a hug." He put his arms around me and held on tight. I smiled as I thought about how we must look to a passing burglar or the postman. Lovers lost in an embrace, not friends lost in a universe of endless possibilities.

I fixed my eyes on the hallway in Tara and Weldon's house. The sun cast its magic in the shadows on the floor and the sound of the farm filled the distance. It moved into my vision and the wormhole performed its curved and silent dance in my head and my heart.

"Oh, dear me!" Simon slid dramatically to the floor. "I remember now why I don't like to fly."

"Simon! You won't even travel on a *train*; your chauffeur sent his children to private school on the basis of your neurosis."

"Well," he said, clutching his forehead, "You meet some terrible people on the train."

"Don't be such a diva!" I helped him up and he clung on to the banister.

"Millie!" Tara came out of the kitchen and gave me a hug. "You must be Simon." She held out a hand and he kissed it in an old-fashioned gesture that usually worked a treat on the para-military wing of the local Woman's Institute. It was effective with Tara too. She beamed. I made a rude noise in the back of my throat and Simon gave me a look that fell into the parental scale somewhere up near, 'any more out of you and we go straight home.'

"Come on into the kitchen and have a cup of coffee," Tara offered. "The men are in from the fields after the evening rounds and eating their heads off."

Simon turned around to me and made a face, mouthing the words 'the men are in from the fields,' with a wicked grin. It was my turn to make the parent face, which had about as much effect on Simon as it would have had on a twelve-year-old truant with a bottle of illicit cider.

I sighed with relief at the sight of Okan and Rari, something cruel and cold at the back of my mind had been taunting me with the thought that they wouldn't be here when I got back. I sat down next to Okan, who put his arm around me and kissed the top of my head. He was eating a large plate of homemade bread and stew. "I hope you haven't left any samples up there." I pointed to my hair. He pretended to pick out a few bits just for effect and because he knew I would find it irritating. I thumped him on the arm and then helped myself to the bread and cheese that Weldon offered. It was confusing to have had breakfast, morning coffee and an evening meal in a few hours, but I tried not to let the temporal differential interfere with my diet.

"Simon. You've met Okan and Joao." Tara was doing the introductions as I suddenly seemed to have lost my voice.

Simon nodded to the two men. "It seems odd that neither of you are bleeding," he said sarcastically.

"Give it time," Okan answered, "I'm sure we can put that right."

"This is Weldon." Simon got up and shook hands in a formal way. Weldon was equally solemn, nodding and shaking with the same gravity.

"This is Rari."

The two men reached out across the table and I felt with a momentary pang, that I had lost something. It was as if a spark of recognition passed between them, an identification of something shared. A place I couldn't understand. It was only a moment, but it made me realise that I had seen Simon with associates before, even partners and the odd one-night stand, but I had never seen him impressed by anyone.

Simon ate stew and bread and then fruit and coffee, he listened to the farm talk and made some serious suggestions about crop rotations that made me wonder where my old friend had gone. He shrugged when I looked at him questioningly. "My parents had a farm." He went on to talk quietly about the dropdown craft now parked in the outer barn, explaining the possibility that it might have something that Zatar could use to track us. When Rari smacked his forehead in a dramatic fashion, Simon added, "I think I may be able to identify a code sequence for you." A *code sequence,* I had trouble controlling my incredulity. "It's been a long time since I did anything like it, but I'll help if I can," he finished.

My head spun, the trip through the wormhole could do that to you, but even more difficult was when someone was not what they appeared to be, or what you needed them to be, as if the world had changed shape around you. It wasn't that I didn't really understand; it was more as if, when so much was not the same you wanted the people to be consistent.

"Well now." Simon sipped coffee without the telltale wince he usually reserved for anything that didn't come from a speciality shop in Old Compton Street. "What happens next?"

I listened carefully to the silence that followed. We all took our own mental step backwards for a fraction of a second.

"Okan and I are heading back to our own verse to get a tracking device." Rari added, "We'll try and sever the link on the returning mechanism. Unlike the others we can be yanked back at a moment's notice."

Simon nodded. "I have heard of that. It was set up to help any of the dreamwalkers who had got into difficulties, it also had a communication component." He looked at Rari who shook his head and managed to express disquiet and fascination in equal measure at the thought. "As far as I knew," Simon continued, "It was destroyed when the bomb went off in the conference centre. It had been part of an experimental phase; there were lots of original ideas to link in with a new way of thinking. The prototype was taken along to the meeting. The central planets science guild in this verse held the meeting on Earth." He shook his head. "I had an idea that some of the technology had survived, but it seems odd." He looked thoughtful.

"What?" Okan sounded edgy, but I could understand why, I felt a little sharp myself, enough to cut a slice off the thickening atmosphere around the table.

"I think it means that while some of us were bleeding, someone was helping themselves to whatever they could carry." He shrugged. "When that bomb went off, we all realised it was time to disappear. I was with Nancy; we came out here to the settlements for a while and then I moved on to Millie's verse with her parents. It became obvious that someone was looking for them and Millie's verse is more difficult to access."

No one spoke for a moment. "I wonder what else is out there that we don't know about," Simon muttered, shaking his head.

It was veritable wave of information; I pulled the plate of small cakes toward me and began carefully removing the icing from the top of one with a knife. Simon reached across and smacked my fingers. "Don't just eat the sugar you'll get hyper and I'll have to pay someone to sit on you."

Rari laughed and Joao said, "She's always doing that."

"You should have more sense than to let her; really Millie!" I managed not to scowl, but I was pleased that everyone who had been letting me get away with it looked slightly guilty. Simon had always managed to make me feel about nine. I was glad to see he had the same effect on everyone else. I knew anyway it was nothing about cake and everything about control. Simon could reduce a team of shark eyed accountants to a bunch of children, faced with scrambled egg and semolina. It was working with the current audience.

I sighed. It was hard to fit all the things that didn't belong, into the places in your life where you were used to having tidy thoughts. I knew that Simon had known my parents for a long time, but my understanding of the past was that they had met because he had moved into the village and needed a doctor. I hunted back for any giveaway memories and couldn't find even one. He had made no real contact with me until my parents had died. I was just going to have to accept that the truth was, they had been running all over the multiverse together.

"Is Donald Theadus still here?" Simon asked. Weldon nodded. He surreptitiously edged a slice of icing towards me which he had surgically removed from his own piece of cake, while maintaining eye contact with Simon; I made a mental note not to play poker with him as I mainlined sugar. "He was the one who warned your parents of trouble, Millie. He was a good man."

"We think he's been giving Zatar information," Joao said.

Simon shook his head. He suddenly looked old and tired. I felt the panic well inside me, the way you do when the people who have cared for you, appear to need you to look after *them*. "I guess we all do what we have to, to survive," Simon said. "Are you sure?" He asked Okan.

A small exchange of unspoken communication passed between Weldon and Okan. Rari shrugged. It was a dance of semiotic proportions. "Yes," Okan answered.

"I'm still going to need to talk to him," Simon replied. He pulled the coffee pot towards him and helped himself. "I need to ask some questions about what happened after the guild broke up. I was staying out of the way in the port here on Ganymede and Rilla and Tom had set up a small splinter group in the same place, Nancy was able to collect information on people using the bar as a cover."

"I thought Theadus was responsible for some inappropriate behaviour on your Earth towards dreamwalkers?" Joao asked Weldon.

"I think there was some talk that he gave people up to the government that followed." Weldon shrugged. "I don't know. It could just have been gossip."

"He warned me *and* Millie's parents, he warned a lot of other people too. I think he was a very brave man. I suspect he still is." Simon sounded so sure. Sad but sure.

"Does Charlie Morris still work with your organisation in your verse Okan?" Simon asked.

Rari moved back from the table as if someone had hit him. His face was full of fear. Okan's usually healthy suntan blanched into a deathly white. "You could say that," he told Simon, "He runs the whole programme now." I tried to touch Rari's fingers which were gripped to the edge of the table. He was incapable of response until I peeled one hand away and held onto it, just hoping he would stop drowning long enough for me to rescue him.

"Really?" Simon appeared intrigued.

"Simon!" I sounded a little panicked myself. But it was hard to see the two men who I respected for their courage and intelligence look as if they had both lost the gamble.

"Okay, maybe we just caught a break." Simon went into thinking mode.

I could see that Okan and Rari were cold with the possibility that they had just handed over their plan to someone who knew the head of the organisation they were trying to get away from. I threw a lump of precious icing at Simon's head and scored a direct hit. "Simon!" I pointed at Rari and Okan.

"Right." Simon sat up and pulled the icing from his hair handing it back to me as if it had been something returnable. "I think I should go with you. Back to your verse. If anyone can get Morris's knickers in a spin, it's me." Simon looked inappropriately pleased about something, glad and grim. My heart did the type of yoyo that usually precluded a response involving sirens and very worried people.

"How is this going to play out?" Okan asked after a pause in which the whole room held its collective breath. "You don't think he's going to be suspicious of someone turning up after so many years?"

Simon looked up. "Not me." His eyes glittered. "He always knew he would see me again one day."

Most of the time I forgot how powerful a man Simon could be, being gay was a piece of something he held apart from the rest of him. It was difficult to reconcile the barely concealed menace with the man who sang karaoke after too many strawberry daiquiris.

"So how do you suggest we get you there?" Okan looked puzzled then resigned. "You've actually been to my verse," he sighed, "I thought you'd met Morris in this verse."

"He's a dreamwalker?" I asked and then added, "You've been to Okan's verse?" I felt as if the sirens would be too late for any kind of hope, as my heart was definitely going into meltdown. "Information overload," I said and leaned my head on the table closing my eyes for a moment. I could feel Rari's hand on the back of my neck in the way of comfort returned.

"Charlie's not actually from your verse Okan, he's from mine," Simon spoke with a quiet at the edge of a storm bite to his voice.

"Okay!" Tara got up. "I think I'll make some brandy. Anyone want to join me?" All hands were silently raised. No one spoke. She busied herself with hot water and honey pouring a generous measure of aromatic alcohol into each mug. We all looked on as if we were playing a part in a necessary lifesaving ritual.

"I'm just going out to check the pens one more time." Weldon got up and went towards the back door, carrying his drink with him.

"Do you mind if I come with you?" Simon asked, as if we had been talking about the weather and the local cricket team's chances in the league.

"Sure." Weldon indicated a hand towards the door much as a waiter in a restaurant would do, and they went off into the night, leaving a trail of emotional debris.

"There's rain on the wind," Simon said, looking out, as he closed the door behind him.

"Millie, can you come and have a look at some of the new designs the weavers have sent me," Tara asked. She held the two mugs of brandy and indicated that we should leave the kitchen with wiggling eyebrows and a humourless grin. Okan snorted at her attempts to be subtle, but he smiled in a tired tight way and I kissed the back of his neck as I left.

"They need some time to get their heads around all this," Tara explained.

"*I* need some time to get my head around it." I took the brandy from her as we crossed the hall into the study. Flora squeaked and looked up from her vantage point in the chair by the fire. Cecil was curled on the back of the same chair, one paw extended outwards in an effort to balance in his sleep.

"Is Simon what he appears to be." She sat down and tried again. "I'm saying, can we trust him?"

"With my life, always and forever," I said. Flora gave a squeak that seemed to punctuate my words and Tara nodded her agreement. She handed me a screen that was a larger version of the com everyone carried. I tapped the keys and the screen sprung into a holographic tizzy settling down to show the different designs that the weavers had sent Tara for her approval.

"Well." I must have looked confused.

"What?" Tara stood up and reached over and scooped up Cecil as his efforts to maintain his balance were losing ground to gravity and sleep.

"I didn't think we were actually going to be *looking* at designs. I thought we were just getting out of the way."

"We are not meant, some of us, for a purposeless moment," she said tartly, then smiled, "Though some purposelessness is probably as important as the filling every minute part."

The designs were good but without that innovative spark. I tried to describe what I couldn't see, without much effect.

Tara looked puzzled. "I don't think I understand," she said, "It's difficult. Ziggy used to help with the process. She had a real eye for what was interesting."

The study was at the front of the house and I could hear the quiet voices of Weldon and Simon out on the farm, eventually they came to sit on the veranda so that all that separated us was a window.

"How are you going to get to Okan's verse, won't it be difficult if you've not done it for a while? I'm not an expert on this thing you do but isn't Millie the only one who can dreamwalk someone across?" A creak of a rocking chair told me that Simon had sat down.

"I need to wait until the others are ready to continue, Weldon. I don't want to cause divisions before we've even started. Okan and Rari are reeling from the possibility that I might be a liability to them."

"You're right," Weldon said, in a tone that suggested quiet respect from someone who really understood waiting.

I looked at Tara. "I think we should go and sit with them." She nodded, picking up the holo-screen from the floor and putting Cecil into the chair when she got up. He settled contentedly into the space where she had been. Flora was having none of being left behind and hung onto my hair with a grumpy hoot when I tried to put her down.

The sky was full of the moon and the curve of Jupiter filled the horizon. Weldon went to get more rockers and we sat in the silence of the stars in the stillness of a spring night.

"May I see?" Simon gestured for the holo-screen that still had the last design hopping around in a crazy dance. Tara handed it over and Simon went through the program with a few 'um's and 'ah's. None of which sounded very positive. "Girl you need help; this stuff is one step from a Sunday afternoon knitting contest. Do you have an adjuster on the program?" She showed him the keys and he went to work pulling things apart. He and Tara seriously bonded over the cashmere designs while Weldon and I looked on, happy to be a couple of spare wheels on the journey.

"Okay, I think I'm going to have an orgasm," Simon said. "This is looking good!"

"Cashmere tends to do that to him," I said sarcastically.

Tara laughed, "I think I understand what you mean. It is rather special, isn't it?" She played with the dancing display going over the different alterations with an innocent pleasure.

"I want to put in an order for this." I pointed at one of the hooded jumpers that had large covered buttons and a curved sleeve. It was in a deep raspberry colour.

Weldon stood up as the three men came out to join us on the veranda. He and Rari got more chairs and they sat down in their collective silence. "The fixers we have in our verse and the tracking devices come from the meeting that was bombed out?" Okan asked Simon. Round two, I thought.

"Yes. I would think so. Zatar is a cunning little shit but I don't think he has the scientific brilliance to make any more of the

308

fixers and I think the tracking device he has is one of the origi-
nals," Simon answered clearly. "Your parents were experimenting
with other ideas, Millie. A wormhole device was one of them. It
looks as if Zatar has been able to work out how to use it. He
arrived in Millie's verse in rather an odd fashion yesterday," he
added, "I mean yesterday of course, in a purely non temporal
differential way." Tara and Weldon nodded in complete understanding. My uncomprehending brain was having a serious effect
on my eyes.

"Yeah, we saw that too," Joao answered, "In Millie's kitchen. It
looked like a tunnel."

"No," Simon said tartly, before Rari could take a breath, "I don't
know how it works. Only that it must be limiting if he's still using
fixers to send his foot soldiers through. They must have had their
DNA altered to fit a previous owner, because the fixers bond with
the recipient on a genetic as well as the subatomic level."

"That's what we thought." Okan nodded. "Many of the children
in our original group have disappeared." Simon grimaced as if the
information was a painful confirmation.

"Don't forget, it's Millie he's after," he said into the dark night.

I could hear the soft sounds of the goats moving in the fields,
settling into the quiet with their kids curled around them for safety
and comfort. More stars filled the sky as the horizon changed and
the heavy curve of Jupiter drifted onwards. It felt as if the most
powerful piece of music was playing but I couldn't hear it.

"Do you think we can dreamwalk you into our verse? Without all
the alarm bells going off," Rari said hopefully.

"Oh, I think the bells will go off," Simon snorted, "But we can get
what we want."

"Do you *understand* that *my* verse wants Millie too, they and
Morris think that she's the key to taking over the power in all of the
verses. We've been looking for her for years!" Okan sounded exasperated and frightened. It was hard to hear.

"Have you given him anything?" Simon asked gently.

"No, I substituted Tara's daughter Ziggy's DNA, for hers. I took
some hair from the brush in her bedroom. I'm sorry Weldon, Tara, I

really am," Okan went on, "The scientists think it's just another dead end. But *he* won't give up. He wants it so much."

Both Tara and Weldon looked deeply shocked. She stumbled over the words, "But won't they know; Ziggy doesn't have the dreamwalk gene." There was an intense oily silence as the facts began to pour themselves all over the innocent. The lighted match of pain not far behind. "Ziggy's a dreamwalker," Tara whispered. I took her hand and squeezed it in mine and tried to give her my strength.

Not one word was said about the fact that the gene must have been inherited from Ziggy's father, Joao. It was thick in the minds of everyone there, but no one spoke. I handed Flora from my lap to Tara's so that she could hold the 'elephant in the room' in her arms and take some comfort from the warmth.

"Do you know why it is easier to go from Millie's verse to this one?" Rari asked after a short amount of time. "We were thinking it has something to do with the temporal differential being less complicated when you cross the energy barrier into a faster temporal environment." Rari looked hopefully at Simon.

"Are you certain you never met Millie's parents, because you really sound like them." Simon shook his head. "The geek stuff is not really my area of expertise. I'm more cashmere designs." He pointed at the hologram of the pink jumper still doing its attractive dance on the floor by Tara's feet. Rari tried not to look disappointed but failed miserably. "Okay," Simon sighed, "I think that you're on the right track. As far as I remember, we have to pass through a time dilation field between the energy barrier and the other verse and it's a harder push to a slower verse."

Rari smiled and got out his personal com and began tapping keys so that mathematical formulas did their own whirl of light; looking, to my eyes, even more attractive than the jumper designs, because I was a geek too.

"We have to start making plans," Joao said. He seemed to have recovered from the news that his daughter was like him in every way.

"I don't see how, unless I know what Simon intends to do," Okan replied, with a fair level of suppressed tension.

"Oh my, a testosterone spill, how quaint," Simon drawled.

I reached across and pinched him hard on the arm. "Don't be such a bully! *They* don't know why you think this is possible and it's causing unnecessary grief." I paused, "Which would include me too, why do you think this man is going to be intimidated by your being there?"

Simon rubbed his arm theatrically and looked out into the dark night. "Well," he said eventually, "You have to remember sometimes that what you fear the most is what looks back at you from a mirror."

Rari said, "I've had the misfortune to spend a large amount of time with Charlie Morris and I'm pretty sure that he's not afraid of anything."

Simon sighed, he reached for the com with the cashmere designs and began fine tuning his previous efforts, tapping keys with no effort and watching the results with a critical eye. In the end we were all watching him, until it was a cathartic noise of future comfort. "The only person Zatar wants to get his hands on more than Millie is Charlie Morris." The silence that followed felt close to the singularity, curved and full at the edges with a darker core sucking you in towards the middle.

Tap, tap, went the keys on the com. "Zatar thought he was dead, though he must have worked out by now that he's not. They always wanted the same things those two, even when they were children, fighting over the same toys."

"They're brothers," Weldon said quietly.

"One of the most destructive relationships you can have, sibling rivalry forever loving someone and hating them at the same time," Simon whispered.

"I know how that works," Joao said bitterly.

We didn't talk anymore that night but no one slept much either. The expanding house took in one more lost soul and the silence of the dawn was punctuated with early risers looking for coffee and comfort.

I walked into the kitchen in my pyjamas and a pair of too big slippers that belonged to Ziggy. I had found them under the bed, abandoned in some past moment of vulnerable ordinariness. I had been looking for Flora who was playing hide and seek with an unwilling and grumpy, Cecil.

Okan was dressed and coming in through the back kitchen door with Weldon, they were talking about the farm; I tuned them out until I had poured coffee and sniffed the fumes. Okan kissed the top of my head and I grumbled into the mug. Weldon laughed and gave me a hug as he got more coffee for himself and Okan. "What's the matter Millie?" He began to sing an irritating little song which sounded as if it was a nursery rhyme, "You've got to wake up in the morning and put a smile on your face, or you'll be your mummy's disgrace and you won't be your daddy's darling." He looked at me. "Okay, you're not buying it!" He began dishing food out for a breakfast feast and I took my scowl upstairs for a hot shower.

The table was full when I got back. Simon, never usually an early bird, was guarding his coffee as if someone might be stupidly inclined to take it away. I sat down next to him and sang Weldon's rhyme. "Right," he said carefully, "That was truly terrible."

Joao reached over and gave me a plate of toast with the butter and honey already spread and I offered my coffee cup for a refill. Tara was nearest the stove and she poured. She seemed almost happy, as if something had filtered through the continuing grief and loss at last, it was a realisation of sorts and I recognised the feeling of a new hopefulness.

"What is everyone doing today?" I asked, trying for a little hope myself.

"Okan, Weldon and I are going to visit Professor Theadus," Simon answered. The coffee was beginning to work its magic because his voice sounded almost normal, back to its usual slightly irritating sarcastic drawl.

"Can I come?" I asked. A small exchange took place. It went from Simon to Okan to Weldon and then spread like a ripple around the rest of the table. I ground my teeth in irritation as people revisited their possible Millie babysitting duties and found the new plan satisfactory.

"Sure," Okan said.

I reached for more honey and some of the farm made cheese and pinched a newly cut piece of bread from Joao's plate while his back was turned at the stove making eggs. He did a silent film double take and then looked at me suspiciously. I buttered completely without guilt.

"Do you use the normal wormhole exit in your verse Millie?" Tara said. It stopped all thought. Everyone looked up. "I imagine, from what you've all said that Millie can come and go at any point, whereas Joao used a fixed wormhole point when he started dreamwalking." It sounded as if it was a question, but it was not. Simon nodded and so did Rari, we were all wondering what direction this was going in. "Somewhere in your vicinity is a fixed wormhole exit? A place where someone might come out by accident," Tara said. Simon and Okan nodded this time. "Don't you see?" She said, "Ziggy might be there!"

It was odd that no one had thought about it. The fact that we had all been suffering from information overload courtesy of Simon might have been an excuse, but we all began thinking about the possibility. Then the probability. "I suppose she might not have known that's what she was doing, but dreamwalking around here is not the way it is in Millie's verse, people realise it goes on." Simon smiled, in what I know he thought was a comforting way, but the staff in the bookshop referred to it as his 'smiling tiger' look.

"There's another possibility," Joao said, his face white with fear. In the morning shadows of sunshine spattering the kitchen table his expression was a floating mask. "There are several other verses she could have gone to, including mine."

Tara held onto her hope and sat still and calm, as if she had been given another chance. Weldon was looking out of the window far away into the distance, but I could see by the shape of his shoulders leaning relaxed against the back of the chair, that he too was getting something positive out of the thought. We all search for answers from the silent past and in the absence of any noise at all, impossibilities will do. I reached out and held Okan's hand for some human contact and he squeezed mine within his, making the potential for being alone as unlikely as the snow-covered mountains moving.

The clutter of the morning divided us into farm tasks and the university visit. Tara and Rari went off to see to the goats and Joao began clearing breakfast, he checked the com in the kitchen for a weather report, while Weldon and Okan went out to get the two farm runabouts ready for the trip into Twin Rivers.

"Does Professor Theadus know we're coming?" I asked Simon.

"Your Okan didn't think it was a good idea." He was on his fourth cup of coffee and he snagged a piece of toast from the plate before Joao put it in the recycler. He seemed to have brought a complete change of clothes with him and was going with the 'on the farm' outfit which consisted of a cravat and a V-necked cashmere with cords and boots. He looked the part. I had borrowed some of Ziggy's jeans and a t-shirt. Her trousers were too long for me and I had folded up the bottoms. The slippers slopped on my feet as I got up to go. It felt as if somewhere maybe there was someone who was trying to fit their big feet into shoes too small for them. I really hoped so.

Flora was eyeballing Simon and with her most persuasive hoot she tapped him on the knee for an offering. He picked her up and held her close to his face. She reached out and felt the shape of his features with her tiny trunk breathing gently on him, testing for whatever it is little things need to find when they make friends. The results were mutually acceptable and he kissed her soundly on the head. Toast and honey were offered and graciously received. I remembered why I loved the man for the millionth time and did some kissing myself before I went upstairs. He smiled and patted me on the face with a slightly sticky hand. As I went out of the door, I heard Joao say, in a rather puzzled way, "What was that for?"

"No idea mate," Simon replied, he added helpfully, "She's a woman, I don't understand them."

"*None* of us do," Joao said. "More coffee?"

"That would be splendid."

Their talk disappeared into the background of the farm as I

reached my room. I didn't know when it had become my room. As if the person that it really belonged to had vacated it in all the other ways that we left things behind. I grabbed my backpack and put on a windproof jacket that I had brought with me on a previous visit. My boots were under the bed with a still grumbling Cecil. He was hiding from Flora, who, as with most of us never knew when to quit. I felt for the boots and found a furry purring face instead. I crawled further under and joined him. Flat on my stomach I scrubbed at his ears until the purr became one of contentment rather than irritation.

"What are you doing?" Tara asked, as she came into the room.

"Talking to Cecil," I explained.

"You can't do that sitting on top of the bed?"

"Actually, it's quite nice under here," I sighed, the atavistic memory of cosy, small spaces and safety surfacing for a moment.

"Really," she said and scrabbled under the bed next to me.

Cecil's purr had changed to include an element of disbelief, but he stayed curled up around my left boot. "You didn't know Ziggy was dreamwalking?" I asked as we lay on the floor next to each other, our legs sticking out into the room.

"No, I should have guessed, but she never *said* anything. It's the way things are here now, it's not quite acceptable anymore." Tara tried to shrug but the base of the bed got in the way. "I think they still monitor them on Earth. I guess she thought it would be easier if no one knew."

"Tara, does she know that Joao is her biological parent?"

"I think she worked it out, but she never asked. I just didn't feel it was important. Weldon is her father. She loves him."

"Still, it must have been pretty confusing."

"Yes." Tara nodded. "Yes," she said again, as if she'd had the conversation with herself a thousand times before.

"What are you *doing*?" Okan's voice was incredulous. He stood by the door, or rather his feet did, I couldn't see the rest of him.

"I was just looking for my other boot," I sighed, sliding out from the place of safety followed by a slightly sheepish Tara. She held out the boot by way of explanation.

"Yeah, I can see that." Okan shook his head. "One day you're going to have to explain the female psyche to me. Because I *really* don't understand it."

"You're not supposed to, it's a secret," I said crossly.

He helped me to my feet and I put my boots on and tied the laces. A small clunk of a noise made us all look around with the suspicion of people one jump ahead of a psychopath. Tara raised the patchwork quilt to see if Cecil was in need of help. A small com was resting on the end of Cecil's tail, he looked furious. Tara picked it up and offered it to me. "It's not mine," I said, holding out the com I kept attached to my belt in a small pouch that Weldon had given me. Okan shook his head as Tara looked at him.

We examined it carefully. The holo-screen on the top popped up with the initials Z W in neon pink. "Oh," I said, "Ziggy must have kept a diary."

"I guess she did," Tara said, fingering the little device. "Do you think it would be okay if we looked at it? I mean it might give us some idea of what verse she was dreamwalking to?"

"I think it's something you should to do on your own, just remember she was a teenage girl when she wrote it." I tried not to wince at the things I was glad I had never written down about my own parents when I was sixteen.

"Don't worry if it doesn't make sense," Okan added, "We can always help with the sites for the wormhole exit."

"Wouldn't you have heard about it if she ended up in your verse Okan?" Tara asked.

"Not necessarily," he said. Which made me feel as if I should take a look behind me, a sensation, I realised, that Okan must have experienced all his life.

Rari came into the room. "Weldon and Simon are getting 'pissy' downstairs. Actually," Rari smiled, "Simon is, and the only reason I know this is because he said so, Weldon is waiting with his usual patience and understanding."

"We're on our way," Okan said.

Tara and Rari came out to see us off and Joao walked over from the barn. I could sense a general nervousness as if dividing our forces made all of us feel weakened. I climbed up on the back of the runabout behind Okan and Simon made a mountain out of a mole-hill, doing the same behind Weldon. He huffed and grumbled, "Bloody advanced civilisation my foot, get yourself a windscreen and a sunroof for goodness' sake!"

"Rari why do you suppose Zatar hasn't tried to mess with this lately," I pointed at my fixer. "He was all about whizzing me into next week not that long ago."

"It didn't work," Rari said, exasperated, as if I should have known.

"Of course, what was I thinking."

"Oak, watch your back," Joao said, leaving out all the things he didn't say scattered on the ground around us, as if they were the discarded betting slips of a true addict.

"You too," Okan replied, making me feel as if I was missing something.

"Is anything else going on, apart from the eventual impending doom?" I asked.

"No, that would be it." Okan said, as he gunned the engine and the powerful little vehicle lifted up on its hover-jets.

We passed the dropdown ship and I waved to Buddy because he looked a little lonely sat next to the outer barn. I saw Rari making his way towards the ship with a tool box in his hand and as I looked back towards the farm, I could see Tara waving from the veranda, I waved back and as we rounded the bend in the road she disappeared from sight, her hand still outstretched in my mind.

The fields and trees filled my view, the hover-screen that the runabout produced in a creepy futuristic way was easily as efficient as my verse's glass windscreen version and the com made it possible to converse between the two vehicles as if we were sitting next to each other. Simon whinged for a while about the discomfort until the beauty of the countryside got to him and then he was equally as eloquent about that. Weldon endured it all with his typical patience. In the end it was me who complained of a numb behind and requested a loo break after two hours. I leapt off and made myself comfortable behind a convenient bush.

Okan was pouring coffee and eating cake with the typical male disregard for the fact that someone had actually made it, he barely tasted it and he definitely didn't chew. I took a sample of each and walked up and down while I chewed respectfully and sipped with appreciation.

"Are we nearly there yet?" Simon whined as he got back onto the runabout.

Weldon did his best to hide his incredulity but it wasn't easy. Then he laughed, "You're just like my little sister, she couldn't sit still and hated being on these things."

"If I remind you of such a discerning and admirable person then I'm flattered," Simon replied with the right amount of gravity. He had obviously worked out what had happened from the holo- pictures of the young Nolie that had never been added to. I felt strongly about giving him a hug when I saw Weldon nod his head in agreement. But I was arguing with Okan about who should drive. I won.

I leaned into the imaginary corners so that I could give myself a well needed adrenaline rush. The fields were in the process of a crop rotation that would have had farmer Payne's head spinning in my verse. I tried to make a mental note about asking Weldon the details of the seasons, but the problem with mental notes is that was exactly what they were, things to remember written in the air.

The best place to leave the runabouts was the clearing on the side of the road where we had put the dropdown when we'd had the run in with Zatar's mercenaries. I shook my head and insisted we park in the university grounds. No one argued much. It was as if the memories of blood-spattered grass and falling friends squatted, fat-toad-like, in the thoughts between us.

The parking grounds were full of neat little vehicles that belonged to the students and tatty battered ones that belonged to the faculty, it was ever thus. I tried to park nicely but it didn't pass Okan's tidy test and he got off the back as I turned the hover foils to neutral and got back on, reversing the runabout so that it faced out towards the open field on one side of the buildings. Weldon had already parked in the same direction. I wondered if I would ever live in a time where a quick getaway wouldn't be required.

The inner corridors of the university were as dusty with hidden noise as before. We walked up the stairs and along to Professor Theadus's door. I knocked and without waiting for an answer pushed it open.

It was as if we had just left him minutes before, not days or weeks. He looked up and gave a knowing smile. "Simon, I wondered how long it would before I saw you again. When these young people began pestering me, I knew you wouldn't be far behind." He moved around his desk and came over to us.

"It's good to see you too, old friend." Simon leaned down and hugged the professor gently as if his bones would break. Which, I thought, given his condition they very well might.

"Please, sit." The professor indicated the possibilities to do so and we went about removing files and books from the places where they had regrown after our last visit. Simon took the chair that virgin sacrifices had used in far-away places. It gave me a weird sense of foreboding; I wanted to pull him away from it and into something that didn't have such a history of betrayal. I know we only gave inanimate objects power by believing in the hate that they bring with them, but it made me shiver.

"We weren't sure you would still be here professor?" Weldon made the statement a question.

"Ah well, Zatar's nasty little henchman came for a visit right after you left, but I am adept at giving them what they want without giving away too much," he added with wry bitterness, "All they see is a twisted old man."

"You're playing a dangerous game Donald." Simon reached out and tapped the crooked fingers gently.

"Well, those of us left behind didn't have much choice, Simon. I came out here to the settler's planets to get away from the parody of science that the guild became." He leaned back in his chair as if his back hurt him. "It's as though they want to turn back the clock on progress and close the door to the future."

"We have that in my verse too," I said, because it sounded as if he were saying something he had said a thousand times before, but no one listened anymore. I wanted him to know that someone had heard him this time.

He nodded sadly. "We do seem to love to reinvent the wheel over and over again."

"Have you seen Zatar?" Simon asked. Okan didn't move a nerve ending but he seemed to be listening for footfalls as well as answers.

"Yes, spiteful little monster!" The professor spat out the words. "Still, you have to give him points for consistency; he has never thought the type three verse should be sharing technology with the rest of us."

"You always know where you are with a psychopath," I said. The professor nodded and smiled as if a particularly dim pupil had just shown a spark of ability.

"He seems overly interested in you, my dear." Professor Theadus sat still, but the words churned the air as if someone had thrown a stone into water. "I spoke to Nancy," he added, "I understand why he thinks you would be useful to him. Your mother was an amazingly gifted scientist."

Simon smiled at him. "Okan thinks you're going to betray them."

"Ha!" The professor laughed without mirth, "I was playing hide and seek before you were born young man." He emphasized the point with a finger. "But you're right, things are changing, we have to choose sides." He held out a hand in an old-fashioned gesture, Okan stood up and took it carefully. "I will *never* give you up. Without you and your kind we have no future."

The silence that followed was the emptiness of an auditorium before thunderous applause. It made my eyes water with emotion. Professor Theadus had probably just signed his death sentence and we all knew it.

"Does he have any real backing in my verse?" Simon asked, "I hear he's been using the portal device that Rilla was working on."

"As far as I know he's on his own, he managed to get a small group of like-minded bigots to listen to him and he stole the device from the conference after the blast. Someone's been working on it, but I don't know who. I just can't see the central planets in your verse getting behind him. Let's face it," the professor smiled again.

"It would have been over by now if they had. No, this feels like a power play."

"Doesn't your government here know what's going on?" I asked. "They must have realised that there were still dreamwalkers coming from the other verses."

"I don't really know what it's like in your verse Millie, but I would guess politicians are pretty much the same wherever you are. The warnings of the guild fell on deaf ears." The professor leaned forward wincing against the pain that must have been immune to his treatment programme. "They seem to be content with the usual political speeches about health, education and the military campaigns against the borderers. Multiverse immigration is not very high on the list these days." He sighed and reached for a drink of water; we were all silent because there was so much more he needed to say. "One of our philosophers once said, 'a somnambulist has two real choices, go back to bed or wake up, anything else is trouble.'" Everyone nodded wisely in agreement, except me. No one had said anything of the sort in my verse.

"Are you saying," I said, " That they're walking around in the dark and are likely to do some toe stubbing?"

"In a non-philosophical sense, yes." Professor Theadus grinned. It suited him, his face lit up and the pain lines receded for a moment. I could see why Simon liked him: he must have been an interesting and funny man to have been around before someone blew up his dreams and smashed his future.

"You're going to have to kill Trevor Morris, Simon." The oxygen was sucked out of the room and I felt a real need for a lungful of air. The professor had used the conversational tone of those who see violence as an inevitable conclusion formed from the continuous study of people. Simon nodded, so did Okan and Weldon. It was a coffee morning with the local chapter of misfits anonymous, a farmer, a professor of anthropology, a dreamwalking warrior, a gay bookseller and me. Just the usual suspects.

"Let me know what I can do to help," the professor said, grinning again.

"Did you give up dreamwalkers on Earth during the pogrom that followed the bomb?" Simon asked, in his usual subtle style of communication. I could see Okan wince.

"I tried to give up Trevor 'Zatar' Morris, as you can see it didn't go so well." This time we all smiled along with the professor. It was as if any barriers had been removed, finally all of us were on one side. "He took all that technology with him. He must have had help but I don't know who it was."

Simon checked his fingernails and frowned in momentary concentration. I thought, maybe we were not *exactly* all on one side. No mention was made of Charlie Morris, Zatar's brother. "Do you think he set the bomb?" Simon's voice was quiet. I felt my eyes close. It made sense; it was just that the headache in the room had decided who was going to be its next victim. I pushed my hand against my forehead and tried not to whimper from the pain of fear filled, information overload.

"I have often wondered; again, it would have been difficult for him working alone, but I am guessing not impossible. It was just a political move to blame the terrorists, they were never that effective," the professor huffed, "Or that organised."

All the questions had been asked and answered. We got up to go and the professor slid from his chair and came to see us out. The door was about eight paces from the desk so he didn't have far to walk. Weldon handed him a small pot of liquid. "This will help with the pain." The professor nodded his thanks and looked surprised that anyone had noticed how he was feeling.

I gave him a hug which also puzzled him greatly. He and Okan shook hands again and we went out into the corridor leaving Simon in the office with his old friend. A quiet exchange took place; for a man whose 'sotto voce' could be understood by passing jet planes he was remarkably difficult to hear. But I could feel the sadness, the echoes of time past and things that were lost. Whatever the question had been we could hear the professor answer an emphatic "No." My money was on Simon having asked him to come with us.

The quick getaway wasn't necessary, as there was no sign of anyone wanting to kill or maim us. I sat on the front of the runabout until Okan got the message. He sighed and climbed onto the back seat putting his arms around me as if he needed to hold on for his own feeling of safety when we both knew it was really for mine. My mental cage had been so well and truly rattled in the previous days my teeth felt loose. I patted his hand from time to time, trying to remind myself of the fact that my dad used to tell me, there was no point in doing the things in life you were sure of, because they took no effort, it was supposed to be about attempting the things that you were not confident you could achieve. Right at that point a sure thing sounded wonderful.

Simon was quiet; he didn't say a word until we stopped for a break. I watered my favourite tree and then came back to the runabout for some coffee and a Tara made sandwich full of the farm's cheese and pickle. I had seen Weldon concocting something impressive with a vat of boiling vegetables and fruit and lots of jars, so I knew the pickle was homemade too. It took a serious ability to make a good cheese and pickle sandwich. Tara could have given a masterclass. "Are you going to be okay eventually?" I asked Simon.

He nodded. "It's not easy to see a once vibrant man so defeated." He dropped his head and I was horrified that his eyes shone with tears. Simon was not an emotional man. He did the impression of a slightly over the top hysterical gay guy for effect and sometimes to get his own way, but actually he was as tough as old leather. I'd never seen him so vulnerable.

We watched as Weldon pulled cakes from the back of the runabout container. It was the small sweet variety that I was rapidly becoming addicted to. They were rich sponge with a soft butter icing in the middle, when you bit into them it usually squidged everywhere. I took two. "Your arse is going to look like *that* if you carry on eating these things," Simon said, pointing to a cow grazing nearby; its tail towards us demonstrating the appropriate proportions. The softer side of Simon's personality had been put safely under lock and key again.

We got back to the farm as the evening feeding was beginning. I followed Tara out to the barn where a few of the not so big kids were waiting for time to catch up with them, so that they could go into the fields with the others. Tired looking mother goats fed their young and we fed them. Tara checked for any problem children and I stretched my legs and generally got underfoot. "How did it go today?" Tara asked eventually.

"If you count the fact that we didn't get shot at, it went very well." I held out a medical kit as she cleaned up a slightly sticky eye on an excited youngster. "Simon thinks Zatar set the bomb that killed all those people at the guild meeting on Earth and started off the pogrom."

Tara stopped. "Are you sure?"

"I don't think anyone's sure," I said. "But it didn't seem to come as such a surprise to Okan, or," I added, "Weldon for that matter."

"Weldon has a way of absorbing information and coming to his own conclusions on things," Tara said, "He's been saying for years he didn't think it was the terrorists."

"Well Simon was at the meeting, so I'm guessing he knows something about it." I shrugged.

Rari came in and helped us finish off, he carried several of the kids that Tara deemed ready for the big wide world out to the field, followed by a few relieved mother goats and two laughing women. He looked as if he was the Pied Piper. Neither of them got my cultural reference when I explained it, but Tara had a similar tale and Rari another version. Somehow the verses grew separate and the same, the interweaving fabric of the wormholes creating patterns into more than atoms and quarks.

Okan came over to us while we stood watching the goat mothers in the field at the back of the farm, as they introduced themselves to the locals and the babies hopped with fear and excitement at the new freedom. He had a tray full of glasses filled with a rich dark wine. Weldon and Joao came down the steps from the kitchen, followed by Simon who was carrying some food in bowls on another tray. I could feel a sense of unease on the wind that brought the sounds of the cows from the distant parts of the farmland.

"It's tomorrow, isn't it?" I asked Okan. He nodded and I leaned my head on his chest for a moment.

Simon patted my shoulder gently. "Have some of these. Weldon just made them."

"What are they?" I asked, gulping down wine and tears at the same time. The wine was as strong as the colour. It went with the edge of the planet on the horizon and the new moon in the sky just on the turn into evening.

"It's some bread fried with herbs and garlic I think."

Simon ate several and handed samples around. We all crunched appreciatively. Simon stood for a moment contemplating the view and drinking in the sky. He said to Okan. "Have you got it?"

"Is there any other way?" Okan asked. My stomach churned. Simon shook his head and held out a hand. Okan passed him a tiny grey box.

I looked inside as Simon took the lid off. "If you do this you will become as vulnerable as the rest of us," I said, "You might as well paint a target on your back!" The fixers were no more than small dots with a tiny spike of wire protruding from one edge. There were three embedded in the gel.

"It looks as if Charlie Morris is running out of the technology he stole," Simon said, licking his finger and removing one of the fixers. "I can't travel safely without it, Millie, it's been too long since I did any real dreamwalking. You were the only reason I was able to get back here without leaving something important behind in the singularity."

"I know we're running low on them," Okan said, "because we have to account for each one when we return. I always assumed they were just difficult to make, but I realise it must be because we're not actually able to replace them and for some reason he could only take a few with him when he left the bombed meeting."

"It seems that Zatar found a way around the problem," I said bitterly, thinking of all the dead dreamwalkers sacrificed by Zatar's greed.

"I know for a fact that Charlie Morris has tried without success," Rari said, equally resentful.

Tara looked on in a sort of horrified fascination as Simon tapped the side of his head with the small dot, he winced as the connection was made and he became a blinking light on a holo-screen some-where. She whispered, "Do you think Ziggy has one of those?"

"If she has," Okan said sadly, "It wasn't me." He looked tired. He and Rari exchanged a glance that covered the emotions of hardened warriors on the edge of a battle. One of those fights where even the most experienced are not sure they are going to win.

I felt my heart squeeze around the thought that so much of what I cared about was right in front of me and I could lose it all in one sweep of a cosmic moment. I ate more of the crunchy bread and took my fear out on the taste of herbs that had never grown in my mother's garden. "Do we orbit Jupiter?" I asked, puzzled for the first time about the fact that we, as in the moon, Ganymede, didn't seem to have to suffer the dark side of the planet at any time.

"No," Weldon said helpfully, through a mouthful of his own barely chewed bread. It was similar to watching a washing machine with a full load. "Sorry," he said, when he remembered that I found speaking while eating, completely awful.

"Let me help," Okan said smiling, foodless. "We rotate on our own axis and so of course does Jupiter and we both orbit the sun at the same speed but in tandem." He took a big swallow of wine and sighed with the satisfaction of someone who appreciated the subtle tones of something someone has made with care and experience.

"Come on let's eat." Tara gave up on the feelings of the things not said and did her best to make ordinary seem possible. "I have to go and see the weavers and knitters tomorrow with the new designs and I need an early start. There will be grumbling as I already submitted my old ones three months ago."

We collected our pre-meal debris and headed for the veranda and the back kitchen door. I saw Joao and Okan drop back, they stood by the wall for a moment and the soft murmur of whispered secrets followed me into the house. It was not really that interesting to eavesdrop on people when you knew for certain that it was you, they were talking about.

I helped Tara with the soup and Rari cut the bread in neat hopeful slices. A thick runny cheese as smelly as old rugby socks sagged seductively in the middle of the table. "It's the first of the new variety we're experimenting with," Tara explained when I scooped a lump and tested it. "Well?" She asked me.

"Lively!" I said, when I could speak.

"I think if you leave it there much longer, we'll have to chase it around the room," Simon said dryly.

Weldon made something spectacular with poached eggs and a locally grown spinach, which was not so much eggs Florentine, as eggs mid-galactic. While he was serving the dish Okan and Joao came in and sat down with us. Okan gave me a hug. "Millie," he smiled as he spoke to soften the words, "Do not go *anywhere* without Joao."

"Of course," Joao said helpfully, "I will be happy to hold the soap while you're using the flannel."

"Very funny."

Simon looked surprised as if the possibility for humour had been left behind on the other side of the quantum singularity. "That was quite amusing." He sighed, "Actually, no it wasn't." He dipped a spoon into his soup and Tara missed her mouth with the bread as her laughter pulled us into a meal with friends that you wish for in a lifetime of shared memories and precious food.

I looked at Okan, his expression was mostly smiling, but I bit back a clever remark because his eyes said 'don't mess with the rules.' He knew that the chance of me doing what he asked was slim to none but he needed to feel that the possibility was out there, along with the tooth fairy.

We spun it out for as long as possible, eating more food than was healthy or comfortable, Simon and Weldon drank too much just to see if they could. A river of coffee followed the wine.

I watched as Tara checked the doors and windows; Weldon and Rari had gone out to the field at the back of the farm to see to the goats and Okan and Joao had taken a runabout and were checking on the stock in the far fields. Tara tapped off the light switches in the kitchen and we went up to bed. She gave me a hug and I followed her into the bedroom she shared with Weldon. It was a huge room with a sitting area at one end and a large attached bathroom. Windows on two walls of the room looked out to the front of the house and the side, you could see the mountains in the dark distance and the snow on the tops seemed to have begun reaching down into the valley. I wondered again about the changing seasons. At home it was autumn, here it was still spring and so far, there had not been much in the way of extremes of temperature.

Tara ran a bath and I wandered out to see if I could find Simon, he had gone up to bed before us, weaving a wobbly path with a slight slur in his footsteps. On the second floor there were three bedrooms, two with bathrooms. The room I called mine, Tara's, and there was a separate bathroom next to the bedroom Joao was still using. A small stairway led up to the third floor in the roof, where there were two more bedrooms and another bathroom. Weldon's parents had built it with lots of potential, hoping for maybe a larger family as the farm had grown around them. Tara had told me that Weldon had lived here alone for several years after his parents had died. It must have been an empty time.

I opened a door, there were twin beds tucked into the eves of the roof, tidy, with book shelves and comfy chairs; a large window looked out onto the back of the farm and the fields with the goats now peaceful for the night. A shade-less lamp was on between the two beds. The shape was a little holographic dance of colour and it cast attractive rainbows onto the walls and floor. It gave illumination without being harsh. There was no sign of Simon.

The other room was a slightly smaller size but with a large double bed in it. Simon was fully clothed, face down and snoring into the covers. I went over to him and rearranged the downie so that he was under it. His shoes were by the bed and the neat leather backpack sat on a chair. I pulled the blind down, shutting out the mountains and the moon. Tara wasn't interested in great swags of curtain or clutter but the rooms seemed to be cosy in their simplicity of wood floors and white walls. I turned off the lamp by the bed and the holograph disappeared into a small disc on the bedside table. "Don't you dare leave me Simon, I would be completely alone without you," I whispered into the shadows as I left, closing the door quietly.

Tara was sitting on the sofa in her room drinking tea, she poured me a cup as I sat down and we drank the aromatic brew, which I hoped would stop the roiling stomach, a combination of too much food, red wine and fear. She patted my hand. Neither of us spoke, we just listened to the house stretching itself in the cool of the evening. "What is this building actually made of?" I asked.

"It's a type of vegetable fibre. We use the blocks when they're still organically alive. They interconnect," she knit her fingers together, the way a child does, "It makes the structure flexible, but stable and strong. You've been here when we had a tornado," she explained, "It's the safest way to build. The roof is made of the same fibre but with a solar strand woven into the blocks. It provides any power we need, that and the wind turbine at the edge of the farm."

"Is Simon, okay?" She asked into the loaded silence. I shrugged and made a face. She laughed, "I imagine having him as a friend means there's a lot of shrugging!"

"He has that effect." I drank more tea and we listened as the farming team returned from their different tasks. They were obviously in the kitchen getting the famous brandy treatment from Weldon.

"It must be hard having your life taken over by a bunch of dangerous strangers and your house filled up with noisy visitors?" I put the tea down and stretched.

"It makes me feel whole again," Tara said simply, "I love the sound of voices in the kitchen as I wake up and the sense of each room in the house full of hopeful thoughts and dreams." Her eyes filled with tears. "The only thing that I can't live with is the silence." I think my mouth had fallen open; it was such a pain filled statement. "Every day I think of the things I should have done, that I could have done when Ziggy was here. But I was starting a business and it filled me up and I didn't have space for my child and I should have."

I moved over to sit next to her and put my arms around her and held on tight, because I could remember that's what I had wanted when my parents had died, someone to hang onto. "I will go back to my verse and see if I can find out if she turned up there. I'm not sure where the main wormhole exit is but Simon will know."

"I keep thinking the reason that she can't be found is either she doesn't want to be or she isn't anywhere to *be* found." Tara's voice held the edge of pure anguish of the parent who 'doesn't know.'

The door opened and Weldon wandered in looking as if he wasn't sure, he should be there. He smiled at me, but it was a smile without mirth. "It's okay," Tara said, "I'm just having a moment about the chicks leaving the nest again." She wiped her eyes and went back to being a mother hen. A transformation that was visible.

A voice from the other side of the open door said, "I have *never* been referred to as a chick before." Okan stuck his head around the door frame. "Is it safe to come in?"

"I'm over the deep meaningful shit," Tara laughed, using words she had picked up from me.

"What a relief." Rari pushed Okan out of the way and came over, throwing himself down on the sofa into the non-existent space between Tara and me. He manoeuvred himself a seat and yawned loudly. I put my finger in his wide, open mouth and he made a great big thing out of spitting it out.

I could have kissed them both. The worry left Weldon's face and the pain lifted from Tara's. It was as if someone had put down a basketful of puppies. Joao completed the picture by coming in and bringing a small snack in the shape of sandwiches and cake. "You *can't* be hungry!" I said.

"It's just so I don't fade away in the night from lack of food," Joao chewed without closing his mouth and Okan took a cake and pushed it in swallowing almost immediately, which would have given most people indigestion filled sleeplessness.

"You two could start up your own club, 'bad eating habits for beginners,' it could catch on."

"Hey, I'm from New York," Okan said, with another cake half consumed, "Chewing with your mouth open is a constitutional right." I thought back to my travels on that continent and realised that he had a point.

We tried to make the night stretch out into even thoughts but the craggy sort got in the way. The ones that cut your fingers and burned your lips. I left Tara's room full of never spoken words and went into mine, which was dark and silent. I took a boiling hot shower, letting the water run over me and not bothering to wash much, because sometimes it was about water therapy, not cleanliness. Without turning the lamp on in the room I pushed Cecil from the middle of the bed over to one side. He grumbled a bit but it metamorphosed into a contented purr. The blind was furled up on the open window letting in the night and the moon had reached a near perfect clarity of brightness. The inner geek in me thought about the albedo reading again; but not out loud.

Flora pulled at the covers until I leaned over the edge of the bed and scooped her up. She settled sleepily in the curve of my arm and as I rubbed her head, her breathing became a soporific orchestration with the cat's purr. I could hear the quiet 'goodnight' noises of the others as they went to bed and tried to leave the fear in the corridor.

The door was slightly open and Okan leaned into the room. "Are you asleep?" He asked.

"You're joking?" I shuffled over to the side of the bed as he sat on the edge dragging off his shoes. He stretched out on the top of the covers and pulled me towards him, earning several black marks from the cat and the pachyderm for inappropriate, reckless, sleep interference.

"It would be easier to get an interview with the pope than try to get a few moments alone with you."

"You have a pope!" I was really surprised. Something Rari had said one day had led me to believe that religion no longer played a big part in their development.

"Yes. But I don't think he has the same profile in my verse as he does in yours," Okan explained.

"What do you mean?" I was wide awake now and shuffled a bit too much, earning myself audible grumbles from the small furry things.

"I can't believe this; I came in here to have a romantic moment full of impossible to keep promises and I end up talking about religion."

I was quiet. Romance wasn't something that I had considered helpful under the circumstances, because of the inconvenient possibility of us not getting away with what was planned and not coming back.

He listened to my silence and sighed, "Okay, we don't have the same religious progression that you do, there was no Dark Ages really and no extremism. The main form of religion was the Cathars, they believe that the world is split along the lines of matter and spirit, good and evil."

"What about the Knights Templar, they were associated with the Cathars in my verse?"

"Yes, we had that too. But you have to understand religion in my verse is very benign. We've had no wars over who worships whom for I don't know, two thousand years."

"It must have been a pretty peaceful existence," I said thoughtfully.

"No. People just found something else to fight about. We've had three world wars and the last one nearly wiped us out; it was a bit like Joao's verse, you're very lucky."

"Give it time. I imagine we can catch up if we really put our minds to it." I tried for dry and witty, but it sounded bitter even to my ears.

"I guess anything remotely romantic is off the table?" Okan sounded wistful.

"I don't think I could actually do that right now, but I'm okay with sex."

He laughed, "I'd better shut the door."

We stood in an early dawn at the foot of the stairs in the farmhouse. Okan took the small gel-com from Weldon with the details of the oceanic power source on it. "Thanks for this," Okan said. He looked at me and nodded as if we had come to an understanding, which maybe we had.

Simon stood next to me and held my hand in a cold grip. I didn't bother to try and stop my tears. He kissed my fingers and moved to stand next to Rari. It was an old dance with new rules.

Without words we divided into those who would be leaving and those who were staying. Tara looked destroyed and I put an arm around her, we were knitted together in our feelings of fear and loss.

I saw Weldon put his hand on Joao's shoulder as if to stop the younger man from jumping into the ring with his friends.

One moment they were there and the next, not there.

The wormhole exit came out on the street in front of the main doors. A man moved politely out of the way as if three people appearing in front of him from nothing was an acceptable part of his early morning. He didn't glance back, but he did hurry away. New Yorkers preferred their secret societies to remain secret.

Simon looked up at the structure. It was on the corner of 77th and Central Park West next to the Natural History Museum. He remembered that in Millie's verse it was still the New York Historical Society. The park was rich with autumn trees that rustled in the cold air. The time differential was similar to the type zero verse his bookshop was in. He watched as the two men braced themselves as if against an oncoming invisible storm. The main doors of the neoclassical building opened automatically and Rari and Okan moved inside. Simon followed.

"Welcome back." One man stood at the entrance, a small com in his hand. He was dressed as a history professor in a barely successful inner-city school would be, in faded corduroy trousers and a tweed jacket. He was tall, with the hidden wiry strength of a basketball player. Simon could see the outline of a laser pistol in a holster under the threadbare jacket.

The building retained an air of careful intellectual study. Large stone steps up to a foyer echoed underfoot. It was spookily quiet in the absence of anyone else.

The man shook hands with Okan as if he was an old friend. Okan looked as if he was trying not to confront the school bully.

The man said, "I wasn't expecting to see you so soon." A

wall of light moved as the three of them stood for unknown inspection, it passed through and over them and the man nodded. "All clear." He leaned back on the curved counter that stood to the right of the foyer, where there was a computer screen and papers scattered on the surface, waiting for a non-existent receptionist to tidy up and issue tickets and careful advice to the customers visiting the equally non-existent exhibits.

High up in the walls the small aggressive cameras performed their impartial duties and the rooms buzzed with hidden interest.

"Who are you?" The man asked casually, looking at Simon.

"Simon Knowles, or actually Charlie Morris would know me as Seager Wells." He held out a hand and the man took it, the veneer of visiting an exclusive club slipping a little at the mention of his real name.

"Craig Brown," the man said, "I look after security for the organisation."

"Yes, I can imagine that you do," Simon said dryly.

Okan and Rari remained quiet and impassive, part of the chess game, but hoping not to be the pawns no one remembers in the endless moves played by queens and bishops, knights and castles.

Okan tried to relax his face, make the muscles smooth, knowing that the cameras would be seeing every tense nerve and analysing every twitch for the hidden meaning. Every time he came back it had become more difficult to hide his feelings behind the necessary wall of pretence. Once or twice, he had nearly lost it all with a moment of impatience. He could feel Rari radiating fear and loathing beside him. The man who 'looked after' the security for the organisation also conducted the interrogation interviews. Rari had been 'reprogrammed' several times by Craig Brown to cure him of his sexual tendencies; something that was considered a weakness and therefore a possible security threat. He tried not to smile at the security man's obvious horror faced with the overt gayness Simon was putting forward.

Okan knew that Simon had his own agenda; he and Rari had talked long and hard about the possibilities, but in the end, they were too far down their own path with too much to lose if they didn't take the opportunity now. He just hoped that the man's obvious love for Millie would protect them all from whatever the bigger picture might be. Okan was very familiar with the broad view of things and heartily sick of it.

Rari in his fear was still able to appreciate the finer points of Simon's strategy. He just didn't seem to care that his obvious contempt was making the security officer very angry. A small device in Craig Brown's ear was giving him orders and he didn't like that either.

"Come this way," he said at last. "Okan, do you have something for the director?"

"Yes." Okan didn't volunteer what it was and this made the security man even angrier. The back of his neck was red and his shoulders were stiff with disapproval as they walked down the corridor to the left of the foyer and then up a wide stone staircase which was lit with atmospheric care, as though ladies in evening gowns would be admiring themselves in the long gilt mirrors. The cameras twitched silently as if scenting weakness. The men reached the first floor and stopped.

A large set of double doors opened onto a stunning room, double windows looked out over Central Park and you could see the outline of the careful forest as the sun began to rise over the city. The furniture in the vast room could have belonged to the Edwardians who had built the house.

"Seager. Good to see you." A man came around the side of the desk where he had been supposedly deep in thought. Okan could see that the director was trying for the higher ground and not succeeding. Craig stood to one side and slightly behind them.

"Charlie Morris. You haven't changed a bit." Simon made

it sound as if it was an insult and Okan tried not to think about the possibility of being reprogrammed himself. It seemed it was going to be difficult to avoid. The director was going to see their association with Simon as a serious internal contamination.

Charlie Morris didn't have the cobra evil of his older brother Zatar, his was a more ordinary, everyday kind. The man who closes the door of the gas chamber on a job well done and then goes home to his wife and children after a busy day of killing people. He was as short as his brother, but with close cropped pale hair and eyes, flat as a shark's.

As a leader he had used the tried-and-true method of divide and conquer, he sensed weakness, the way a predator does, as an electronic flash in a brain process without any emotion. He exploited it, turning people on each other, as if he was a Roman emperor bored with the usual death of warriors. It was therefore easy to keep people frightened; they would give each other up to preserve their own fragile existence. He liked the feeling of power that the fear gave him.

The organisation he had moved in on when he first came to the type one verse had been a fledgling dictatorship, it had been a simple matter of getting rid of the weak director and taking over. The technology that he passed on to the military and the scientific community was enough to keep him interference free. Of course, what he passed on was a fraction of what he had kept.

"Coffee?" The director asked, gesturing towards a table by the open fireplace.

They arranged themselves in the deep leather chairs and sofa and Simon leaned forward before anyone could touch the coffee pot, saying, "I'll be mother." He poured the hot liquid into fragile china cups and passed them around. Rari tried not to let the incongruousness of the situation show on his face; he sipped coffee and watched the careful interactive fishing expedition unfold.

"Zatar hasn't worked out that you're still alive?" Simon poured himself another cup and leaned back in the chair.

"No, and it would be nice if it stayed that way." Charlie Morris tried for a casual response but failed. The possibility for killing turned the air into emotional soup.

Okan realised something that he had missed before, fear. Charlie Morris was very frightened. Of Simon. In his life Okan had been reprogrammed twice, once not too long ago when he had let his guard slip to one of the R and D staff about how much he loved the idea of farming the land in Tara's verse. The man had been really interested and had asked lots of questions and it had taken Okan a minute to realise he was being baited. Too late. He had spent three days in the isolation unit with Craig Brown for company. He sipped his own coffee and tried not to snap the handle of the cup in his impotent anger.

"I'm surprised to see you with one of those," the director said, pointing at the fixer on Simon's face.

"I couldn't seem to get back into the dreamwalk without it." Simon smiled. "I don't suppose you've tried it since the meeting in the type two verse that you bombed?"

Charlie Morris spilt his coffee slightly and his hand shook as he put the cup back in the saucer. "Something that cannot be proved; but you're right, I haven't been out of this verse for a very long time. It seems that it's an ability you lose as you get older, without the fixer. You were in the type zero verse I take it?"

"Ah, you want to know where Millie is," Simon said, "Your brother seems to have had the same idea. Why is that I wonder. Hardly a case of great minds thinking alike," he laughed. Craig Brown did his best not to hit out but he moved carefully so as to make reaching for his weapon easier.

"Hopefully we can come to some arrangement." Charlie Morris's voice took on an edge. So far in his life there had been nothing that he could not buy, bargain, intimidate or kill for and he didn't think anything would change.

He may not be winning on points, Rari thought, but he was, in the end, holding all the cards. The cup slipped from Craig Brown's fingers and he looked surprised before he slumped to the floor. Or not, Rari thought, as he watched the director hopelessly fighting the same effects. His head dropped back on the chair and his eyes closed on a furious impotent rage. Simon got up and removed the gun from the security officer's body and threw it at Okan who caught it one handed, putting the coffee down with the other hand at the same time.

"This is what you might call a crime of opportunity," Simon said cheerfully. "What?" He asked, looking at Rari's horrified face, "You weren't planning to stay anyway!" He kicked at Craig Brown with his foot. "Is this the man who tortured you?" He asked Rari, with the careful expression that would have made the staff in the bookshop scurry to all points but where he was.

Rari crouched next to the security man and felt for a pulse. "What did you give them?"

"One of the potions from Weldon's collection." Simon smiled. "From the locked cabinet in the distillery at the back of the house."

"The cabinet marked 'poisons, handle with care?'" Okan asked dryly.

"That would be the one." Simon was smiling. He reached down and checked the pulse on Charlie Morris's neck.

"Does he have a security medical monitor?" He asked Rari, who nodded. "What about him?" Simon indicated the man lying on the floor with a wayward foot again.

"No." Rari stood up. "Just the director and a few key members."

"Good, because I may have given him a larger dose." Simon's kicking was more of a statement this time.

"He's going to die?" Rari asked, trying not to let the moment of hope well into his eyes. He shook his head.

"What?" Simon asked.

"I'm just wondering where my humanity has gone."

"Yes, it's a real tragedy." Simon touched the younger man's arm and a moment of understanding passed between them. They both nodded as if they had spoken several important words. Simon sighed, "It's because the things you haven't done are always more difficult to live with than the things you shouldn't have done."

Rari nodded. "I think I understand that, actually no, I don't and you're beginning to sound like Millie."

"What about him?" Okan asked. He leaned over the director whose lips were turning a very definite shade of blue. "Is he going to die?"

Simon sniffed, "Yes, but not yet."

Okan felt the shadows of something only talked about pass through his heart, the now or never sensation and he wondered much as Rari had, where the sorrow in death feelings had gone. Probably out with the rest of the mental rubbish after three days in a reprogramming tank. "What do we do now?"

"Well, we need to act as if nothing is out of the ordinary, what would you be doing?"

"If anyone had just seen that, about thirty years in an isolation unit," Okan huffed.

Rari laughed without humour. He went to the door and listened, then shook his head. "I can't hear anything." He shrugged. "It's your call Okan. I say we go with this, but it's up to you."

Both men looked at Okan as if some unwritten rule had just appointed him team leader. He hefted the gun and examined the pattern on the Turkish carpet for a moment as if a self-help message had been woven into the wool along with colour and design. "Okay, we need to take the com with the new power source to R and D and then we have to have a medical. If this was a normal day, I would be writing reports and Rari would be debriefing the geek squad."

"Right, we'll go with that, then." Simon moved to check the leg of the security man as his kicking had revealed a second gun. He handed that to Rari. The dying man's face was suffused with blood. "You might want to step back; I think this might be messy." The security man gave a dramatic cough and a gout of blood followed, he slid into death with no more than a sigh as the breath left his body. Simon got up without a second glance.

"You have something of the psycho about you," Okan said, as he went over to the desk and began tapping at a computer screen.

"Actually, the definition of that particular personality disorder is someone above average intelligence, who can appear to be charming and socially skilled, each of which I obviously have in abundance, oh and of course amoral, someone who cannot experience guilt, though as you can see, I am wracked with just that emotion," Simon said, grunting with effort as he went through the pockets of the dead security man and then moved to check Charlie Morris.

Okan snorted, "If I hadn't seen the way you look at Millie, I might actually believe that!" He cursed, "Rari, do you have any idea what Charlie Morris's password was for the security settings?"

Rari came over to the desk, he checked the computer and then took out his com, tapping keys and attaching the small unit to the big one. "That should do it." A small scroll of code passed across the screen and the computer lit up.

"Thanks." Okan programmed in the relevant sequence as Rari went back to the door and stood guard with the security officer's gun.

After a few moments they were ready. "Right, remember what I said." Okan stood the other side of the door to Rari and Simon. "There are cameras on every floor and in every room except this one. There are security barriers, the same as the one we passed through in the foyer, into the R and D section and the medical unit, this," he held up Craig Brown's security tag, "Means you can go anywhere." He attached it to the inside of Simon's shirt. "You will be seen as a special visitor approved by the director, just try and look the part and no one will question anything, they're too scared, it's the only thing we have on our side."

"This room," Okan waved a hand around, "Will be in lockdown with a red flag on the computer in the security office. It's not that unusual after we've returned from a long dreamwalk. Hopefully there won't be an emergency. Basically, Rari and I have set up a 'do not disturb' sign."

"Let's hope it works," Rari said, "The fact that Craig Brown is still in here and not interviewing you in the specialist wing will ring a few bells with someone."

Okan went on. "Security on all floors is minimal due to the cameras, but don't think it's weak Simon, they have a fast response. There are security staff at the R and D doors and the specialist wing. The tracking device is in the planning office next door to R and D; are you sure you can disconnect us?" Okan pointed to his fixer.

"Just get me in there," Simon answered, "I may need help with the computer connection."

He looked at Rari who nodded, then dashed over to the director's desk and retrieved his com. "Sorry about that!"

Okan made a face, then said, "What about him?" He dipped his chin towards Charlie Morris. "How long have we got?"

"Maybe a day maybe a little longer." Simon shrugged unhelpfully.

"Great," Okan said. "How are we going to know?"

"Well, I guess when all the bells go off and the barriers come down that might be a clue!" Simon hissed. He looked at both of the other men. "Okay, more like a day." He shrugged. "Poisoning people is not my area of expertise."

"You have a very biblical attitude to justice." Okan shook his head.

"I didn't think you had an organised religion here?" Simon said, puzzled.

"Oh, we do, just not the same as the one in the type zero verse," Rari explained, "But," he added dryly, "There's quite a lot of 'smiting' in our bible too."

Okan tried not to grind his teeth and Rari tried not to smile. It was a three-act play, but with only enough script for two acts. Both men had been part of a gang of three for so long they danced in mismatched harmony without Joao. Simon would just have to be the extra leg.

"R and D are going to want to talk to you Simon, try not to be funny, they don't have a sense of humour down there. As far as they are concerned you would have been interviewed by the director and Craig Brown so they aren't going to question you on matters of security and they'll be too scared to ask you why you're here. Be careful, these people have survived by scoring points with the boss." Okan gestured towards the director. "They won't think twice about picking up on something that might get them somewhere better."

"I suppose you could call it an interview," Simon said thoughtfully, looking at the bodies of the dead and dying men, "I always think these things go so much better with coffee, it's more relaxed."

"It's like talking to the elephant," Okan grumbled.

"Ah, the delectable Flora." Simon smiled. "I am indeed in good company."

"Okay, are we ready?" Okan and Rari seemed to be reluctant to leave the false safety of the director's office. The sun had come up and was frustratingly getting close to mid-morning. It was as if they had brought the time from Tara's verse with them.

"As I'll ever be," Simon said cheerfully.

Okan stopped with his hand on the door. "Look, we both

know," he pointed to himself and Rari, "You have something else going on here. Otherwise, you wouldn't have come." He added carefully, "I don't suppose it ended with that." Once more he gestured towards the dying Charlie Morris.

Simon sighed, "There is something of the 'vast eternal truth' about why I'm here yes, but," he said, "I'll try not to get you killed."

"Bloody hell!" Okan swore. "That's just a poetic way of saying 'the bigger picture.'" He shook his head. "I hate that." Simon patted him sympathetically on the shoulder and Rari smiled. They looked as if they were going to a rugby match when their team was playing at home and everyone expected to lose.

Okan opened the door and they moved out into the corridor, he closed the door respectfully behind them and a red light came on above the carved wood frame. The ever-present cameras twitched and turned to watch them pass.

The morning was full of the things you were supposed to do when you were waiting. Tara made breakfast and coffee and we sat, as if we were the survivors of a disaster, around a now too big table. Joao and Weldon went out to the far fields to check the stock and I went through to the back of the house to feed the goats. The mothers grumbled loudly at the lateness of their breakfast, as if they had all been issued with internal clocks of atomic accuracy. "Do you want some help?" Tara asked, as she stood on the veranda, a shawl wrapped around her shoulders. It wasn't because she was cold, the morning was mild with a warm wind, but I understood that sometimes you needed to cover yourself for comfort.

I was nearly knocked down by some enthusiastic kids and she laughed, coming over to me and grabbing the other end of the feed bin. "I feel as if I need to keep running to the hall to see if they're back yet," I said, "It's stupid I know."

"I've been twice." She smiled a watery smile. "Do you think we'll ever see them again?"

I was stunned that she had asked; I stood in mid feed as the bad-tempered hungry goats butted against my legs for their breakfast. "Of course!" I said weakly, but my voice must have betrayed my real thoughts because she nodded in a way that indicated 'as I feared.' I realised she had lived with the fact of someone *not* coming home for so long that it didn't take so much of an emotional leap to see it happening again.

We began the feeding process and the goats settled down and so did my nerves, I leaned over the tiny kids and tickled their ears and they danced in childish delight at something new. "I wouldn't want to be young again," Tara said. I looked up confused. She laughed at the expression on my face. "I was just thinking about how difficult all that fitting in was. Trying not to be different and it's only when it's almost too late you realise, you're not supposed to fit in; it's about being extraordinary." I knew she was talking about Ziggy, not herself.

"I think the only thing I miss about being a teenager, is not having to carry around the baggage of my own failures," I said quietly. She nodded. It felt as if it was the weight of a lifetime. I thought about Professor Theadus, willing to give his life for something he remembered believing in and then Muglier, in Joao's verse, who had possibly given up *his* life to buy me some time; the thoughts of which became a trail of tears that could follow me through the rest of my life.

Weldon came out to the back of the house from the kitchen; he didn't say anything until he got to the wall. His face was impassive.

"Did either of you go into the cabinet in the distillery?" Tara looked shocked. "You'd better come and see," he said.

Joao was making coffee and a second breakfast when we went into the kitchen; he raised his eyebrows over a large slice of toast.

The distillery was at the back of the house opposite the kitchen, the door was slightly open and Weldon swung it wider. I had only been in the room once, when Tara had asked me to get some salve for a goat she was treating with a severe cut on its hoof. The cool walls were covered in labelled shelves full of different pots and bottles.

Dried herbs hung from hooks in fragrant bunches. Weldon worked on the herbal process with great care and attention to detail. The table in the middle of the room held his distilling apparatus and instruments for weighing and measuring as well as a computer and some technical equipment I didn't recognise. It was neat and clean, with the empty jars waiting in tidy rows on the edge of the work surface.

Opposite the window, which looked out on the back of the farm to the fields of, for now, contented goats, was a cabinet with the legend 'poisons' painted in large gold letters on the top edge. A small gel-computer-lock was attached to the door. It was one of those locks that required a key code to be tapped in, in sequence. It was still locked. Weldon opened it using a series of six letters and a thumb print. I couldn't see any indication that someone had broken in.

The bottles and jars were all black and labelled with skull and crossbones so that no one would be in any doubt. The shelves looked tidy, but Weldon pointed to two not quite spaces where the bottles had been moved to compensate for the missing item.

"Do you know what they took?" Joao asked, his mouth still full of toast and honey. He didn't seem surprised or even worried.

"It was one of the haemorrhagic poisons, very fast acting, some-thing I was working on to put down cattle in extreme cases." He added an explanation. "If you have to shoot them out in the fields it can cause great distress to the herd. This," he pointed to another space, "Was a sleeping draft that was still too unstable to be useful." Weldon was calm but worried. "Do you have any idea why they took them?"

"No." Joao shrugged. "I don't suppose it was Rari or Okan because they don't know enough about it." He pointed at the labels. "These don't make any sense to me."

"I used the Latin names and added a few of my own when I made a new strain." Weldon was stunned.

"What you're saying is that Simon did this?" He looked at me and then so did Tara and Joao. I shrugged, trying not to look guilty, but I remembered Simon translating the rugby results into a sort of pidgin Latin just to irritate me one Sunday morning. He was good at it, it had been *very* annoying, I had chased him around the garden with a particularly juicy slug that I had threatened to put down his over pressed cords if he didn't leave me alone. He had screeched like a nine-year-old after too much party cake.

We stood in silence contemplating the possibilities, Weldon's 'do no harm' attitude at direct opposition to Joao's 'well if it's necessary.' Tara and I were together physically as well as metaphorically, somewhere in the middle.

"I guess we'll hear about it when they get back." Weldon shut the cabinet door and locked it again. He patted the wood, half saying to himself, "I wonder how he got in?"

Joao snorted, "I don't think a gel-lock would present much of a problem for someone like Simon."

"What do you mean?" I asked, almost insulted. I had one of those relationships with Simon where you feel as if you can pick out their faults yourself, but when someone else does it you bristle with indignation as if they've suddenly grown wings.

"You know, the person who crosses off the faces on the 'most wanted' posters which are plastered all over the walls of specialist organisations?" Joao said.

"A bounty hunter!" I was stunned.

"Yes, Simon reminds me of one of those men. Though I don't suppose he does it for money."

I was incredulous for a moment then spluttered, "He wears a cravat!"

Tara began to laugh and the so did Weldon, eventually I had to join them it was so infectious, Joao's rusty squeak was a reminder of the places he had spent his childhood, where laughter didn't happen all that much.

Tara and I walked out to the front yard and into the far barn where the dropdown had been parked, it looked a little forlorn in its neglect. I could see Joao sitting on the rocker on the veranda cleaning his guns and watching us from a suitable distance; that was the one where shooting someone would not be a problem. I felt obliged to explain to Buddy just exactly what had been happening and where I'd been. He was very understanding.

I checked the outside and then went in through the doorway, the pilot's chair beckoned and I sat down, putting my hands on the controls and feeling the familiar frisson of contact between the craft and me. Tara stood looking over my shoulder and I was so involved with the sensation of being a part of something space worthy that I didn't notice her going out again. A movement in front of the windows as I looked up, made me aware she was outside and a moment later I realised she wasn't alone.

The man was covered in blood and he barely stood upright. Tara was holding him as he slid to the ground. I stumbled out of the pilot's seat and ran out of the dropdown door. My sudden rushing about must have caught in the corner of Joao's eye because I heard him shout and then I heard his footfalls scrunch in the stones of the roadway.

I reached Tara first but only just, Joao must have used his super-skills, because he was breathing down my neck in a second. I helped Tara move the man into a more comfortable position on the grass. His legs were tangled up beneath him and he was heavy. Joao stood looking around with his weapon in his hand and then he sped off into the trees. I could see him searching for others as he disappeared and reappeared in the sunlight, as though he was a tiger in the long grass.

The matted dreadlocks and strong features made me realise that the man under the layers of fresh and dried blood was Marl. His face was a mess and he had been severely beaten. One arm was clearly broken and there was a wound on his left leg above the boot that was dripping onto the grass, the red flow seemed to soak into the earth as if the ground was suddenly thirsty.

Tara pulled her com out of a pocket and then removed a small weapon from the holster on her ankle. "Damn!" I said, "I always seem to forget that I could possibly need a gun."

"Might be a good idea to remember from now on," she muttered as she called Weldon quietly on the com. "Don't want to shout," she explained, waving a hand around.

We moved Marl gently onto his side as he slipped in and out of consciousness. I could see Joao making his way back towards us. He kept turning around and looking into the woods behind him and it made me shudder with fear at the unknown that was out there again. Tara tapped me on the shoulder. "Hey, you're shimmering! Don't do that, it makes me nervous." Her voice had the edge of tears.

"Sorry. I think my freeze, flight or fight DNA has a few bells and whistles." I squatted down beside Marl and shook him carefully trying to get a response.

"Well, mine doesn't," Tara said, "So don't leave me." As I shook Marl again, she said, "What are you doing?"

"*He's* going to want to know if there's anyone else around," I pointed to where Joao was standing, once again looking towards the barrier of trees, "I don't think he's going to be too gentle about it." She nodded and I handed her the gun as I tried to get a flicker from Marl.

"Millie? Tara whispered, "Rari once said if you had to run to try and take me with you to the empty verse, do you think that's even possible?"

I shrugged. "I don't know, I've never dreamwalked with anyone who doesn't do it themselves, except for Cecil and he's a cat."

Weldon's rich voice came from behind making us both jump and Tara to point a weapon about three inches from his nose; he pushed it away, his face was a tight non-smile as we both sighed with relief. "If it comes down to it Millie, just do it. You hear me?" He was so serious and insistent that I nodded. "Promise?" I nodded again. He sighed with relief and then hunkered down next to me, checking Marl for a head injury. "Looks worse than it is," Weldon said as his hand came away covered in sticky blood.

"Good! Because it *looks* dreadful," I said.

Weldon put a small gel dressing on the wound and another on Marl's leg. He cradled the broken arm in a thin transparent splint. "We need to move him to the house. I can get a better idea of the damage with the emergency kit."

Joao was close enough to hear the last remark and he shook his head. "Wait." He squatted down and began checking Marl's pockets. He removed one boot, the one without the blood and cut into the sole, then checked the other one in-situ. He then did a thorough search of the man's clothing.

"Okay?" Weldon said.

"No, but I guess it will have to do." Joao really did look worried *and* angry. He constantly checked over his shoulder which made my neck itch as if I was standing in the crosshairs of some super sniper.

Marl opened his eyes and struggled to focus. "Tara," he whispered. As she knelt down next to him, he grabbed for her hand.

"What happened?" She asked him.

He laughed; a disturbingly hissing noise that ended with a bubble of blood in the corner of his mouth. Weldon tutted and helped Marl into more of a sitting position to ease the pressure on his lungs. Marl nodded his gratitude. "I had a disagreement on policy with Torin and his weasel of a brother."

"Gasat?" I asked.

"You know him?" Marl winced with pain, but he refused the pressure syringe that Weldon offered him.

"We've met," I said. "What are you *doing* here?"

"I came to warn you." Marl's voice got weaker and he struggled with each breath.

His eyes began to close again. Joao moved in and pushing Tara to one side he shook Marl. "Warn us about what?"

"Those two have no code, no sense of the rules." Marl struggled with his own anger. "I was stupid, I didn't see that they were planning behind my back. They made a deal with some traveller, an evil little shit called Zatar."

"Oh no," I said, interrupting Marl.

"You know him too?" Marl asked.

"We've also met," I said dryly, trying not to let the fear swallow me whole. It was not that it was unexpected, it was just that I didn't feel ready, or prepared.

"What was it?" Joao said and then shook him, his voice raised, he asked again, "What was the deal, Marl?"

"The borderers are on their way," Marl managed to get out before he fainted.

Joao moved as if he'd swallowed a temporal differential of his own. He swept up the unconscious man and with Weldon's help slung him over one shoulder. He handed the gun he was holding to me and began running for the house.

Tara and I ran after him. Weldon made his way towards the barn. I saw him go inside and come out a moment later with a large bag. He shouted to Joao, who was on the veranda by now, "I'll start planting the defence line."

"I'll be right with you."

"I'm going to warn the town!" Tara shouted as we got into the house. "Put him in the kitchen." She followed Joao down the corridor and in through the kitchen door. I was a close but breathless third.

Joao let the unconscious man slip off his shoulder onto the sofa and I tried to arrange his untidy limbs into something that didn't look as though a rag doll had been discarded by a bad-tempered child.

"Ask Til to get what he can from Twin Rivers, their security net has long range sensors. Tell him they might miss Gold Cliffs altogether and just come straight here." He was about to go through the kitchen door and Tara was keying in Til Duster's main com when he said quietly, "Ask him if he can spare any people from the town militia."

"Don't you think that if they're just going to hit us, they'd use a small craft, to slip in unnoticed?" I took the emergency kit Tara handed me and began taking Marl's observations with the small handheld unit. Blood pressure and pulse, it beeped its results, which were not good. Marl was obviously bleeding internally.

Joao stopped. "I think that's a possibility, in fact that's what I'm hoping, but they could also think that they might as well get as much as they can while they're here." He left in a hurry and I heard him shout as he went outside, "Weldon, I'm going to make a start at the back of the house."

I tried to suppress my fear, to make it work for me. "Tara! Marl is bleeding internally; do you have any of those medical nanobots Weldon was talking about?"

"In the distillery, on the shelf near the door, the unit is labelled, there's a pressure syringe already prepared." I ran off into the corridor and I heard her say, "Til, thank the gods you're there!" It surprised me that in a verse where religion was seen as unrelated to science, people still felt the need to thank some deity.

The unit was a large box and was indeed right by the door in a labelled slot on the shelf. I checked the contents. A clear pressure syringe was held in one compartment, its nanobots invisible in a pale green liquid. There were several small gel-boxes in different colours also set in their own labelled sections. It looked as if the nanobots were graded in size and complexity. I closed the door and went back to the kitchen.

Tara was still talking to Til, his gentle face was grey with worry. "I'll do what I can Tara, but you know we're still very thin after the last hit. I'm going to get the children and the vulnerable to the caves. As soon as I've contacted Radley Donahue in Twin Rivers, I'll get back to you, he's the new militia leader over there, plus he's a bit of a science geek; no offence Millie." He raised his hand in greeting.

"None taken Til," I smiled, waving back.

"Donahue has some new equipment; he was trying to tell me about it at the last militia meeting. Made my eyes glaze over. But I think it's something to do with identifying the different power signatures the borderer's craft give off, should make it easier to see how bad what's coming is."

"Damn!" I said as my nervous fingers slipped on the syringe and I checked the different labels in the hope that the right one would jump out at me. Tara came over and took the kit from my hands. "You would think," I said, "That a civilization that can move a moon, correction, two moons, set up a mirror system for sunlight and make medical nanobots," I waved the jar around for emphasis, "Could say *which ones and how many*!" I tried not to shout but my fear had made me loud.

"*We* didn't move the moons, Millie," Til said patiently, "The travellers from the type three verse did that and it's not so much about our technology, it's that the borderers have developed some sort of blocking device in the last few years, we just can't see them coming."

"I imagine we know who to thank for that," I muttered.

"What?" Til almost shouted.

"Do you remember that nasty little man who was looking for me in the bar?" I asked him. He nodded. "The next time you see him, shoot to kill."

"Are you sure?" He said, looking at me, to judge my sincerity.

Tara went over to the com screen; she had been calculating the different strengths of nanobots and putting them into the syringe. "Don't miss, Til," she said quietly.

"Understood. I'll speak to you as soon as I've got everything underway, or before if necessary."

I had heard many accounts over the years of people talking about the blitz. How they sheltered in the London tube stations and listened as the dreadful noise of the V1 bombs cutting out overhead which meant it might not be you this time. Some people ended up running through the streets, sheltering in doorways, a pointless but somehow comforting form of protection. Most of us had never experienced the sense of utter helplessness that goes with waiting for something to fly over and attack you. It brings out a primitive fear.

I stood and watched Tara push the pressure syringe into Marl's neck. The nanobots would repair any tissue damage, whether it would be in time, we would have to wait and see. His own strength would mean more now than anything else we could do. I got out the stitch kit and cleaned and repaired the cut on his leg. "What about this?" I pointed to the gel-splint on the man's arm.

"I think that the best thing to do would be to straighten out the break while he's unconscious. Can you hold his shoulder for me?" I cringed at the sound of bones scraping together but held on as Tara pulled the splint tighter around the break. Marl groaned and came awake. "I'm going to give you something for the pain," she told him. He nodded but his eyes barely focused.

I went to get a blanket and took off his remaining boot and the rest of the bloody clothing, while she filled another pressure syringe with a small dose of one of Weldon's herbal remedies. "It's very strong, I don't want to give him too much; it could affect his breathing. Weldon is so much better at this than I am." In an incongruous move I put the dirty stuff in the washer. "So even if we're going to die it's good if the clothes are clean?" Tara asked, with a small smile.

I held my hands out, palms up in an expression of my own exasperation. "I don't really know what I'm doing," I said. A small bright disc caught my eye; it must have fallen out of Marl's torn and bloody trousers. I picked it up. My fingers activated the hologram. Ziggy's smiling face sprang into view. "Okay," I said, "I think we know why he came."

Tara reached out and with tender fingers touched the dancing light that showed her daughter, it rippled in a rainbow of colour and meaning.

"Look at the state of this man's body!" I said, as I moved the blanket to cover Marl's nakedness. He was a mass of bruises and cuts, some of them several days old. I thought about it for a moment. "He's been kept somewhere, for quite a while and continually beaten. Whatever time we thought we had before they get here, I don't think we have that much," I whispered.

"We'd better see if we can help outside," Tara said. She covered Marl with one more blanket, even though it was a warm sunny morning the man looked pale and cold, shock was beginning to take over. I knew from my parents' frustrated experience that it could kill as easily as any bullet. "Don't worry Millie, the nanobots are fast workers, they'll do the job." I nodded and then so did she; both of us hoping she was telling the truth.

The hallway was full of precious gold sunlight, with the shafts of dust motes swirling in the draught from the open doorway to the farm. I heard a worried hoot from the top of the stairs and Flora's questing trunk curved around the banister. A whisk of a tail meant that Cecil was there too, but had sent the braver elephant to do the dirty work. I ran up the stairs and scooped then both up, a move which Cecil considered very much undignified. Flora could smell Marl's blood on my unwashed fingers and her hoot became one of fear.

I made a nest for them in my bathroom out of cashmere blankets; I added treats and a water bowl. Flora always used the bottom of the shower for her early morning ablutions anyway so I pointed this out to Cecil, along with the fact that if he went to the loo on Tara's towels or blankets, being turned into a winter hat was not beyond the realms of possibility. He seemed to understand. The two of them felt safer in the small space, they settled into the nest and I turned to go. Flora hooted and skittered on the smooth floor, asking to be picked up. For some reason it made the tears flow down my face and for a moment I squeezed her much too tightly; she politely pretended she didn't mind.

"Everything okay with the furry babies?" Tara asked, as I came back down the stairs. She had waited for me and I think had one more check on Marl.

"I put them in my bathroom."

"Good idea." Tara reached the veranda and we stopped for a moment and watched Weldon dropping small discs on the ground and covering them with a layer of dirt using his foot to sweep it over them. He had moved some distance since we had left him and Joao to it. "Do you think Okan, Rari and Simon will be back soon?" Tara whispered; her voice was lost in the realisation of things to come.

"I hope so," I said, unhopefully.

"What can we do?" I asked Weldon. He handed me the pack of discs and took another from his back.

"Start with the edge of the drive near the farm, work your way up the road."

"Are these things dangerous?" I looked into the bag.

"They're frequency operated," he explained, "You need a sonic signal before they go off." He jumped on one to demonstrate. "See, no bang."

"Very adult," Tara said dryly, "I can remember someone blowing off their foot with one of those."

"Yeah, you're right, maybe not a good idea, every now and then you get a dud." Weldon looked slightly embarrassed.

"I'll start to get the goats out to the far fields," Tara said, "We might not have time to get them all away."

"What do you mean?" Weldon asked.

"Some of the injuries on Marl were several days old, maybe even a week," Tara explained.

Weldon nodded, he looked up at the sky, "Not as much time as we thought, then." It wasn't a question and no one answered him. I just took the extra bag of antipersonnel mines and went up the drive away from the house. I couldn't see the point of mining the road as the type of shock troops the borderers would send didn't seem as if they would bother with a designated pathway.

I dropped the devices and covered them as I had seen Weldon doing, the road curved away from the farm and I was nearly to the trees when I saw the runabout. It had tipped over onto its side. It solved the question that had been dancing attendance on my consciousness about how Marl had travelled all the way from Great Port to the Weldon's farm.

The vehicle was battered from an argument with one of the stout trees that sheltered the buildings from the fierce winds, which could spring up from nowhere. I remembered the one that had developed into a tornado on my first dropdown trip in Buddy. I turned on the engine and it coughed into life, settling on its hover-jets and waiting for me to tell it what to do. I sat on it and sprayed stones and leaves around as I spun back to the farm house.

Weldon was waiting with a gun and Joao was close to the veranda as I reached them. My smile faded when I realised what a scare, I had given them. Not a big borderer's ship fright but a smaller, strangers coming one. "Sorry," I said as I turned the jets off and hopped to one side as the runabout settled on the ground. I pointed to the small logo on the power unit. "Marl must have stolen it from the port."

"When this is all over," Weldon said, "I'm going to have a talk to those port workers, the thought that some of them are trading with the borderers is going to come out in all sorts of ways, none of them good."

"Yeah, and I'm coming with you," Joao said. They both nodded as if some pact had been signed in the smell of blood on the air.

Weldon rubbed the back of his neck. "If I look up at the sky one more time my head is going to fall off."

"There will be a few borderers who'll want to help you with that," Joao laughed with black humour. "Put the runabout in the barn with the others Millie, no point in advertising our visitor." He gestured towards the back barn behind the ones that usually held the goats.

I turned the jets back on and waited for the runabout to lift before I got on. It wasn't as easy to ride as the farm runabouts, more of a Harley as compared to a moped. I wobbled a few times as I eased it in through the barn doorway. Buddy had been put away by one of the others and was sitting forlorn, peeping out of the large doorway as if looking for company. Rari's alterations and additions to the computer made it possible for it to be flown by any one of them, but Buddy didn't like it and neither, according to Tara, did they. I patted his nose. "I won't let them get you."

The runabout tipped slightly as it settled and I heard a thud as something dropped off from the underside of the vehicle into the beaten earth floor of the barn. Tara had told me the floor surface was treated with the same vegetable fibre the house was made of, but gradually, as time went on, the general detritus from farm animals gave it the look of a place that would have been acceptable in nineteenth century Kansas.

I picked up the large dirty bag and realised that it was covered in dried blood, the caked dust floating away as I touched it, in evil little swirls of lifelessness. Whoever it had belonged to was probably dead because there seemed to be globs of a grey jelly-like substance that I recognised as brain matter; it doesn't look like anything else. I cringed in horror and wiped my fingers down the side of my jeans, trying to remove the thought as well as the actuality.

The object inside was awkward and I put the bag back on the ground to open it, looking carefully at the underside of the runabout first to see where it had come from. A jury-rigged sling and bits of tape were lying loose and impotent now that they had done their job.

A shadow fell across the doorway and I started up, with my hand on the weapon Tara had made me put in a harness on my ankle.

"Only me Millie," Joao said. He waved a hand in front of him to demonstrate that he was in fact who he said he was. Then shook his head as if he realised how stupid he must sound. "What's that?"

"I don't know, it was tied to the underside of the runabout that Marl came in on."

"It could be a bomb, Millie!"

"Calm down, it would have gone off when he crashed the runabout *or* when I dropped it just now," I added and Joao winced.

"Some of these things are calibrated to go off on detecting a biometric signal Millie," Joao explained, taking out a com and tapping keys.

"I didn't know that," I said, moving my hand away from the bag as if it could make a difference. Even a small incendiary device would have taken out both of us and most of the barn given the combustible material that we were surrounded with.

"It doesn't seem to be giving out any power source signature." Joao put the com away and I wondered for a moment if mine did that or if I'd ended up with the basic model.

Weldon came in through the doorway, making both of us jump as though we were guilty children; it was Joao this time that pulled out a gun.

"Sorry," Weldon said, "I think we need to start announcing ourselves or risk getting shot," he paused, "What's that?"

"Millie found it. We were just going to take a look, it was attached to the bottom of the runabout, so I'm guessing that Marl was trying to get it to us." He indicated the rigging that I had shown him and the two men peered down at the brown crust on the sack.

"Is that?" Weldon said, looking at the blood. I nodded. "That looks like?" I nodded again as he pointed out the brain matter. "Great," he sighed. "You've checked it for a biometric signature?" Joao nodded this time. "Okay, let's see what we've got."

I pulled the sticky dusty folds off the top of the bag and a square framed object came into view; it appeared to be a larger version of the com everyone carried, but more complicated. It had a range of gel-keys on three sides and a curved clear surface with the thread veins of the bio-computer component. It was similar to the capillaries and nerves in a human arm, that carried power and information from and to the periphery of the body. Only in this case it was carrying information to the heart of the structure.

"You're sure it's not live?" Weldon said to Joao, who looked at the device as if he'd seen a deadly snake crawl out. "Are you okay?" He patted him on the shoulder, but there was no response. "Joao!"

"Oh crap!" Joao whispered.

"What's the matter? What is it?" I said, touching his arm, listening as the fear crept up on silent dark footsteps.

Joao sighed and put his head in his hands. "It's a tracking device."

"You mean," Weldon tried again, "The same as the one Okan and Rari have gone back to their verse to steal?"

"Yes." Joao leaned down, his face a mask of nausea. "Talk about lousy timing." He fought hard not to be sick.

We stayed in our different worlds for a moment, each thinking the same thoughts and trying not to let it swamp us. I stood up first and then reached out a hand to Joao to help him to his feet. His fingers felt warm and alive in mine and for a few seconds I realised how far I had come from the dreamwalk days of my childhood and was grateful for the chances my parents had given me; my genes, yes, they had edited a few, but I was beginning to understand that on a cosmic level I was part of something that began with the stardust on the winds of space and ended with the hands of friendship in the dust on a barn floor. We were in a conversation with the quantum universe, or maybe everyone was, you just had to listen.

"Does anyone here remember we have a little problem or are we all due for a short rest?" Tara's voice sounded puzzled and worried; from her point of view, we must have looked as if we were a frozen tableau in a rather over staged gothic play.

"We found this." Joao had taken possession of the discovery and I didn't mind. "It's a tracker," he explained.

"Does it work? Can we use it to see if the borderers with the fixers are on the way?" Tara came over to look, ever practical, she had thought of the most important possibility.

"I wish the professor was here," Joao said, "He'd get it working in a second."

"Who do you think it belonged to?" I asked no one in particular; I seemed to have a gift for the pointless enquiry.

Everyone stopped again. "That's a good question," Weldon said.

"Do we know how many there are?" He asked Joao. Joao shrugged and so did I and eventually Tara did the same.

"Well, we know that there's one, or maybe two, in Okan's verse that were stolen from the meeting after the bomb and Zatar has one. Who else?" Weldon asked.

"The type three verse may still have one?" I said, "But I find it hard to believe this is theirs." There was more nodding and shrugging. "I suppose this might have belonged to Zatar?" We all looked at the bloody and brain spattered bag.

"I can't imagine we would be that lucky," Joao said.

I pulled the tracking device out of its macabre container which I abandoned on the barn floor and we went in silent agreement back to the kitchen, where I placed it on the table.

We all looked at Marl lying on the sofa, white as a ghost and still as death, as if he'd materialised from thin air and I felt terrible that I had completely forgotten his existence.

Tara smiled at my expression. "Don't worry, I checked on him before I came out to see you. He actually seems to be doing a bit better."

"He looks terrible!" I said.

"The internal bleeding has stopped." She shrugged.

It was the edge of everywhere feeling that came to mind. You did what you could for the people around you, but even with the technology the type two verse had, it was still frontier country and so much depended on your own inbuilt survival instincts. I wondered how effective mine were.

"Okay, Joao will see if he can get this device set up and I'm going to link up the defence grid in the front to the farm," Weldon said, as he left the room. I could hear him in the study as he collected whatever technology he needed to do the job.

"Millie and I will finish up moving the stock to the far fields," Tara said to Joao who nodded, looking as if the enormity of the task was just beginning to dawn on him.

"Think like a geek," I suggested helpfully.

"Oh, right, thanks for that, Millie." Joao made a face.

"It can't be that difficult, just start by turning it on." I must have sounded exasperated.

"I could give you the variables on just how many combinations," he counted, "Seventeen keys would give you but I can only add up into the squillions." Joao was getting frustrated, which meant it was time for me to leave.

After eight hours of rounding up three flocks of goats and moving them into the far fields, the thought of pressing a few computer keys seemed the better end of the deal. My shoulders ached with carrying half a dozen complaining kids at a time and putting them on the back of the runabout that Tara was riding. The mothers followed their bleating offspring and we hopped one field after another until they were as far away from the house as possible. A steady stream of smelly disgruntled goats filtered through my brain until all I could see were resentful slashed pupils glaring at me.

We overfed them with the rich pebbles that Tara had thought-fully brought with her on one of the return journeys and this seemed to appease the mothers, but the kids were inconsolable with fear and loathing for their new surroundings.

At every moment, our eyes turned up to the sky with any noise of passing traffic, or the wind making too much fuss in the leaves on the trees that surrounded the fields. We were behaving the same way as the kids, resentful with fear.

At last, tired and dirty, it was time to head back to the farm-house. I got onto the back of the runabout as though my age had increased by about seventy years, staggering with tiredness. "Please, if there's a higher power, don't let them attack us until I've had a shower and at least three bowls of Weldon's stew and dumplings," I said. My tongue was furry with the dust that several hundred goats can muster and no amount of water can dispel.

"Are you religious?" Tara asked over her shoulder making the runabout wobble and me to grab onto her for safety. "Oops, sorry," she said, righting the vehicle.

"I really can't do oops right now," I said, "I'm not sure I can do religion either."

"Weldon's ancestors were Jewish and my grandparents had a catholic upbringing, but neither of them was practicing."

"I'm surprised you still have a religious history here," I said, "It seems more appropriate to a type zero verse," I added sadly, "We still have wars over religion."

"That can't be true!" The runabout wobbled again as she tried to look at my face to see if I was joking. "What about you Millie, what do you think?"

"I think that I'm an agnostic in the Darwinian sense of the word; that there's something out there; I don't know what it is; I don't mind that I don't know and I'm happy to wait to find out. I don't require anything that was created and written by men as an explanation."

"You've obviously given it some thought," Tara laughed.

"I also think that it's important to do the right thing *because* it's the right thing and not because you think you're going to be punished if you don't, or rewarded if you do!"

"Do many people feel the way that you do, in your verse?" Tara asked.

"No," I said.

"Pity." She pulled the runabout around into the front of the farmhouse and we both sat there for a moment, too tired to get off. I leaned onto her shoulder and we both cried silent, dusty tears as if we were a couple of teenagers who know they're in trouble for being late back from a party that wasn't actually worth it.

A loud bang had both of us leaping from the runabout and flat down on the road, guns out and ready for a battle. My heart thumped so hard in my chest that it took a moment to realise that I couldn't see anyone to aim at.

"Sorry!" Weldon shouted, "I was just testing the sensors and I didn't know you were back." A plume of smoke and flame spiralled up around him as he stood near the far barn. A small crater loomed at his feet; anyone who didn't know where they were buried, was going to be in several inappropriate lumps all over the place. I felt an unnerving satisfaction at the thought.

Tara and I staggered up and I grabbed the bobbing runabout. "You go and get showered and I'll put this away," I said.

"Are you sure?" She asked me, the tiredness seeping out of her along with the light on the horizon.

"Yes, I want to hit your husband and I don't want witnesses," I said. I could hear her laughing all the way into the house as I manoeuvred the vehicle through the barn doors.

"We've moved two of the runabouts over to the back field by the tree line," Weldon said as he followed me into the barn. I nodded; my fear back in my throat. "Don't hesitate to get to the empty verse Millie, don't think about Joao and me. We'll manage." Quiet words that were full of meaning, and 'manage' turning into a euphemism for dead.

"I'm not sure if I can take Tara with me," I said, my eyes full of tears, "I'm so afraid of trying and failing." My own word substitution was obvious to both of us.

"Rari thinks you can and that's good enough for me." Weldon gave me a hug and wiped my eyes the way my dad used to do, when I had been experimenting with early forms of flight.

"I miss them!" I whispered, not sure for a moment if I was talking about my parents or my friends. He hugged me for a bit longer and then I said, "If Tara asks, I thumped you for giving us such a fright. I'm too tired to actually do it but I think it's important to say that I did."

He nodded. "Absolutely."

"Is there any food?" I asked hopefully.

"I made a vegetable stew with dumplings and a banana cream pie."

Weldon fiddled with the sonic detonator in his hand, tweaking the controls until he was satisfied.

I stood there with my mouth open. "You know you do sacred work, don't you?"

"Yeah." He shook his head. "There's something *really* spiritual about cooking dinner in-between setting antipersonnel mines."

We made our way back through a twilight of stars and a gibbous moon, the curve of Jupiter part of the orange splashed horizon. Joao met us on the veranda; he was stretching his arms above his head and groaning. "Well?" I said.

"I managed to turn it on."

"In *eight hours,* you've managed to turn it on!" I think my disappointment was as dusty as my face.

"Yes, and that was just luck," Joao added, "I *really* need Rari." He dropped his head with tiredness and frustration and scrubbed at his eyes.

I staggered up the stairs, stripping off as I went and got into a shower, the temperature of which would have been suitable for boiling eggs. Flora and Cecil were stir-crazy at being let out from the safety of the bathroom and skittered around the bedroom churning up the downie with their enthusiasm. "Get over it, you two!" I shouted as they spun around my damp ankles nearly tipping me over.

"What about angels?" Tara said, coming into the bedroom with a hot drink, the strength of the fumes alone could have removed paint from a barnacled boat. She was half joking and I think expecting a cynical answer, that was the problem with the question of belief, once you've opened the door it was difficult to close.

"Yes. But my angels don't have feathers or wings." Tara looked surprised and puzzled; she sat down on the bed and cuddled Flora who was having a well-deserved rest. "Is there any progress down there?" I asked. "I saw Joao, he looked discouraged."

"I guess it's a start." She shrugged. "I spoke to Til, he's got some help from Twin Rivers, they've offered to program their security net to cover us."

"That's mighty neighbourly of them darlin,'" I said, in what I felt was a more than reasonable impression of John Wayne.

Tara looked very puzzled. "Marl is awake."

"I keep forgetting the man exists!" I sat down on the bed and tied the laces of my boots, I thought it was important to get properly dressed again, as it didn't seem to be a good idea to get into a pair of pyjamas if you thought you were going to have to do some shooting and running. "It's as if he's become completely invisible when you're not in the room with him."

"I imagine that's how he's managed to survive on the streets for so long," Tara said dryly. She sipped her drink and smoothed Flora's ruffled nerves. Cecil had settled on the pillows and was washing as if he would never be clean again. I stroked his head and was rewarded with a low uncertain purr.

"There's no sign of *them* yet?" I said, saying what felt as if it had become the unsayable.

"Not yet."

"Are you two coming down for supper?" Weldon shouted up the stairs, making both of us jump and Cecil growl.

"Coming!" I shouted back and scooped up the cat and the elephant as Tara carried both of the unfinished brandies. The smell of hot food and kitchen comfort wafted up the stairs toward us and we swam gratefully through the waves of reassurance. Most of the lights were off in the house, because it didn't do to advertise, but the kitchen had a warm glow of low lamplight.

Marl was sitting up, or really, he was leaning in a more upright position, his toffee-coloured skin a pasty yellow and his hair matted against his head. But his eyes were open and focused. I went over to him and gave him a hug which I think surprised both of us.

"I thought you'd know how to use it." He pointed to the tracking device on the table and shrugged, a painful movement that made him gasp.

"Yes," I drawled, "I think we thought that too."

"You do know I can hear you?" Joao said, with a scowl that made him look a lot like Cecil, who was sitting on the back of the sofa and watching Marl with orange eyes.

Cecil was on tabby alert, fur standing out so that he seemed twice his size. Marl watched him back with the mixture of admiration and something that was probably calculation. "I didn't know you collected exotics," he said, checking out Flora who was standing back from the young man as the smell of old blood still hung in the air, her trunk twitching in alarm.

"We don't," Tara said, going over to help Weldon with putting the food out on the table. The unlicensed cat and the stolen pachyderm took a corner of the sofa and began to wash each other.

"Right," Marl said. He took the unspoken advice and pretended he hadn't seen anything.

"Do we know where this came from?" I asked the room, pointing at the device.

"Marl?" Joao said. Marl shook his head indicating that Joao should talk; it was too much of an effort for him. Joao went on, "Marl told me earlier, that he took it from a borderer who was with the group Torin had contacted."

"You *took* it?" I asked carefully, "That's an interesting choice of words. There was *brain* matter all over it!"

"Millie!" Tara said, her spoon halfway from the bowl to her mouth.

Marl smiled, one that didn't include his eyes. "He didn't want to give it to me."

"Was this before or after you got away from Torin and Gasat?" I could hear the underlying note of doubt in my own voice, and it was not surprising that everyone ceased eating.

Marl wasn't able to eat, so he didn't actually stop. Weldon had rigged up a hydration system that consisted of a bag of fluid attached to a gel-pack straight onto the skin of his neck. It was disconcertingly sucking in and out like a living creature. He smiled again. "I killed three borderers and Gasat. After *four* days of being kept in a cage the size of that." He pointed to the cupboard where Tara stored the crockery. He didn't sound angry; he sounded cold and matter of fact, which made me shiver.

Slowly the spoons clattered in the bowls again and we ate in silence for a while. "Where are the other two?" Marl asked.

"On a visit home," Joao replied in-between mouthfuls of bread and stew.

"That professor guy, he'd be able to get it to work." Marl was only voicing what the rest of us were thinking but I patted Joao's shoulder in a gesture of solidarity.

"You're right," Tara said dryly, "We got the second team."

"Tara!" Weldon said, laughing.

Marl looked bleak for a moment as the rest of us gave each other the verbal abuse that only really close friends can carry off. Tara got up and put the largest pie ever seen in any verse, on the table, a towering confection of cream and toffee and banana. Marl sighed

365

with frustration and I sighed with desire. I have always loved anything with a high calorie count.

The silence that followed the first mouthfuls was cathedral-like in its reverence. Marl's face held the expression of a man with no friends left in the world. He muttered quietly, "You're killing me here."

"I think someone else already had that covered," I said, through cream and toffee. Marl sniffed and leaned back on the cushions, a small smile curving from his mouth towards his eyes for a change.

"Tell me about your angels?" Tara said, ruining the possibility of table peace forever that evening.

I was not sure why my feelings about ideology always seem to cause me trouble; maybe it's just the fact that I don't believe in any conventional sense. I took a deep breath and several mouthfuls of pudding. "I think that an angel is the one perfect moment." Blank faces all around. "The one you're aware of which fills you with love and longing in equal measure for something you can't understand. That 'heart in the mouth' moment of pure joy." Some slow nods, even Marl was listening. I put the spoon down in my empty bowl and sighed, "The sun rising on an orange sky over the hills of home. The way that puppies breathe when they're sleeping. The first time I flew a plane on my own. My mum's face when she didn't know I was watching her watching me," my voice cracked.

"Knowing that someone out there, cares about you," Marl said in a whisper.

"The lights of home after a long day," Weldon sighed.

"The sound of a cat's purr when you wake up in the night full of lonely fears," Joao added.

The silence that followed was even deeper than the one following the pudding. Then Tara said, with a catch in her voice, "The first time your baby smiles."

Weldon took pity on Marl and gave him a teaspoonful of the banana cream, just enough to make him grunt with frustration but his gratitude was three dimensional and he moved carefully towards the edge of the sofa and sat up with help. "Is there any chance that I can get a shower?"

Joao looked at Weldon for his say so and got a considered nod in return. "Okay, I'll give you a hand."

Marl looked even more grateful. It took them ten minutes to make it to the foot of the stairs and they were still climbing when I went out to check the stock in the far fields with Tara ten minutes later. I heard Joao say with some exasperation, "Right we need to rethink this, I'm going to carry you." Marl's protests were still audible when we had left the farmhouse.

The sky was full with stars and the ever -watchful planet filled one horizon from edge to edge. I stopped for a moment, lost in admiration at the sight. "It still affects me and I've been here forever," Tara said. She stood next to me and we both looked up and took in the magic of the universe and the power that it held over all of us.

The runabout was draughty and I clung on with my hands tucked around Tara's waist. All the cattle were settled into the small night time groups that they seemed to favour. The goats were another story, restless and nervous they wouldn't calm down and their resentment radiated out to the different flocks as they drifted back and forward trying to find a place of safety.

"I know just how they feel," I said, watching them.

The house was in near darkness when we got back, I pushed the runabout into the barn using the red beam on the emergency torch Tara had given me. It cast a wicked light into the corners of the building; threatening shadows crept up from behind the feed bins and the other vehicles making me jumpy.

I joined Tara at the door to the barn; she was watching the woods at the end of the farm driveway. Her head was turned slightly to one side, trying to lose the blind spot in the centre of the eye that can fool you into thinking anything on a dark night. Over to the edge of the trees some of the shadows seemed too uniform to be branches swaying in the wind. They detached themselves and as if they were phantoms coalescing into human form, moved towards us.

My mouth went dry and I dropped to one knee, sighting the weapon in my sweaty fingers on the nearest figure. Tara went over to a small unit on the wall by the barn door and pressed a red key. It must have done something because it flashed on and off for several seconds before going dark again. She slid up to the edge of the door and positioned herself side on for the smallest target. Her weapon rested against the frame and I heard her breathe out quietly for a better aim.

For skirmish troops they were pretty hopeless, because they made no move to hide from us and they must have known we were there, it hadn't exactly been a quiet ingress into the barn. I held off from firing, the sixth sense that everyone should listen to, making me cautious. They stopped a few yards from the drive. "Tara?" A voice called. I looked at her and we both shrugged, it was not the sort of conversation that you usually had with a borderer. "It's Granger. I'm a friend of Marl's." We stood in silence. He spoke again this time in a more impatient voice. "We came to help, because of Ziggy." They waited in silence for us to speak.

"What do you think?" I whispered to Tara. She shook her head, holding up a finger asking me to wait a moment.

A sound from behind us made me turn to see if we had been ambushed, it was Joao and a barely standing Marl. "Granger?" Marl sounded surprised, puzzled and something else, pleased.

The whole group moved into the light from my torch by mutual consent. Joao and I still held our weapons out but Tara had put hers back into its harness. Marl held his gun pointing straight down at the ground. Not away but not aggressive either. It made me think that maybe he wasn't that certain himself. I looked at Joao, his eyes glittered in the dark and he moved his head towards the back of the barn. I realised that he was letting me know where Weldon was standing.

"Don't want no trouble," Granger said. "Thought we'd see if we could be of any use here." He pointed at the other three men.

"Civin, Wills and Kasper." They nodded and we nodded back. "Don't hold with what Gasat and Torin did," he added.

Wills moved into the light, he was middle height and stocky with strong even features. "We know the borderers are coming here for her," he pointed to me, "Don't hold with that either," he shrugged, "Even if she's the one that caused all the extra kidnappings over the years as Marl said."

In the shadowed light they didn't look so young, the weight of unnecessary years and impossible decisions grooving lines where there shouldn't have been any; the sort of men who never expected to actually grow old, so they brought old with them just in case. It reminded me of Okan and Rari and I felt a great pain for the loss sweep over me. That and the reminder that I was being looked for and other likely candidates had been taken because of me.

Joao turned to Marl. "It's your call. I recognise these men from the skydancing towers, but only you can say if you trust them or not." I knew that if Marl even demurred a second, a shot in the back of the head was all these men could hope for and they must have realised it too, but they stood there waiting for Marl to pass sentence on them. It made my heart break for the agony of it.

Marl spoke simply, "I trust them with my life."

"Maybe you could call off your shooter then," Granger said, with a smile in his voice.

"I could do that," Joao replied, with that warrior-to-warrior tone. He moved a hand up in the dark and flicked a red-light torch on and off twice.

The atmosphere changed almost at once. The men moved to shake hands with Marl as if they were buddies at a board meeting; it was a quaint old-fashioned gesture that was full of pathos. Joao watched as Weldon came out of the black shadows at the far end of the barn and moved quietly to check out the road. He came back after about ten minutes and shook his head to Joao's silent enquiry.

Tara broke up the meeting when it became obvious that Marl was not able to stand up any longer. She scooped him towards the house and the men followed like goslings after a mother duck. Joao and Weldon stayed behind and Weldon said, "Are we going to do this?"

"I don't see that we have any choice?" Joao looked down at the ground. "What do you think Millie?"

I must have looked surprised because he smiled. There are not many men who had the strength to ask a woman what she thought, as it took a person who was at peace with their own ego. I'd met more than one in the type two verse in the previous few months, but it caught me off guard that he actually cared.

"I think," I said, "That they don't know what to do without a leader, that Marl fits that bill and that they will fight for him until they drop. They have a code and a set of rules and someone broke those rules and that breaks them because all they have is each other and what they believe and they will try and make amends. To do what's right. They see honour and integrity and they understand it, and although we may not agree with some of what they've done to stay alive they *will* fight for us." In my head I added 'and they will probably die.'

"That's pretty much what I thought, not including all the flowery stuff," Joao said, completely without irony. Weldon nodded his agreement. I shelved the fact that for a minute there I had felt the differences between men and women shrink; it was sometimes still as wide as the Grand Canyon.

"I'm going to check the perimeter," Weldon said and disappeared into the night. He was a moving shadow in a matter of moments and then he was nothing. I shivered.

Joao pointed to the house. "Come on, let's get something to drink and check on the kids." He put an arm around my shoulders and gave me a squeeze. "They'll be back soon. Okan won't stay away a moment longer than he has to." We both tried to believe that what he was saying was true, because we both needed to. Truth could be a moveable feast at the best of times.

The house was full of whispers and dark spaces that reached out to touch you on the shoulder when your back was turned, so that I felt as if I needed to look behind me all the time for what wasn't there.

The dim light in the kitchen gave a false glow to everyone's features and Tara was feeding the gang of men with big bowls of stew and fresh bread that had miraculously appeared from the oven. My head was spinning with tiredness and the level of fear that you can't quite swallow. Wills and Granger made a space for me at the table without breaking stride in either eating or talking. They were catching up with Marl as to where he had been kept and where they had looked for him; it came as sudden and damming news to them that he had killed Gasat.

"Torin?" Granger asked.

"He wasn't there," Marl said, "When I left." He looked at me to check if I was bothered by the description of his escape. As far as I could see, it was just another euphemism for killing and death to live with. Granger and Wills shrugged and that passed for the only comment on Gasat.

Tara and Joao and I sat and listened, Tara because she thought she might hear something about Ziggy, me because I was too exhausted to do anything else and Joao because he still didn't trust them.

The com on the wall chimed; a small intrusive sound that stopped everyone in mid-breath. Tara went over and answered it. Til Duster's gentle face was tired and lined with concern. "Something in the outer atmosphere, no confirmation on the ship so far. I thought I'd better give you the heads up. Could be nothing," he said.

Tara moved the com so he could see the rest of the room. "We got some help," she explained.

"As soon as we know what's happening, I'll be back on the line," he added, "It could just be there's lots of space navy around at the moment."

"We appreciate it Til," Joao said.

"Oh, one more thing, bad news I'm afraid, that professor friend of Weldon's?" He looked down at something and then read out, "Professor Theadus." I could feel my vertebrae stiffen with the inevitably of it. "Found dead in his office at the university, it looked as if it was a break in. They were after something because he was tortured before they killed him," he finished lamely, "I'm sorry." He nodded goodbye, the screen went opaque and the room breathed out.

"Weldon!" Tara said. We all looked around at the open doorway to the house. He must have come in while Til was speaking. His face was grey with pain and then he swallowed it and his face changed.

"I set the sonic alarms and the mined perimeter. We shouldn't have any surprises."

"Granger and I will take the first watch." Wills stood up. He looked for a moment at Joao and then back at Weldon.

The possibility for another road was deliberated and not taken in that moment. "I will show you where the antipersonnel mines are and the perimeter sensors," Joao said. Weldon nodded his agreement and the men left quietly and went out into the night together, a small army on the same side for all the usual imperfect, impossible reasons.

"So, what do we do now?" I said to the rest of the room.

Tara's smile was thin and strained; the two men, Kasper and Civin, who were finishing their meal, looked from one to the other of us.

"We wait," Tara said.

The three men moved slowly down the stairs as if thinking carefully about what had been said to them, by the one dead and one dying man. Simon was looking around, trying to get the feel of the place, he didn't think anyone watching him would see his behaviour as anything but normal. He glanced at Okan and Rari, neither man was smiling or joking the way they did in the type two verse, but then he didn't think they would do much of that here. The walls prevented any kind of laughter, it was as if the stone leaned towards you with a hidden malevolence. He tried not to shudder.

Okan was wondering just exactly how long they had until someone got up the nerve to disturb the director. Maybe a day, maybe less. He sighed, if they hadn't done what they came to do by sunset they were dead anyway. He could see Rari thinking through his own survival possibilities and coming up short.

The lower levels of the building were a few degrees colder than the upper floors and their footsteps clicked on the polished marble. Okan pointed at a set of double doors with a sign above 'Research & Development.' He nodded to the guard who stood to one side of the doors, silent and suspicious. The guard looked up to the doorway light as the three men passed by him, a flicker of surprise crossed his face as the light remained unchanged when Simon went through.

He didn't query the access, Charlie Morris had done his job well, no one questioned anything if they wanted to stay in work, or worse, alive.

A bright busy room surprised Simon. It was full of scientists; the reason he knew they were scientists was the constant babble of geek talk and a propensity of white coveralls that made everyone look as if they were kindly snowman psychopaths. He wished that he hadn't surrendered the guns to Okan and Rari but the chances of him surviving if someone saw him with a weapon were slim to none. 'For now,' he said to himself, later, he was going to have to find something useful.

"Hey Okan!" A large genial man with the eyes of a mean school bully waved and came over to them. He shook hands with Okan and Rari and waited for an introduction to Simon.

"Riddick, this is Seager Wells." Okan remembered to call Simon by the name that Charlie Morris would have used.

Riddick nodded and smiled. "Good to meet you." Simon grinned back and did his best not to do the 'ugh' dance after he had extracted his hand. Millie would have been proud of him he thought. "What have you got for us?" The scientist asked.

"It's a new power source," Okan explained, handing over the device to the greedy man, who pawed and stroked the com, as if someone had given him a luscious inebriated blonde with dubious morals. Simon tried to bite back the remarks about slobber and sighed again about Millie's inevitable pride in his reticence.

A small crowd had gathered and the com was passed from hand to hand as the holo- readings and information were gloated over. A steady hum of 'geek speak' filled the air. Rari explained a few of the readings that seemed to be a matter of difference between the type two verse and his and Okan's. Simon watched him pointing to the different components of the power source. He looked over to Simon and then his face darkened and he flicked a glance at the cameras. Simon tried not to let his fist clench. He could see Okan watching the different exits and trying not to be seen doing it.

"The off verse is still interesting then?" One of the other scientists asked. It seemed an innocuous question, but everyone listened to the possibility of an answer. It was the type of careful fishing expedition that was obvious and easily deflected.

"We have to get a medical," Okan said, finishing the conversation before it started. No one pushed or joked, no one dared. The scientists went back to the equipment and terminals and the three men went out into the corridor and the waiting guard and the invisible clicking footsteps around each corner. Simon sighed, he'd been here about three hours and so far it had been about as much fun as a tax audit.

The end of the next corridor was an unguarded door into the medical department with the usual helpful sign above. Okan moved one eyebrow in warning to Simon as they went through to the anteroom and began stripping. Simon put his clothes neatly on the shelves provided and followed the nearly naked men into a clear cubicle that filled with steam and then cleared just as quickly. A light similar to the one that had checked them out in the main hallway passed over them and a breathy female voice said, "All clear." A door on the other side of the sterile box opened and they walked through.

Several of the scientists came over, this time in blue romper suits. The breathy female was one of them. "Okan it's good to see you."

"Good to see you too, doctor." Okan sounded friendly and he smiled in a careful, guarded way.

"Rari." She added, nodding.

Rari was as stiff as a board and Simon watched him as he leaned away in an almost shudder. "Doctor Smithfield. This is Simon," Rari realised his mistake and stopped mid - sentence.

Simon held out a hand. "Seager Wells. Rari calls me Simon, it's my middle name." He oiled his language in a way that usually got him around the little inconvenient things in life, as in murder and train tickets.

She was clearly capable of out oiling him. "Carole Smithfield. Charlie Morris and I were just talking about you this morning, he told me so much I feel I know you already."

She shook his hand and Simon resisted the temptation to check he still had his fingers. He realised that nothing from now on was going to be even a little easy and the body count was going to be more than the two men upstairs, because as sure as the sun came up in all of the verses, he was going to have to kill this woman. Her evil didn't just extend to torturing Rari on whatever pretext, it was the deep malevolence of the truly convinced. Charlie Morris had surrounded himself with every nasty possibility in human nature. He looked at Okan and Rari and felt a terrible sadness for their obvious plight, and an abiding respect that in the face of so much wickedness, they had managed to hang onto something good.

Simon was aware of the fact that he was standing in his underwear while everyone else had more than the usual amount of clothing on, a not unpleasant sensation but one that would affect the quick getaway he had worked out in the section of his brain he labelled 'hopeless plans,' the type, he thought wryly, that usually made the gods laugh.

Okan submitted to the blood test and then stood in the curved wall unit that performed a full body MRI scan. They still used this after each return from dreamwalking on the pretext of checking for changes in the body tissue, but Okan knew it was in the hope of finding an excuse to open someone up. Smithfield had once confided to him it was her dearest wish to examine the brain of a dreamwalker under the latest sub molecular microscope. A device he thought with humour that he and Rari had brought back from the type two verse a few years ago. He watched as Rari and then Simon was checked carefully.

They stood in the same anteroom getting dressed. Simon realised that his clothes had been searched thoroughly and then neatly returned to the shelves. The security tag was pinned to the inside of his shirt but it was askew as if someone had put it back in a hurry. He watched as Okan and Rari made little of returning their guns to the harnesses they both had under their jackets.

"I'm surprised that you are both still carrying a weapon in the building?" Smithfield had removed her blue suit and was strutting about in stilettos and a skirt that would have made Saffron, Simon's punk receptionist, blush.

Okan shrugged. "We may have to leave in a hurry, depending on the director."

Rari nodded in agreement. Simon admired the perfect lie, one that was really the truth in disguise.

Smithfield wasn't falling for it. "I shall have to ask Charlie about that when I see him." Okan shrugged. She turned to Simon, her annoyance at not getting a rise out of Okan still twisted in her mouth. "I would have thought Craig would want to be interviewing you in the specialist wing?"

"He very well may still do that." Simon used his most winning smile. It seemed to make her angrier and he saw Okan shake his head a little, trying to tell him not to bait her. Which was too late.

She whipped around glaring at each of them. "I think," she hissed, "Something's going on here and I'm going to find out what it is." Her clicking heels followed the other lost, angry sounds out of the doorway and along the empty corridor.

Rari sighed and sat down to put his boots on. He looked at Okan, they used the practice of many years not speaking, to convey the thought that the possibility of this lasting more than a few hours was over. He could see that Simon wanted to ask them something but he put a warning hand on the man's arm, the cameras in the medical unit were very sensitive, they would have to find one of the dead spaces in the corridor for a quick conference. Simon hid his frustration under another bright grimace and they walked out through the double doors.

The corridor crept around a corner and Rari stopped in the middle, he pulled the com from his pocket and pointed it at the camera on the wall a few feet away, it buzzed and turned to face away from them. "We've got two minutes," he said.

Okan started. "It seems things have changed since the last time we were here, there have always been factions, that's how Morris kept control over people, but Smithfield has a much more definite air than she used to and I don't think that she will be put off by the red conference light for too long," he paused, realising that he had nearly said home, but he'd said here instead. Home was the type two verse now and Millie. He knew Rari was aware of the emotional slip by the wry expression on his face. "Simon, we need to get to the tracking device, can you go into R and D and disconnect us from the recall mechanism?"

"I need a weapon," Simon said by way of an answer, "The one the guard is holding will do."

Okan went on. "We're going to have to remove both of the guards outside the R and D and the specialist wing. Once we start this, we'll have maybe twenty minutes before the security team get it together, they will be relying on Craig Brown to tell them what to do and he's-"

"Unavailable," Rari said helpfully. "That's nearly one minute." He had his com in front of him counting down the time.

"Right, everyone ready?" Okan asked. The three men looked at each other and nodded. "Let's go."

The guard outside the doors to R and D was standing half in and half out of the required mentally alert state and was truly bored. He was not surprised to see the three men return from the medical unit, but it took him more than a second to realise that as they passed to go back into R and D something was wrong.

Okan leaned forward as if to open the double doors and moved to one side to let Rari walk through, Simon watched as the guard looked up automatically for the security barrier to go from red to green to release the door mechanism, in that split second, he moved in and reached around the guard, snapping his neck in a sickening crunch. He let the dead body slide to the floor quietly and the three men waited a moment to see if he had a medical alert attached to him. Nothing, no alarm. "So far so good," Simon said. Rari opened the door to a cupboard helpfully labelled as cleaning crew. He pulled the body over to the doorway and propped him up between the floor robot and some canisters of nasty smelling liquid. "Is anyone likely to be using this in the next half hour?"

"No," Rari answered, "However, a red, open door, warning light will have appeared in the security room and if they feel like coming down here and investigating, we will have a problem."

"What are you," Okan asked, with a sense of exasperation, "A paid assassin?" He checked his own weapon.

"No one actually pays me to kill people. I always think that it's a perk of the job," Simon said cheerfully. He wiped his hands on the guard's jacket then relieved him of his weapon, checking it for a charge. They pushed the door closed on the dead guard. It was a tight fit, Simon huffed, "Fat knacker!"

Rari found himself laughing and shook his head at the feelings. He saw that Okan had much the same expression of puzzled disgust, it was as if they were suffering from a collective madness.

"Are you bothered; did you know him?" Simon asked Rari.

"I knew him yes, he was one of the security team that

presided over my last reprogramming, and no, I'm not that concerned." He tried for not bitter too, but was unsuccessful. Simon nodded his understanding.

Rari and Okan stood outside the R and D entrance and Rari pointed his com at one of the cameras again, clicking it into a position away from the laboratory doors. Okan indicated another door on one side that said planning. He then pointed to the corner in the corridor that led to the specialist wing. Simon nodded.

Rari said, "We have about ten minutes until the guard will be missed, that camera is going to notice he's not standing outside in two, but it will take the security team another seven or eight to signal him for an answer. Hopefully they won't make any connection to the red light on the cupboard door opening."

"What about the scientists, are they likely to be wandering about any time soon?" Simon asked.

"Not if they want to keep their jobs," Rari said. "They have to have a good reason for leaving the labs in the middle of a shift." He added, "It's not likely but not impossible, be careful. Smithfield now seems to be able to do what she wants so that's new, other people may be equally empowered."

Okan said, "Can you take care of the security guard outside the specialist wing on your own?" Simon smiled.

"Okay, Okan snorted, "Stupid question. Once we go through that door," he pointed again at the planning room, "Things are going to get complicated. We're not going to have much time to make it to the main entrance." They were all silent for less than the moment it takes to breathe in and out. "Ready Rari?" Rari was looking again at the com counting down the time. He nodded.

Simon sped off down the corridor and Okan and Rari went in through the doorway. The planning section was quieter than R and D, but there were still several scientists in white suits working on the computer units.

"Hi Okan, what are you doing in here?" One of the men asked him. His name badge said Martin. Okan didn't know him very well. He held out the weapon and motioned the man over to the other end of the room; the man's face was a picture of puzzlement.

"Are you crazy?"

"Don't do it." Okan said quietly to a woman who was edging towards the doorway and a security alarm. She stopped; rabbit in the headlight still.

"Move away from the units," Rari asked politely, he waved his gun in the direction he wanted them to go. They all walked over to one wall, trained by the careful instinct of self- preservation that the director had encouraged over the years. They were the prisoners on an island hoping to please the guards. Okan stood carefully watching them while Rari looked for the tracking device.

"You're going to spend the next seven years in the specialist wing after this," Martin said. "That's if the evil doctor doesn't get you first," he added wryly.

"I can't see it!" Rari said. He pointed the weapon at the nearest scientist, a man who had been in the planning section for as long as he could remember. "Sefton, where's the tracking device?" The man looked at Martin and then at Okan, he did an almost humorous mental summing up about his loyalties and his fear of punishment, then indicated a container on the work surface behind Rari.

The device was cushioned in a sectioned compartment with a sealed lid and a handle for easy removal. Rari checked that it was the real thing by flicking the unit on for a moment, he programmed the device to accept the subatomic information of the verse they were in and a small holo-screen popped up with red lights flickering on and off.

"It looks as if Wethers and Smallwood have just left to go to Millie's verse," Rari said, tracking the readings the holo-screen rolled up. "We're the only dreamwalkers in this verse right now."

"Is that good?" Okan asked.

"I don't know," Rari huffed, "I guess it would be better not to have anyone else to worry about and," he added wryly, "Wethers has never been very fond of you."

"He thinks I gave him up to Craig Brown after the first trip he made to the type two verse," Okan added bitterly. "Just one of the many ways the director kept us fighting amongst ourselves."

"Kept?" Sefton latched onto the word. He looked carefully at Okan and then Rari. "Past tense." The room was silent for a moment; then something crept across Sefton's face, a fleeting expression that may have included hope, Rari wasn't sure. He and Okan said nothing.

"Can we track the signals in the type two verse from here?" Okan asked, not taking his eyes off the group of men and women standing with unnatural passivity in one corner of the room.

"No," Rari answered closing the case, "Well not that I understand. The person who designed it might be able to program it to read the different verses, but I think you can only read the verse you're in." He shrugged, lifting the small case off the work surface and backing up towards the door. "Simon might know something."

"Who's Simon?" Martin asked. "I heard you came back with someone; does he have new technology?" The questions were asked with the hunger of the truly obsessed.

"Me and my mouth again," Rari said, as he backed up to stand by Okan, "We'd better get out of here or Simon is going to end up in a petri dish."

"You'll never get out of here," Sefton whispered, his voice as cold as the empty echoing corridors the other side of the door, "Even if Charlie Morris is in the past tense, Craig Brown will kill you before he lets you go."

"Stay inside the laboratory," Okan said calmly, "Otherwise I will shoot you." Martin nodded, his whole body indicating 'not my problem.'

Rari blasted the alarm on the inside of the lab doorway as they left, he paused as the two of them went through the double doors, aiming the com at the camera again. "I don't know how long they're going to keep falling for that in the security office, their heads must be spinning by now." He opened the door lock mechanism and moved the control wires around so that it stayed locked and the scientists couldn't get out.

"Will that last for a while?" Okan asked.

"Well, Sefton is as least as smart as me and Martin is very clever, so," he shook his head, "No."

They went out into the corridor and peered around the corner, the guard in front of the specialist wing was glaringly absent. Okan nodded. "It's going better than I thought."

"Are you crazy?" Rari spluttered, "Don't say that! These things have a way of coming back around and biting you."

A loud siren shrieked making both of them cringe and Rari looked accusingly at Okan, who shrugged and mouthed, 'Sorry.'

The door to the specialist wing sprang open, Simon sprinted out carrying a small black box and firing over his shoulder at two heavily armed scientists, both of whom dropped in an untidy, sickening heap of blood and bone. Okan looked behind him for a moment at the doorway to R and D as if he couldn't understand why Simon was coming out of the wrong laboratory. The computer that could separate them from the recall mechanism was in the R and D unit and without it being reprogramed they could be pulled back at any time, which meant they would never get away.

Simon reached them and Okan pushed the winded man into the wall and took over firing at the open doorway to the lab. The scientists were hunkered down using the doors as cover. Simon caught his breath, "It might be better to move away before the bang."

"What bang?" Okan looked exasperated as he kept up a steady stream of fire. The cat was well out of the bag and down the road, the sound of the siren was almost drowned out by the sound of gunfire.

"What did you do?" Rari asked. He was crouched on one knee facing the other way towards the R and D laboratory doors and planning, covering the backs of the other two men.

"It's astounding what you can find in cleaning cupboards these days, I mean don't people realise how dangerous some of this stuff can be?" Simon asked, smiling winningly, his forehead was shiny with sweat and he was still breathing hard. He lifted his weapon and added his fire to Okan's.

"No, they probably don't, but I think that's because they haven't done the 'how to cause mayhem in the shortest possible time' course!" Okan sounded desperate. "We'll never get out of here now," he muttered. Words that could have been missed under the combination of the ear battering that was going on.

Simon said, "Don't worry you will get out of here, let's get to the main entrance, I am guessing it would be impossible to dreamwalk inside the building?"

"I imagine you've tried," Okan said bitterly, "Now you've got what you came for." He pointed to the box. Simon shrugged in an almost admission.

"Well, you'd better go," Okan said, "Rari and I might as well stay here and try and disable the recall mechanism."

"Okan," Simon said, in-between bursts of fire, "There isn't one."

"What!" Rari shouted, his concentration broken for a moment. He looked away from the doors to the laboratories and the corridor, just as the first of the security teams came down the stairs, their weapons fire heaping noise upon noise.

"No mechanism, nothing to keep you here. It was something Charlie Morris put about to add a layer of control," Simon had to shout.

Okan had no space in his mind for thought processing but

his brain wouldn't give up, he tried to remember if he knew of anyone who had been returned. There was lots of hearsay; but no empirical evidence. He wanted to shout with frustration.

"There's no time for this," Rari said to Okan carefully, "Let's go home."

"Now would be good," Simon said, "Because I wasn't kidding about the big bang."

The security team of six men were wall hugging and moving forward in a military pattern of 'advance to contact.' Okan recognised it because he'd had the same training as the men who were coming towards him. They used the corner that led to R and D and planning for cover. In a few moments Okan realised he, Simon and Rari would be overrun in the squeeze of the two groups. Behind them was the dead end that led to the medical department. A shout from the specialist wing made Simon wince. "Okay that means we really are out of time. I suggest you cover your eyes and open your mouth." He dropped to the ground and curled into a ball and Okan followed suit a half second before Rari. They both took Simon's advice and hoped that the measure would save them from losing their sight and their eardrums.

The pressure from the 29,000 feet per second velocity blast wave of the bomb was quite literally deafening, and the following vacuum air sucked them back down the corridor in the moment after a fraction of a second passed.

"Fire!" Someone shouted and woke the men up from their daze. The specialist wing was gushing smoke and flame, it licked around the doors and hesitated as it met more oxygen rich air in the corridor, before rushing forward.

"Shit!" Rari shouted, grabbing his weapon from the floor where he had dropped it, his clothes were shredded from his back and he had a nasty cut over one eye from flying debris. Okan was in a similar state, one trouser leg was gone and his arm was bleeding, small bits of the composite door were sticking out from his elbow. They staggered to their feet and looked though the smoke. No one fired from either side.

"Well, maybe my calculations on the explosive load were a little on the heavy side," Simon said, sounding annoyingly cheerful. His clothes looked as if they had been freshly pressed and a small smudge on the side of his nose was the only mark on him. Okan decided not to beat him to a pulp until a more convenient moment.

"The specialist wing will be full of something that looks similar to internal organ soup after that," Rari said, coughing. He tried not to let the feelings of revenge surface, but his face must have betrayed him because Simon patted him sympathetically on the shoulder, carefully trying to avoid the lacerations.

"Oh no!" Rari groaned. He held the container that the tracking device was in, it wasn't bomb proof. A large piece of broken door had been propelled into the metal box. It was still sticking out of one side. Rari threw it in fury at the wall.

"I guess you must think there was no possibility that was salvageable?" Okan said, his own bitterness threading out through the words.

Rari scrubbed at his forehead with bloody fingers, leaving a trail of stripes in the sweaty dirt already there. "Not a chance."

"Think yourself lucky," Simon said gently, "It could have been you." He patted Rari on the shoulder again and Rari shook his head, his own feelings of despair leaking out into the air between them.

"Was any of this about us?" Rari asked Simon, who didn't answer but clutched the black box he held and tried not to look guilty. Rari looked away first. "That's what I thought," he said.

They moved back up the corridor towards the security team, testing the potential for return fire. One of the team was lying in an unnatural position in the middle of the floor; his back was at an impossible right angle to his legs and he was bleeding into an ever- increasing red halo of liquid around him, as his heart pumped blood to keep his internal pressure up; his fingers clawed at the ground as if trying for a safer hand hold. Half his face was missing.

The bomb had blasted outward on a specific trajectory, but Okan realised that they had been lucky to get away with so little damage. Even lying on the floor with the corner to the medical laboratory shielding them from the main part of the explosion, they could all have died. He tried not to punch Simon, but if looks could have killed, they would have. Simon tried to look sorry but didn't succeed. The man who was dying on the floor behind them had not been so lucky. More aggressive than his team, he had reached the angle of the corridor just as the bomb went off and paid the price.

Okan dropped down as weapons fire hit the wall above his head and Rari moved to shoot from a lower vantage point. They were still trapped, just in-between a fire and the security team this time. "How many are there left?" Simon asked. He was behind Rari and watching back down the corridor towards the specialist wing, the medical laboratory and the fire.

"I think we still have a big problem," Rari said.

"There's definitely no way out back in that direction?" Simon asked.

"The director wasn't a big fan of more than one entrance and exit," Rari explained.

"I can imagine," Simon said, sarcastically.

"Oh no!" Okan hissed with frustration as the doors to planning and R and D opened and the scientists came out. They were slightly behind and to one side of the security team and they crept along as if fearful of the consequences. "Could this get any worse?"

"Well, not to add fuel to the fire," Simon joked inappropriately, "Get it?"

Okan looked over his shoulder, his eyes dark with anger. "Simon!"

"The fire is getting closer," Simon finished, straight faced.

"Is Charlie Morris dead?" Sefton called to Okan and Rari, shouting to be heard above the noise of the emergency siren and the occasional bang of something in the specialist wing igniting. He held a piece of what looked as if it could be metal cabinet in his hand. Okan realised that all the scientists were similarly armed with whatever they had been able to find.

Okan glanced at Rari who shrugged his opinion; it didn't make sense whichever way you examined it. Okan shouted above the sound of guns and the ever-increasing smell of fire and smoke, "Yes, he's dead."

"So is Craig Brown," Rari added for good measure.

The effect on the scientists was puzzling; they rippled towards the unprotected backs of the security team and began to attack them.

"Get out of here, Rari!" Sefton shouted to the stunned men.

"Quickly!" Riddick from R and D said, "Smithfield will be back and her medical staff are very loyal to her."

He was about to say something else but one of the security team had broken free from the overwhelming odds and he shot Riddick in the chest. Riddick sank to his knees. Sefton hit the man who had fired with the makeshift weapon he carried. It was a hard, vicious blow, one backed up with years of memories of cruelty and oppression. The man spun around under the force of the impact, his face caved in on one side, mostly dead when he hit the ground.

Okan and Rari reached the scientists and the four remaining security team, who were on the floor and disarmed. They muttered angry threats until one of the scientists fired a gun into the leg of the nearest man. "That's for my friend, Lowell," the scientist said bitterly. The security man grunted and clutched his leg, trying to stem the flow of blood.

Okan knelt on the floor by Riddick. "Thank you," he said, the word sticking in his throat with its inadequacy.

"Good luck," Riddick whispered; his hand on Okan's as he slipped slowly into the comforting darkness of whatever happens to us next.

The men raced up the stairs for the front entrance, Rari raising a hand in farewell to Sefton as they rounded the corner. He bumped into a stationary Okan and nearly knocked him over. Simon was standing next to the desk, his gun lazily held down by his side and an expression on his face that would have had the accountants in the bookshop running for the safety of Millie's office. He looked, Rari thought, as if he could eat broken glass and get some nutritional value from the meal. Rari sighed and watched the face of Carole Smithfield as she snarled orders to the security team. He saw, rather than heard, Simon counting quietly almost under his breath. He seemed to be saying 'one, two,' Rari hit the ground as the word 'three' materialised inside his imagination, and fired as he fell.

Nothing about the night made any sense. "Tell me," I said to Wills, who came over to me, as I stood by the window in my room, "Am I getting up or going to bed? I know it's a strange question but I just can't remember right now."

"Well," he said helpfully, "I'm not sure either counts, because you haven't actually *been* to bed yet and you went to sleep standing up. A gift I might add, I very much admire." I could see his teeth smiling in the darkness.

The men had taken it in turns to walk the perimeter and Tara and I had done the rounds with coffee and food until we took over one of the shifts in the middle of the night so that they could all get some sleep for two hours. It felt as if it was the worst sort of waiting. A tooth grating silence of epic proportions.

Flora and Cecil had gone back to the safety of the bathroom and

I wished that I could join them. Flora was holding onto one of Cecil's paws with her trunk and he had his tail curled around her eyes. I wanted to cover my own eyes and hide. But fear always finds us wherever we go. My heart ached for Okan, Rari and Simon and their continuing absence, which could mean nothing but bad news.

A rumble of thunder brought me back from my thoughts to the window of now and the man standing next to me. He turned away from me and walked over to the door as the two men downstairs shouted up to us and then began to run. "Move Millie!" Wills said, "This is it!"

I raced down after him.

Tara was waiting at the bottom of the stairs; she handed me a large rifle-like weapon with the tiny clear laser bubble attached to the stock, a bag of ammunition and a replacement power unit. It was an ergonomically pleasing shape, made out of the same light alloy as the other weapons and most of the farm machinery. It was also a lethal combination of projectile and light under pressure. Weldon had said dryly, 'that I should use the skills I had been given and kill people from a distance.' He had expressed the opinion several hours before, and I had laughed and replied 'that the thought of a rooftop and a weapon was the unfulfilled dream of all maladjusted teenagers trying to make it through secondary school.' Now my comment didn't seem quite so inappropriately funny.

Tara's face was the grey colour of no sleep and early hours and the thoughts of not making it. She hugged me as if we were drowning already and then went down the dark corridor to the back of the house, where a barricade of thick layers of fibre was standing between her and the borderers. Joao was already there and he raised a hand, but said nothing. He and Weldon had put barriers up at all the windows and doors, ready in place as a fall back. I hoped we wouldn't have to use them. Because by the time we were firing from the house some of us would be dead. Marl was lying on the sofa in the kitchen again; he looked as if holding a weapon was slightly more than he could manage, but he held one anyway and he too raised a hand to me as I stood by the door for a minute, because we take our moments when we can. Kasper was on the roof of the farmhouse, having demonstrated similar skills to mine in his ability to hit anything he shot at.

Wills went out into the night that had become early morning and I followed him. Granger and Civin were outside standing at the edge of the road leading to the house. "Get up on the top of the barn roof," Wills said, he looked up as he said it and therefore so did I.

The ship was huge, and unlike Buddy, it had a clean clear line from stem to stern. I was stunned to find myself admiring the beauty of the craft, it was a 'ship of the line' with two ridges on either side as if someone had borrowed the jets from a 747 and added to the idea.

"Crap!" Wills said, "A warship."

"How many borderers are there on it?" I asked, as the craft came towards us, a dark leviathan of the night sky.

Wills looked at me. "Maybe thirty, if," he added, "We're really unlucky. Go! Weldon has put a ladder up to the loft; you'll have to climb out of the storage hatch onto the roof *and* don't forget to pull the damn thing up after you!"

He ran off to join his friends and they disappeared into the shadows. They would use the cover of the woods to drive the borderers onto the mined perimeter. Weldon was going to be joining them. Even an optimist would have had to admit there were too many of them and too few of us and I didn't get the impression that there would be any effort made to take prisoners, except of course for me. I closed my eyes for a moment and tried not to let myself drift back to the type zero verse and then thought about the fact that I didn't call it home anymore; the tears of fear and frustration made a sneaky move to overwhelm me. I choked them away with more anger at the feelings of being hunted from verse to verse and that this would have to be the end of it, one way or another.

I saw Weldon come out onto the veranda, he was heavily armed and he was talking into his com. The engine noise from the spaceship was not loud but it drowned out the feelings of hope and filled them with a primitive fear; which I was sure was part of the borderer's strategy. They were the soldiers of the painfully obvious.

If Weldon was talking to the town, which the ship had just

passed over on its way to the farm, it would still take them the better part of much too long for anyone to get near enough to help.

I wished with all my heart to see Okan and Rari behind him in the hall and in my delusion, for a moment, I thought I *could* see them.

They were already firing their weapons, but there was no noise, as if I was watching an old black and white silent film; Rari stretched out on the floor, Okan crouched by a big curved desk, Simon curled on his side near Rari. I couldn't see their faces properly, but it felt as though it was a dream within a dream and I shook my head to get free. It seemed for a second that Okan could see me too and he looked puzzled and frightened and shouted my name.

The dark night rushed back in and the sound of the ship heading for the fields and a landing site filled my thoughts and fed my fear. Weldon had said that the borderers didn't fight with any sort of cunning, they just used overwhelming numbers to get the result they wanted and that they had been taking heavy casualties lately as the settlers were getting better at fighting back. I hoped it wasn't wishful thinking, because it had seemed to *me* that it was the borderers who were getting better at it.

The ladder was a rope and metal combination, which was not that easy to climb with one hand. I slung the rifle over my shoulder the wrong way up in my haste and then hoped I didn't shoot myself; I sweated and swore up the last few rungs and I pulled the ladder up after me, securing it to the hook in the rafter. My climbing skills were nearly as good as my shooting ability, due to the profusion of trees on Exmoor and a father who thought you were never too old to have fun while learning.

My hands were sticky and shaking when I reached the roof. It was shaped in two small peaks with a channel between, damp from old rain and slippery with green slime. I checked the far barn that was over to the other side of me. Buddy was tucked away in the downstairs of the building with the doors bolted.

I wiped the muck off my hands and made a mental note to tell Weldon that he needed to add the green slime to his list of irritating, time consuming tasks that had to be done. Then wished on all the stars I could see and the curve of the planet for good measure, that we would all be there to do the jobs list sometime soon.

A small red light blinked off and on from the roof of the farm-house and I took my own torch out and sent the same signal back to Kasper. He was in a better position than me in as much that he could move all the way around the roof of the farmhouse and had a clear view of the ship landing, 'better position' being a poor choice of words.

The thick jacket cushioned me against the rough surface of the roof, it wasn't cold but I shivered as I set up my weapon and put the ammunition within easy reach. The barn was made of the tough fibre that the house was constructed of and Weldon had said it was barely flammable but if the borderers started throwing 'big stuff' to get out of there and into the woods. He'd added that I should take Tara with me, but only when she wasn't listening.

I realised that although I could see all of the farmyard and the buildings, I would have to move back up the channel in the roof to the other end of the barn, if the borderers stayed in amongst the trees and tried to stage the fight from there. Weldon had said that their usual method was to rush the buildings. I found myself hoping they stuck to that, because we didn't have the people to deal with the unusual.

I felt, rather than heard the ship land, as it made the ground shake with its rumble of engines, more fear inducing tactics which was effective in my case. I could see the lights from the craft as it went into the field behind the farmhouse. I thought it was a strange choice for a landing site but what did I know. We didn't do much in the way of battle tactics in the bookshop in Exeter. Except of course at sale time and Christmas when I suppose every shop worker had a taste of trench warfare.

I waited; moment after moment for what would happen next; my throat was full of marbles every time I swallowed. I tried not to shake but my hands seemed to have taken on a life of their own. I appealed to the force for good out there in the verses that I wouldn't be a coward when the time came, and I wouldn't let anyone down, not least myself. Then I asked that they would get on with it because the deafening silence was worse than the rumble of the ship.

My heart was making the sort of noise you only read about in survivor stories. A huge bang made me scuttle back from the rim of the roof. I swore, a lot. The sound had come from behind me. The borderers were not rushing the house; they were creeping through the woods. It seemed that strategy had been introduced into the mix. I scrambled over to the other end of the channel trying not to skyline for the snipers the borderers might have brought with them. Weldon had said it wasn't likely but they hadn't done anything likely thus far.

I put on the night vision lenses; they fitted neatly into your eye socket, like a superior set of skiing goggles, uncomfortable at first, I had practiced walking about with them around the house, trying not to trip over my feet. They were based on the structure of the lobster's eye, which was similar to a series of reflecting mirrors in a sphere; the facets produced a very distinctive image for the brain to interpret. The lenses compensated for the bangs and crashes of bright light with something that reacted the way a superior pair of sunglasses did, only much faster. It was the sort of equipment that would have been popular with international space stations and special forces in the type zero verse. The lenses were a present from some friend of Weldon's and were experimental so he only had two, the pair I was wearing and a pair for Kasper. The others were relying on older equipment and instinct. It was easy for me to see the figures moving through the woods, borderers, who had built in night vision of their own in their cat-like eyes. Men made by people for a war no one cared to remember.

The possibility that they were going to rush the house was over before it had a chance. They were moving in battle order, down towards the three men who were waiting in the woods behind the barns. It seemed that plan B was going to be starting really soon. I cursed all the best swear words I knew well and a few that I didn't.

Weldon and the gangers had stood over a holo-diagram of the farm and its land and buildings. They had devised several plans using the words 'advance to contact,' 'withdraw' and more chillingly 'kill zone.' It made me look at the men slightly differently; at least one of them probably Wills, must have had some sort of military background before joining a gang on a settlers' moon. My own experience of special forces was limited to the complete works of Andy McNab, which I'd bought in a 'three for two' moment. I tried to remember any helpful hints on the best way to deal with shooting at people but nothing much came to mind. Weldon's thoughts on the matter were another story. He had said in the dark kitchen when I sighed my most painful sigh that, 'cold blooded killing was impossible to cope with unless you had the empathy of a psychopath, if you were going to kill someone it helped to be angry.' He told me to 'find your anger,' and I had promised I would look.

I watched carefully as the three gangers made a move forward firing rapidly and then withdrawing just as fast, I saw one borderer fall in a deadly heap to be left behind by his friends. I lifted up the weapon in my hands and looked for the warm central glow of the body which filled the line of sight on the rifle and I steadied my breathing and closed the circle in my mind. There was no sharp crack, just a small puff of power and noise from the laser and another borderer tripped over his feet and spun backwards. I felt nothing. Which was worse than feeling awful.

A steady rain began to fall in gentle drops and I wiped my fingers and pulled the hood up over my head, then changed my mind and removed it again, it was as if I needed as high a level of all the senses I could get. The borderers moved with more caution, maybe their eyes were not as effective as I had thought because they didn't seem to realise that there was someone on the roof of the barn. I guessed that the cat-like structure of their night vision was based on movement. I could almost feel their puzzlement, the resistance from the settlers was usually painfully thin and this was different. They stopped for a moment strung out in the trees, crouched and standing, soldiers waiting for something. I wondered if they were talking to someone inside the ship for advice, but they moved on again as if the orders had been along the lines of 'just get on with it.'

I heard small sounds of gunfire behind me and realised that another group of the borderers must have moved down the tree line on the other side of the farm. It was Kasper I could hear on the roof of the farm, firing carefully at moving targets and Weldon, who was on his own. The plan in the farmhouse had been based on the idea that the gangers would be able to draw the borderers down on the barn side of the buildings and bring them into the farmyard where Kasper and I would do, what we were supposed to. Weldon was hoping he would be able to join up with the gangers on the road. It wasn't working out. I searched my cold wet memory for alternatives and my pocket for a com.

I was about to make contact with Wills when the com vibrated gently in the palm of my hand. "Millie?" A voice barely whispered, "Is that gunfire I can hear on the other side of the farm?" It was Wills.

"Yes," I whispered back, "Weldon is by himself. I can't see how many, I'm over on your side, but if you were right about the numbers of the borderers, he could be up against fifteen or so." A slight pinging noise interrupted my words, "Make that fourteen."

Wills snorted, then spoke, "Can you tell Weldon, I'm on my way and see if it's clear on the road?"

"Wait one," I said and cut him off. I moved back down the roof channel in a crouch that made my knees ache and took a look. I beeped Wills on the com. "It looks okay. I have only one small blind spot at your end of the road, so be careful." He clicked his com to say he had heard me, three clicks as arranged in the planning, which was Weldon again and then was silent.

I watched carefully for a moment and then opened the com to speak to Weldon. He sounded out of breath and was obviously running.

"Yes," he said, in a hoarse whisper.

"Wills is on his way," I whispered back, "He's heading to the road now; try not to shoot each other." He clicked three times and then turned the com off.

The advance and withdraw continued without Wills, three more of the borderers were killed. One by me. I wasn't counting people, just shapes and shadows. The gangers pulled the borderers towards them and down to the edge of the farm. They cut across the grassland and backed into the ring of antipersonnel devices. I removed the sensor unit from my pocket and followed the instructions Weldon and then Wills had given me.

Behind me the sound of gunfire was coming nearer. I tried to concentrate as Civin and Granger ducked into the cover of the far barn firing from their first real vantage point.

They looked up at me though they couldn't have seen me that well; they just knew I was there. Civin lifted his hand, he pulled it down in a chopping movement and I pressed the sensor key on. The whoomph of fire and pressure threw bodies in the air in sharp relief against the flame and smoke that rose into the sky; if they had time to be in pain no sound could be heard. I saw Granger slap Civin on the back as they ran towards the farmhouse one at a time, passing each other in a game of tag with guns.

I could see the shapes of three borderers, who hadn't come out of the tree line and they moved carefully using as much cover as possible. The secret was out about me, and they kept their heads down. I spoke into the com, "What shall we do about the remaining borderers Civin? They're not moving and I can't get a fix on them."

"We're going to circle back and get behind them," he whispered. I scrambled in the familiar knee aching crouch towards the other end of the barn and looked towards the farmhouse.

Civin and Granger were crawling along through the grass, with little or no cover. I waited until they were out of my line of sight with the barn roof in the way and then ran back down the channel in what was becoming an irritating game of which knee would crack first. I watched the borderers and the two gangers and tried not to be distracted by hearing the firing that was going on behind me in the woods on the other side of the fields. Civin and Granger made it to the tree line and began to work their way down the edge. I swore as the borderers used the natural undulations in the ground to protect them. Even being on the roof of the barn gave me no advantage. As Civin got closer I lined up the sight on the rifle on what little warmth I could see and took a shot. The two gangers reached the borderers and began firing.

I felt the helpless sense of desperation that comes with not knowing. I couldn't tell one warm shape from another, even with the disparity in size and height it wasn't possible to tell them apart. Only one person walked away. I watched the silent life fade from the bodies on the ground with the tears streaming from my eyes and clouding the night vision lenses. I took them out, put them carefully in my pocket, and moved back to the other side of the roof and the view of the farm. I waited, with my heart pounding and hope a bitter taste in my mouth.

Granger reached the end of the far barn and raised a hand. I could see him in the half light, he was bleeding from a wound in his leg and his face was twisted with pain. I raised my own hand and he slid along the line of the barns and across the farm road towards the cover of a few trees and the main road to the town. I lost him in the shadows and the tears on my lashes that were mixed with the falling rain. They say you can't mourn for someone you don't really know, but you can.

I raised my head and wiped at the rain and the tears and looked towards the tree line on the other side of the farm. "Weldon," I said quietly, "Granger is on his way over to you."

"Just Granger?" He whispered.

"Yes."

Weldon and Wills must have met on the road; they were moving up to the crown of a small hill that edged into the landscaping of the garden; it sat between the fields on one side and the farm road on the other. I realised that I was holding my breath when I could see bright spots of light at the corners of each eye.

Wills would run and Weldon would crouch and fire then the other man would move past as the first one crouched and fired. They looked so vulnerable. A string of shadows seemed to be pressing close on them. Laser flashes split the grey and I realised there was more light moment by moment. The dawn was coming. Soon we would be able to see them clearly and they, of course, would be able to see the few of us.

Granger closed in on them from the side, he spoke briefly on his com to warn Weldon and Wills not to shoot him by mistake and then moved to join in. I lifted the rifle to my eye and concentrated on the best way to help.

I could see the outline of the men lying down in the wet grass firing at the oncoming borderers; then something odd happened. The borderers seemed to melt back towards the road. The men stopped firing. Weldon looked behind him then up at me and I shrugged. The com vibrated in my pocket and I pulled it out. I could see Weldon was holding his com.

"Shit, we're in trouble!" Kasper said, "Can you see this?" His voice was choked with emotion.

I looked around me, back at the road, down to Weldon who was moving up to a crouch and using a pair of powerful binoculars. I turned to the farmhouse; behind the building was the ship and standing outside was a group of at least thirty borderers. They must have been packed in like frozen sausages.

The borderers moved forward; a wave of battle-hardened mercenaries who had been kept in check for far too long. I heard Joao and Tara begin firing from the rear of the house and I saw Weldon and Wills crawl to the other side of the hill turning to face the oncoming horde, their backs to the road. I watched for a second and then lifted my shaking hands to the rifle and the spreading group of borderers who streamed towards the buildings.

We fought. My arms ached and I aimed and fired, reloaded and fired again. The borderers used the building, they used their numbers, we used our vantage points, but they kept coming. Tara set the antipersonnel mines and a massive line of heat and flames ignited. Broken bits of people lay around in evil reminders of fragility. I saw Kasper firing over and over and then he flew backwards hitting the window of the attic room; he slumped down and lay quieter than sleep. My fingers wiped away more tears and sweat and I tried not to shout out loud at the pain of not knowing him.

The front of the farm was full of noise and gunfire and bodies. I could see Weldon and Wills on the brow of the small hill but not Granger. I cried some more and swore, because we were losing. Where were Til and the people from the town? I ducked my head and looked at my watch. Shook it and checked again. Impossible. It

398

was less than an hour since I had climbed the ladder to the barn roof.

I looked up, tracked the movement of a borderer and fired, he fell in a rush of blood and bone against the veranda of the house. A shout made me cringe and the door to the house opened. Marl was tossed out as if he was an unwanted dog; he crawled for a moment through the puddle of his own blood; then sagged to the ground and was still. Joao was pushed out after him, he managed to stagger to his feet, the side of his face was covered in blood and his left arm hung uselessly by his side. I stopped firing and so did Weldon. Then Tara was held out and everything went silent.

She stood battered and bleeding with a borderer using her as a shield, something of a joke as she only came up to his shoulder, she hit out; the borderer punched her on the side of the head and she sagged as if without life. Joao lunged for the borderer with a cry of pain that I could hear echoed in Weldon's chest, it was a pointless effort because he was knocked to the ground where he didn't move. I raised my rifle finding one more puff of the 'anger' Weldon had recommended for killing and sighted the target. My teeth were clenched and I shook but the head of the borderer still exploded in an unfeeling mass spattering the wall of the farmhouse and covering Tara as she fell. An instant attack of nausea had me spitting bile. I couldn't stop the shaking of my hands. I put my head down on my arms and waited.

A voice I didn't recognise called out, "If you come down now, we won't kill them." I raised myself up a few inches. The farm road was full of borderers. They held Weldon and Wills. There was another figure, frighteningly familiar; a small, spiteful looking man gazed up at the barn roof with a polite smile. Zatar.

"Get away!" Weldon shouted at me angrily. "What are you waiting for?" His voice cracked with emotion and the borderer holding his arms behind him raised him up on his toes in what must have been an agonising embrace.

I looked towards the veranda; Joao lay as he had fallen. I saw one of the borderers lift Tara and bring her over to Zatar, she struggled in his arms and Weldon tried to get to her. "I *will* kill them if you verse jump," Zatar said, in a conversational voice.

My sigh must have filled the void in-between the universes, as I stood up and moved towards the hatch. I heard Weldon shout, "Don't!" But he didn't finish and I moved even faster as I untied the step ladder to the upper level of the barn. A borderer stood to one side as I climbed down. Then he did a strange thing, he held the ladder so it didn't swing and reached out a hand to take my rifle. It was disconcerting. I stood with shaking legs for a moment before I moved to the steps to climb down to the ground level. The borderer stood patiently to one side not touching me, his eyes averted.

I could see two more borderers on the floor of the barn as I came down the narrow steps. Up close they were huge. I hadn't been near a live borderer, they were nearly seven feet tall, built the way a nine-year-old would draw a warrior in a game of war. Their faces were a confusion of feline, lupine and human. No one touched me on the ground level either. I was expecting violence and anger and I got silence.

The morning light of the yard fell on a scene from a first world war photograph. People lay around in the creeping horror of continued death. The smell of drying blood and old cheese, which the bacteria that decomposing bodies gave off after a very little time, was hanging around with the sickening buzz of clouds of busy flies.

Zatar stood with barely concealed impatience as I came out of the barn entrance. He was holding Tara's arm as she wavered; her face was bloody and shocked, she kept glancing at Joao as if she expected him to stand up. He didn't. I know because I looked too.

Weldon was angry and he shook his head at me. "Millie, you have to go," he said quietly. Zatar raised his gun and aimed it at Weldon. I moved, and my feet felt encased in lead; it was as though I was in one of those dreams where you know all the evil is behind you but you can't get away, only this wasn't a dream and the evil was in front of me. My hands came up as the gun snapped off a shot, but I was too late. Wills had broken the hold of the borderer standing by him and moved between Zatar and Weldon. I screamed as if I was a demented wraith. Wills flew back into the dirt on the road and the blood bubbled out of his mouth. I knelt beside him. His eyes were still open. I stroked his hair and he smiled. Then he left his body, along with all the others, to go wherever we go next.

"Well, that was touching," Zatar said. He looked up at the sky, "I think we'd better be going, take her," he pointed at Tara, "Keep them apart; if they get close enough to make contact," he pointed at me, "She'll verse jump." He was right I would have. It was what Weldon was counting on.

We moved off in a group towards the farmhouse and the borderer who had met me at the bottom of the ladder held my arm very carefully. He looked at one of the other borderers who returned it with a creepy cat-like expression.

I stopped and so did the borderer. Something *else* was very wrong. I turned around. That whole world slowed down again and I pulled away from the borderer and began to scream. The gun in Zatar's hand was held out and pointing at Weldon. "Don't you dare! You kill him and I *will* dreamwalk!"

Weldon looked at me and a shadow of a sad smile crossed his face, he mouthed words I couldn't understand and I threw myself at the two men and raked Zatar's cheek with nails I didn't know I had. The gun went off and I fell. I screamed and so did Zatar, his was one of anger, as was mine, along with the fury and pain. Weldon was lying beneath me, our legs tangled and the pulsing dark iron smell of blood mixed with my tears, I crawled to be alongside him and touched his face. He sighed, all his last breath felt warm and real on my skin and in my heart for always.

I was dragged to my feet and then lifted and the borderer carried me towards Tara who began to keen like a wounded creature. She rocked on her feet and I tried to reach for her but they wouldn't let me. I could feel blood dripping down my forehead and I realised it belonged to me. One of the other borderers pushed a dancing Zatar out of the way as he screamed into my face spitting orders at me that I couldn't hear. I tried to look back at Weldon but the borderer carrying me held me tight and the other one pressed a dressing to my wound.

One of the group of borderers tried to get Tara to walk but she couldn't move, she just rocked and keened like the broken bird she was and I cried into the chest of someone I had been trying to kill for the last few hours.

The ship had a huge cargo door at the back; it swallowed us whole without a gulp. My head was spinning and the wound had begun to hurt as if it was splitting my skull in two. Another borderer came over and the one who carried me put me down, I slithered to the floor. The shorter borderer had slightly more refined features, still feline but different. He seemed to be in charge. He lifted the dressing on my head and grunted; squatting on the floor of the ship he opened a small box and reached for a device similar to the stitch kit in Tara's emergency bag. He swabbed and closed the wound and then shone a small light-stick into my eyes. Then he got up and pointed to the borderer who had carried me and then at me, the man nodded. The rest of the mercenaries clambered into the hold, backing up with great care until they were all inside.

I could hear the ship rumbling as it started up and then Zatar shouting at the smaller borderer, "I want that place levelled!"

"No."

I looked up, my head spinning. The borderer had answered in a deep clear voice, but it sounded strange as if he didn't use it very often or he had a sore throat.

"Do it!" Zatar said, in full psychopath mode, frothing at the mouth so that bits of spittle landed on the borderer's uniform.

"No. We need some of the things that these people have; if we annihilate them, we will not be able to have these things anymore," he added carefully, as if he was quoting from a set of rules, his voice sounded rusty, "You do not conquer a people by destroying them." He walked off followed by a furious Zatar and my head spun a bit more.

I looked out towards the fields, at the place where my pain lay on the ground not breathing and I realised I could see the farmhouse silhouetted in the outline of the closing cargo door; standing by the side of the building were Okan and Rari. There was no sign of Simon.

Tara was half lying against the inside of the ship in a state of complete breakdown. Her eyes were open but she hardly blinked and didn't focus on anything. I watched as one of the borderers moved a jacket and some packing material and made a pillow out of them for her. It just stunned me. They were quiet and careful.

My own borderer sat down next to me and began to set out an injection kit on the floor of the ship. "I don't need anything for the pain." I tapped his arm. I thought the fact that I might have concussion from the gunshot wound would make it a bad idea. He shook his head and pointed at himself. I looked carefully for an injury. He seemed blood free apart from the smear of mine on the front of his uniform. I think the fact that they were wearing uniforms had filtered through the mist of shock.

"I'm fine," I said, not really understanding, as he carried on with preparing his syringe. He shook his head and pointed at himself again. Then he set the pressure syringe on his arm and pressed.

"What is that?" I asked.

He tried for a sound and made a noise like a squeaky door. Most of the borderers standing near us stopped to listen. He pressed his throat like a surgeon applying cricoid pressure and tried again.

"Anti-testosterone," he said at last. His voice sounded as though an artificial synthesizer had been added, as if he were a criminal trying to disguise it in a kidnapping case.

"Why?" I asked, pointing at the syringe.

"The space is so small," he indicated the cargo bay, "We would kill each other." I must have looked stunned. "It is how we are made, like you, but different."

"Well, no," I said, "Not exactly like me, I don't like small spaces but I have never felt the need to kill people because of it."

"Only one, want to kill only one." He pointed at Zatar who was still shouting at the borderer in charge. Then he stunned me by smiling. It wasn't a pretty sight as his teeth were feral and pointed and my head made strange connections about good and evil.

I watched as the rest of the borderers injected themselves with the drug, they seemed to be calm and controlled but the fact was we were packed in. My borderer and I were the only ones sitting down and the rest had to bunch up into one corner to let Tara lie down in another. "Your voice," I said, pointing at his throat. "Why?"

"Made to be silent *and* to fight," he explained.

I curled against myself for a moment; it was one piece of information too much. I had no feelings left, no fear, no pain, no anger, nothing. I needed someone to rescue me from the inside of my own head. I closed my eyes and thought about Weldon's face and the word he had said. 'Tara.' He must have known he was going to die and wanted it to be the last thing he thought about. I felt so tired.

"Mothership, soon." My borderer tapped my arm and pointed up. I nodded and let my head drop back against the side of the vessel and tried not to let the threatened darkness take over. It came in waves; I envied Tara the peace of an empty mind. I wondered if she would ever come back from it and tried not to think about that either.

I couldn't see the expression on Okan's face as he stood with Rari by the farmhouse, but I could see the shape of desperation in his body. My tears must have leaked down my face because a gentle tap on my shoulder made me open my eyes. "I hold on," a voice said. Another of the borderers was leaning over me. He held me carefully against the bulkhead and my borderer pushed against me from the other side blocking me in like a child's harness. Two of the group were shielding Tara as if she were made of glass.

"Doesn't your pilot do the docking very well?" I looked at the other borderers who were grabbing straps and handholds and bracing themselves for what looked as if it might be a hard landing.

"He needs more practice," my borderer said and the other one snorted as did anyone within earshot. I laughed and the irony of that was not lost in the darkness in my head.

The cargo door opened and the lights of the docking bay filtered through. The other borderers picked up their kit and my borderer picked me up when he realised that I didn't seem to be able to walk. He gave his weapon and belt to the one standing next to me. "Medic?" He said and my borderer nodded. I watched as Tara was lifted and then realised that my head was beginning to hurt really badly. I looked up at my borderer, his eyes began to blur in his face and I called him Cecil and smiled and he looked worried for a cat, which made me laugh, and that made the pain worse.

I could hear Zatar giving orders and shouting at my borderer, "Don't let her pass out she might dreamwalk."

The corridor was busy with other borderers who looked curious in a feline way but not hostile or resentful or angry. My nausea was similar to the seasickness version, first you think you're going to die then you wish you were. I could hear voices but the faces became indistinct and I held on because I couldn't leave Tara. I knew that if I let go, I would never be able to get back to the ship and she would be lost to me forever and I wasn't going to let that happen.

A face swam into view, still feline, but closer in type to the one in charge on the warship and I heard him say, "We have to sedate her."

"No!" I shouted at the same moment as Zatar and then laughed; it was the only time in my life I had been in complete agreement with a psychopath. I don't think he got the joke though because he shook my arm and tried to get me to look at him.

"If you leave, I *will* kill her," he whispered. His face was close to mine and I could see the track my nails had carved in his cheek.

"Get your disgusting breath away from me before I match up the tribal marks," I whispered. He moved. I realised that I had never been less afraid of anyone. There came a point when you've done all of the fearful you're ever going to do.

The room began to take on a settled appearance and became less fuzzy around the edges. It appeared to be exactly how you would imagine a medical centre on a busy starship should be. Functional, filled with quiet soldiers getting fixed up, or in one case, dying. The beds were close together but seemed to have a screen mechanism between them because they put up an opaque barrier so that the dying borderer could have some small privacy.

Several doctors or medics moved around the patients treating them with much the same equipment as the settlers used. I saw the one who had assessed me pick up a neat portable device that must have had the same capability as an MRI scanner. He brought it over and made a single pass across my head. "Hmm," he said, which confirmed all my suspicions about doctors in every verse, anywhere, they learned to say that in their first lesson. He leaned over me making me cringe back into the bedding. "We'll just give you something for the pain and monitor you for further symptoms. It is a concussion from the bullet."

"Is Tara, okay?" I whispered; as anything louder caused my head to spin.

He turned to look behind him. "We've sedated her, she's in shock." He turned back to me. "Some of them don't make it."

"Them?" I whispered.

"The taken," he said, in the flat emotionless artificial tone that made them all sound similar. His eyes flickered in the same way that Cecil's did when he had found a really big piece of buttered toast left unattended, but knew didn't belong to him.

He moved off and I lifted my head and tried to judge the distance between my bed and Tara's, a matter of several dozen paces but something in the region of a marathon in my present condition. Her dark hair was spread smoothly over the roll they used for a pillow. Her eyes were closed and her face had the blank look of someone far away. My head ached. I noticed the glances she got from the medics and even from the patients, it puzzled me even more than all the other things I had seen. It looked as though it was longing, not lust.

My borderer came over to me and sat on the floor by the bed. He seemed quite content to be there and began to clean his weapon in much the same way that Okan or Joao would have done. I nearly let their faces swim into view then blocked the thought; that way madness lay in wait.

"Are you on duty?" I asked him and pointed at myself. He nodded and gave the half smile that made him look so very nearly human, but not quite. "Do you have to take the anti-violence drug all the time, or just when you've been down to Europa?"

He pressed his throat with his fingers again and cleared it. "All the time." He pointed around indicating the mothership. "Still small space. We have to fight or take the drug or die. Sometimes drug not enough. Have to fight each other anyway." I must have looked stunned because he added again, "How we are made."

"That's awful!" I said.

He looked puzzled for a moment and then smiled and nodded and went back to cleaning his gun, his face impassive in concentration.

He had removed the disgusting muck that all the troops seemed to smear in their cropped hair in battle conditions and was wearing a looser set of overalls instead of the tight uniform that he'd had on before.

"What's your name?" I whispered. He looked puzzled again and then pointed to a set of hieroglyphs on his overalls. "I can't read that," I explained.

"Bird of the Wind," he replied proudly, "I am named for a great warrior." He pointed at me. "Who are you named for?"

"I had *thought* I was named for my great grandmother," I said, looking back on the past and wondering if I should add it to the ever-growing list of things that didn't really exist.

He nodded, his disappointment for me was nearly enough to make me smile. "It's a bit of a mouthful," I said, "Can I call you Birdy?"

He gave this serious consideration. "No, I don't think you can," he said eventually.

It made me laugh and then I began to cry, because I was stuck on a starship full of borderers and Tara was dead inside and other people I couldn't think about, were dead everywhere and I just wanted to go home. Only, I didn't know where that was anymore.

"Birdy is yes!" My borderer was standing up leaning too close and I cringed away from him. He looked devastated. A cat without the cream. "You all hate us," he said quietly.

"You should understand," I said, equally quiet, "The slaughter, laying waste and kidnapping, it's difficult for most people to get their heads around."

"You made us," he said stubbornly, as if this was an answer.

"It looks as if that would be me too," I replied bitterly.

He sighed and nodded and sat down again. The room was full of curious whispers and the cat-like avoidance of eye contact that meant unfettered interest if you were a feline. I tried not to give them another show but it was hard to hold onto the taste of endless loss and loneliness. I sighed, "What happens now?"

Birdy shrugged. "You see captain. Then, I don't know."

I nodded. "I imagine Zatar is somewhere out there planning the removal of my genetic code and whatever else he fancies."

Birdy looked disgusted. "No one is allowed to take your code away, it belongs to the tribe, to the future."

"Yes," I said carefully, "I'm sure that Zatar is going to be very careful to do the right thing by the tribe *and* the future." Birdy thought about this but he seemed to be unable to grasp the irony and just shook his head. It was part of the total tragedy of the borderer's situation, that they had been programmed without a sense of the absurd, in the type zero verse it was practically a recruiting necessity. I have always thought that irony was a prerequisite for a 'successful' war.

I suddenly felt really tired and I closed my eyes, drifting off into one of those dreams that are full of things you can't get away from, dark shadows and drifting ghosts. I saw my father and he was cross about something, his face morphed into a cat and then into Zatar who was also angry. "I told you not to let her pass out!" He shouted and I could feel someone shaking me.

"She is asleep!" My eyes opened to see Birdy holding Zatar nearly off his feet and the look on his evil twisted face meant that he would not survive for long if he didn't back off and I needed Birdy.

"What's the matter Trevor, have you lost your teddy?" I said.

A ripple of movement made me look around Zatar to see a refined version of the borderers coming through the medical bay doorway. He must have been important because Birdy stood up straight with his head bowed. Even the men lying in the beds were doing their best to radiate respect.

"Come and see what all your hard work has got you, captain!" Zatar was strutting, which was not a pretty sight.

I looked the borderer captain right in the eye and held out my hand. "It's an honour to meet you sir." There was a stunned silence. Whatever had been expected, and I imagine a certain amount of verbal abuse would have been the norm, it wasn't this. My dad had told me once, never to call anyone sir unless you know for sure they've earned it. I felt under the circumstances he would have understood.

The captain took my outstretched hand; he didn't shake it or kiss it, just held it carefully for a moment. I kept on looking him in the eye; his expression was one of curiosity and something else that I would have called amusement, except for the fact that it didn't seem likely. "Captain of the Tar Dal Tribe," he said, "I am called Wings of Fortune."

I smiled and nodded. "Millie Rushcroft."

The feline preoccupation with anything that flew was going to be something of a pattern, I thought.

Zatar was having trouble with the situation and wanted me back in the role of captive and therefore controllable. "She killed many of your men captain," he said, looking at me as if the tools for removing my DNA were already laid out on the operating table.

"Millie of the Rushcroft tribe, is therefore worthy of our respect," the captain said quietly, it was a voice barely above a whisper but everyone in the medical bay heard it.

Zatar was losing ground and he knew it. "Remember our agreement captain. I get control of the wormholes and we share the possibilities."

"You know," I said dryly, "If you have to keep telling people you're the psychopath in charge, Trevor, it loses its impact." Zatar was speechless, which was something that must have been a new experience for him, judging from the expression on his face.

The captain grunted and looked at me again, I looked back trying to be all the things a warrior would admire, even though my head ached and my heart was full of the continuing silence of loss. He leaned towards me and I did my best not to flinch and he smiled.

"When you are released by the doctor we will talk more."

"I look forward to that sir," I said, causing more of a stir in the medical bay.

Zatar followed the captain out, he looked over his shoulder and said, "Don't get too comfortable."

If it hadn't been such a bad day for threats, I would have laughed at the melodramatic impact of the words. "I'll be here," I said and waved.

Birdy looked down on me and then smiled. "Why do you make that man angry? He is dangerous."

"Because I have no power," I shrugged.

"I don't think that is true," Birdy words trailed off into silence, his face puzzled. Then he sat down on the floor again and finished cleaning his weapon. I held out my hand for one of the pieces and after a moment's hesitation he handed it to me. I reached down for a spare cloth and began rubbing the tubing of the weapon, inspecting it for non-existent particles of dirt. I could feel the eyes of the borderers in the medical bay watching me but I didn't look up because they would have seen the shine of tears and the fear within. There are some places you need to keep fear to yourself and the medical bay of a borderer's ship was one of them.

I stood next to Tara's bed and reached out a hand though I wasn't allowed to touch her on Zatar's orders. She stirred and her eyes opened but she didn't see me. I leaned down as close as I could get and whispered, "I will kill Zatar for what he did, I promise."

Tara spoke quietly but with some strength, "Make it an interesting death." She closed her eyes again.

"All death is interesting," a voice said, making me jump. It was the doctor who had examined me. Oddly, though at first, they had all appeared to be the same, I was now beginning to be able to distinguish the slight difference in their features. He said something in a guttural language that sounded similar to Dutch, pointing at the name tag on the front of his uniform. I must have looked confused because he thought about it for a moment and then said, "I'm called Star Flight in English."

"*That* is a very beautiful name," I replied, holding out my hand which, after a moment of stunned surprise, he took carefully in his.

"I have never met anyone else like you," he said.

"I'm not sure that there *is* anyone else like me," I replied with a wry smile.

He laughed, "Really, we don't see many who are not afraid and angry and," he paused, looking at Tara, "Ill."

"Well, I *am* actually *all* of those things," I said quietly.

He nodded and then pointed to where Birdy was standing waiting patiently. I took his hand again and said, "Thank you for looking after me." Once again this caused an expression of incredulity. Which was good because I needed his incredulity, *anything* to keep me in a place where it would make it more difficult for Zatar to get what he wanted.

The passageway was full of busy people. All of them borderers. There were no women, no 'taken.' I had been in the medical bay for a few hours, which was not long enough to get my balance. The pain in my head was still a violent jagged edge of sharp light at the corner of one eye, and a brief exploration of the bandage over the wound had me whimpering, I realised that the groove in my skull would probably be permanent.

It was odd how you could feel nothing and yet still be in agony.

"Birdy. Where are all the taken?" I asked, as I followed him through the maze of the ship. The passageways were low lit and almost tubular, with sliding pressure doors to either side where I could see tantalizing glimpses of activity as we passed. We were headed to some quarters allocated to me by the captain, though I think Zatar had other ideas.

Birdy turned to me without stopping, he looked puzzled. "They are in their own living areas; it is early on the ship. Too early for the women to be about. Just soldiers." He waved a hand to include the other borderers.

"They're not prisoners?"

Birdy stopped, he looked horrified and embarrassed. "No, they are part of all this." He waved the hand around again.

"They're your guests then," I said. He nodded, looking relieved. I added quietly, "Who can't leave."

He sighed, examining his feet and then glanced up at me. He seemed angry for a moment. "We need them."

"Yes of course you do!" I said, unsympathetically. Thinking, I can just guess why *that* would be. Why had men taken women for every war in the history of all the universes.

He tried to explain, "If we have them, we *don't* kill each other." I stopped in my tracks causing something of a borderer's traffic jam.

"What are you saying?" I was confused.

"It's the way we are *made*," he said, sounding exasperated. "It is chemical. The touch makes some," he struggled for the right words, "Endorphins in our system. Without them we either fight or die."

I stood for a moment listening to the waking feelings connecting my thoughts, and the first one that came alive at his words was disgust.

"Are you saying that you were designed so that if you didn't fight you would die and the only cure is the proximity of women?"

"Yes," he said, relieved. "Though it was only discovered by accident. Before that we had to have an arena every few days." He struggled with the words again, "An organised fight. Even if we just watch fighting it will keep us from, frenzy."

"That is just, plain *evil*," I said eventually, he nodded his agreement and we resumed walking.

The explanation was much more complicated than I had thought. Someone had built in a hormonal fail-safe, one that was guaranteed to get rid of the evidence of the act, but the 'lab rats' had worked out a solution. It was a cure that didn't suit anybody really. I wondered if their scientists onboard the ships had tried to put it right. "Have your scientists tried to adapt the genetic engineering," I trailed off at the look Birdy gave me. "Obviously they have," I said, "Stupid question."

"You are new here, you can ask lots of stupid questions," he said, which made me laugh, thought he didn't understand why, he just looked delighted that I had laughed. Birdy must have been getting a hormone overdose.

"Birdy, does it make everything worse if the women are angry and frightened?"

"Yes."

Make that a double fail-safe, I thought.

After that I shook hands with every borderer that passed us. As this was quite a few and the word had obviously got around, that here was a woman who didn't seem angry or frightened and was willing to share her, whatever, it soon became a bit of a problem. There was no pushing or shoving, just a sense of hopeless resignation and a grateful acceptance of not very much it seemed to me. I just reached out while Birdy stood stoically by my side and I felt as if I was the lady of the manor, handing out alms to the poor or a sacrificial lamb on the way to the slaughter, a take your pick moment. All I could think of was making it more difficult for Zatar to get to me and affecting as many people as possible with my female mojo, so that they were hopefully, on my side.

We moved slowly down towards the quarters that I had been assigned. A voice interrupted the progress for a moment. "I see you're making friends?" Zatar drawled. He was leaning against the bulkhead with his arms folded. A snake coiled ready to strike. Birdy made a strange noise in his throat. I couldn't identify it at first, but a few of the borderers in close proximity to us began to copy him. It was the deep vibrating sound of a cat's growl. Zatar looked slightly alarmed, even a murderer with the sensitivity of a toaster would have understood. He looked at me, his black eyes glittering. "I'll be back soon," he said and turned to go.

I laughed, Zatar was furious. It's a well-known fact that psychopaths, much like your average capitalist and most malevolent dictators, don't have much of a sense of humour. Zatar turned around and stared at me, he wasn't used to people not being frightened of him, I wasn't used to it either. I couldn't say exactly when it stopped. Maybe about the time he had killed Weldon. It was swallowed up by my own hate and need for revenge.

He came right up close to me trying to claw some ground back, but it was difficult as he was looking up my nose and I could see a small bald patch on the top of his head. I could also see something more important, or rather not see it. No fixer. I smiled. "The wormhole technology you use for your own personal verse hopping; that would have been stolen from the meeting on Earth in this verse, the one where most of the dreamwalkers died?"

He blinked. "I suppose Seager told you that."

"*Simon* did mention something, but I got a good look at it when you tried to kidnap me from the kitchen in my verse. You remember; I hit you with a baseball bat?"

Zatar nodded. "The science laboratory is on the floor below this one, tomorrow we can continue this discussion, just the two of us."

He turned and walked away.

"I *also* do not like that man," Birdy said.

The living quarters were small and neat, with well thought out facilities and most importantly, a window. I leaned over the seating area and looked out. Jupiter was a massive presence and the moons that were the settler planet Europa and Leda its moon, seemed to be strung out in conjunction with the mirror system that I had heard of but not seen before. The mirrors that amplified the sunlight were closer in design to crystals, than the sort of household object that you looked into to straighten your clothes. You could clearly see that the moons were orbiting the sun *alongside* Jupiter rather than orbiting the gas planet as well. The science of holding a moon in space so that it didn't orbit a larger body was mind-bogglingly difficult to imagine. It was just possible to see the twin settler planet, Ganymede and its moon Elara and one of the space satellites. I wondered what they thought of a borderer's mothership hovering above them.

Birdy showed me proudly around the rooms, there were two if you counted the bathroom, as if he was a Manhattan estate agent in a cold water walk up. He really wanted me to like it, so I did. I admired the fixtures and fittings and the view and the furniture, which was bolted to the floor. It was a rabbit hutch in the sky.

I sat down and folded my feet under me. Birdy had left after saying that he would bring me some breakfast. My face was stiff and aching with the mask of an expression I had been wearing. I let it slip and put my head onto my knees. I pushed the sense of the wormhole into another place in my thoughts. Then, as I tried not to think of anything, I found myself focusing on Buddy. I stood up and went to the door, and leaning against it I listened. Silence. Though what I had expected to hear through an airlock pressure door I was not sure. The quarters were standard for the 'brain' class, Birdy had explained. The slightly refined feline features belonged to them. Birdy was 'troop' class. He had showed me the computer system that was used by the previous occupant, then apologised, saying that I wouldn't be able to use it because I didn't have the appropriate biomechanical connection. I had stood smiling throughout the explanation, thinking about Buddy.

I held a hand over the console and let the powerful fizz move from my fingers to the keys. The universal menu came up, or at least that's what I thought it was, because it was written in the same hieroglyphs as on the holo-screen in the dropdown craft. I tapped keys at random, the computer equivalent of giving a typewriter to a monkey and hoping for Balzac, whilst looking around the room for the Rosetta stone. Sadly, there was nothing available, but somewhere out there were Buddy's friends *and* I could fly any one of them.

Birdy came back with a tray of food, most of which was edible and some of which I recognised. He sat with me while I ate and tried to make conversation, asking me about my own verse. He obviously hadn't been part of the group that had attacked the house on the moor, but he seemed to know something about it. "Why were they trying to kill me?" I asked after I had drunk the liquid that tasted nothing like coffee.

He shrugged. "The frenzy gets to some of the troops, they lose control." He frowned. "But we are better than the mercenaries, they don't care if you die or not. Zatar stopped using them; he couldn't get them to do what he wanted."

"I remember," I said, thinking about the enclave in Joao's verse and Muglier lying in the dirt telling me to get out of there. It seemed to me that I would be avenging more than the loss of Weldon, and I wondered when I had become the type of person who calculated death into their daily schedule. Maybe we all had a war zone lying in wait in our hearts.

"I'm surprised your captain does what Zatar wants," I said carefully.

Birdy frowned. "They both travel in the same direction for a while; it doesn't mean they want the same thing."

"Can I go and meet the other women?" I asked casually.

"Certainly," Birdy answered without hesitation, "Your friend had been moved there this morning," he added, "I don't know if she is much better though. Most of the taken are at the recreation area."

We walked out of the quarters and along the corridor and up one level to double airlock pressure doors that opened onto a large space. I had talked and shaken hands along the way with as many borderers as I could and word had got around again, there were smiles and nods of appreciation, I thought to myself, when you're lost in the middle of the ocean, keep paddling.

I stood looking at the groups of women scattered around the walkways. They talked and laughed as if it was a necessary part of the survival technique for living on a borderer's ship. It felt as if it could have been a busy market place, if it wasn't for the guards.

The recreation area was two levels high. Plants and seating were placed against the walls in an attempt to give the impression of planet life, by someone who had clearly never lived on the surface of anywhere.

I was surprised by how few women there were and wondered at the words 'some of them don't make it' that the medic had used as an explanation. Birdy pointed at the seating by the far wall and I could see Tara leaning back with her eyes closed. She looked as if standing up would require lots of help.

I ran; walking wasn't possible. Birdy came with me to keep me to the not touching rule. She opened her eyes just as I got to her and her cry was that of a wounded animal when one of her precious creatures has made it back to the place of safety. She staggered to her feet and we stood apart just out of reach. Birdy had his arm across my chest trying for an inconspicuous look, which was a bit like seeing a hippopotamus in a tutu, not something you're likely to miss. It made me want to laugh which in turn made me want to cry. I thought about it carefully and did neither.

The silence between Tara and I was the one that goes with loss and the feelings best left unsaid. Then she murmured the unsayable, "Do you think that they're both dead?"

"Weldon," I couldn't finish. His blood was fresh on my mind and in my heart.

She nodded, her head drooping, then gradually realised what I hadn't said, her eyes lifted and fixed on mine. "Joao?" She whispered, stunned, "Do you think, but I was sure I saw," she stopped, Birdy was looking at the floor, his arm still between us.

"I know, I saw it too, but I have a feeling," I said.

"A dreamwalker feeling?" She asked.

"Yes." I shrugged. The truth was it was more than just a feeling, as if the wormhole connected something other than just the verses.

Tara sat back down, and leaned forward resting her elbows on her knees. I moved to one side to give Birdy a break from the rules and he sat down on the other end of the bench, careful not to brush against Tara. She rubbed her eyes. "I'm so very tired!"

"Tara, this is Birdy." I gave it all the unspoken meaning I could get into the words and Tara, amazingly considering her shock and exhaustion, understood. She didn't know why, but she looked up and then held out a hand and after a moment's stunned hesitation, Birdy held her hand in his for a second or two.

I told her about the genetic manipulation and the fail-safe device in the DNA of the borderers and as much as I could about Zatar and my quarters, keeping it light and hoping she could comprehend the meaning behind the words. Mostly she did, I could see a few puzzled questions form and then collect in frustrated silence behind the ever-present pain in her eyes.

A voice gently interjected into the conversation, "Is it Tara Weldon?" The woman looked hopeful and sorry at the same time.

"Ginnie!" Tara said with a smile, "It's good to see you." Tara back peddled. "Not *here* obviously," she fumbled.

"I know what you mean." Ginnie smiled. She looked at Birdy and asked, "Would it be okay if I sit down?" He nodded and she sat next to Tara, careful not to make contact with Birdy in any way. "I was hoping for news of home," Ginnie said.

Tara told her gently about Til and Solly and then some general news about the town. Ginnie drank it in as if she had been without water for far too long. I told her about reading the boys a story one evening and when she looked puzzled, I explained that Lu Wang was living with them without giving the reason why. Jarry Wang's injury from a borderer's attack wasn't a good topic for conversation at that point.

She nodded. "Solly always wanted a little brother."

We were quiet for a moment, each thinking the disconnected thoughts of people who find themselves somewhere they weren't supposed to be. I tried for another hint to Tara and I sighed, "I hope Buddy's okay."

She looked startled for a second then came back quickly. "He'll be fine, Til will feed the stock." We all tried not to look at Birdy, who was studying his feet carefully.

A bell rang and the women began gathering their personal items and heading toward the exits on the two different levels. They kept as far away from the borderers as possible. Guards and guarded. Ginnie helped Tara to her feet and I wished I was able to hug her, not just for her comfort, but mine too. I could see that she understood but I added the hint, "Tell Ginnie about how Buddy can do tricks," I smiled.

"For a goat he's really smart," Tara said sarcastically.

I really needed to find out what the women knew about the ship and the possibility for escape. But I couldn't figure out how Tara would be able to get the information to me. Or what timescale I was working to. Zatar's plan for universal domination might not be fully on course but he wasn't stupid, just psychopathic on several fundamental levels. I could see myself being tied to the railway tracks listening for train whistles.

The walls of the quarters were closing in on me after a few hours and the evening stretched without books or company. I paced up and down finding myself returning to the computer terminal for more pointless attempts at looking for the map of the ship and the red dotted line that led to the docking bay and the space to surface craft marked 'this one.' Birdy had gone on a work-related errand and I found myself missing him. Which made me feel as if the madness was closing in. I had never usually found the sensation of small spaces too difficult but my breath came in short gasps and suddenly I was in the area of a full-blown anxiety attack. I sat on the floor, which was nearer than the furniture and tried not to suffocate.

The door slid open after a polite beep and Ginnie came in with a woman I didn't know, they abandoned the food trays on the table and came over to me. Ginnie pulled a mask from a wall cupboard marked with a hieroglyph that I had thought was more empty storage. The mask came with its own small pressure unit and I began to breathe again.

"Okay, thanks," I said eventually, moving to a chair, still gripping the mask in my hand just in case.

Ginnie looked around the room and then back at me. She went to fetch the food and some cups of the disgusting brew they used instead of coffee. "How long do you think we've got until the borderer is back?"

"Birdy? I've no idea," I said. I took sips of the drink which was still awful but at least hot.

"Tara wasn't allowed to come with us; they think you'd be out of here." The other woman introduced herself, "I'm Becky by the way." We shook hands. "Is it really possible for you to dreamwalk with someone?"

It looked as if Tara had given them the full and unexpurgated version of my life. I shrugged. "I don't know; I've never tried it."

They both nodded and as if the conversation was not bizarre enough, they began to tell their story.

Most of the taken were very young and over time many of them had been moved into the different tribes on the motherships. As with the history of so-called civilisation in all verses, assimilation being the way that people developed their survival potential. The small group I had seen in the recreation area were the sum total of women who were not prepared to change their lives, and only permitted minimal contact with their captors in exchange for luxuries. A barter system that seemed to work pretty well for everyone.

Ginnie and Becky were silent after this short biography and exchanged looks. "Tell me?" I said.

"In the last few months three women have disappeared. We don't know what happened to them and I don't think the borderers do. We were wondering if you might be aware of something," Ginnie said.

"Do you mean they were dreamwalkers?" An unpleasant thought surfaced. But I didn't voice it.

"I think if they had been they'd have left as soon as they got here," Becky said.

"They'd have left *before* they got here," I sniffed. "You say the borderers don't seem to know what happened to them either?"

"We don't think so; they appeared to be as worried as we were. The captain did a ship wide search," Ginnie said, "They were just nowhere to be found. Lately they have been using more guards in the women's quarters at night." She added, as if she just realised it, "Also during the recreation periods."

I thought about the unpleasant possibility again and wondered if I should voice it. Then I realised that these women were as strong as you could be to have survived the capture and imprisonment of their circumstances. "How long has Zatar been on this ship?"

"That nasty little scientist?" Becky looked puzzled. "About eight or nine months."

"The women. When did they start disappearing?"

Ginnie and Becky looked at each other. "We are housed in quarters similar to this, all together, on the deck below this one, mostly two to a room," Ginnie said. "Tara is in with us for the moment, we didn't want to leave her on her own. It's always hard at first." She shook her head. "It would be difficult to say when the first one disappeared, she was in quarters on her own. But maybe six months; the last two were sharing and they went missing together," she looked at Becky then added, "It was just over a month ago."

I sighed. The basic development of a psychopath is a childhood filled with setting fires, torturing small animals and bedwetting. How they turned out depended on circumstances and sometimes, luck. Several successful businessmen in my old verse could have fallen into the definition in their youth. It's what happened next. The torture of small vulnerable things sometimes needed a place to go. I shuddered.

"What are you saying?" Ginnie whispered.

"I don't know," I whispered back, feeling tired to my bones. I put the mask over my mouth and nose again because I found it made breathing easier. I looked at the food on the table. "Can I have some of that?"

"Sure." Becky went to get one of the trays.

I picked at bread that tasted of sawdust and tried not to think about the farm and Okan and wanting someone to rescue me, because rescuing myself was looking more and more difficult, never mind all the women who deserved a chance to see their homes again and the borderers who were supposed to fight or die whatever. I wiped a tear and tried not to look like a fool.

Thinking back to the recreation area, I asked, "There are twenty-three women not including Tara and me?" I chewed the food that hadn't ever been farm fresh. Ginnie nodded. "I don't suppose either of you can read the borderer's written language?" I added.

"I've been studying it. I was a teacher at Gold Cliffs," Ginnie said, "I thought it would pass the time, then when I realised, I stopped." She left the part out about no one coming to rescue her and take her home. She pointed at the computer console. "We don't have the biochemical connection to work their technology."

I went over to the holo-screen and put my hand on the smooth surface. It buzzed under my fingers and the screen came alive in its three-dimensional light dance. The main menu poked fun at me. Ginnie and Becky did the local verse's equivalent of incredulity, which is pretty much the same sound wherever you are, then came over to join me.

"Is there anything on this that looks like a map of the ship?" I asked.

Ginnie frowned for a moment then pointed at one of the groups of hieroglyphs. "I think you need to start here." I tapped keys and she frowned for a few more minutes as we made our way through the system. Finally, a complicated matrix of lines indicated the corridors and rooms on the ship. The distance from the living quarters to the docking bay was dizzying.

"Becky, could you go and listen just in case?" I asked politely.

"Sure," she snorted, "Don't want the vermin to find us out." She stood with her ear to the door and nodded 'okay.'

"They were made that way," I muttered.

"What?" Ginnie and Becky said together, puzzled.

"Someone made them so that they either fight or die of the consequences of not fighting. You can't blame them for looking at an easy solution."

The two women were both horrified, Becky's face filled with red anger, her freckled skin and coppery hair betraying the feelings within. "I lost my husband when they took me; they kill without a second thought."

"That is exactly what they were *designed* to do," I persisted quietly.

But you can't overcome the prejudice of many years in a moment. Becky was getting shrill. "Don't you get it, they're monsters!"

I sighed, "I just think there might be a better way. Look," I added, "I understand, I was hunted in every place I have ever thought safe and not just by the borderers. I lay on my stomach in the dark and shot at moving shadows. I killed to keep the farm on Europa safe and to protect my friends *and* I lost someone I love," I tried not to sob, "I'm just trying to explain, maybe that's what they're doing too."

We were silent for a while, not long, because women don't require much time to look at things from someone else's point of view; we've had a lot of practice over the centuries.

"I need to think about it," Ginnie said, "It's been a way of life." She patted my arm and I smiled my best watery smile.

Becky shook her head. "I don't think I can forgive them for what they've done." She was still very angry.

"I don't think you should," I said. She looked even more confused.

"I *don't* think some of the things they've done can be forgiven." I struggled for the right words, "Comprehending and condoning is not the same thing."

Becky sighed, "I know, I know," she said tiredly, "I just can't, let's leave it at that?"

There are some people it's not possible to win over and you shouldn't try.

I stepped back from the console and the holo-screen spiralled into the work surface. I thought about what to do next and an idea came to me, not a good idea, as it fell into the category of 'do or die.' "I need you to pass a message to Tara," I said. I tried several versions in my head.

"You can trust us," Ginnie smiled.

"What are you going to tell the other women about me when you get back?" I asked.

"That you have a plan and you're a dreamwalker so it might work," Becky said. I shook my head slowly. "Um," she said, then tried again, "That you looked well and were resting?"

I nodded. "I need you to say to Tara I'm going to do what I promised. Then I need you to speak to the captain." They both looked worried. "You must wait until the right time before you do."

"How will we know?" Ginnie asked.

"You'll know," I said. "I need you to say, 'I won't let him down.'"

The two women were close to tears, it was one of those moments when you finally understand that situations without hope require hopeless solutions. To give them their due they never asked 'what about us' and never put themselves first. I have always thought women were amazing and I always will.

The door pinged and Birdy walked in after a second's hesitation. He hovered just inside the room. I smiled at him. "I've had visitors and food."

"I can see," he said.

"Though I think you need to have a word with the cook, the bread could be used to build a small support wall." I banged it on the plate where it made a suitable resounding noise.

"You're making a joke?" He asked hopefully.

"Just a little one." I held up my finger and thumb a fraction apart.

The two women got up to go; they both gave me a hug. Becky took the tray nearest to me and said, "I'll leave the drink," she nodded to the other tray, "It's in a heated flask, you might want it later."

They passed Birdy still hovering by the doorway. Becky swept by him without a glance and Ginnie touched his arm very gently. Birdy looked stunned. There are things you can't change and some that you can.

Zatar came into the quarters sometime in the middle of the night. I knew it was night time because Birdy had left earlier telling me to get some sleep, saying he would be back to go with me to the scientist's laboratory in a few hours. I had turned the lights down to give myself the illusion of a safe cave for a short while. I can't say I slept. Zatar banged the lights up, getting an emotional charge from my momentary look of shock. He was deluding himself that I was surprised. I was fully dressed and even wearing my boots.

The borderer that Zatar had watching his back had something wrong with him. His eyes flickered in an alarming fashion and he had little strings of spittle at the corners of his mouth. One sharp eye tooth protruded over his lips. He looked as if his cat DNA had rabies.

I could see how three women had disappeared without a trace. I smiled at both of them. "Night time high jinks?" It was funny how easily you could make a psychopath angry. The blow came swiftly but was not unexpected. I fell back between the table and one of the chairs and it was the borderer who leaned down and grabbed me by my hair dragging me upright. Their psychotic double act was well rehearsed. It was agony. My eyes filled with tears and my heart filled with hate. Weldon, as always, was right, you needed to find a great deal of anger if you had to kill someone. I was completely on schedule.

The corridor was nearly empty, no one challenged Zatar and I was surprised by the reaction of the few borderers we did meet. They looked puzzled and one or two maybe even seemed worried, but no one stopped him. Then eventually I saw two borderers, one of them Birdy's friend from the landing craft, conversing at the end of the living quarters. They looked at me and then the other one went off while Birdy's friend stood watching. I hoped they wouldn't find Birdy too soon.

We went down a level using a set of steps into a wider corridor, the doors on either side were double sized and the lighting was different as if no one slept here. Zatar took great delight in shoving me through a set of pressure doors so that I skidded across the floor on my knees, which banged painfully against the fixed work surfaces.

The room was large with masses of holographic equipment spinning out data in a variety of languages, some of which I could understand, a jumble of food containers and old cups of half-filled drink were a surprise. The floor was dirty, and a sticky mess that I could feel under my hand, could only be one substance. I didn't think the borderers could have checked in the scientist's room when they were looking for the missing women. I gave them a moment of my sadness and then added them to the list in my heart.

I got up slowly and turned around as if admiring the fixtures and fittings. "Very nice Zatar," I said, cheerfully, wiping my hands on my jeans. It infuriated him and he came close, his eyes narrow slits. I smiled down at him. "Zatar. Why did you pick that name for yourself? I suppose Zaphod Beeblebrox was already taken and Trevor Morris really doesn't have the same effect." His hand came back again and he hit me to the ground with a closed fist. My head filled with red bubbles and I did my best not to lose consciousness. I let it creep in just enough so that I looked as if I was about to dreamwalk.

"You verse jump and I'll just jump with you," Zatar shouted, he had one hand on my shoulder, the other closed around a device on the work surface that looked similar to the sort of belt you gave a pugilist, after they've done their best and the other person is lying in a pool of blood on the canvas.

I thanked all the deities I could think of, because I couldn't have taken much more. I hadn't had any idea what it looked like or even if it was small enough so that he carried it around in his pocket. The wormhole unit was surprisingly clunky but I thought the prototype for something so amazing could look the way it damn well pleased.

Zatar wasn't actually wearing the device and that was what I had needed to know.

I got up to my feet, not having to pretend to feel exhausted and defeated, as it flowed out of me. There were some answers I might not get but it would be worth a try. "Did you kill my parents?"

Zatar smiled. "Let's just say that life is unusually cheap in the type zero verse."

I couldn't say I was stunned and the numb sensation of sorrow was gradually being supplanted by the anger that would be needed, my fists relaxed and I tried for more as he seemed to be in a chatty mood. "Did you have help," I waved a hand around, "With all this?"

He looked down and then back up at me, his face puzzled. "Yes," he shrugged, "For a while, but," he looked at Igor, "They weren't too careful around my friend here."

I bowed my head and added the three more innocent souls to the ever-increasing list of people not to forget. "What were their names?"

"Enough of this," Zatar said impatiently, shrugging off the death.

I stood and waited. "I assume we're just missing the too loud opera music. Isn't that what psychopaths do when they set to work on their victims?" I actually laughed without meaning to when his eyes slid to a unit on the work surface which had pretty horizontal waves dancing above it. "Let me guess, Madame Butterfly?" Zatar snarled, there was no other word for it; I was worried for a moment that I had pushed him too far but he was under control after a great deal of effort. He hated the fact that I wasn't frightened of him and it seemed to confuse Igor too.

"Tell me," I asked gently, throwing another spanner into the psychopath mix. "Why do you need me? Can't you get the wormhole technology from the type three verse?"

He surprised me by answering. "Your parents and the few dreamwalkers at the meeting were the only ones who knew the research. There's nothing left except," he added with a theatrical pause, "You."

"Is this about the wormhole, or is it something else?" I asked, with the sort of prescience that you should usually keep to yourself.

Zatar had begun positioning units in place while he was talking; he tapped keys and snapped equipment together. Then he stopped. "Clever girl. Seager said you were smart." He thought for a moment and then went to a wall unit with a key code on the outside. He opened it and pulled out a black box about a hand span wide and deep on either side. He held it out to me. "It's about this," he said.

I moved towards him and he held up a warning finger as Igor went to stop me. I reached out for the box and Zatar let me take it. I turned it in my hands. The feeling of power it gave off was mind blowing, literally. I could see stars spinning into the room and feel the swirl of the quantum universe through my fingers. Zatar sensed something and he snatched it back, as though he was a jealous child with a favourite toy. I could understand how he and his brother Charlie Morris had ended up in separate verses. They were two halves of an evil egg.

"What is that?" I whispered. Knowing the answer but needing to hear it anyway.

"It's a quantum singularity weapon. Or it will be when I get the last component." Zatar smiled and the rest of that necessary hate turned inside me adding strength and resolve as it spun.

I realised the pieces of the puzzle were all there. The odd behaviour of Simon morphing from bookseller in a Devon city to something indefinable but dangerous, his, not entirely necessary, journey to Okan's verse under a thin pretext of being able to deal with Charlie Morris. He wanted something that he knew or suspected was there and I was betting that great, or rather evil, minds thought alike. I didn't know what or who Simon really was apart from my friend, but he was a big piece of the puzzle. Okan had known it, he couldn't quantify it but he knew.

Simon had told me at one point that Zatar's real name was Trevor but not until the trip to Tara's verse had he said what the man's last name was and his connection to Charlie Morris. I had referred to him several times as Zatar without Simon correcting me. There was so much information that had been held back until 'the right time,' I couldn't remember when I knew things and when I didn't.

The unrelenting pursuit of me through the different verses made me understand I was linked to the weapon by its makers. Though I didn't think it had been a weapon when my parents had worked on it. Anything with great power can be made to go bang by someone determined enough.

I was beginning to see several other puzzle pieces. Both Charlie and Trevor had found something at that meeting, and had planned separately or together to get the experimental technology, when the spoils were being fought over or divided up or just stolen, Trevor had got the wormhole belt and Charlie the fixers. I was thinking the weapon would have been something on an information chip from the type three verse, which they both ended up with a copy of.

Planck Energy. Energy derived from black holes, at which point space/time becomes foamy and unstable, frothing with minute wormholes. Something that was connected to an integral part of the deviations in me.

It was why I was being looked for by Okan and Rari, Charlie Morris had worked it out too. I was the last 'component.' I wondered what Trevor Morris had told the borderers. I didn't think for a moment the conversation had included the words quantum singularity weapon. Charlie and Trevor Morris were dreamwalkers from the evil end of the gene pool.

My head ached and my heart hurt and I watched as Trevor 'Zatar' Morris tapped more computer keys and added more units to the experiment as I was adding pieces to the puzzle. He turned toward me with the singularity box in one hand. "I think we're just about ready."

I looked behind me to see where Igor was and just as I moved

Trevor Morris grabbed my arm. The doors slid open on Birdy and his friend and they shoved at Igor to get to me. The 'biological crazy' went from one to the other in a second. Birdy pushed a knife into Igor and Trevor Morris was distracted just enough for me to reach his other arm with mine. I gripped him firmly and his expression was one of puzzlement for a second. We must have looked as if we were the odd couple at a barn dance who couldn't remember which was their left foot and which was their right.

He realised what I was going to do in the moment before I did it and his mouth fell away from his teeth in a parody of a smile, as though his face was the death grin on a rotting corpse. I turned to Birdy but I couldn't think of anything to say and he shouted my name as he stabbed Igor again and kicked him out of the way. His friend was in the corridor sounding the alarm.

We moved, Zatar and I, into the rumbling silence; the dark shadow of the wormhole drifted beneath my feet and around my head at the same time. I let myself move closer and closer to the edge of the event horizon and the accretion disk until I could feel my bones pulling me into a shape I couldn't possibly survive.

Zatar was a weight against me, he shouted and screamed in stunning silence and I could see tears and snot flowing away from his face and I didn't care. I waited, until I knew if I waited any longer, I would never leave there. Then I let go. He clung on to me but I peeled his clawed hand from my arm and punched him in the face with a closed fist, twisting my hand as my dad had taught me, to maximise the effect and protect my knuckles. I kicked out at him in slow motion until the fingers slipped and the arms wheeled in the darkness and the endless silent scream became a maw swallowed by the mass below.

I could see the shape of the man elongate into 'spaghettification' pulling him in all directions at once and he disappeared into the huge power of the accretion disk that turned on a moment in time. He still held the weapon in his jealous hand. Without a fixer he was helpless. The older you were, as Nancy Lawson had said, the less able you were to dreamwalk without one.

I closed my eyes and began to reach for the farmhouse. I became aware of a sense of quiet disapproval and then something else pervaded my thoughts; I could feel sadness. It washed over me. I opened my eyes and looked at the wormhole and then closed them and reached for the farm again.

The hallway was dark with a light showing under the kitchen door. I don't know what I shouted but it must have been something. The door to the kitchen flew open and Okan and Rari shot out as if on wires in a stuntman's trick.

I said, "We have to go now!" Then Okan was folded around me and I couldn't breathe because he squeezed me so tightly, my nose was squashed against his chest. I pushed him away and there were tears in his eyes which nearly broke me. "Please, don't do that," my voice petered out; it took a great deal of effort, but he got it together.

"Is Tara with you?" Joao asked quietly from the doorway.

My knees gave way and I sat on the floor which was the most convenient place at that moment. I sobbed. For all the lost possibilities and the wonderful people, who had done selfless amazing things, the pointless killing and the terrible waste, then I stopped, suddenly; because I didn't have time and because we still had Joao.

"I'll take that as a no," Joao said, as he slid down the wall and sat next to me. Patting my shoulder in understanding.

Okan was squatting opposite me, his leg held at an awkward angle. Rari was leaning on the stairs, he turned on the lights and we stared at each other. Shipwrecked sailors in the lull of the storm.

They were battered and bruised, Rari looked as if he had broken some fingers and his face was filled with weary resignation. Joao had one arm in a sling and his eyes were half closed with the swelling. Okan had been shot, again; I could tell it was a leg wound because his trousers had been ripped to accommodate a bulky dressing and the half squat was a complete giveaway.

He studied me carefully and then said seriously, "You look terrible."

I laughed, it sounded as if someone was opening a door without working hinges. "We have to go. Can you get Buddy up and running?" I asked Rari.

"Where are we off to?" Okan asked me, the way you would speak to a child who had just had a bad dream.

"Back to the borderer's ship to get Tara," I said impatiently. "What?" I asked their stunned faces.

"I don't know if that's a good idea," Rari spoke gently, going with 'this person is shocked and I need to protect them,' which was actually very irritating.

"They're expecting us!" I said in exasperation, getting up.

"That's what I'm afraid of," Okan said, getting up with me and shrugging when the other two looked at him for an explanation.

I looked around me, suddenly realising something. "Where's Simon?" I asked in horror, wiping my face with a grubby sleeve.

"He didn't come back with us," Rari said.

"What do you mean?" My breathing stopped.

Rari shook his head. "When we dreamwalked, he didn't come here." He shrugged. "We don't know where he went. He had something that he found in our verse. I think it was important."

"Yes," I said, as the puzzle got another big fat piece, "I think it was."

I went up the stairs two at a time and Okan called up after me, "Feel free to let us know what you know."

"I think," I said at the top of the stairs, "It was a quantum singularity weapon."

The three men stood still as stone, in the half light of the early morning hallway they were cast in deep shadow and filled with the dark of impossible tiredness. "Bloody hell!" Rari said. "Are you sure?" I had never really heard him swear that way before, but he also seemed deeply shaken and I hadn't *ever* seen him like that. I nodded. "Do you think it's somewhere safe now?" He asked me.

The question was filled with meaning. "Do I think Simon took it somewhere that no one can use it?" I asked. Rari nodded. "Yes," I said, "I think he has."

I went off into the bedroom and half in trepidation pulled open the bathroom door. A frightened squeak greeted me and I grabbed the little creature who was cowering in a corner along with an equally frightened Cecil. They listened to the tears and laughter and a promise of better days and then I found my bag of travel things and after one longing look at the shower, I changed my clothes for some that were less bloody and smelly as fast as I could.

The three men were in the yard in front of the barns. I couldn't recognise the places where the dead had been, there was no sign. No tell-tale dark stains, no lingering thoughts of death snatched from life. The biodegrading microbes had obviously been doing their job again, but I didn't ask any questions and they didn't say. It wasn't the time; that would be later.

"It's early morning here isn't it?" I asked Joao, trying to get my bearings. The time on the ship and the nightmare of the last few days meant I couldn't remember when I was. The fight with Zatar was still fresh in my mind and if I turned for a moment to the worm-hole inside me, I could still see him wheeling away into the disk. I shuddered.

"Are you going to tell us what's going on?" Okan asked; trying not to sound as if it was conditional.

"We'll have time on the trip up there," I said. "Maybe you could tell me what happened to you."

"I'm not sure we've got *that* long!" Rari said dryly.

Buddy was waiting. He said 'hi' when I held my hand over the surface of his hull and I said, "Hi yourself." Which made Joao snort, then he winced with pain as the movement in his face pulled at torn muscles and damaged skin. The pilot seat was a welcome relief and I sank into it, I tried not to yawn with suppressed tension but the sound came out anyway.

"Hm," Okan said, looking at me, then he leaned down and kissed me. "I love you," he said.

'My brain froze. The inside of the ship was quiet. "I'm not sure I really believe in all that," I was stunned, "I think it's mainly about brain chemicals, but thank you," I finished lamely.

"Okay," Okan said, smiling, "In that case, my brain chemicals are crazy for your brain chemicals." I put my hand out and he took it and I kissed his closed fist as it curled around mine.

"Ha," Joao said, "Geek dirty talk, you two are perfect for each other."

"What did you do to your hand?" Okan asked, frowning. My knuckles were cut and covered in dried blood, which was mostly not mine.

"It happened when I killed Zatar," I said quietly. "Technically I didn't actually *kill* him, but he was hanging on to me and I punched him, which is not that easy to do in zero gravity." I almost sobbed on the last word because the emotion was just below the surface and every now and then the wind rippled the water.

"Let me get this straight, Zatar's dead?" Rari asked, after a stunned silence.

"I think so," I answered, somewhat distracted, as connecting with Buddy was making my head spin.

"Is he, or isn't he?" Joao sounded impatient.

"I don't know, he's in the accretion disk of the wormhole. What do you think?" I looked at Okan for confirmation and then turned around and checked with Rari and Joao.

"I think that very well might do it," Rari said.

"Okay, good," I whispered, going back to my link with Buddy. The ship was sliding out of the barn on little spurts of power and I manoeuvred through the doors carefully, trying not to scrape anything. "Is her tongue out?" Joao asked, "Because I'm not going anywhere if she's got her tongue out."

It was.

Rari said, "As a strategy for concentrating *I* have always found it very helpful."

It was as if our lost collective mojo had finally found us.

"Ready?" I asked, not waiting for an answer. The ship went up in a near vertical climb and I could hear both the men in the back swearing at the fate of being pinned into the seats. Okan just laughed.

They told me what had happened in Rari and Okan's verse and then I told them as quickly as I could what had taken place at the farm, most of which they must have worked out by the trail of death. Til had come from the village with some men to help them 'put things to rights' as Rari said. They had used the microbes to break down the bodies of the borderers and then burnt them as we had with the ones in the dropdown craft when we had first found it. I didn't ask about Weldon or Wills or the others and they didn't tell me. Some things were best left alone until grief had its time.

Okan held my hand for a moment. "I wish we had been there," he said.

"If you had, you'd have died too," I replied bitterly, "So I'm glad you weren't. I did see you for a moment in the hallway in the house; as though I was watching your shadows."

"I saw you too," Okan said. "We were stuck in the entrance to the building in my verse, there was a homicidal doctor calling the shots."

"What happened?" I asked, tongue out again, as I swam Buddy through the weather net.

"Simon killed her, with a double tap to the head. Very professional for a bookseller," he added dryly, "He also finished off Charlie Morris."

"He likes to keep busy," I joked with appalling humour, which made Rari snort with laughter.

I said, after a moment's thought, "We have two tracking devices that are not much use for anything anymore."

"Actually, ours never made it out of the building in our verse," Rari said, "But thanks for the other one."

I explained about Marl and the gangers and tried not to choke on the tears which were threatening to cloud the words. More silence followed; it was a necessary pattern for all of us.

I told them about the biochemical time bomb the borderers had been designed with and after another short silence Rari asked me, "Are you sure about this?" I did my best to explain the details as I had understood them.

We were all quiet for a moment and I didn't know what they

were thinking but I was wishing that Simon was with us. I really wanted to talk to him. I needed to see him; to make sure that he was okay; he was all the family I had left. I couldn't imagine that carrying a quantum singularity weapon would make you very popular anywhere. The continuing strand of thought made me remember something else. "Zatar also had a quantum singularity weapon," I said, "It was on the borderer's ship."

"Please tell me it's not still there," Okan whispered. I could literally *hear* the three of them reassessing the situation to include a suicide mission to get the device.

"It's in the accretion disk with him," I replied carefully.

"What's the plan?" Okan said at last, when I had pushed the little craft towards the coordinates that I had found on my holo-trip around the inner workings of the mothership. At least I hoped that's where we were headed. It had been a guessing game, with me trying not to give away to Ginnie, what I was doing, but still needing her help on the translation. "What makes you think they won't just blow this ship out of the system as soon as we get close?"

"I'm hoping that the fact that it's a borderer's craft might buy me some time to get a transmission off."

"It just might work," Joao said grudgingly. "Then what?"

"We ask the captain of the Tar Dal Tribe of borderers to give us the taken women in exchange for help with a cure for the chemical imbalance and access to female volunteers in the interim." More stunned silence.

"*That's* the plan?" Rari said, when he was finally able to speak. "Why would they *do* that?"

"What can I say, I'm winging it," I added, "Of course, when I made the plan, it included a gay guy from the type three verse, who may or may not have access to just the sort of biochemical information we would need to help the borderers."

"I'm having trouble imagining the borderers without the DNA deviation to hold them back," Okan said. "I'm not sure it's a good idea for them to have no self-destruct button."

"I don't think they *want* to fight any more," I tried to explain.

"It's the way they were made. They want what everyone does, a life for themselves."

"Do you *really* believe that?" Rari asked.

I contemplated for a moment or two and remembered back to my conversations with Birdy. "Yes, I do."

"What about the settlers, what would persuade them to even consider it?" Okan sounded exasperated.

"I was hoping that maybe Ginnie would help," I said.

We had nearly run out of stunned silence, but not quite. Okan spoke, "Til Duster's Ginnie?"

"Yes," I replied. He nodded. Then Rari and Joao did.

They didn't speak to each other; I knew they were thinking it was huge gamble to take on something you were not that sure of. But they never said so. We had, all of us, taken so many risks trying to get to this place, wherever 'this' was, maybe one more chance wasn't too much of a leap. I wished for once, the voices I listened to that kept me out of trouble, would just shut up. Those voices usually saved me as my mouth was never likely to.

I put my tongue out again as I saw the borderer's mothership. It looked *huge* and *very* grumpy.

The hieroglyphs I had written on my palm in what was hopefully ink, were sweated into slightly different shapes and I squinted at the possibilities. Even if I'd had time to have a shower back at the farm-house I wouldn't have dared, the margin of error was too close to transfer the figures across to something else.

I asked Okan to change the console information from English to the borderer's language; he looked back at Rari and Joao who both shrugged. "Okay," Okan said quietly, "Let's try this." He leaned forward and banged the surface with a fist, it shook the hologram for a moment and it did an uncertain dance; then settled into the unreadable.

"Oh, great, very high tech," I grumbled. No one was listening as they were giving each other congratulatory smiles behind me. I input the hieroglyphs carefully, making one or two corrections until I was satisfied and then tapped the communications key. "Tar Dal borderer's mothership, this is Millie Rushcroft on the incoming space to surface craft. Can I have permission to dock?"

The silence that followed could have filled the Royal Albert Hall in London, in the moment before they played Land of Hope and Glory on the last night of the proms.

I don't think anyone in the history of the borderer's settler's conflict had ever returned to a borderer's ship willingly. Okan snorted, "Good luck with that!"

We listened. Eventually after what must have been three minutes which were the longest of my life thus far, the captain's voice said, "We will arrange for you to dock." He didn't sound *that* surprised, so I guessed that Ginnie had delivered the message.

"Captain? If you have any procedures for craft crashing into the docking bay, it might be a good idea to put them in motion."

One more cavernous silence and a different voice replied, "Understood."

"Oh great," Joao muttered.

The mouth of the mothership loomed large but somehow slipped to the left and right at inopportune moments and I sang 'I am a lineman for the county' under my breath to keep me on a straight course. Okan was trying hard not to grab the controls. He had banged the console one more time in an effort to get the readings readable and the holo-screen was expressing some irritation along the lines of 'make your mind up' and kept changing its own tune every second or so. I just tried to get into a deeper connection with Buddy and not worry too much about the small stuff, as in the speed and angle of descent.

I had asked if any of them would like to take over the docking procedure when the whinging got a bit heated, but Okan had pointed out that none of them had the biomechanical connection with the craft, and though they had been able to fly it on short hops on Europa it wasn't a good idea. They were as quiet as they could be under the circumstances and just kept it down to a few whimpers and whispered swearing. Okan's left foot however was tapping invisible brakes long before we reached the docking bay doors.

I slid across the floor and wheeled a few times in neat circles towards the control room where a group of interested borderers had gathered in what I thought was misplaced curiosity. Their faces got larger and larger and their expressions more stunned as I got closer to the crash wall that separated us. I saw the borderer who was guiding us in on the landing mark, throw himself out of the way with impeccable timing, in what looked as though he was performing a spectacular high board dive. It would have given him a ten from the judge on any day of the Olympic week. My singing got a little louder but I felt sure I finished on a high note worthy of Glen Campbell, as we were still the right way up when I came to a halt; or nearly the right way up.

The borderers were on the ship in a moment and with great presence of mind Okan sat in his seat along with Rari and Joao, until the door was open and an 'escort' was sent in to collect us. Birdy was through the entrance first and he came over to me as I stood up. I put my arms around him and he hugged me back. Something that electrified the three men, but they didn't move, didn't resist and kept their incredulity to a minimum. "I was, worried," Birdy said, trying on the word for size. It was a good fit and I hugged him again.

"Is everyone okay?" I asked him, meaning Tara.

"She is fine. She told me you would be back as soon as you could. I think I didn't really believe her," he said, bewildered.

I shook hands with the two other borderers, one of whom I recognised as Birdy's friend. "Thank you for acting so quickly." He nodded and smiled, which was not such a disconcerting experience any more.

"These are my friends." I pointed at the three men, Okan followed my lead and held out his hand. The borderers looked uncomfortable.

"Is something wrong?" I asked Birdy. Then I worked it out. "Do you think it will make a difference if it is a male person, you have contact with? That it will make the chemical imbalance worse?" Okan put his hand down.

"I don't know, it has never happened before," Birdy said.

"Would you like to give it a try?" I asked him.

Birdy thought about it for a moment and we stood there waiting, as if we were diplomats about to swap nuclear secrets for a good cause. "Yes, I would. Your friend Simon said it is time for changes." He held out a hand and Okan took it, they shook and then both moved a step back.

I smiled; then my mouth dropped open. "What did you just say?" I spluttered, "Simon!"

"Yes," Birdy said, "He is here. He arrived just before you did. On that ship." Birdy pointed to a small craft of an unusual configuration.

"Well now," Rari said, "This should be good."

"Really Millie, what a mess you've just made!" Simon walked into the docking bay and was in full gay mode. The captain stood slightly behind him looking as if it had been something of a day of firsts. Simon came over and tapped me on the head in annoyance, Okan's face was one of bemusement, Joao of stunned incredulity and Rari appeared delighted. He shook their hands. "Very nice to see you all again. *Very* nice." It was as though we had just arrived at the vicar's summer garden party on Exmoor. "Though I don't see why you *are* here." He bounced on the balls of his feet and turned back to the captain.

Simon was puzzling the bemused borderers who were probably getting the biochemical equivalent of a mixed message.

The conference room was full of chairs fit for the grumpy giant in any children's story, the same as the ones in Buddy. My feet dangled which made them ache and even Okan's were only just touching the floor. He looked worried and it was reflected in the faces of Joao and Rari. I was fairly sure they hadn't carried any weapons onto the mothership and that must have been making them nervous, as we were surrounded by borderers.

The seats were taken up with a group of the brain class and two of the troop class including Birdy, who sat next to me on the other side to Okan. Ginnie and Tara were sitting opposite us. When we had reached the room, I had rushed over to her and this time no one tried to stop us. It was impossible to find anything to say that didn't include feelings that were best left out of a public performance.

The meeting between Tara and Joao though, was desperate, they stood close to each other but didn't touch; you could feel the emotional fireworks hissing and spitting with guilt and love, longing and loss. It stuck in the throat of everyone there; the borderers must have felt as if they'd overdosed.

Simon was all business. "The captain and I have come to an arrangement."

"That was fast," Okan muttered. I kicked him under the table and he winced.

"Sorry!" I whispered back, when I realised that I'd chosen the leg with the bullet hole in it. Simon gave me a look that would have provided a frozen solution to desertification. I smiled my most innocent look and he snorted.

"In exchange for an antidote to the chemical imbalance they are going to be travelling to my verse to help with the war. They have agreed to send back any of the women who wish to go and provide answers for the families who want to know about their missing loved ones." Tara leaned forward but didn't say anything. I saw Joao, who was sitting next to her reach for her hand.

"What war?" I spluttered, finally hearing the important part about a half a minute after Okan and the others. "There's a war in the type three verse?" Somehow this was increasingly horrifying the more it filtered through. You expected the people who were smarter than you to be, just that.

"I would have thought," Okan said, voicing everyone's feelings, "That a type three verse would be past the slugging it out stage."

"Apparently not," Simon said dryly.

"Captain Wings of Fortune can only speak for the Tar Dal Tribe," Simon said, "But he has agreed to arrange a meeting for me with the other tribes and to intercede on my behalf." The captain nodded his agreement.

No one spoke. The elephant in the room that was the quantum singularity device, was never mentioned by me or Simon, Okan, Joao or Rari and no one gave a moment's thought to Zatar.

"What happens now?" I asked carefully.

The farm was quiet except for the sound of the goats in the fields behind the house. I stood in the early morning by the graves of my friends. The little plot of emotionally dusty stones, were carefully placed on a hill overlooking the farm and the valley, and out towards the far mountains whose snow-covered peaks were forever part of the sense of time standing still.

It had been several weeks since we had returned to Europa from the borderer's mothership in Buddy. He was parked back in the barn waiting for the next emergency. It had been days of one thing after another and somehow, I had found a constant supply of reasons not to come out and make peace with my dead.

Simon had stayed with the captain, and made it quite clear that he didn't want any of us around to hear while they talked.

Tara and I had spoken to the women on board without the borderer guards present and it was no real surprise that several of them had decided to remain. They had formed clandestine relationships with the men who had held them captive. I spoke at length to all of those who were going to stay on the ship. I wanted to be sure they were not suffering from, what could have been Stockholm syndrome, but without a qualified psychologist it was only really possible for me to see that they were not stressed, or pressured about their circumstances. The worst suffering was experienced by the women who were leaving them behind. It made for many difficult goodbyes.

We ferried the leavers down to Europa in several trips over the first week. I was on my own for the second landing on the borderer's ship and every one after that. Okan, Joao and Rari had decided to stay at the farm and contact the relatives of the taken. Trying to keep the news as low profile as was practical, so that people could filter back into their lives if they chose. It was also easier for the borderers not to have the men around, although nothing was ever said.

By the time I got back on the return leg the second time, there were several scenes of reunited families taking place in the front of the farmhouse. Some of the more complicated encounters were from people who had come to the farmhouse looking for women who had not come back. Okan, Rari and Joao had dealt with angry fathers, husbands and partners, who wanted answers and we didn't have any. We speculated that several disappearances that had been attributed to the borderers may well have been about something else. There was one 'father' who made me shiver at the thought of sharing a house with him and I wished the 'ungrateful wretch' a safe place wherever she now was.

The borderers were true to their word and sent all the information they could on women who had decided to stay and those who 'hadn't made it.' We found no trace of Ziggy. Tara said nothing but her eyes became clouded most of the time and you couldn't reach her. She eventually took a guilty look at the diary that Ziggy had left behind, but apart from the teenage anxiety about being different, the only teenager in history to be right, nothing much else was revealed. It took days to see Tara smile through the disappointment and endless sadness of continuing loss, and it must have felt to her as though the last door was closing.

I went back up to the borderer's ship for the final time, not because there was anyone else to bring home but because I knew I should. Okan hadn't wanted me to go but he didn't stop me. I watched him as he stood by the barn, his arms wrapped around him in a voiceless expression of frustration.

The runabout was in the far fields as I passed over the cattle. Joao and Rari were checking on the stock, Tara was in the house with the three women who were still waiting for someone to pick them up. There was enough emotional trauma floating around to sink a reasonably sized flotilla and some of it was mine.

The trip back into space was filled with the memories and broken promises of a regret filled future, but we don't get to choose the life we live, mostly it chooses us. I know I cried into the silence and Buddy listened and didn't judge me. That was what friends were for, even the ones without faces and fur.

My landing got a nod of approval from the borderer, who actually didn't have to dive out of the way on that occasion, he came into the cabin of the ship and talked to me about the modifications that had been made by Rari and Joao. He was curious about my ability to make a biomechanical connection but I wasn't up to the conversation and he motioned me out to the main area with a smile.

Simon met me on the edge of the docking bay and we stood not talking for the length of time that would make strangers uncomfortable. I pointed behind me at the little cone shaped craft Simon had come back to the type two verse in. "Rari wants to know if that ship came through the wormhole with you, and if so, he's very interested."

"I'm rather impressed that he worked it out," Simon smiled.

"Don't leave," I said, looking at my feet and watching tears drip onto the tops of my shoes.

"I will never leave you my darling girl. I just have to go away for a while." He put his arms around me and kissed the top of my head and when I moved my face out of the way of the buttons on his shirt, I could see a group of borderers watching with undisguised interest and worry at the flood of emotion that must have been swirling around, as if bees were searching for a broken hive.

I glanced up at him. "Have you ever felt anything when you went through the wormhole?"

"Have I *felt* anything?" Simon asked, looking worried himself. "What do you mean?"

"When I was there with Zatar I thought I could sense something," I tailed off.

"I imagine that emotions were running somewhat high at the time, are you sure that wasn't it?"

"I was aware of disapproval," I whispered. It sounded really stupid when you put it into words.

Simon sighed, "*I* would have thought a round of applause would have been more appropriate under the circumstances." He saw my face. "Alright. I'll ask it a few questions the next time I'm on my way through!" I scowled.

"Really Millie you look just like your mother when you do that," he laughed then gave me another hug. "She used to say that the history of accretion and the history of stars are connected and at the centre of every galaxy is a black hole, each one born at the beginning of the universe. So why not conscious thought, who are we to think it's only humankind that can express emotions?"

Captain Wings of Fortune came onto the deck and he smiled at me. "It was good to meet you Millie, I wish a safe journey through your life, for you, your tribe, and your warrior." It took me a moment to realise he meant Okan.

I smiled back at him. "My warrior asked me to say 'good speed on your way.'" Which I thought must have been something nautical from his verse. The captain nodded as if I had imparted a diplomatic speech at the most detailed level. I held out my hand and he took it in his enormous one and the gentle pressure from both of us made for a more appropriate communication.

"Is the war in your verse very bad?" I asked Simon, fishing for information. The borderers and the gay guy looked at each other and decided that it was in my best interest not to know too much. It made me grind my teeth in a very expensive way.

"I will contact you in a few days," Simon replied after some thought. In anyone's language that meant things were *very bad*.

"Please be careful," I said quietly to both of them.

They walked me to my ship and I began to notice that several more borderers had crowded onto the docking bay deck. Birdy was standing by the doorway to the dropdown craft. I thought sadly that this was actually a goodbye moment and none of these people thought that they would be coming back. I looked in panic at Simon who gave me a smile filled with love and pride and that made me more frightened than I had ever been at any time in the previous few months.

I whispered, "You don't think you're going to be able to pull this off?"

"We have to protect the other verses, as we made a stupid mistake," Simon explained.

The deck was completely packed by then, borderers pushed into the spaces where the cargo was stored and I saw several of the women who had elected to stay behind standing with their partners. I turned in a full circle drinking in their feral bond and letting my feelings wash over them.

"Could I ask you to say something to my people?" Captain Wings of Fortune asked me politely. I must have looked puzzled because he explained, "They see you as something made like them but connected to the wormhole and therefore special."

"But you know I'm not?" I asked him, stunned. "There is nothing unusual about me." He shrugged in a way that expressed the unspoken words of gentle denial.

I looked at the borderers and then at the floor. "This is a poem that was written in my verse a long time ago, by a warrior who was going off to war and didn't expect to come home again." I thought about Weldon and then Muglier and Wills lying in the dust of a road they hadn't taken and the sound of guns that lived forever in the heart of anyone who has ever fired one.

I spoke, *"If I should die, think only this of me; that there's some corner of a foreign field that is forever England. There shall be in that rich earth a richer dust concealed; a dust whom England bore, shaped, made aware, gave once, her flowers to love, her ways to roam, a body of England's, breathing English air, washed by the rivers blest by suns of home. And think, this heart, all evil shed away, a pulse in the eternal mind, no less gives somewhere back the thoughts by England given; her sights and sounds, dreams happy as her day; and laughter, learned of friends, and gentleness, in hearts at peace, under an English heaven."*

When things look dark, and you're flying into storm clouds, or sailing into the unknown, only Rupert Brooke can speak for us.

A sigh moved as the wind through long grass does, filling my head with its sound until it became a sea of noise. I stepped through the doorway of the craft.

The trip back to Europa was filled with the conversations we have with ourselves when we know no one else can help with the answers. In my head I understand that I am made of the same particles as star matter and in my heart, I realise that there must be something in that. If there is a force for good in the universe and a

445

force for evil, then there are no real reasons not to ask for advice from the endless space of out there.

I turned once and then turned back again as the emptiness behind me made no sense. Until it did. How it had happened I would never know. At least not for now. But they were gone. All of them. The ships. The borderers. Simon.

My coffee cup was full and I sat down carefully next to Weldon and patted the mound of soil that was covering the place where he lay. "Gosh I miss you my old friend," I whispered. "Sorry about the diatribe, but I thought you'd like to know what took place after you left."

I looked at the other memorials with the names of his family on them and then at the names carved on the stones towards the back of the plot. The gangers were in one row. Tara and Joao had tried to find out something about them, to see if there were any families who would want to know, but without much success. It was as if they hadn't had any past. Now they were part of the land and time would make them special, because we wouldn't forget them. 'They shall not grow old, as we that are left grow old.' I put my head on my hands and cried. Goodbyes all over again and coffee. I picked up my now empty cup and went back towards the house.

Tara was out on the veranda, her hands shading her eyes, when she saw me, she waved and then shouted, "Hurry." She pointed into the house. "Simon!"

I ran.

The hallway was full of people. Okan, Rari and Joao, Tara and me. Flora was winding herself around my feet and I picked her up. Simon was here, but not here. He seemed to be half in and half out of the verse and kept glancing over his shoulder and shouting, "It's not working! Boost the signal or something!" He sounded exasperated and he looked tired. There was a new scar on the side of his face near the eye.

I reached out a hand to touch him, but Okan said, "Give him a chance, I don't think it's functioning properly."

Eventually the image settled into something that didn't ripple and Simon sat down on a chair I couldn't see which was oddly endearing. He held out his arms to me and said, "I wish I could give you a hug, but we're rather busy right now."

"How's it going?" Okan asked.

"That's what I need to talk to you about, and I imagine you have lots of other questions."

"What made you make a move to interfere with what was happening here?" Rari asked, earning himself a look of deep respect from Simon.

"As always," Simon said, "The nail squarely on the head. It was the quantum singularity weapon that got our attention."

"The fact," I said, slightly hurt, "That I was being chased around the verses by a homicidal maniac was not top of your list then?"

"Millie, don't be so melodramatic," Simon said crossly, "You would always be top of *my* list, just," he added, "Not top of *the* list."

"Thank you, I think!" I said, earning a smile and a hug from Okan.

"The weapon?" Rari persevered. "Has anyone actually used it?"

"Yes," Simon said, "We did."

Okan looked as if he was going to be sick and Rari and Joao were stunned. I couldn't get my head around the possibility. "But why?" I asked. "What viable reason could you have for using it?"

Simon shrugged. "We were stupid, we were testing it to see how it worked."

"What *happened*?" Okan asked, not sounding sure he wanted to hear the answer.

"We created a tear in the fabric of space/time into another dimension."

Waves of incredulity filled the silence that followed, and into that absence, Simon talked to someone we couldn't see, he was asking for a few more minutes. "Sorry," he said, turning back to us, "This takes up a lot of energy and we don't have much to spare at the moment."

Rari shook his head. "You idiots," he muttered.

"Quite." Simon shrugged.

"Has it started to affect your gravity?" Rari said, as his voice disappeared into a whisper, "Your scientists must be going crazy!" Simon didn't say anything, but he didn't really need to. My grasp of inter-dimensional physics was almost non-existent and even I knew they were in trouble. I just hoped a type three verse had more in the way of resources than a few dreamwalkers and a really smart gay guy.

"Who exactly *are you*?" Okan asked. He was leaning against the wall of the hallway and trying to rest his damaged leg which was taking longer to heal than usual, despite the medical nanobots Tara had given him. Tired bodies always needed more time to get better.

Simon looked at his fingernails. "Good question," he said, thinking about it and coming to a decision, "I work for an under-funded government department."

There was a bark of disembodied laughter from behind Simon, and a voice said, "You've got that part right!"

"We run sleepers in the different verses to keep watch. Things have been getting more difficult lately with the war, but there are still a few of us left from the old days.

"Your parents, Millie, hid you in the type zero verse. After the explosion at the meeting in Tara's verse, it seemed the safest thing to do. We were mostly scattered, but a few of us got together eventually and began to organise. It didn't take too long to work out who had done it and where all the technology had ended up.

"There wasn't as much as you would think. Even then the governments in the different verses weren't sure about us. Charlie Morris took most of the fixers and a copy of the quantum energy information. Zatar took the wormhole belt and another copy of the device. The craft I came to the borderer's ship in was a single experimental vehicle and no," he held up a hand to Joao, "I can't tell you how it works, not today anyway."

"Simon," Rari said patiently, "Just exactly whom are you fighting?"

Simon smiled. "Once again with the nail on the head. We're fighting the creatures that came through the space/time rift."

448

"From the other dimension," Rari said, as if confirming his worst fears.

"How's that working out?" Okan asked, after the usual speechless pause.

"We're getting our arses kicked," Simon replied.

"I can imagine," Okan said.

"Actually, with respect, Okan, you can't." Simon looked tired and what frightened me more, defeated.

"No, you're right, I can't," Okan whispered, shaking his head. "Is there *anything* we can do?" He asked, earning Simon's undying respect and my gratitude.

"We must keep it from happening in the other verses. In time we may need to do some quiet dreamwalking to keep a safe watch." He pointed at the fixer on his face. "These will make it easier. We will need the ones you have left and your help."

Okan nodded, looking at Rari and Joao. "We can do that."

"Is this it?" Rari said, "Is this is what you and the other dreamwalkers have been doing, Nancy and Millie's parents and the others, keeping watch?"

"Yes," Simon said simply, "Yes, that just about covers it. Are you okay with that?"

Rari made a face and then smiled. "I guess I am."

We all were. It was as if the reason for my being had just been made clear to me. A click of a switch and the light was turned on.

The sense that things had just become so much bigger and the stakes so very much higher swamped me and I leaned on Okan for strength, he put an arm around me. The chance for peace, the dream of other days, filtered through the corridor of the farmhouse along with the sighs of tired people. But the worlds are full of people dreaming of peace and that is always the first step on the ladder of hope.

"How are the borderers?" Joao asked Simon, he too leaned on the wall and then slid down to sit on the floor, it was as if someone had given us permission and everyone began to settle in more comfortable floor-like positions.

"They have a genetically coded war sequence, and we unlocked it." He shrugged. "They're very good at what they were designed for."

"But you're not winning?" I asked, my throat closing over with anxiety.

"No. Not yet." Simon looked behind him one more time. "I have to go, we're out of energy and I'm getting a red light from the techs."

Simon stood up. "Can I speak to Rari in private for a moment?" He asked sheepishly. I held out a hand to him and he put his palm against mine for a second. There was no contact but he smiled. "I love you darling girl and I will be there as soon as I can." I nodded because speaking would have released the great gulps of loss that welled up inside me.

The rest of us trooped into the kitchen and we talked loudly about crop yields and the goat cashmere designs to give Rari and Simon some privacy, all the while straining to hear any giveaway words.

The door opened and Rari came in looking genuinely happy for the first time since I had known him. Being who you really are takes courage, but as far as I could see it's mostly worth the trip. He took the coffee Tara offered him and we stood in silence for a moment, then Okan and Joao started dividing up the work for the day.

The distillery at the back of the house was cool and comforting in its sameness. It smelled of the concoctions that Tara now prepared alone, though I had been taking lessons. Joao helped occasionally. He and Tara had fallen into the gentle dance that was love and guilt, but they were working it out and we gave them space, and I just hoped that they could survive their interrupted history. We talked about Weldon as if he was still there some days and it became a painful process of letting go. I missed him in the way that I had my father, and with Simon gone most of the time and barely there when he was there, my 'coffee' trips to the hills behind the house and the grave markers, became a regular occurrence.

We all slipped into the patterns of life that made sense to each of us apart and as a group. The farm was tended in the same way, goats and cattle didn't notice who fed them and looked after them, just as long as someone did. We came together in the evenings as we had always done, to talk about the day and eat. If the space where Weldon had been was ever present it didn't matter because life was always full of the people who lived in our hearts.

In the weeks that had followed our conversation in the hallway, Simon had been to the farmhouse twice. He had been desperately tired and slept the sleep of hopelessness. The war was not going well. He wouldn't tell us the details, a feature that drove Okan up the wall with frustration.

Simon, Okan, Joao and Rari organised visits to Okan's verse, Joao's and to mine. They were able to recruit four of the dreamwalkers from Okan's type one verse in the aftermath of the 'change of leadership.' The new man in charge, a dreamwalker himself, was someone Okan had grown up with and trusted to a certain extent. He didn't tell me until late one night, but the organisation had tried to persuade him to take over the job.

On one occasion I had gone with Okan and Joao to my verse and set up one of the recruits in my old house, he was going to write science articles for magazines and newspapers. Simon had put him in touch with several contacts. I wandered around as though I was a stranger out of place and time and I couldn't wait to get back to the farmhouse on Europa with the blue-green sky.

I pulled bottles from the shelves in the distillery at Tara's request and she measured the dosage and mixed cures quietly. "Do you think there's a chance that Ziggy is still out there?" Tara asked me. I sighed; we had looked as much as it was possible to do so. She couldn't have gone to the type three verse because of the block and it was unlikely she was in the empty verse I had visited once. She had been sixteen when she joined the gangers and maybe nearly nineteen when the borderers were supposed to have taken her, though they had checked their records and there was no information on her.

It could be that she had ended up in my verse, but Okan and Rari had spent some of the time that they were in the different verses, checking records and leaving messages in a variety of places for her to get in touch. There were only so many crossing places a dreamwalker could exit without a fixer or another dreamwalker to help them. Ziggy would be twenty-three if she had survived and probably would have got in contact if she had been able to. Teenage rebellion didn't travel that well.

I sat and looked out of the window at the goats. They were shaggy in their winter coats. The sky was a clear blue-green and the snow was thick on the mountains. The seasons were a confusion of mostly spring and summer but we had one winter about every six seasons. The vildenbeasts were coming down from the mountains to look for easier food sources and that meant they headed for the farms. Okan and Rari were out in the far fields checking the traps and warning grids. Joao was feeding the goats some of the disgusting supplements they needed to get them through the winter.

Jupiter took over eleven years to go around the sun so most people used the central planets three-hundred-and sixty-five-day year on one level of reference and the Europa seasons as another. It took some getting used to.

I let my mind wander and I found myself thinking about Professor Theadus, who was yet another casualty in the debris of my past. Something pushed through the guilt. "There is one place we haven't looked," I said, "Do you remember the professor telling us about the other type two verse?"

Tara sat down and moved pots so that she could put her elbows on the work surface. Her face showed the strain we all seemed to be experiencing. Simon had used his contacts in the government of the central planets to warn them of the war in the type three verse. Okan had told the new boss in the organisation in his own verse but they had decided to keep the information from the controlling power. It was a secret of killing proportions and the weight of it ate away at all of us.

"Is there any way we can try and contact her?" Tara asked.

"I'll see if Simon has a sleeper he can speak with, but as far as I know they had cut off all communication after the bomb."

"That's it then," Tara said, as if to herself.

I leaned forward. "No, that's not it; I promised I would help and

I will; for as long as I breathe, I will *not* give up." I held her hand and we made a silent pact not to let the past get away from us. Sometimes all you needed were the answers, because not all stories came with tidy endings.

"Come on," I said, "let's get Buddy out and go for a spin!" I pulled her to her feet and we grabbed coats and food and went out to the barn. I saw Joao at the feed bins and we waved. He came over to us dusty and grinning.

"Running away again, are you?" He kissed Tara on the top of her head and pinched one of the cakes she had in the food basket, swallowing it without chewing and grabbing another one, then he helped us check out the dropdown.

"I'm surprised the borderers let you keep this heap of junk!" He said, as he tapped the hull. "Give us some fizz Millie," he asked me in an echo of a past question, when we had stood in front of the dropdown and they had discovered I could connect with the ship, which felt as though it was such a long time ago.

I did hear him say to himself when he went inside, "How you doing Buddy?" But it was whispered and I smiled and didn't tease him about it.

Flying was a love affair that ended badly; it made your heart hurt with its memory. I took off and soared over the farmhouse and we saw Joao in the front waving an empty sack and I wiggled the stubby craft instead of waving back.

The fields spread out in their green splendour and the mountains seemed nearer because the snow was so far down the slopes.

Even the hills that surrounded the town were covered with a light sprinkling of white.

It took no more than a few minutes to get to Okan and Rari and they looked up to watch us land in one of the fields without cattle, who were usually grumpy and skittish about any arial intrusion. Okan's face was worried as he came over to the doorway and it slid back as his hand tapped the keypad. I managed to speak before he did. "That word you used when we were going back out to the borderers craft."

453

"Er?" Okan said, puzzled, as Tara gave him the basket of food. Rari joined us and began helping himself to sandwiches and coffee.

"The L word," I said, "It goes for me too." I smiled and put my arms around him.

He tutted, hugging me back with a soppy smile on his face. "That's all I'm going to get I suppose."

"Take it mate," Rari laughed, "Trust me, it's a good deal!"

I sat in the kitchen in the early morning, the dawn was an orange streak on the horizon and the house was quiet. Okan had got up to see to a warning light in the far fields, and then he and Joao had gone out on the runabout with guns and coffee, hoping not to find any dead cattle. The winter had been harder than usual and the vildenbeasts had taken their toll on the stock.

Cecil was asleep in the fruit bowl; his fat rolls a furry waterfall over the edge. He snored gently, surrounded by apples. Flora slipped grumpily into the room, she usually slept with Tara but had been woken by the activity and now wanted a cuddle, food and to get Cecil from his sleeping place. I picked her up and we shared my coffee and last night's pudding.

We went out onto the veranda to finish the drink and to admire the sunrise, manufactured by a long-ago scientist out of crystal mirrors and imagination, it was a spectacular sight. I raised my cup and thanked whoever it was for the privilege.

The com in the kitchen pinged for attention and Flora grumbled again because she had just got comfortable in the crook of my arm, having given up on Cecil, who was more than capable of pretending she didn't exist if it suited him.

I went back into the kitchen and tapped the on key. Ginnie's cheerful face was irritatingly awake, pretty and smiling. I grinned back. Ginnie had walked back into her life with a skill and determination that took your breath away. She had made it her goal to let as many people know what the dreamwalkers had done for the system. The lack of borderers and raids meant we were experiencing a surge of popularity. I had no illusions about it lasting, people had amazingly short memories when it came to complicated situations, but it was a good place to start. She seemed excited, her face was flushed and she didn't bother with the usual 'good morning' and 'how are you.'

"There was a child here yesterday. A very young boy!" She could hardly speak and her eyes filled with tears, then Til came on the com. He looked exasperated but somehow just as excited.

"I don't understand, what boy?" I poured more coffee in the hope that it would help my level of comprehension, and put Flora on the table to pester Cecil from a better vantage point.

"He's about five in central planet years, maybe thirty seasons?" Til seemed to think that would make it easier to understand. I must have looked even more puzzled. "He was playing with Lu at the stables. Look Millie, I took a picture." Til's face disappeared and a holograph appeared of a gorgeous child, muddy and laughing in the dirt with the horses and a smiling Lu Wang handing him a shared toy.

"Oh my," I said, "Do you think he's a dreamwalker?"

We had speculated about the fact that there were no more dreamwalker children after our generation had been decimated by Zatar. All the fixers had been recovered from Okan's type one verse and the rest of the technology from the borderer's ship had been collected by Simon and given to Okan for safe keeping; it had been quite a pitiful collection. After that, we had hoped that one day the natural gene would assert itself and more children would appear. This little boy was the first anyone had seen. I was delighted.

"I'll get Joao out there tomorrow to see if we can put a fixer on him. Has he been coming regularly? Are there any more?" I was full of questions.

Til's face came back on the com, his hologram was full of frustration again. "Millie! Look at his *eyes*."

I looked at the holo-picture of the little boy. At a child with one green eye and one blue. Joao's eyes. *Ziggy's* eyes.

ACKNOWLEDGEMENTS

We seldom get the chance to put things right. This was made possible by Robin Phillips of Author Help who 'helps' with experience, intelligence and patience. (AuthorHelp.uk)

The cover is once again the brilliant design work of Henry Hyde. (HenryHyde.co.uk)

Kat Morgan, 'earth magic lady' for her kindness and the great website, Twitter and Instagram. (Kat@seasideweb.co.uk)

Patricia Gilpin, for teaching me how to read.

Kip Gilpin, for teaching me how to shoot!

Eric Cottrell for sharing his knowledge and understanding of all thing's sci-fi and for explaining how to punch someone without breaking my knuckles!

Gill Baderman and Sara Pearcy for being the lifelong friends who believe in you when you don't!

Bernie Martin, for his insight into Simon, despite the fact that most of what he told me was unprintable!

To my fellow dreamwalkers, the multiverse is out there waiting.

This book was originally written between 2004 and 2006. It was published for the first time by Stephen and Irene Clark of Paradox Publishing in 2008.

S. P-H

ALSO BY S. PARNAM-HARRIS

Dreamwalkers

A Short Book of the Dead

The Starfire Diaries

The Voice in the Mirror

The Here of This Now: Science Fiction Stories

Find out more at sparnam-harris.com.